Kate Glanville was born in West Africa to Irish parents. She now lives w??? her three ??? ??? years she ha? ???cused as a successful ceramic artist supplying tiles and tableware to many leading shops and galleries around the world. From childhood she has been passionate about writing stories. Kate is the author of four captivating and moving novels.

Praise for Kate Glanville:

'Poignant, warm and unpredictable. I enjoyed it hugely'
Julie Cohen

'Beautiful . . . with heart'
Tracy Rees

'A real page turner. Ideal holiday reading'
Lovereading

'A warm and touching family drama . . . Moving'
Laura Wilkinson

'*A Perfect Home* by Kate Glanville is one the best stories that I have read so far this year'
Goodreads reviewer

'An enchanting book full of twists and turns'
Goodreads reviewer

'A beautifully told story of new beginnings and old secrets'
Goodreads reviewer

Also by Kate Glanville

Heartstones
A Perfect Home
Stargazing
The Cherry Tree Summer

Kate Glanville

THE
CHERRY TREE
SUMMER

ACCENT

First published in 2021 by Headline Accent
An imprint of HEADLINE PUBLISHING GROUP

1

Cataloguing in Publication Data is available from the British Library

ISBN 978 1 4722 7986 6

Typeset in 10.5/13pt Bembo Std by Jouve (UK), Milton Keynes

Printed and bound in Great Britain by Clays Ltd, Elcograf S.p.A.

HEADLINE PUBLISHING GROUP
An Hachette UK Company
Carmelite House
50 Victoria Embankment
London
EC4Y 0DZ

www.headline.co.uk
www.hachette.co.uk

For my wonderful children, Harry, Daisy and Tomos.
A constant source of support, love and joy.

Prologue

London 1992

The cold air stung her cheeks as she stepped out onto the doorstep. Inside, someone had started to sing 'White Christmas'. The singing faded as the black front door closed behind her, leaving only the berry wreath swinging back and forth in one last wave goodbye.

'Careful, darling.' Her husband turned as he bumped the empty pushchair down the steps. 'It's icy.'

'We'll be fine.' She held on to the wrought-iron railing with one hand, clutching the bundled-up baby in the other as she carefully descended the steps. Her long fur coat skimmed her ankles and she worried that she might catch her high heels on the hem. From the pavement her husband watched. She saw a frown pass across his handsome face before he spoke.

'It was only meant to be a quiet drinks party with my parents' friends. You really didn't need to perform.'

She paused, steadying herself before the next step. 'They asked me to sing. It would have been rude to say no.'

'But, darling, I know how it stirs up all those memories. I don't want you to be upset.'

'I didn't mind, it was fun.' At the bottom of the steps she crouched to strap the baby into the pushchair. 'There you go, my gorgeous boy. Not long and you'll be home tucked up in bed ready for Santa to bring you your first stocking.'

Her husband pulled on his leather gloves. 'And you know my

father doesn't like it when his Steinway is used for anything other than Chopin.'

She looked up and forced a smile. 'They enjoyed it though, didn't they? The woman in the twin-set was dancing.'

'But you didn't have to do your entire back catalogue; they were hardly your typical kind of fans.'

'They seemed to know all the words.' The plastic buckle of the pushchair slipped between her fingers. 'Sorry, cariad.' The baby boy wriggled, frustrated inside his quilted snowsuit as the buckle slipped again. She kissed his nose. The baby laughed. She whispered in his ear. 'You liked my singing, didn't you sweetie? You always do. Mummy's biggest fan.' She kissed him again.

At last the buckle snapped into place and with one last look at her son she stood up. She felt dizzy, slightly sick after too much champagne. The words of the final song reeled around her head.

I am dancing on the moon

'I'll take him now, darling.' Her husband touched her cheek with one gloved finger, pushing back a lock of her long auburn hair. 'You look exhausted. We should have left earlier.'

'I'll be fine with him,' she protested, but his hands were on the handles of the pushchair.

'Come on, little man, let's get going.'

'Wait a second.' But he was already ahead of her, striding down the empty street, pushchair wheels clattering over the paving slabs, his overcoat swinging in time to the tune in her head.

In my sleep I feel you kiss me

She murmured the lyrics as she set off to catch up; her new Manolo Blahniks made it hard to walk fast enough.

And your lips whisper a love poem

Her breath came out in little puffs of smoke that reminded her of the illicit cigarette she'd enjoyed on the balcony with the wife of a businessman.

Then I wake and find you're with me

Frost glittered on the railings, and the cobbles in the gutter glistened in the streetlight.

2

We ask the band to play our tune

A thin mist swirled ahead of her, thicker at the end of the street. Her husband and the pushchair were shrouded in the distance.

We are moving in the starlight

Across the street she heard a woman shriek with laughter as a small group spilled out of the entrance of a pub.

And I am dancing on the moon

Car headlights were coming out of the mist, a yellow taxi sign emerging from the fog. The lights cast a glow on the woman and her two male companions.

'Martha?' the woman shouted from the opposite pavement. She was wearing a tight red sequined dress and carrying an enormous handbag. 'Is it really you?'

In the distance her husband called to her. 'Darling, just ignore them. We need to get home.'

'Martha Morgan. One of our own.' The man had a Welsh accent; he started to sing.

Calon lân yn llawn daion

Martha glanced ahead; her husband was waving his hand, beckoning her to hurry up.

Tecach yw na'r lili dlo

The man was still singing. Martha joined in with the next line of the song.

The taxi passed and the group stumbled across the road towards her.

'I can't be doing with those funny foreign lyrics,' the second man said.

'You English moron; you're talking about our language,' the Welshman turned his back on his companion and taking Martha's hand in his he shook it vigorously. 'The whole world wanted to speak Welsh when your band sang that at Glastonbury. You were bloody fantastic.'

'Thank you, but I must go,' Martha said. 'My husband and my baby are waiting.'

'I was such a fan.' The woman's words slurred a little as she

3

spoke. She held out her arms. 'I love you, Martha Morgan, you're a goddess.'

Martha laughed and let the woman hug her; the woman smelled of beer and smoke and Opium perfume. It reminded Martha of the dressing rooms she and Cat had shared.

'And I love "Moondancing",' the woman said. 'I had my first snog to that song.' She began to sing the lyrics that the middle-aged businessmen and their wives had just been enjoying in the drawing room.

In my sleep I feel you kiss me
and your lips whisper a love poem

Martha sang too as the woman began to lead her in a waltz. After two verses they fell apart with laughter. Martha teetered backwards on her heels. The Englishman put his arm around Martha's shoulder.

'I always liked that one about the waitress in the cocktail bar.'

'That was The Human League, you pillock,' said the Welshman. 'Martha was in On The Waterfront.'

Martha was still laughing. 'I'm amazed you remember, it's years since we split up.'

'Martha!' the voice came muffled through the fog.

Martha stopped laughing and peered up the street. Her husband was a ghostly figure silhouetted under the streetlight. She could hear the baby crying. 'I must go.'

'Can I have your autograph?' The woman was fishing around in her handbag, pulling out the contents, dropping a can of hairspray and a bunch of mistletoe onto the pavement. 'I know I've got a pen in here somewhere.'

'I'm sorry, I really have to go.' Martha detached herself from the man's arm. Martha began to sway; she wished she hadn't had the last glass of champagne.

'This'll have to do.' The woman produced the stump of a black eyeliner and a dog-eared Christmas card. 'Can you sign here?'

4

Martha hastily scrawled her name.

'Can I give you a peck on the cheek?' the second man had retrieved the plastic mistletoe from the pavement and held it up in front of Martha.

'I have to go,' Martha repeated. She couldn't see her husband or the pushchair any more.

'Just a quick kiss from a fan.'

'No!' Martha set off as quickly as her shoes would allow. Another car was coming down the road. The headlights were very bright, shining in her eyes as she searched for her husband in the distance.

'I bet those girls from The Human League would let me give them a kiss!' the man called after her.

Martha squinted against the car's headlights, hoping her husband had waited for her. There was no one under the streetlight now, no sign of anyone ahead. She couldn't hear the baby crying any more, or anyone calling out her name. He would be angry when they got home.

She started to run. Her foot slipped on something leaking from a black rubbish bag that had frozen to the cobbles, pain shot through her ankle. She stumbled into the road and cried out. Screeching brakes drowned out the sound. Headlights swung towards her. The car was spinning in front of her, the lights going round; an image in her mind of a fairground ride long ago, and then she was spinning, flying through the icy air. She heard a scream and the Welshman cried out *My God, it's hit her!*

With the cold, hard smack of the pavement, she thought of her baby's beautiful face. Then she didn't think of anything at all.

Chapter 1

The Dordogne, 2019
Saturday

It was hot, even in the shade of the terrace. Sweat prickled under Martha's bra and trickled down her spine. She stopped sweeping the fallen vine leaves and pushed her sunglasses back to watch the young man.

He worked with ease; not even the midday heat seemed to slacken his pace as he hammered the broken shutter back onto the wall. He'd already re-erected the vine-covered trellis and repaired the torn gazebo. Martha wondered how old he was. He took off his shirt to reveal multiple tattoos on his narrow chest and wiry arms; doves and flowers, a stag's head and a Celtic symbol. His jeans hung low on snake-slim hips, revealing the wording on his boxer shorts. Barely a man, more like a boy. Martha wondered if he might be the same age as Owen.

Martha began to sweep again; the bristles of the brush against the slabs sounded like the introduction to a song she and her mother used to sing when they walked along the beach at Abertrulli. Martha remembered pushing Owen in his pushchair along the sand and singing it to him. In her mind the song went round and round.

Under the boardwalk . . .

In the poplar trees the cicadas provided backing.

Martha could still see Owen laughing up at her, his cheeks ruddy from the wind whipping in from Cardigan Bay, huge brown eyes full of mischief as he pulled his mittens off for the hundredth time.

She stopped sweeping, and stood staring into the distance, remembering the days when she had been able to look after Owen like a proper mother; retrieving his mittens, putting them back on with a giggle and a kiss. She'd loved those long weekends spent on the beach with her son. Sometimes she'd fantasised about buying a little cottage in the village for the two of them; escaping from London for good, escaping from Andrew. If only she had.

The sound of banging brought her back to the present. The man was still hammering the shutter into place. In a film the man might have been Owen; the son who'd come to seek out his lost mother after so many years. But Martha could tell by the tattoos and the piercings in his ears and the cheap cut of his jeans that this was obviously not Owen; it was not someone who'd been brought up by Andrew Frazer in his rigid world of privilege and tight convention.

She glanced at the man again. He had his back to her; an inky reptile snaked its way across his shoulders. He turned and Martha saw it was a dragon, blue scales like bruises on his skin. She wondered what he might think of the tiny butterfly she had at the top of her left thigh – would he be surprised? He probably thought she was ancient, older than she really was with a face already lined and her hair a short grey cap. Martha hacked at her hair with the kitchen scissors every few weeks, barely looking in the mirror as she did it. It had been many years since she had visited a hairdresser. In the past, she had loved the fuss of Anton at John Frieda trying different shades of red before a photo shoot, or Cat smothering her big flicked fringe with hairspray just before the band stepped on stage. In those days, Martha had spent many happy hours in front of mirrors while other people attended to her make-up and stylists decided what she should wear. Now she barely thought about clothes, shrouding her body beneath long, black layers. No one could see the butterfly disappearing into the dimples on her thigh, or the jagged, purple scar along one leg.

In the village, Martha always wore dark glasses. The old men on the boules court would watch her walk past, her limp drawing their attention, or the women shopping in the market would look her up and down, but they didn't engage her in conversation.

Martha had heard the local children call her *La Sorcière* – The Witch.

'I'm going to make a start on the pool,' the young man called out.

'Don't turn on the pump until you've got all the leaves out of the filter,' Martha called back. She hoped he'd be able to make it look more like the pristine turquoise rectangle depicted on the Dordogne Dreams website before the guests arrived.

The previous evening a storm had raged, keeping Martha awake as the wind rattled the stained-glass windows of the old chapel and rain poured down the terracotta roof tiles. Lightning had lit up Martha's bedroom and she'd worried that Pippa would be frightened by the thunder, even though Martha had brought the rabbit into the chapel as soon as the storm had started. Her leg had throbbed with pain and the longing for the small white tablets seemed to fill her restless dreams.

I am in control. I will not give in.

She'd tried very hard to focus on the mantra they had taught her at the rehab clinic, to focus on the thought of Owen, the possibility of seeing him again.

I am in control. I will not give in.

In the early morning, Martha had limped up the path that led from the chapel to the old converted convent. She could smell the cloying stench of raw sewage wafting from the septic tank in the meadow; no doubt it had flooded with the vast amount of rainwater that had gushed down the drive all night.

Climbing the steps, Martha picked her way through the broken trellis and fallen vine on the terrace and surveyed the battered shutters and sagging terracotta roof. The swing she'd had made for Owen was now broken. It had never been used. She was sure there were new cracks along the ancient walls and half the roses that had clambered up the yellow lime-wash lay in a tangled heap on the muddy ground.

Faced with the devastation around her, the craving for the tablets was almost unbearable. She thought about getting into her car to find Jean-Paul with his slippery smile and inflated prices; he'd charge even more if he saw any desperation in her eyes.

She lit her first cigarette of the day and tried not to think about the broken shutters or the tattered roses or the awful smell or how to tell the guests, who would be arriving that afternoon, that they would have to find somewhere else to stay.

I am in control. I will not give in.

She'd spent weeks cleaning and polishing and dusting and touching up the peeling paintwork. It had been exhausting; many times, she had nearly given up, but she had been spurred on by the thought that when she was back on her feet financially, she could at last reply to Owen's postcard.

She'd turned from the scene around her trying not to think of all the wasted hard work or the letters from the bank, or Owen.

I am in control. I will not give in.

Martha focused on the view. A thick pink mist lay across the valley. The ancient cherry orchard that formed the boundary to her steeply sloping garden was visible, but she couldn't see the patchwork of sunflower fields and vineyards that led down to the valley with the oak wood – known for the truffles that could be found there in the winter months. Only the tower of the medieval church clearly protruded through the haze.

A noise made Martha turn. A motorbike was coming very slowly down the steep, pot-holed drive. She watched, hardly having the energy to be worried or even curious about the rider or what they wanted so early in the morning. Unexpected visitors would once have had Martha's heart racing with anxiety. When she'd first moved to the house a steady stream of fans and nosey tourists, who had found out who owned the old convent, would peer down the drive, hoping to catch a glimpse of her. In those days she'd always kept the big gates locked. Latterly the fans were few and far between; it had been so long since Martha had even shut the gates that their hinges were permanently rusted open.

The bike stopped at the bottom of the drive and a young man in a T-shirt and jeans took off his helmet.

'*C'est privé*,' Martha called. '*Sortie. Allez-vous.*'

'Is this *Le Couvent des Cerises*?' the young man called back.

'I said, it's private. Go away!'

'I wondered, do you still need a man?'

'What?'

'I was in the bar. I saw the card.' Martha could tell from his accent that he was from Scotland.

'Get off my property before I call the police.'

The young man looked around the bedraggled garden and sniffed. 'You have a problem with your septic tank.'

'I said go!'

The man shrugged then put his helmet back on. He started up the engine and began to turn the bike around. Behind her Martha heard a creak and then a crash. What was left of the trellis collapsed onto the patio table. A glass lantern that had been hanging from the overhead joists smashed on the paving slabs. The man's words echoed around Martha's head. The card. It had been weeks since she had pinned it to the noticeboard in the bar. *Handy Man needed. Odd jobs and general maintenance. Good English essential.* She'd given up on finding anyone and had done what jobs she could herself.

'Wait!' Martha struggled down the terrace steps. 'Just hang on.' She had eight hours; with help she might be able to get the mess at least partially cleared up. Her leg prevented her from going very fast.

The engine revs grew louder. She waved her arms. 'Stop!'

The bike pulled away, quickly gaining speed; Martha reached the bottom of the steps, breathless after her exertion. She shouted, 'Don't go!'

She started to hobble down the path, but it was too late; her words were drowned by the engine noise and with a cloud of dust the bike disappeared through the gateposts at the end of the drive.

'Bloody hell!' She put her hand out to steady herself on the wooden fence that ran between the path and the pool. With a splintering noise the fence gave way and fell into the flower bed, snapping the first hollyhock that had come into flower.

'BLOODY HELL!!'

11

Suddenly the air was full of noise again. Martha saw the bike coming back, faster this time. It skidded to a halt not far from where she stood. The engine died and the man took off his helmet again. He smiled, a small lopsided grin. Martha took in his dishevelled blond hair, tattoos, studded nose and eyebrows.

'I just wanted to let you know that a tree has brought your phone line down.' He pointed to the top of the drive. 'It's knocked the pole over too.'

Martha folded her arms, trying not to look too desperate for his help.

'Well, it looks like I can't phone the police to get rid of you now.'

The man produced a phone from the back pocket of his jeans and his grin widened.

'I could lend you my mobile.'

'No need,' Martha shook her head. 'There's no signal.'

The man slid the phone back into his pocket. 'I'm a good worker.'

Martha peered at him doubtfully. He didn't look very strong. More skinny than muscly. He looked in need of a meal.

'What's your name?'

'Ben,' he said, kicking down the bike stand and dismounting.

'You're a long way from home.'

'Just doing a bit of travelling.' He nodded towards a large ruck-sack strapped to the back of the bike.

'Where are you from?'

'Scotland.'

'I can tell that. I mean where in Scotland?'

'I've lived all over.'

'A bit of a nomad then?'

'I suppose,' the crooked grin appeared again. He picked up a broken piece of wood. 'I'll get this fence back up for you if you have a hammer.'

When Martha had written the advert on the card, her idea of a handyman had been of someone older, maybe one of the expat English builders who gathered in Sally and Pierre's small bar to drink red wine, compare house prices in the area and wind up Pierre by criticising the French. This thin young man, with his multiple tattoos and piercings, was not quite what she'd had in mind.

Martha thought about the letters from the bank and the phone calls from the mortgage department. She had promised to pay some of the arrears as soon as she had the first payment from the holiday company. If only that snooty woman from Dordogne Dreams hadn't insisted on withholding her fee until the first guests had given a good review.

'It's not our usual sort of property,' the woman – Tamara – had sniffed, as she took in Martha's collection of assorted antiques and bric-a-brac. 'I suppose we could market it as shabby-chic.' She'd run a long coral painted fingernail along the dresser leaving a line through the dust. 'You'll need to do a lot of housework.'

A couple and their young son would be arriving later in the afternoon; they were Martha's only hope.

'Can you help me clear up this mess?' Martha waved an arm at the storm damage strewn around the garden.

Ben nodded.

'And sort out the septic tank?'

Ben nodded again.

'I have a lot to do inside,' Martha pointed towards the house. 'Making up beds, clearing the kitchen and a hundred other things I can't even remember. Everything has to be ready by three o'clock so there'll be no time for slacking.'

'If you don't like the way I work you can just tell me to get lost.' The man's innocent smile seemed at odds with his illustrated arms and piercings.

Martha pursed her lips.

'OK, it's a deal. Your first job is to clear the vine from the table on the terrace . . . and find my bloody cigarettes!'

13

Chapter 2

They sat in the dappled shade of the vine looking out across the cherry orchard to the valley beyond. Sheets and pillowcases hung from the washing line strung across the garden and several bulging bin liners – and a quantity of empty wine bottles – were lined up along the steps up to the terrace.

A bucket of food scraps stood on the steps, ready to be taken to the compost heap. Martha could smell the discarded vegetable peelings rotting in the heat but at least the smell of sewage had disappeared since Ben had prodded at the blocked-up pipes.

The church bell rang for the Angelus, reverberating around the hillside. Martha peered at her watch.

'Right, we've got three hours left. Hopefully they'll be late, I've still got to make up the beds, take the rubbish out and deal with the compost. But I think we're in control.'

'I'll take the rubbish.' Ben swigged from the bottle of beer Martha had given him. 'And the compost.'

'You've done so much already.' Martha cut two thick slices from the bread. 'I think you deserve some lunch first.' She pushed a plate of cheese towards him and passed him a small bowl of salad. 'I haven't even asked you where you're staying. Have you got somewhere in the village?'

Ben was already chewing on a chunk of bread and cheese, pushing it into his mouth as if he hadn't eaten for days. When he finished, he wiped his mouth with his hand. Martha waited for his answer but instead he nodded towards the open kitchen door.

'There's a rabbit in your house.'

'Hey, there you are, cariad!' A small brown rabbit with two white socks and a floppy ear hopped across the terrace. Martha scooped her up.

'This is Pippa. I rescued her from a pack of dogs in the village. If I'd got there seconds later, she would have been ripped to bits.'

'Poor thing.' Ben leant forward to offer the rabbit a lettuce leaf from his plate.

'She was tame, probably a pet who had escaped. I put up notices, but no one ever came forward to say they owned her.'

'What's wrong with her ear?' Ben peered at the little rabbit, nibbling enthusiastically on the leaf.

Martha stroked the drooping ear. 'The dogs nearly ripped it off.'

'Bastards!'

Ben tore off another chunk of bread and spread some goats' cheese on the doughy surface.

'Would you like some melon?' Martha asked. 'I've a Cantaloupe that has just reached perfection, I've been waiting for it to ripen for days.'

Ben nodded, his mouth full of bread.

'I'll get it in a minute,' Martha said. 'Then I have to clear all my food from the kitchen, and I mustn't forget to cut some flowers for the table. It's the *little things like vases of flowers that make all the difference . . .*' Martha made a face, 'according to Tamara.'

'Must be odd,' Ben said. 'Giving up your house to other people.'

Martha shrugged and gave Pippa another leaf. 'I just hope they don't let their child chase Pippa.'

'Who are they?' Ben asked.

'A family from London, that's all I know.' Martha put the rabbit down on the flagstones. 'I told Tamara I didn't want any children staying here, but she said I'd be narrowing my opportunities when the school holidays kick in. They have a six-year-old son, he must go to a private school because it's still pretty early in the summer.'

'Loaded then?' Ben took a swig of his beer.

'You'd think so, but they're getting a bloody big discount in

15

return for writing the first review! And they don't even have to pay if they're not happy. Tamara's idea to get *Le Couvent des Cerises* on the *rental radar* – as she put it.'

'That's not very fair.'

'In my experience life has a habit of not being fair.' Martha smiled thinly and took the packet of cigarettes out of the pocket of her trousers. She offered one to Ben. He shook his head.

'I gave up.'

Martha lit a cigarette and inhaled.

'I gave up for a while,' she said. 'But then I decided there's only so much you can do without.'

Ben looked at her from under his mop of pale hair. His eyes were very dark, like two deep chocolate pools. It was unusual in someone with such fair colouring; it reminded her of Owen, golden hair and huge brown eyes, though everyone said his hair would be dark like Andrew's when he was older. Martha hoped that Andrew wouldn't have also passed on the darkness of his personality; the cruelty that had lurked beneath the geniality and charm. She prayed her son still had the loving and easy-going nature he'd had as a baby. In her memory he'd spent far more time laughing than crying; his sunny humour, never faltering despite the increasing chaos of his world.

It seemed impossible that her baby would ever have become a young man like the man in front of her; though she doubted that any son of Andrew's would be bumming around France on a motorbike. She knew that Owen was ensconced behind a desk in the city, being trained in all things financial to follow in his father and grandfather's footsteps. She had googled Owen Frazer a few years previously and found a blurry picture of a young man on LinkedIn; slicked back hair, perfect teeth and a CV that included Wellington College, Exeter University and now a senior job in the family firm. Since then she had looked at the LinkedIn page over and over again but the picture had never been updated.

She was about to ask Ben how old he was when a rumbling noise made them both turn towards the gates. A black Range Rover was slowly lumbering down the drive in a cloud of yellow dust. Martha took in the tinted windows and personalised number plate – RANJ1. The car looked over-sized on the narrow driveway; it was steering carefully around the potholes as overhanging branches scraped alarmingly along the gleaming paintwork.

'Fucking twiddly twats and bollocks,' Martha whispered. 'They're early!'

Sally and Pierre had thought she was mad to rent out *Le Couvent des Cerises*; it was far too much work for her to take on alone.

'How hard can it be?' Martha had asked four months before as she stopped for her weekly coffee in the tiny bar.

'Well . . .' Sally had been tentative; she and Pierre were drying beer glasses, working in unison, swiftly replacing the glasses back on the mirrored shelf behind them. Sally's breasts jiggled as she moved – they seemed to have a life of their own beneath her blouse. Her curves were a delicious contrast to her older, angular husband's Roman nose and greying hair. 'It would be really hard work,' Sally continued. 'We used to rent out rooms upstairs and it was . . .'

'Hard like you do not imagine!' Pierre butted in, his thick French accent booming around the empty space. 'And for you it will be more. First, you must make the house clean and not decorated with the cobwebs, and then you must make the pool blue and not green, and then there is the beds and the sheets and the towels and the mending of your leaky roof, and the drippy taps.'

'It's the leaky roof and drippy taps I need to pay for,' Martha said. 'And the bank is threatening to repossess the house.'

'Oh no!' Sally swung her tea towel over her shoulder and came out from behind the bar to top up Martha's coffee cup. 'Don't you make enough money from the royalties, or whatever it is you rock stars get?'

'I was never a rock star.' Martha blew on the steaming black coffee. 'It was just a pop group. And Lucas and Cat claimed the credit for writing all the songs, so they got all the money. I only get royalties from the one hit that had my name on it.'

Sally sat down beside her and folded her softly rounded arms.

17

'But I heard "Moondancing" on the radio the other day. Don't you get money every time it's played?'

'A bit, but it's not much. The royalty cheques get less every year. The only thing I can think to do is rent out the house. I've found an English holiday company who'll put it on their website.'

'I can't imagine you sharing your home with strangers,' Sally said. 'You always say you *like* being on your own.'

Martha took a sip of coffee. 'I know, but needs must when there's bugger all in the bank, as my mother used to say. She had three jobs when I was growing up. Even though she was a single mother I always had nice clothes, we ate well, and I had ballet classes and piano lessons – God knows how she managed.'

'But are you sure you'll be allright with strangers in your house?' Sally looked concerned. 'You don't want to end up back on the drugs,' she whispered the last word.

'They weren't *drugs*,' Martha protested. 'Just painkillers.'

'I know, but you've sorted yourself out and done really well these last few months.'

'Thanks to you, persuading me to check into the rehab clinic.' Martha smiled at Sally over the rim of her coffee cup. 'Even though they were—'

'—just painkillers,' Sally finished off the sentence with a roll of her eyes. 'But I can't help thinking that renting out *Le Couvent des Cerises* will be more stressful than you think. Have you thought about any other options?'

'The checkout at the Intermarché . . . grape-picking?' Martha sighed. 'I think I'm a little too old to open a brothel.'

Pierre leered forward with a grin.

'I think you might be having an idea there.' He raised his eyebrows. 'Madame Martha, the name, it has, how you say? A ring. I think I know some potential customers . . .'

'Pierre!' Sally scolded. 'Don't be so silly.' She turned to Martha. 'But you can sing!'

'I used to sing,' Martha corrected.

'Surely you still can. Why don't you sing here?' Sally's cleavage began to jiggle again. 'You could sit on a stool in the corner. Henri from the boulangerie could accompany you on his guitar. In the summer you could sing outside, get a crowd. I'm sure people would pay. And when the truffle festival is on in January you'd make a fortune from all the visitors we get then.'

Martha shook her head. 'Absolutely not.'

'Martha does not need to sing in our petite village,' Pierre frowned at his wife. '*Mais non*, she is needing the big tour. 1980s music is very popular. Everyone is doing concerts; Kajagoogoo, Bananarama, even Rick Astley, he is back. What about if On The Waterfront is getting it together again?'

'But how could we be a band without Lucas?' Martha paused and stared into her coffee cup. 'He *was* On The Waterfront.'

It had been six months since Martha had received an email inviting her to Lucas Oats's funeral. She rarely looked at the news and hadn't seen the reports that the band's lead singer had been found dead in his Surrey mansion. Martha didn't go to the funeral; she couldn't bear the thought of seeing Cat sweep in, dripping in her success, whilst the rest of them had faded into obscurity and middle-age. And there would have been the press; they might have brought up all the horrible stories that had been plastered over the newspapers when the band broke up, they might have remembered the incident at the BRIT Awards, they might have remembered the other awful things that happened in the years that followed.

Despite the letter she'd received from Cat, Martha had stayed at home. She didn't want Cat's charity; she had winced at the thought of accepting Cat's offer of a private plane from Bergerac to Heathrow, a suite next door to hers at the Savoy. We can be a support to each other, Cat had said, get through the funeral together, side by side like the old days. Martha had ripped the letter into pieces and thrown it in the bin without sending a reply. In the old days Cat's idea of support had not been hers.

Sally picked up a sugar lump from a little bowl in the middle of the table; she popped it into her mouth and began to suck, deep in thought. 'Your paintings!' She slapped her hand triumphantly on the table. The sugar cubes jumped in the bowl. 'You could sell them. We could have an exhibition here in the bar.'

Martha made a face. 'I don't think I'm that good. Until the clinic suggested using painting as therapy, I hadn't picked up a brush since I dropped out of school.'

Sally's jubilant expression fell. Martha reached over the table and squeezed her hand.

'Thank you for trying to help, but renting out the house really is the only answer.'

'Huh!' Pierre twisted his red cloth into the bottom of a glass until it squeaked. 'I worry for you, Martha. Those British people are all fussy-pots, nothing is ever right.'

'Hey!' Sally aimed a swipe at him with her cloth across the bar.

'Not the people from Rochdale, *ma petite*.' Pierre was laughing.

'And not the Welsh either.' Sally looked pointedly at Martha, but Martha wasn't listening. She was gazing out through the narrow doorway of the bar into the brightness of the village square beyond. A small boy was playing in the fountain, splashing in the water, throwing up rainbows in the air.

Smiling, Martha turned back to Sally and Pierre.

'Don't worry. I have it all planned. I'll move out and make the old chapel my home for the summer. I can't even see the house from there. I'll hardly even notice the guests.'

Chapter 3

Martha stubbed out her cigarette and thought of the unmade beds and the stinking rubbish and empty bottles and the washing still on the line. The Range Rover looked enormous parked beside Ben's motorbike and Martha's old Saab. The engine died. Everything was very quiet, apart from the unremitting chirrup of the cicadas. Martha waited.

After a long pause the driver's door swung open. A tall man in dark glasses and a white linen shirt stepped out. A few seconds later the passenger door opened and a tall woman in a neat shift dress and ballet pumps slipped down from the seat; she had a perfectly cut auburn bob. Her hair swung from side to side as she looked briefly around, then she opened the door behind her to whisk a baby out of a car seat, cradling it against her in a rocking motion.

There had been no mention of a baby.

Martha thought of cots and highchairs and changing tables; she had none of those things to offer. The baby looked big enough to crawl or maybe even walk. She thought of the steep stairs and lack of stair gates and wanted to light another cigarette. She shifted her gaze and saw a little boy clambering out of the other passenger door. He looked like his father with his good looks and thick, glossy locks. He ran to the woman's side.

The man yawned and stretched and looked around. The woman said something to him, and he stopped stretching and reached back into the car to retrieve a flowery sunhat and a bottle of sun cream. He handed them both to the woman who put the sunhat on the baby's head and started to rub sun cream onto the baby's chubby arms and legs.

The man suddenly spotted Martha standing on the terrace.

'Hi there,' he called, raising one arm in a wave. He strode forward up the path and mounted the terrace steps two at a time, white shirt billowing in the warm breeze. He approached Martha with a confident smile. She took his outstretched hand and noticed that his teeth were very white and very straight. His grip was firm.

'Good afternoon, I'm Ranjit Chandra.'

'You're early,' Martha said and then hastily added. 'Welcome to *Le Couvent des Cerises*.'

Ranjit took off his sunglasses to reveal his large brown eyes and thick, black lashes. He held up his hands in apology.

'I'm sorry. I know we're not supposed to be here until three o'clock, but we were worried about driving down from Calais in the storm.' He gestured behind him to where his wife remained beside the car. The little boy was trying to show her the pool beyond the fence, but she was busy adjusting the baby's hat. 'We had the children to consider, so we drove down yesterday and booked into a hotel for the night – *Château du Pont* – do you know it? It's very nice, only a few miles away . . .' Martha shook her head. 'Oh well, I'd recommend it. We weren't sure how long it would take to find you but with the excellent directions from Dordogne Dreams it was really very easy.' His smile broadened.

Martha glanced towards the car again. The baby was crying now, trying to pull the hat off her head. Martha looked back at Ranjit.

'I'm afraid the beds aren't made up yet and there's still some cleaning to finish.'

'No worries, we won't get in the way. Maybe we could sit here and admire the stunning scenery.' He swept his arm expansively towards the valley. 'Or by your beautiful pool. The website didn't do this place justice.'

'I'm glad you like it.' Martha felt relief flood through her – at least the initial impression was good.

'And the house.' Ranjit turned to look at it. 'It's . . .' He paused as

22

though searching for the appropriate words. 'It's no doubt steeped in history.'

Ranjit was staring at the deep crack on the wall above the terrace; his eyes seemed to be flicking back and forth along it. Martha pointed to the other end of the building in the hope of distracting his attention.

'That section at the end is Roman and then there are some medieval additions. It became a small convent and the little chapel was built around 1700 when a local dignitary paid for the convent to expand.' She knew she was rambling, but the words kept coming. 'Then after the French Revolution the nuns built an extension on—'

'Fascinating,' Ranjit interrupted. 'You must tell my wife all about it, her degree was in Medieval History. I'm just a humble accountant, Paula's the academic. She's also very interested in houses – in fact she's designed a beautiful extension for our kitchen, right down to the hand-painted tiles.' He raised his eyebrows and lowered his voice. 'You can imagine how much they cost!'

His wife and son appeared beside him. The baby had stopped crying and was staring intently at Martha from underneath the brim of the hat. Martha tried not to let herself look into the huge brown eyes.

'What's going on, Ranjee?' the woman asked. 'We can't stand around all day, Tilly needs to be changed and Reuben needs to find his book, he hasn't done any reading today.'

'Ah Paula.' Ranjit put his arm around his wife. 'I was just saying that you are the one with the interest in history and architecture in our family.'

Paula's shoulder gave the slightest of twitches and her husband took his arm away. Paula looked at Martha.

'If you could show us to our room I can see to Tilly. She needs a nap.' She kissed the baby's hair. 'You're a sleepy girl, aren't you, precious?' The baby girl went on staring at Martha, eyes huge and wide-awake.

'I don't have a cot,' Martha said.

'Tilly doesn't need a cot.' Paula kissed the baby's head again. 'She sleeps in bed with us, don't you, poppet?'

At the sound of skidding wheels, they turned in time to see another car, a silver sports car, coming through the open gates at surprising speed.

'Fantastic! I thought they'd broken down again.'

Martha watched as the Porsche bounced towards the bottom of the drive and crunched to a halt. Martha noticed that the car's soft top was incongruously half up and half down, partially revealing the driver and his passenger and what looked like a back seat stuffed full of luggage.

'There are more of you?' Martha looked at Ranjit.

'Is that a problem?' Ranjit flashed his brilliant smile. 'HEY, JOSH!'

Martha's reply was drowned out by Ranjit's cheer as the Porsche's driver clambered out of the side window. The man was deeply tanned with a pale beard and tousled sandy-coloured hair.

On the other side of the car a woman was opening the door. The driver rushed to assist her. Martha noticed he was wearing espadrilles and that his shorts looked uncomfortably tight. After the young woman had disentangled herself from his helpful hands she stood on the drive, barefoot in a short floral dress. Looking around she pushed her long chestnut hair behind her ears to reveal a very pretty, pink-cheeked face.

Ranjit turned his attention back to Martha.

'It does say on the Dordogne Dreams website that there are more bedrooms if needed?'

'Well, I suppose there is one,' Martha said, thinking about the yellow bedroom that her mother used to stay in long ago. It would need dusting and airing, and she didn't have enough new bed linen. This extra couple would have to make do with old sheets and fraying pillowcases. She also remembered that the light bulb had long ago rusted into the socket in the ceiling. She supposed Ben might be able to get it out and replace the bulb. She turned to look for him, but he had gone, as had the rubbish bags and the compost bin.

There was a shout, a child's voice. Martha turned back to the Porsche and saw that a small boy with long white-blond curls had begun to squeeze his way out of the tiny space in the back. He jumped out onto the dusty drive, unzipped his shorts and began to pee, with an impressively large arc of urine, in to an azalea bush.

Martha gasped.

'Noah, don't do that!' There was another voice from the back of the Porsche and an additional figure clambered out, long limbs struggling to unfurl themselves from the cramped space. It was a girl; skinny black jeans and a curtain of long turquoise streaked hair that half-hid her face. Her T-shirt read 'Don't Ask'.

'Fantastic, the gang's all here,' Ranjit grinned.

'Ahh . . .' Martha couldn't seem to form coherent words.

'I'll tell Josh that we'll have to wait an hour before the rooms are ready.' Ranjit was walking away, guiding his wife towards the steps with one hand lightly on her back, his other hand was firmly gripping his son's. The little boy was jumping up and down with what looked like excitement, squealing Noah's name over and over.

'Whaaa . . .' Martha tried again.

On the drive the little boy had finished peeing. He looked around and spotted the swimming pool. He set off towards it at speed but the girl with the 'Don't Ask' T-shirt was in instant pursuit, catching him and holding him tight against her, ignoring his cries of protest and attempts to bite her arm.

'Dad, help!' she called out to the driver of the Porsche, but he was busy nuzzling his female companion. Even from a distance Martha could see that she was too young to be the mother of the children.

'But I don't have enough rooms,' Martha called after Ranjit. He turned and came back up the steps despite the protestations of his son who was trying to pull him back, presumably towards Noah. His wife followed.

'But you just said you have more rooms if needed.'

'I have three at a push. Not enough for the extra children.' Martha nodded towards Noah, struggling to free himself from the older girl's firm grip.

'I told you we should have said no to Josh,' Paula muttered under her breath.

'Darling, it'll be OK,' Ranjit reassured his wife and then turned back to Martha. 'Josh is my old friend from university, he wanted to join us at the last minute. We usually holiday with him and his wife Carla. We try to meet up every year.' Ranjit lowered his voice. 'Due to some personal problems Josh declined this year. But then, a few days ago, he suddenly phoned up and asked if he and the children could come.' He paused. 'Without Carla.'

'He didn't mention his new *friend*.' Paula pursed her lips.

'In the photographs on the Dordogne Dreams website the house looks huge, so we told him it would be fine.' Ranjit smiled at Martha.

Martha sighed. 'As I've explained, the problem is . . .'

'Maybe if the two boys and Elodie shared?' Ranjit suggested.

'Elodie is fourteen. I'd imagine she needs a room of her own. I'm sure Carla will be expecting Josh to provide adequate accommodation for their children while they're with him.'

Martha could see, from the way Josh was whispering into his companion's ear, that providing adequate accommodation for his children was probably the last thing he had on his mind.

Paula was looking around the terrace. Martha could see her taking in the empty bottles, the remains of Ben's lunch, the cigarettes and ashtray. Paula lowered her voice.

'I'm not sure it's really *us*, Ranjee. It looks a bit . . .' She stopped and ever so slightly wrinkled her nose.

'As I've said, I haven't finished cleaning yet,' Martha protested.

'*Château du Pont* said they have vacancies all week,' Paula continued in a loud whisper. 'They have such a big pool, and a spa. And the dinner last night was excellent.'

'Darling, don't be hasty,' Ranjit grimaced. 'It was a bit pricey. And we are trying to save money this year – remember the extension is costing a lot.' He turned his dark eyes to Martha. 'If Josh and his friend . . .'

'Alice,' Paula muttered.

'Ah yes, Alice. If Josh and Alice have the third bedroom and the boys share, would you have anywhere that Elodie could sleep? Anywhere at all?'

Martha glanced up at the little dormer window in the roof and thought of the room in the attic, very small and very full of stuff.

'There is a room I use for storage, but it will take a while to clear.'

'Come on, Ranjee, let's just leave.' Paula smiled at her husband for the first time. 'I'd feel so much better at *Château du Pont*. Tilly loved the toddler splash-pool with the fountain, and Reuben had such fun in the children's playground.' She glanced at the broken swing hanging from the oak tree and turned back to Martha. 'I presume we can get a refund?'

'Sorry?' Martha stared at her.

'As you can't meet our needs we should be eligible to get our money back.'

'I haven't actually paid yet,' Ranjit hissed. 'I did a special deal with Dordogne Dreams, I meant to tell you.'

Paula shot her husband a look of surprise.

'Oh! But we should be eligible for some sort of compensation; we've come all this way and the property is completely unsuitable.'

Ranjit took his phone out of his pocket.

'I'll phone Tamara in the Dordogne Dreams office. I'll tell her we have a problem already.' He held the phone up and turned around in several different directions. 'I can't seem to get a signal.'

'There isn't any signal here.' Martha started to clear the debris of the lunch, hoping that she wouldn't be the one expected to pay the compensation. 'And you didn't tell me about the extra guests.'

'Then let's look at the terms and conditions on the Dordogne Dreams website,' Paula said, ignoring Martha. 'Ranjee, give me the phone.' The baby started to cry again.

'The Wi-Fi will be down along with the phone line.' Martha picked up the pile of plates; Pierre had been right about the *fussy-pots* British. 'And if you're looking for 4G don't bother.'

'This is unbelievable!' Paula was now turning around with Ranjit's phone trying to find the elusive signal; she seemed undeterred by the wails of the baby. 'And I need to keep in touch with my father, he's project managing the kitchen extension while we're away.'

Martha shrugged. 'I'm sorry but that's just the way it is.'

A sudden smash of breaking glass made them all turn around. Ben was picking up the pieces of a broken bottle.

Martha hadn't even heard Ben come back. Ranjit and Paula were staring at him. Reuben was staring too. She wondered what they were thinking. No doubt the *Château du Pont* had much more salubrious-looking staff.

Ben put the broken glass into a box and walked over to Martha.

'I could help you clear the room,' he said quietly.

Martha shook her head, already reaching for her cigarettes.

'Come on, Ranjee.' Paula had already started down the stone steps. 'I really don't want to stay.'

Ranjit shrugged apologetically at Martha and together with his son followed Paula back down towards the car.

'Are you sure you want to let them go?' Ben said. 'After all your hard work.'

'She's so rude!' Martha slid a cigarette out of the packet and placed it between her lips. 'I really don't want her to stay!'

'I thought you needed the money.' Ben's voice was very quiet.

Martha looked at him, then up at the sagging roof and the rotting shutters and an especially wide crack in the wall. She thought of the letters from the bank and the mounting bills. She thought of a life away from *Le Couvent des Cerises*. She thought of Owen, her longing to see him.

She took the unlit cigarette out of her mouth and put it back in the packet before forcing herself to turn around.

She called down to the group assembled on the drive. 'The attic room will be ready in an hour.'

Paula looked at her husband and shook her head. She started to strap the baby back into the car seat. Ranjit lifted up the little boy and put him into the Range Rover. Josh now seemed too busy with the roof of the car to notice there had been a change of plan, he was getting Alice to turn the engine of the Porsche on and off while he tried to pull the soft top down.

'Are we going?' his daughter asked. She had her little brother in a headlock now.

'Yes, we are,' shouted Paula firmly.

'Say you'll cook dinner for them,' Ben said.

Martha stared at him.

'But I'm a hopeless cook.'

'Just say you will.'

'I'll cook dinner,' Martha called out.

'Sorry, what did you say?' asked Ranjit. The baby was still crying and Reuben's sobs could also be heard coming from inside the car. *But I like it here.*

Martha glanced at Ben – he nodded eagerly.

'I can help you,' he said quietly.

'Dinner will be provided,' Martha shouted. She hesitated, waiting for Ranjit to say something. 'Every night,' she added when there was no response. When there still wasn't a response, she found herself calling out, 'Free of charge.'

Ranjit turned towards her but before he could speak a huge splash came from the direction of the swimming pool. The teenage girl was standing empty-handed.

'Sorry,' she mumbled with a shrug. 'I couldn't hold him any longer.'

Another splash followed and Paula shouted out.

'Reuben! That's very naughty to get out of the car! And you're wearing your new T-shirt!'

'Looks like the boys are happy here,' Ranjit said laughing. 'And if we can have the extra bedrooms and our dinner cooked, we might as well stay.' He looked at Paula.

Paula looked suddenly exhausted. 'Well, the extension is already over-budget, and I really don't enjoy cooking when I'm on holiday, and Reuben is too wet to get back in the car.'

'That sounds like a *yes* from the chief,' said Ranjit doing a thumbs up sign towards Martha. 'But are you sure about the cooking?'

After another reassuring nod from Ben, Martha returned the thumbs up sign.

'Looks like we're staying,' Ranjit called to Josh.

'Sorry mate, what did you say?'

Josh had resorted to lying on the back seat pushing at the roof with his feet. Alice was peering under the bonnet trying to follow Josh's instructions. Josh squeezed out of the Porsche through the window.

'We're staying now,' Ranjit repeated.

'I never knew we weren't. Hey, Elodie,' Josh called out to his daughter. 'Where's Noah? I thought you were watching him.'

'Come on,' Martha said to Ben. 'Let's get started on the room and then you can explain to me how the bloody hell I'm going to feed four adults and three children with no culinary skills to speak of and a practically non-existent budget!'

Chapter 4

The wooden stairs creaked under Martha's feet as they climbed towards the attic. Ben followed her though he kept stopping to look around.

'Wow,' he'd murmured as they'd walked through the large and colourful kitchen. For years Martha had trawled the local antique shops and flea markets and accumulated a myriad of unusual items of furniture and objets d'art. High-backed tapestry chairs, stencil-decorated cupboards and an ornate carved church pew that ran along one side of a scrubbed pine table. Enamel advertising signs and large majolica dishes hung side by side with eighteenth-century portraits of long-forgotten French aristocrats. If one word described the room, it would have been *riotous*.

The living room was also a cacophony of random items; a golden 1950s cocktail bar complete with matching bar stools and a set of multicoloured champagne flutes. A zebra-skin rug lay in front of a huge stone fireplace filled with giant pine cones and a spray of pea-cock feathers. An elaborately edged gilt mirror hung above the mantelpiece, candleholders attached to both sides of the frame. On the other side of the room a small record player, in a red leather case, sat on a sideboard, beside it a neat stack of Motown records.

'Meet Elvis.' Martha indicated a large stuffed bear. It rose up on its hind legs, its mouth set forever in a twisted snarl. 'He used to be called Wagner but I renamed him after the famous Welsh singer.'

'Elvis?' Ben touched the rough brown fur. 'Not Tom Jones?'

Martha laughed at Ben's confused expression.

'Didn't you know that Elvis Presley's grandpa came from Wales?'

'I don't know much about Elvis or Tom Jones,' Ben said.

'Before your time.' Martha started up the wooden staircase. 'To be fair, Elvis is before my time as well, but I thought there was something about his snarl and the thrust of his hips . . .' she paused, 'he just didn't seem like a Wagner.'

Ben looked quizzically at the bear.

'Come on,' Martha called down the staircase. 'There's only so long they'll be happy staring at the view.'

The heat increased as they neared the top of the house. The air was very still. Martha stopped in front of a dark oak door and fished a large key out of her pocket. She hesitated before unlocking the door and turned to Ben.

'Maybe they would all be better off staying at bloody *Château du Pont*.'

He shrugged. 'It can't be that hard to clear the stuff away for a while.'

'Sometimes I think I should just clear it away for good.' Martha placed the big key in the lock. 'I don't know why I brought it all here in the first place. It's a mess.' The door creaked. 'I started going through it all a few years ago but it brought back so many memories I gave up.'

The door swung open. Dusty sunlight streamed through a dormer window illuminating dozens of dresses hanging from a picture rail that ran around the small room; slinky metallic lamé competed with layers of sequined net and tulle to twinkle and sparkle, while velvet, silk and satin glistened and fur coats looked sumptuously soft in a myriad of colours that could only be fake. Diamanté jewellery dripped from the frame of a dressing-table mirror, glittering in the glass beside strings of gaudy-coloured plastic beads and fake pearl bracelets. A dressing table was covered in gloves and hats and different sizes of sunglasses from tiny round ones to huge 'Jackie O' style frames with peach-tinted lenses. More hats were piled on top of an unmade wrought-iron bed and cardboard boxes, precariously stacked in one corner, looked like they might topple at any time.

Ben gazed silently around the room.

'My mum kept it all.' Martha began to take down the clothes and fold them. 'I didn't realise just how much there was until I had to pack up her house after she died. Didn't know what to do with it, so I brought it here.'

Ben walked over to the bed and picked up a sailor's cap; he examined it then put it back beside a battered top hat tied round with a silver scarf.

'Was this stuff all yours?'

Martha turned away without answering Ben's question.

'It's so stuffy.' She opened the window and took several deep breaths.

She could see the guests arranged beside the pool below, their luggage scattered haphazardly on the ground. Some of the cases and bags were opened, children's clothes left strewn on the grass, no doubt in the haste to find swimming costumes and goggles.

The two boys were splashing noisily in the pool with Josh. He was throwing himself around in the water pretending to be a shark, perhaps trying to make up for his earlier neglect of fatherly duties. Noah and Reuben shrieked with laughter, though Elodie didn't seem impressed. She sat hunched at the side of the pool, legs dangling in the water, her skinny frame draped in a large towel.

Paula sat under the gazebo feeding the baby from a jar. Ranjit lay back on a sunlounger looking at a map.

'Who's up for a trip to a vineyard?'

'That's not going to be suitable for the children,' said Paula.

'Maybe the boys should have a little expedition?' Ranjit said.

'By *boys* I assume you mean you and Josh?'

'Well, I think Reuben and Noah are a bit young for wine tasting,' Ranjit laughed.

'Get on with the shopping list.' Paula looked at him irritably. 'We need things for breakfast and for snacks and lunch. Let's start with peaches.'

Ranjit obediently put down the map and picked up a notebook and pen.

'Peaches,' he repeated and wrote it down.

'Rice cakes,' said Paula. Ranjit wrote down rice cakes.

'J2O,' called Elodie. Ranjit wrote that down too.

'Really? I don't want Reuben having all that sugar.' Paula shook her head. Ranjit crossed out J2O.

'But Noah won't drink anything else,' Elodie said. 'Not even orange juice or water.'

Ranjit added J2O again.

'Do you think she'll provide wine with dinner? I hope she realises how much we'll need.'

From the window Martha wanted to shout out that she would definitely not be supplying wine but then didn't want them to think she was spying.

'Please don't turn this holiday into another lad's booze-up.' Paula looked sternly at Josh. 'We don't want a repeat of Tuscany.'

Josh grinned. 'Ah, Tuscany, never to be forgotten.'

'Kefalonia was my favourite holiday,' said Paula. 'Much more civilised.'

'What happened in Tuscany?' Alice had been quietly reading a book under the fig tree a few yards away from the rest of the group.

Paula turned her head to look at Alice as if she had forgotten the young woman was there.

'My daddy peed on the barbecue,' shouted Noah.

'And my daddy fell in the pool,' called out Reuben.

'And then they both . . .'

'That's enough!' Paula silenced Noah. 'You were much too young to remember.'

'I think I get the picture,' smiled Alice.

Ranjit was chuckling.

'That was such a good holiday. Carla was hilarious when she did the dance of the seven sarongs – what a woman!' He put his hand up to his mouth. 'Oh sorry, Josh. Sorry, Alice.'

There was a pause. Even from a distance Martha could see Josh's cheeks flush pink.

'Please excuse my social ineptitude, Alice.' Ranjit smacked his face with his hand. 'I forgot the whole new . . .' His voice trailed away, he seemed to be struggling to think of the right words.

'It's fine, Ranjit,' Alice said. 'I realise I must be a bit of a surprise.'

'You can say that again,' muttered Elodie.

'Pringles,' Noah suddenly shouted out.

'Yes, Pringles,' Reuben repeated. 'Daddy, write down Pringles – salt and vinegar are the best.'

'Don't be silly, Reuben,' Paula snapped. 'You don't even know what Pringles are.'

'Yes, I do!'

Paula looked suspiciously at Ranjit. He looked back down at the notebook.

'Grapes,' he said, writing the word down studiously.

Paula turned back to feeding Tilly. 'I'd better tell that woman I don't eat wheat. Let's hope it's not too much of a challenge for her.'

'You can usually find a wheat replacement.' Alice started thumbing through the book on her lap. 'There are some very good gluten-free puddings and cakes in here.'

'You're reading a cookery book?' Paula looked at Alice with an incredulous expression.

Alice smiled. 'Yes, this one's fascinating; French and English fusion baking: *Let Them Eat Scones.*'

'Alice writes a baking blog,' Josh called from the edge of the pool.

Paula frowned. 'What on earth do you write about?'

'I try out recipes and experiment with new ingredients and tell everyone what they're like. And I review cafés and cake shops near where I live.'

'That's your job?' Paula's eyes widened.

'Well, not full time. I work as a receptionist.'

'So, the blog is more like a hobby.' Paula turned back to Tilly to wipe the baby's mouth with a wet wipe.

'What's it called?' asked Ranjit, getting out his phone. 'I'll look it up.'

'It's called The Bedsit Bakery.'

'Why's it called that?'

35

'I live in a bedsit.'

'I think it's more of a studio apartment than a bedsit,' said Josh. He turned to the others. 'Alice has thousands of followers and she is an amazing cook, not just a pretty face.'

'*Nearly* a thousand followers,' Alice corrected quietly.

'I forgot there isn't any Wi-Fi.' Ranjit put his phone back in his pocket. 'We'll have a look when it gets fixed later.'

Above them Martha inwardly groaned. From past experience she knew getting the Wi-Fi restored took many angry phone calls to grumpy engineers; with only pidgin French it was a long and frustrating process that could take weeks.

'Alice has brought some of her triple chocolate date and walnut cookies.' Josh seemed to be doing press-ups against the side of the pool, admiring his arm muscles as he did so. 'Wait till you taste them, they're delicious – just like the lovely lady herself.'

Alice glanced at him quickly then turned back to her book.

'I don't eat sugar,' said Paula, wiping her hands with another baby-wipe. 'And Reuben has a nut allergy. We think he may be lactose intolerant as well.'

'We've never had him properly tested,' said Ranjit. 'We don't know he has those allergies for sure. He'd probably be fine with one of Alice's cookies.'

'It's better to be safe than sorry.' Paula looked imploringly at her husband. 'You know that, Ranjee, after everything we've been through.'

'Luckily neither of my kids has an allergy.' Josh sounded very proud. 'And you love cookies, don't you, Elodie?'

Elodie pulled the towel more tightly round her shoulders. 'I told you. I'm a vegan now.'

'More for us then.' Ranjit patted his stomach.

'You're on a diet,' said Paula.

Ranjit's response was drowned out by Noah shouting *Shark attack*, and the screaming and splashing began again.

Martha turned back to Ben.

'Did you hear that list of dietary requirements? And that young woman sounds like a serious foodie. You'd better be a bloody good cook because I struggle with a sandwich for one, let alone dinner for seven!'

Ben wasn't listening. He was squatting down, studying something leaning against the wall. Martha looked down at the framed platinum disc.

'Something else well before your time.' She attempted a laugh.

'I think I've heard of On The Waterfront.' Ben stood up. 'And that song.'

Martha thought back to the morning she'd spent in the hotel in Amsterdam, picking out notes on the piano in the empty bar. The simple melody was so different to the band's jangling electronic beat, but when Lucas heard Martha singing it had seemed to rouse him from the drunken stupor he'd been in since he'd got back together with Cat.

> *I touch your face and close my eyes*
> *Our bodies meet and my heart flies*
> *I take a step into the darkness of the room*
> *And suddenly I find I'm dancing on the moon*

'That's beautiful!' he'd whispered, putting down his whisky glass.

Cat had been lying on the sofa flicking through *The Sunday Times* colour supplement looking for an interview she'd given entitled 'My Life in Lipstick'.

'I'm not singing it like that,' she'd said. 'Let's leave the power ballads to Bonnie bloody Tyler and Cher.'

'I think Martha should sing it this time,' Lucas had said. 'It is her song.'

And that had been the beginning of the end.

A particularly piercing shriek came through the open window followed by children's laughter. Martha pursed her lips and looked around the cluttered room.

'Most of this will go into the big cupboard on the landing.'

Ben picked up a box and started to carry it towards the door.

Martha pulled a dust sheet off a low table revealing several rows of Dr. Martens; a rainbow of colours and some in unexpected fabrics like tweed or velvet, some customised with splatters of paint or graffiti.

Ben came back into the room. 'Shall I put the boots in the cupboard?'

Martha didn't answer. She picked up a patent purple boot; out of all of them the patent ones had been her favourite.

'The boots were our trademark,' she said. 'Cat – my bandmate – and I wore them with old-fashioned cocktail dresses that we found in charity shops.' She put the boot back down. 'When we broke up *Melody Maker* said we were "the essence of the 1980s".'

'You must have been good.' Ben disappeared into the corridor with a box of records.

'I think *Melody Maker* said that about all the bands,' Martha called after him. 'We were just a group of Welsh kids who were at the right place at the right time.'

'But you must have had some talent.' Ben reappeared and started helping Martha fold up the clothes.

Martha shrugged. 'Cat once came second in the local Eisteddfod for reciting a poem and the boys had been in a punk band called The Rippers – West Wales's answer to The Sex Pistols. I was the only one who could read music.'

'Was it the band with the lead singer who died not long ago?' Ben was trying to work out how to fold a very frilly blouse.

'Yes. Lucas Oats.'

'He looked quite cool when he was younger,' said Ben. 'For a man in make-up.'

Martha thought of the first time she and Cat had seen Lucas after he came back to Abertrulli; leaning against the bar in the rugby club he looked like something from another planet. Jet-black hair, shaved on one side, eyeliner and a single huge hoop earring. He was wearing a leather jacket over an elaborate lace shirt; skinny as a beanpole with a face like James Dean.

He'd stood beside the burly sons of sheep farmers, in their checked shirts and flared jeans, unperturbed by their muttered insults and sideways glances. He knew that every girl at the disco only had eyes for him.

Lucas had spent the whole night watching Martha and Cat dancing nonchalantly on the sticky dance floor. They had crimped their hair and wore winkle-pickers bought for pennies in the chapel jumble sale. They pretended not to notice Lucas but just when they thought he was coming over to speak to them he'd vanished.

It was Christmas before Martha and Cat saw him again, leaning against the wall of the newsagents opposite the school. As they came out of the gates he sauntered over, flicked back his long fringe and said, in the cockney accent he'd acquired during his year in England, 'I could use a couple of girls like you in my band.'

A creaking sound made Martha jump. She turned to see a small thin figure standing in the doorway. It was the girl, Elodie, changed back into her skinny jeans but with a different black T-shirt; printed across her chest was the word 'Seriously' with a very big question mark underneath. One eye was completely obscured by her heavy fringe; the other was staring around the room.

'We're not quite finished yet,' said Martha.

'Dad says I have to sleep in here.' Elodie looked down at the floor as she spoke.

'Surely you don't need to sleep right now.' Martha reached up to put the top hat in a box. As she did so the pile of boxes began to wobble. Martha tried to push them back against the wall, but the pile began to sway and the top box crashed down spilling clothes, papers and photographs all over the dusty boards.

'Oh no!' Martha crouched down to try to pick things up. Ben joined her. Elodie remained standing by the door.

'At least give us a hand,' Martha said, looking up at the girl.

Elodie bent over and picked up a sheaf of black and white

39

photographs. She handed them to Martha. Martha flicked through them – they were the first press shots of the band, taken when they'd come to London after the talent scout had seen them perform at the Aberystwyth University Students' Union.

The band were standing in a back alley, rubbish on the ground, brick walls on either side – Martha remembered that bleak February day. The alley was just around the corner from the record label's offices on Greek Street; the photographer hadn't wanted to go to excessive trouble for a new Welsh band that would probably never make it. He had made a joke about them singing in the valleys; Martha thought the boys might hit him.

Lucas stood in a gold-trimmed military jacket and a chequered Arab scarf in the middle of the picture, looking furious. He was flanked by Idris and Posh Paul, who both wore oversized trench coats and tight leather trousers; they held their guitars like sentries holding guns. Sledge skulked behind looking too butch for the ruffled shirt he'd been forced to wear; his arms were folded, drumsticks clenched in one fist.

Martha and Cat were sitting on a fire escape in matching strapless dresses, full skirts and petticoats, ripped fishnet stockings and their first pairs of Dr. Martens. Their manager, Big Bryn, had bought the boots that morning from a Soho market stall.

'You gotta have a look, my lovelies,' he kept repeating as he tore holes in their stockings and did up the long laces.

It had seemed like a dream as they piled into Sledge's van and headed for London. They'd only done a handful of gigs. Martha remembered how she had shivered with the cold on the day of the photograph. She'd worried that the goosebumps on her arms would show in the pictures.

Afterwards, they had drunk Cinzano in the flat the record company had found for them to rent on Baker Street. They ate chips from the takeaway on the ground floor and Lucas and Cat had disappeared into the bedroom while Martha tried not to cry. She'd gone downstairs and bought more chips and watched *Dallas* with the boys on the biggest colour television she had ever seen. Later they had all gone to the Blitz Club; 'he wasn't that good,' Cat had whispered to Martha in the taxi on the way. It was dawn when they got back to the flat. Martha and Cat had tumbled into bed declaring that they were never ever going back to Abertrulli, whatever happened. It was 1980 and they were seventeen.

Martha gathered the rest of the photographs and put them back into the box. The pictures of those early days brought back all the happiness and excitement she'd felt then. So different from how she'd felt in the end, she was glad the glossy publicity shots from that time hadn't spilled all over the floor. She supressed a shudder and stood up. Ben had something small in his hand. It took Martha a few seconds to realise what it was. She snatched it from him.

'Sorry,' he said standing up. 'It was under the bed.'

Martha stared at the tiny knitted mitten. It had been made to look like a dinosaur head; beaded eyes stitched onto the top, a row of pointy felt teeth along the edge. Martha raised it to her face and sniffed. It smelled of musty wool, it smelled of the room – there was nothing else, all trace of Owen long gone. With an aching heart she dropped the mitten into the box and firmly pushed down the lid.

Elodie had wandered over to the Dr. Martens. She stroked the toe of a patent boot.

'Please don't touch,' Martha said.

Elodie moved towards the dressing table and started picking up pieces of jewellery.

'I said don't touch.' Martha snatched a string of plastic pearls from her hand and slipped it into a large leather bag with some other jewellery. 'And I don't want you going through my things while you're staying up here, do you understand?'

Elodie nodded.

'I'll know if you have.' She could see the scepticism in Elodie's expression. 'You can ask the local children.' Martha stared at her. 'They think I'm a witch.'

Elodie looked even more sceptical but then her eyes grew suddenly wide when a loud scream came from the garden below. Martha

41

and Ben rushed to the window. Paula was standing on top of one of the suitcases, tightly clutching the baby and looking wildly around.

'I saw a rat, a giant rat.'

Ranjit was already on his feet and looking under the sunlounger.

'It had huge teeth. It was about to bite Tilly!'

Josh and Alice had joined Ranjit; they were looking under the chairs and in the corners of the gazebo.

'It's not a rat,' Josh said after a few minutes of searching. He was peering behind a large terracotta planter. 'It's a weird-looking rabbit.'

Chapter 5

'A rat!' Martha peeled another onion and handed it to Ben. He chopped with remarkable speed considering Martha's knives were rather old and blunt. 'How could she possibly have mistaken Pippa for a rat?'

He shrugged at Martha's question. 'Maybe South London's leafy suburbs have some very large rats?'

'With long ears and fluffy tails?'

She watched as Ben added several bay leaves to the pan. He had already explained that the slow-cooked caramelised onions would provide the base for a pasta sauce that would suit all the guests' dietary requirements. He was using ingredients that Martha had hastily emptied from the house that afternoon, and herbs from the neglected bed that had been planted many years before.

Ben added sage and rosemary to the pan and stirred the contents.

'Where did you learn to cook?' Martha asked.

'I work in a restaurant kitchen,' he answered, stripping thyme leaves from their woody stems and scattering them across the surface of the sauce. 'I'm just having a bit of time off at the moment, travelling around, looking for new ingredients.'

'So, you've come to France on a culinary journey?'

'Something like that.'

The pop of a bottle being opened came through the open door of the chapel, the distant chink of glasses being placed on the long mosaic table on the terrace. Someone laughed.

'My God, Ranjit! I need my shades to look at that Hawaiian shirt! It's blinding me!'

'Has anyone seen Noah?'

'Josh – is that a spray tan? Or have you been overdoing the carrots again?'

'Ha ha! Very funny!'

'I can't believe the fridge doesn't have an icemaker – I mean . . .'

'Let's open another bottle.'

'Have you seen that creepy stuffed bear? And the zebra-skin rug!'

'Talking of rugs – when did you grow the beard, Josh?'

'Dad, Noah is climbing up the trellis.'

'Do you think this mosaic table is hygienic?'

'Did anyone buy crisps?'

Martha tried to block it all out. She picked up a stick of celery; it drooped in her hand.

'We can't use this.'

'Chopped small and sautéed it'll be fine.' Ben was crushing garlic with the back of a spoon.

Martha set to work with her knife. The smell of herbs and onions was beginning to make her mouth water. In the distance someone was banging random piano keys.

'I told them not to touch the piano,' Martha muttered. The notes turned into something vaguely resembling a tune. The third time it was played Martha recognised 'Ode to Joy'.

'I need to pay you for today,' she said to Ben. 'I can't thank you enough for everything you've done.'

'If there're any other jobs, I'm happy to do more tomorrow.'

'There are plenty – the path needs weeding, the shrubs need pruning, the grass needs cutting, cracks need filling in the walls, and I've been meaning to fill the potholes in the drive with the stones I had delivered months ago. They're still in a pile by the gates . . . which no doubt will be considered unsightly.' Martha gave the celery an especially hard chop. 'And I've got six more dinners to cook after this one.'

Ben scooped up the chopped celery and added it to the pan.

'I can stick around for a few more days if you like?'

'Could you?' Martha's heart lifted. 'I'll pay you as much as I can, but it won't be very much.'

'Whatever you can afford, I'm not that fussed.'

Martha raised her eyebrows. 'Surely you have more exciting places to go? This is what Cat and I would have called *The Back of the Back of Bloody Beyond*.'

Ben shrugged. 'It suits me fine. I'd planned to stay in the area anyway.'

'Where are you going to stay tonight?'

'I was wondering if I could put my tent up here?' he gestured through the door towards the meadow in front of the chapel.

'And camp?'

Ben nodded.

She didn't want to be on her own with these strangers in her house. There was something about Ben's easy-going nature that she liked. His quietness calmed her, and he didn't ask too many questions.

'I don't see why not. You can use the shower and toilet down by the pool. Just not when the paying guests are using it – or should I say non-paying.'

'Great! It's a deal.' Ben sloshed red wine into the pan and a cloud of steam enveloped him; he added a large tin of tomatoes. 'This sauce has got to reduce now for a while.'

'Then I think we deserve a break.' Martha fetched two glasses from the dresser and filled them with the wine. 'Let's take these onto my patio.'

'I can see someone in the orchard,' said Martha, as she sat down on the bench. She leant forward peering into the fading light.

Ben turned to where Martha was looking at the copse of cherry trees beyond the meadow. The trees were in shadow; the ancient trunks were twisted into strange contorted shapes. Some of them had fallen over, their roots rising up out of the earth. The gnarled branches were heavy with the cherries that had originally given the convent its name, and the warm evening air was filled with the thick syrupy scent of ripening fruit.

'I think it's that woman whose boyfriend can't get his roof up,' Ben said.

Martha could see Alice reaching for a cherry. She wondered why she wasn't with the others on the terrace.

'What's the story there, I wonder?'

Ben made a huffing sound. 'The usual one, I reckon.'

Alice walked slowly up the field, lost in thought, unaware of Ben and Martha until she was just a few feet away.

'Oh sorry.' There was a little trickle of pink juice on the young woman's chin. 'I probably shouldn't be eating your cherries.' She wiped away the juice with her finger, licking it off her fingertip with one quick movement of her tongue. She laughed. 'They're just so delicious. They must make lovely jam.'

'I wouldn't know.' Martha shook her head. 'The birds eat them; the rest fall off.'

'Would you mind if I used some?' asked Alice. 'I was thinking about making a clafoutis.'

'Be my guest.' Martha lit a cigarette and thought of the delicious cherry clafoutis that they sold in the patisserie in the village. She'd never thought of making it herself.

Alice glanced towards the kitchen door. 'It smells good in there.'

'Ben is working his magic.' Martha took a sip of her wine.

'Are they getting hungry?' Ben nodded towards the terrace.

Alice smiled. 'Don't worry, I think they're happy with the champagne and salty snacks for a little while longer.'

She turned to Martha. 'Is there any chance of the Wi-Fi being fixed so that I can post some pictures on my blog? It's all so lovely here, I'd love to share it with my followers.'

Martha shook her head. 'I'm afraid I haven't had a chance to get to town to phone the engineer.'

'There you are!' Josh appeared from the direction of the house. He glanced at Martha and then at Ben and slipped his arm round Alice's waist.

'I've been looking for you everywhere.'

Alice smiled up at him. 'I'm going to make a clafoutis with Martha's cherries.'

'Clafy what?' asked Josh.

'Cla-fou-tis,' she said slowly. 'It's a traditional French dessert – just like a big cherry pancake. Delicious. It might go on that top ten list of favourite puddings you've told me about.'

Josh nuzzled her neck. 'I've decided you're all the sweetness I need.'

Alice's fingers reached up to gently push his face away.

'Come on, your glass of fizz awaits.' Josh began to steer Alice towards the house, sliding his hand down onto Alice's left buttock as they disappeared around the corner.

'Prat,' Ben said under his breath and drained his glass.

Chapter 6

Sunday

Dinner was preceded by a long list of requirements: extra pillows, extra toilet rolls, big towels, small towels, a hairdryer, a brighter light bulb, instructions on using the DVD player and a request to cover Elvis with a blanket – the snarling face of the bear was apparently frightening the children. Then there had been the complaints: a dripping tap, mosquitos on the terrace and a 'smell' in Paula and Ranjit's en suite – all combined with general incredulity at the ongoing problem with the Wi-Fi and the lack of air conditioning.

Martha had been apprehensive about how dinner would be received. She had seen the minute flaring of Paula's nostrils as she placed the large bowl of spaghetti on the table. Ben had followed with a salad and Noah, who was sitting on one of the high golden chairs from the cocktail bar like a little prince, looked at the food and pretended that he was going to get sick.

Martha had made her way around the table hoisting the slippery pasta with a fork and serving it onto the mismatched collection of plates in front of the guests. Paula had picked up her plate and checked the back for a maker's mark. She put it back down with a sniff.

Ranjit swapped his rose-covered porcelain for Josh's blue and white willow pattern.

'To help you get in touch with your feminine side.'

Josh swapped them back. 'Get in touch with your own.'

Then Reuben started to cry because he wanted the owl plate that Noah had taken from him.

'Look what you started,' Paula hissed at Ranjit.

Amidst the commotion Martha dropped Josh's serving of spaghetti onto his lap.

'For God's sake!' Josh leapt up and the pasta slithered onto the floor. 'These are my new Paul Smith shorts!'

Martha apologised and remembered a holiday job she and Cat had worked in the hotel in Abertrulli; Martha had been sacked for spilling an entire dish of peas into an elderly lady's cleavage. Cat had lost her job the next day after she'd given a toddler his grandma's G&T instead of lemonade. The two teenage girls had laughed at their dismissals and decided they weren't cut out for catering. Martha wondered what Cat would think if she could see her now. She thought of the tight Botoxed face she'd seen on the Internet; the nips and tucks and fillers probably wouldn't allow Cat much laughter these days.

As Martha approached Paula the woman recoiled as if she were about to be presented with a dish of snakes.

'I thought I said . . .' Paula started to say. But, before she could continue, Ben appeared with a small dish of herb-speckled rice and placed it in front of her.

'Thank you,' Paula said, just loud enough to be heard by Martha.

The noise diminished as the group began to eat. There were murmurs of *this is very nice* and *really quite delicious*. When Martha and Ben returned to clear the empty plates, they were met with smiles and compliments, even the two boys' plates were scraped very nearly clean.

'You're so clever to be able to cook for so many people,' Martha whispered to Ben as they stacked the dishes in the dishwasher.

'I work in a very big kitchen.'

Alice came in carrying the last few plates.

'That pasta was *so* good, better than the meal I had at *Château du Pont*. I couldn't even work out what I was eating last night!' She put the plates beside the sink. 'Can I help take out the pudding?'

Martha sat down heavily on a kitchen chair. 'Pudding?!'

'Ranjit's dreaming of chocolate mousse. Josh is hoping for a lemon tart.'

'They can go back to the *Château du Pont* if they want chocolate mousse and lemon tart.' Martha fished in her pocket, drew out a cigarette and put it in her mouth. She remembered the guests and took it back out.

'There's that big tub of vanilla ice cream you moved down to the freezer in the chapel.' Ben was evidently considering pudding.

'And I have a bar of Toblerone from the ferry,' said Alice.

'We could melt it and drizzle it over the ice cream with chopped almonds on top.' Ben was smiling.

'And I've got my date and walnut cookies,' Alice added.

'They'd go really well with the ice cream.'

'We could serve it in those little glass dishes.' Alice pointed at a pile of green Art Deco bowls on a shelf.

'What about the people who don't eat chocolate?' Martha flicked the lighter on and off. 'Or wheat, or dairy products.'

Ben grinned. 'People who don't want ice cream or cookies or chocolate could have some of that melon you mentioned earlier, Martha.'

Martha slid the cigarette back into the packet with a sigh. 'I'd been looking forward to that.'

But Ben had already left to get the ice cream and the melon from the chapel and Alice was going to fetch the chocolate and cookies. Martha put her head in her hands.

The sound of laughter wafted through the kitchen door from the terrace; Ranjit was telling a long story about an altercation with a chair lift in Chamonix. The boys had got down from the table and were taking it in turns to peep around the kitchen door. Martha looked up and smiled at them; they screamed and ran away. Martha hoped that everyone would go to bed very early.

No one had gone to bed very early and the men's laughter and loud voices had continued long after midnight. Martha had tossed and turned in the darkness of the chapel wishing she had let them go back to the *Château du Pont*. She had put her pillow over her head, trying to block out the noise, but it was impossible.

Her dreams, when she eventually slept, had been fragmented, snatches of images from the past: the tour bus, the recording studio. Abertrulli; the sea and cliffs and multi-coloured houses tumbling down the hill towards the yellow slab of sand. Then suddenly she was in the cosy living room of the little pink council house. The doorbell rang, Martha ran to open it. There was no one there. She stepped out onto the path. Below her a man was walking on the sand. Scrambling down the cliff to the beach, she took a step and found she was sinking. In the distance a baby cried. She couldn't get out of the sand; her ankles, her legs, her whole body was sinking, faster and faster. She tried to shout but sand filled her mouth and ears and eyes . . .

She woke up, her body covered in a slick of sweat, her heart pounding. Dawn had broken; sunlight filtered through the stained-glass chapel window, casting a rainbow onto the floor. Martha sat on the edge of the bed and lit a cigarette. Her hands shook.

I am in control. I will not give in.

Pippa lay stretched out asleep beside her. Martha gently stroked the rabbit's soft fur and inhaled deeply. She blew out a long stream of smoke.

I am in control.

I will not give in.

She shut her eyes and thought about the rehab clinic and remembered what the kind doctor had told her she must do at times like these.

Channel your thoughts elsewhere, find another release. Is there anything you like to do creatively?

With the doctor's voice echoing round her head, Martha gathered the things she needed. She set the easel up outside the chapel door and carefully arranged the tubes of paint beside the palette. She fetched a stool from the kitchen and a jam jar filled with water for her brushes. She set down a patterned blue and yellow bowl on the little patio table in front of the easel. She needed something to put in it. Martha looked up at the cherry orchard; the dawn cast an eerie pink

51

light amongst the twisted branches. When Martha bought the house, she had been told a story about a ghostly nun that roamed the orchard. In over twenty years Martha had never seen any sign of the nun, but then she hadn't been inclined to spend much time amongst the trees. Martha peered towards the little copse, and then with the bowl in her hand she set off determinedly towards it.

She passed the small tent that Ben had put up the night before. A sleeping bag lay in an empty heap at the entrance. She looked around but there was no sign of Ben. Then something caught her eye, a movement to her left, something at the bottom of the drive. It was a figure in tight Lycra contorted into a peculiar position. Martha stopped and stared. After a few moments the figure stood up and windmilled its arms backwards and forwards, jumping as it did so, as though trying to attempt flight. Martha could now see that it was Josh. His arms stopped rotating and after a quick sprint on the spot, he sped off in the direction of the gates. Martha shuddered at the thought of running anywhere and walked on through the long grass.

Martha didn't have to venture far into the orchard; the trees around the edge were covered with bunches of the sweet fruit. The dish was quickly full of glistening cherries and she turned back towards the chapel. The slight slope of the meadow made her breathless, even over such a short distance, and her leg began to ache. She thought of Jean-Paul. If she phoned him, he'd be here within half an hour. Martha remembered that the phone was out of order and forced herself to sit down at the easel and banish thoughts of Jean-Paul and his little pills.

I'm in control. I will not give in.

Hastily she squeezed paint onto the pallet; blue, yellow and green, lots of black and a good squirt of zinc white. The tube of red slipped between her fingers as she twisted the lid to open it. It dropped onto the ground.

'BLOODY HELL AND SHIT AND KNICKERS!'

'Here, let me.' Ranjit, appearing from nowhere, was already bending to retrieve the paint. In his other arm he held Tilly. The baby was dressed in crumpled pink pyjamas, her starfish hands reaching for the paint tube as Ranjit straightened. He held it away from her reach and returned it to Martha.

'Sorry about the language.' Martha avoided his eye.

'Don't worry, I used to play rugby at University,' said Ranjit. 'It's nothing to what I heard on the pitch.'

Martha squeezed a small pool of scarlet paint onto the pallet. Ranjit bounced Tilly up and down on his hip as she tried to lean towards the pallet.

'You're an early bird, Mrs. Morgan.'

'Ms.,' said Martha.

'My apologies, Ms. Morgan,' Ranjit said with his charming smile.

'It's Martha, please, just call me Martha.'

The baby made a lunge towards the easel and Ranjit stepped back.

'Tilly is also an early bird,' he said. 'I'm trying to give Paula a break. Normally I'm rushing off to work and she's the one left trying to cope in the mornings. This holiday I'm focusing on the family – that is what holidays should be about. Don't you think so, Ms. . . . sorry, Martha?'

'I haven't had a holiday for years.' Martha put her glasses on and started to sketch the bowl of cherries in front of her. And she didn't want to think how long it had been since she had been part of a family. She drew the outline of the dish onto the blank canvas with a stick of charcoal.

'I see you are an artist,' Ranjit continued. Martha wished that he would go away. 'Paula likes us to buy paintings.' He paused. 'Not the very expensive ones though. Her father's quite the artist too.'

Martha didn't answer. She concentrated on the canvas, adjusting the position of the bowl, trying to decide what colour to use for the background.

'How much do you charge for yours?' Ranjit indicated the practically bare canvas.

'My paintings are not for sale.'

Ranjit watched Martha draw in silence for a few moments then asked, 'Any chance of the Internet being fixed today?'

Martha shook her head. 'I doubt it. Sometimes it takes weeks to fix after a storm.'

Ranjit sighed. 'I really need to check my emails. For work.' After a brief pause he added, 'It's important that I keep in touch with my clients.'

Martha looked up. 'Surely your clients will understand that you're on a family holiday.'

Ranjit transferred the baby to his other arm. 'Yes, of course, I'm sure they can live without their accountant for a week.' He tailed off uncertainly, then added, 'But Paula needs to contact her father – he's supervising the building contractors working on our extension.'

'I'll inform the head of the French telecommunications service.'

'Thank you, that would be very kind.' Martha's sarcasm seemed to be lost on Ranjit. 'And we still have a leaky tap in the bathroom.'

Martha started to wonder how much Ranjit and Paula might be willing to pay for a painting.

'Ranjit!' The shout came from the terrace. 'Ranjit, where are you?' The woman's voice sounded desperate.

'Paula,' Ranjit called back. 'I'm down here.'

Moments later Paula was running down the path, her feet bare, her cotton nightdress damp and her neatly bobbed hair in disarray.

'Tilly!' Paula swept the baby from Ranjit's arms and hugged her tightly. 'Tilly, Tilly.'

'Hey, hey, calm down.' Ranjit put his arm around his wife.

'I didn't know where she was.' Paula sounded on the verge of tears.

'I thought you needed to sleep.' Ranjit smoothed down Paula's hair. 'I was only trying to give you a break.'

'I thought something had happened to her,' Paula sobbed and then the baby started to cry as well.

Ranjit kissed Paula's forehead. 'Let's go and get a cup of tea.' He turned to Martha. 'Please excuse us. Paula has had a bit of a fright.'

'Is there anything I can do to help?' Martha thought Paula was overreacting a little.

'No, it's my fault.' He looked down at his wife and child. 'Sometimes I just don't know what to do for the best.'

Martha watched the little group walk slowly back up the path.

'Coffee?'

Martha looked around to see Ben standing behind her. His hair was wet and slicked back and he held a mug in each hand.

'Thank you.' Martha took one.

Josh puffed past them, red faced and sweaty though he seemed to be moving at a snail-like pace.

'Good morning,' Martha called but Josh didn't seem to hear. He looked exhausted.

Ben watched the man shuffling up the path, and then moved away to sit on the low wall by the flower bed and stare across at the view, sipping his coffee.

There was the sound of gentle splashing coming from the pool.

'There you are, Josh.'

Martha could hear Josh's rasping breaths as he spoke.

'I like to do a few K before breakfast,' he said.

'Come and join us, the water's gorgeous, isn't it, Reuben?' Martha recognised Alice's softly spoken voice.

'Yes, it's very wet,' said a child, followed by some more splashing noises.

There was more heavy breathing, then some coughing, then eventually, 'Where's Noah?'

'Noah? I don't know, I found Reuben wandering around the house on his own.'

'I was exploring.'

'I haven't seen Noah at all this morning; I presumed he was with you.'

'Noah,' Josh was calling out. 'Noah, where are you?'

'Noah's with me, Dad.'

From her position outside the chapel, Martha could see the little attic window had been flung open. Elodie was leaning out.

'He woke me up in the night. He'd had a nightmare about being chased by a bear.'

'Probably the old stuffed one downstairs,' said Josh.

'No!' Noah's round face appeared beside his sister's. 'It was a real

55

live bear with laser eyes and fire coming out of its bottom, like fart bombs.' He leant out of the window making raspberry noises with his mouth followed by explosive sounds.

'Be careful, Noah,' Josh called up to his son. Noah leant out a bit more. 'Noah, don't be silly, it's dangerous up there.'

Noah laughed and twisted around so that he was leaning backwards from the window, his white-blond curls hanging down like sunrays.

'Noah, you're being naughty.'

Noah made more farting noises with his tongue.

'Noah, stop now, please.'

'Fart, fart, fart.'

'Noah! Please, darling, don't do that.'

Noah leant back a little further. Martha stood up and bellowed as loudly as she could.

'STOP DOING THAT RIGHT NOW! DO YOU WANT TO BREAK YOUR BLOODY NECK?'

Immediately Noah slid back and disappeared from view. Elodie looked at Martha then also vanished back into the room. Martha sat down. Everything was silent, even the splashing in the pool had stopped.

Ben studied his coffee cup.

'Did I go too far?' Martha whispered.

Ben raised his head and grinned.

'Someone had to tell him.'

Martha sighed. 'Something tells me it shouldn't have been me.'

Chapter 7

Despite Martha's warnings that it would be at its hottest and most crowded in the early afternoon, the guests had left for the lake an hour before. Elodie had refused to go, saying she had a headache. Josh had asked Martha if she would keep an eye on her while they were away. He hadn't complained about Martha swearing at his seven-year-old son.

'He can't think I'm that bad if he's asking me to babysit his daughter,' she had said to Ben as they finished off a late lunch of bread and cheese.

'When I was that girl's age no one needed to babysit me. I got up to all sorts and no one bothered.'

'Didn't your parents worry about you?' Martha asked.

'No chance of that. My mum died when I was a kid, then my dad wasn't really around.'

Martha was about to respond when Ben continued, changing the subject. 'Any ideas for the meal tonight?'

'Oh my God, I'd completely forgotten we had to cook dinner *again*!'

'I'll think of something while I finish the strimming.' Ben stood up.

Martha smiled at him. 'You're an angel.'

'A what?'

'An angel.'

Ben smirked, pushing a strand of blond hair back from his eyes.

'No one's ever called me an angel before.' He suddenly looked very young despite the tattoos that ran up and down his arms like comic strips. 'A devil once or twice but never an angel.' Still smiling he turned and walked back towards the drive. Martha picked up the empty plates and the strimmer started up with a cheerful roar.

Elodie was ploughing up and down the pool. Martha could hear her every time the strimmer stopped. The young girl's headache seemed to have disappeared when the others had left.

Martha put down her paintbrush and lit a cigarette. Pippa sat beside Martha in the shade of the easel, her ears twitching as the strimmer stopped then started again. Martha turned around to look for her ashtray and saw Elodie standing beside her. She had a towel clutched round her shoulders; her long turquoise streaked hair was dripping down her back onto the dusty ground. Martha noticed a woven leather bracelet on the girl's thin wrist and thought of all the diamanté and plastic pearls she and Cat used to wear at Elodie's age.

'When will the Wi-Fi work?'

'I don't know,' Martha replied. She still hadn't been into the town to phone for an engineer.

'I need to use Snapchat. I've got to keep up my *streaks*.'

Martha didn't know what Snapchat was, or *streaks*. A long silence followed.

Elodie looked at the painting; her small wet head tilted to one side. 'It's good,' she said.

'Thank you.' Without hair covering half of her face, Martha could see that Elodie was a pretty girl with large grey eyes.

'Can't you dry yourself properly?' Martha looked at Elodie over her glasses. 'You look half frozen.'

Elodie shivered more dramatically. 'I'm fine.'

Martha stubbed out her cigarette. 'Oh well, the sun will dry you soon enough.' She picked up her paintbrush and dabbed another dot of white onto a cherry.

'I did a hundred lengths,' Elodie blurted out.

Martha wasn't sure what to say. At Elodie's age a hundred lengths was the last thing Martha would have wanted to do. She and Cat would have been applying lip gloss and learning the words to 'Chanson D'Amour'.

'Elodie is a pretty name.' It seemed like a safer topic to Martha.

'I hate it.'

'Oh.'

'My mum named me after some stupid French film star. She saw her in a film the day before I was born.'

'My mother named me after Martha Reeves, the Motown singer. Have you heard of her?'

'No.'

'Martha and The Vandellas? "Dancing in the Street"?'

Elodie shook her head.

'My mother loved Motown. She wanted to become a singer – West Wales's answer to Little Eva . . . instead she met a French sailor on a night out in Swansea and became my mum instead.'

Another long silence followed.

'I want to be an illustrator.' Elodie patted her hair ineffectively with the towel.

'I wanted to be an illustrator when I was your age,' Martha said. 'Well, some kind of artist anyway.'

'I'd like to go to art college,' Elodie said.

'I had a place at art college in Cardiff,' Martha continued. 'But I didn't go.'

'Would your parents not let you?'

'There was only my mother . . . she didn't mind, but I did something else instead.'

'What?'

'I joined a band.'

The girl's eyes widened. 'Were you famous?'

'A bit.' Martha paused and added a dash of pink to the rim of the bowl. 'But I often wonder what my life would have been like if I had gone to art college instead.'

'You're good,' Elodie gestured towards the painting.

Martha peered at the picture critically. 'I've only recently started to paint again. It's therapy really.'

Martha pursed her lips. She was saying too much. Elodie didn't say anything. Martha hoped the young girl would never have to find a way to quell any demons rioting in her head. They were silent for a while then Elodie spoke.

'My dad says art college is for losers.'

'What does he do?'

Elodie made a face. 'He's a Financial Applications Specialist.'

'Oh,' Martha said. 'I don't think I know what that is.'

'Nor do I,' replied Elodie.

'And your mother? What does she think about art college?'

'That woman is not my mother,' Elodie said quickly.

Martha took off her glasses. 'I realise that. I mean your actual mother.'

Elodie pushed at a small stone with her toe. 'She says it's a great idea, but then I think she just wants to wind Dad up.'

'What does your mother do?'

'She's a journalist.'

Martha could feel her heart quicken at the word. 'Any particular kind of journalist?'

Elodie shrugged. 'Magazines, women's stuff, a bit of travel sometimes. Interviews with celebrities. Anything that pays, especially now she's not with Dad.'

Martha was very glad that Elodie's mother was not with her dad; the last thing she could cope with was a journalist hanging around all week.

Elodie crouched down and extended her hand towards Pippa.

Martha started to tell her to be careful not to frighten the rabbit but stopped when she saw Pippa's nose twitching towards Elodie's fingers. After a few moments Pippa let Elodie stroke her head.

'She likes you,' Martha said.

'She's cute,' Elodie replied.

An approaching noise made Elodie and the rabbit look up. The black Range Rover trundled down the drive, followed by the sports car, it's top still half up, half down. Within seconds car doors were slamming, children were complaining and a loud conversation between the adults shattered the peace of the afternoon.

'The heat!' Paula sounded exasperated. 'Poor Tilly was beside herself.'

'You couldn't move for fat French people,' Josh's voice broke in.

'Great ice cream though,' Ranjit said. 'Hey Josh, fancy a beer?'

'You bet,' Josh called. 'I'm going to have another go at fixing this soft top first.'

'I'll put a few bottles in the freezer for later,' said Ranjit.

'You're on pool duty,' Paula called out from a distance that sounded as though she was almost inside the house. 'Stay sober!'

Elodie remained crouching beside Pippa and made no attempt to go and see the others. After a few moments Alice came down the path. Her red spotted halter-neck dress revealed plump arms already turning golden in the sun. She was carrying a Moroccan bowl from the kitchen that Martha usually kept her car keys and spare packs of cigarettes in.

'Hi,' she said as she approached. 'Are you feeling better, Elodie?'

Elodie looked down on the ground and didn't answer.

'I see you've made a friend,' Alice continued in a cheerful voice. 'That rabbit is gorgeous, isn't she?' Elodie remained silently looking at the ground.

Alice turned to Martha. 'I like your painting.'

Martha nodded a thank you.

'Elodie's very good at art.' Alice looked back to Elodie. 'The portrait you did of your dad sleeping on the ferry was amazing!'

Elodie shot her a disdainful look.

'How was the lake?' Martha thought a change of subject was in order.

Alice smiled. 'It was wonderful. I swam out to the raft in the middle, so much nicer than swimming in my local pool. But I think it was a bit too hot and crowded for the others.'

'It's much quieter and cooler in the early evening,' Martha said.

'You did say that earlier. I don't know why they insisted on going just after lunch.'

'Well, next time maybe they'll listen,' Martha muttered.

'Maybe,' Alice said thoughtfully. 'I was just going to pick some cherries to make the clafoutis, if that's OK with you, Martha?'

'Fine. Pick as many as you like.'

Ben appeared, wiping perspiration off his forehead. He'd taken off his shirt and tied it around his waist. Martha noticed Alice staring at the tattoos. Ben noticed too and put his hand up to the dragon on his shoulder as if to pacify it.

Alice looked away. 'I'd better go before Josh wonders where I've got to.'

She set off towards the cherry orchard. A cloud of butterflies rose around her as she picked her way through the long grass towards the trees.

'Chickpea fritters,' Ben said.

'Sorry?'

'In a wrap.'

Martha stared blankly at him.

'For dinner.'

'Oh, of course.'

He looked down at Elodie. 'OK with the veggie?'

'Vegan,' Elodie muttered, but she nodded her agreement.

'Chilli-chicken for those who can't live without meat,' Ben continued. 'And a few salads on the side; a bulgur, a Greek, a creamy potato, tomato and avocado and maybe an anchovy and red pepper panzanella.'

Martha stared at him in admiration. 'I'd better go and get the ingredients for this banquet from the supermarket.'

In the distance someone was calling Martha's name.

'Mrs. Morgan, I mean Ms., I mean Martha.' Ranjit was running down the path towards her. 'Sorry to disturb you, it's just that I wondered if you have a mosquito net. Paula and Tilly are trying to take a nap and Paula says the bedroom is full of mosquitos and Tilly has already been bitten *to bits*.'

'I expect she was bitten at the lake. I did say to use bug spray when you went there?'

'Yes, I know, but Paula says the mosquitos are definitely in the bedroom, I can't see them but . . .' Ranjit's voice trailed away and he looked anxiously at Martha. 'Please. Do you have a net?'

'Somewhere, I think, but it may take a while to find.'

Ben slipped his shirt back on.

'I'll go into the village to get the food.'

Martha sighed. 'Would you? You can take my car. The keys are on the dresser.'

'It's OK. I'll get my panniers and go on the bike.'

'Thanks,' Martha smiled at him. 'Oh, and will you tell Sally and Pierre at the bar that the phone is out up here?' Martha called. 'Maybe Pierre could call the engineer and get us on the list for repairing the line and the Internet connection. Pierre can explain it in French so much better than me.'

'No problem.' Ben was already fixing the panniers back onto his bike. Like a cowboy saddling up to go to town. 'In the bar where I saw your advert?'

'That's the one,' Martha nodded. 'Could you pick up two packets of cigarettes as well?'

'Sure.' Ben started to push the bike towards the drive. He waved. Martha waved back. Ranjit waved too.

'Elodie,' Josh's voice called from the terrace. 'Can you help me get this sun cream on Noah? He won't stay still.'

There was a shriek, followed by, 'Oh, for fuck's sake, Noah!'

'You'd better go and help your dad,' Martha said to the girl.

Elodie gave Pippa's ears one last stroke and stood up. Her hair had dried now into undulating waves of turquoise; she shook her head so that it fell forward to hide her face, and walked away, towel clutched tightly around her body.

Martha turned back to Ranjit. She noticed his pained face. He was staring at the packet of cigarettes on the table. Martha could almost hear his disapproval. She thought he was about to mention them, anticipated that he would ask her not to smoke where the children could see her, or not to smoke at all. Instead, Ranjit repeated his question from the morning.

'Do you know when the Wi-Fi will be fixed?' He rubbed his palms together anxiously.

'The Wi-Fi is in hand. Didn't you hear me asking Ben to get my

63

friend to phone the engineer?' She smiled up at Ranjit, trying not to show her gritted teeth.

'Yes, but I just wondered if you had an actual idea of the length of time? Paula is desperate to get in touch with her father.'

'I'll let you know as soon as I have news,' she said. 'And if you give me a few minutes I'm sure I can find that mosquito net.'

'Thank you so much, Mrs., Ms. Morgan, Martha.' Ranjit started to walk backwards up the path. 'I am very grateful for all your help.'

Then he turned and with long, graceful strides headed back towards the house.

When he was a safe distance away, Martha lit a cigarette and wondered why such an affluent-seeming man should choose to book such an indiscriminate holiday for the sake of saving a few pounds.

Chapter 8

It was almost midnight and there was still no sign of Ben.

Martha sat on the little patio outside the chapel with a large glass of Chardonnay and the remains of the leftover salads. There was one chicken wrap left. Martha had assumed that she and Ben would eat together once they had cleared the plates and bowls and stacked the dishwasher, but Ben had said he had to go back to the village.

'I've left my sunglasses in the bar.'

But Martha had since noticed the sunglasses sitting on the low stone wall beside the patio, glinting in the light from a citronella candle.

She picked at the salads on her plate, watching the zigzag road that led down from the village. She would be able to see the light of Ben's motorbike on his way back. She didn't know how much longer his chicken wrap would be edible. She hoped he was coming back, she'd enjoyed his company. She imagined it was what spending time with her son might be like, she hoped that one day soon it would be Owen she would be sharing a meal with.

The guests on the terrace were becoming more raucous, their laughter rising into the night with the sound of glasses being clinked together and accompanying toasts. They seemed to be having a good time; Martha hoped it meant that their review would be favourable and more guests would follow. The more successful her new business venture was, the more confident she would feel about getting in touch with Owen.

She could hear music, presumably from a laptop or an iPad.

Tamara had noted the lack of any form of radio or CD player in the house.

Martha didn't recognise the songs, but then she hadn't really listened to anything new since the early 90s, apart from the French pop songs that played constantly during her weekly shop at the Intermarché.

There were lots of other sounds coming from the house and garden. The two little boys were letting out loud whoops as they raced around, despite it surely being past their bedtimes. The baby was crying, and someone started to sing. Martha wished she could block her ears to the din. The guests seemed determined to assault every bit of *Le Couvent des Cerises* with noise.

'Hi.' Alice emerged from the dark, a plate in her hand. 'I've brought you some of my clafoutis.'

Martha peered at the plate. 'It looks very moist.'

'I'm afraid it was a bit of a disaster. The boys wanted to help but they were a little over-enthusiastic with their mixing and Noah tipped the first lot of batter on the floor. Then Paula turned the oven off halfway through because it was making the kitchen too hot, and when Ranjit tried to help me get it out of the tin he spilled his glass of Merlot on it! I was thinking of making a lemon tart tomorrow but I'm not sure I can cope.'

Martha thought of all the puddings she and Ben would be expected to make if Alice wasn't baking anything. The thought of five more nights of cooking savoury meals, let alone sweet courses, made her heart start to race. She looked up at the young woman.

'You could cook here?' Martha pointed towards the kitchen. 'It's tiny, I'm afraid, there's not as much room as in the main house.'

Alice's eyes brightened. 'That would be wonderful. I'm used to cooking in a very small kitchen at home. I'd be ever so tidy, and it wouldn't take me long. I'd just like to contribute something to the holiday. Otherwise I feel sort of . . .?' She paused, trying to think of a word. 'Spare.'

Martha scooped up a small spoonful of the pudding.

'You'll have to work around me and Ben cooking the dinner – well, mostly Ben really.' She put the spoon into her mouth tasting sugar and cherries and something else that she couldn't quite identify, red wine perhaps? It was delicious.

'I'd be happy to help,' Alice said eagerly.

'I'm sure you'd rather be enjoying your holiday than feeding the five thousand.'

Martha took another spoonful of pudding and let out a small groan of pleasure. 'This is lovely.'

A cheer went up from the terrace, followed by the men's voices singing along to a chorus.

Alice glanced back towards the house. 'I really would be happy to help.'

In the distance, Josh called out Alice's name. Alice didn't move. Martha noticed the young woman's dress was covered in a print of skulls and roses. It reminded her of Ben's tattoos.

'Would you like a glass of wine?' Martha asked.

Alice hesitated then nodded. 'That would be nice.'

Martha gestured towards the spare chair and poured wine into the glass that she'd set out for Ben. Another cheer went up from the terrace. Paula's voice rang out.

'Josh, don't encourage him. Oh no – there really isn't any need for that!'

Martha and Alice exchanged a look.

'They're very lively,' said Martha.

'Yes.' Alice took a sip of her wine. 'I didn't realise Josh could be so . . .' She stopped and then said quietly, 'exuberant.'

'Anything planned for tomorrow?' Martha asked after a few moments of silence.

'Canoeing on the river.'

'Sounds fun.'

'I think I'll just find a tree by the riverbank and sit under it with my cookery book.' Alice twisted the stem of the glass between her fingers. 'It will be nice for Elodie and Noah to do something with their dad. I don't want them to think I'm dominating all his time.'

Martha thought of Elodie's taciturn manner with Alice. She

wondered if Owen had been like that with his stepmother. It must have helped that she had been his nanny first.

'Do you get on well with the children?'

'I don't know.' Alice took a large gulp of wine. 'I only met them the day before yesterday. I didn't know Josh was bringing them until he picked me up to come here.'

Martha raised her eyebrows.

'That must have been a surprise.'

Alice grimaced. 'It was. For them too. They didn't seem to know their father was seeing anyone, let alone bringing them on holiday. Josh said their mum asked him to have them unexpectedly – decided to go off on a holiday with some new partner she has.'

'Have you and Josh been together long?'

'Three weeks.' It was too gloomy to see Alice's cheeks, but Martha felt quite sure that they had flushed a few shades darker. 'No, it must be three and a half weeks now.'

'How did you meet?'

'On a deli-dating-night.' At Martha's confused look, Alice added, 'A dating night at a delicatessen.'

'Oh,' Martha said.

'A very lovely delicatessen. In Battersea. Amazing cheese. Salame cotto to die for, wonderful macarons – a really big display.'

'I see.'

'I know the couple who run it. They set up a date night as a marketing experiment. I only went to take pictures and write about it for my blog. The last thing I expected was to actually meet someone. Josh and I bumped into each other in the cheese-tasting corner. We have exactly the same favourites, Reblochon and Vacherin.'

'That's good.' Martha tried to sound as if she actually thought a shared taste in cheese might be the basis for a rewarding relationship. After all, she had met her ex-husband in an art exhibition in a disused paint factory in North London. Their eyes had met across Damien Hirst's dead shark.

'Do you like seafood?' Andrew had asked with an irresistible smile.

Over crab legs and langoustine he had told her about the films he made; gritty urban stories about disadvantaged families and poverty in former mining communities. He loved the fact that Martha came from a single-parent household and had grown up in a council house.

He described his own family home in Norfolk as run down and shabby; Martha was expecting a two up two down in Norwich. Three weeks later, she had found herself being driven up a drive a mile long and crossing a moat to get to the front door – Andrew's childhood bedroom was in a turret. Martha felt like she had stepped into a fairy tale.

Andrew had been funny and charming; he lavished her with the love and affection she had craved since the band split up. Martha couldn't remember his taste in cheese, but he liked all the same exhibitions, films, and music as she did – surely that was enough.

But after they were married Andrew announced he was giving up filmmaking and going into the family business. By the time Owen was on the way they had bought a house just around the corner from his parent's town house in Kensington. Andrew wasn't interested in going to the exhibitions or the films Martha liked any more, or listening to music. He was always out with his City friends; pheasant shooting at the weekend, golf, tennis, tickets for endless cricket matches. He supported benefit cuts and council houses being sold off, thought that the Poll Tax was a good idea – he seemed to have forgotten the people he'd been making films about. Even before the accident Martha had begun to realise that they had little in common any more. Nearly thirty years later Martha still felt the betrayal; the man she'd fallen in love with had turned into someone else.

'I know Josh is a bit older than me, but he's been lovely.' Martha had been so immersed in memories of the past she had almost forgotten Alice was there. 'He's very different to my last boyfriend,' Alice continued. 'Spud had no interest in food unless it contained potatoes.'

'Hence the name?' Martha ventured, pouring Alice more wine.

'He thought an adventurous meal was a baked potato with chips on the side but then he didn't like the dauphinoise I made him. Or the colcannon. He said *Why ruin a good root vegetable with muck like cream and garlic.*' Alice sighed. 'At least Josh appreciates my cooking. Since we met, I've cooked for him nearly every night.'

'Sounds like Josh has landed on his feet,' said Martha. 'But all the same, a week with his two children will be a test.'

'Yes,' said Alice thoughtfully. 'But at least I'll be away from . . .' She paused and looked down at her glass; the girl's long hair stopped Martha from seeing her expression, but she was pretty sure it wasn't happy. Suddenly Alice looked up with a bright smile. 'At least I'll be away from my boring job as a receptionist, and it's ages since I've been abroad.'

Both women turned towards the drive at the sound of the motorbike. Ben approached through the gloom. He stopped, dismounted and walked towards the table. He looked exhausted.

'Sorry, I got held up. The football was on in the bar.'

Martha pointed to the sunglasses on the wall. 'They were here all the time.'

Ben picked them up and shook his head. 'I'm such a numpty, as my granny would have said.'

'I like that word,' Alice laughed.

'In Welsh it would be *twpsyn*,' said Martha. 'My teachers used to say it to me all the time.' She turned to Ben. 'If you want some wine go and get a glass from the kitchen, or there's beer in the fridge.'

Ben went off and came back with a bottle of beer. He leant against the doorway and almost drank the bottle in one swig.

Martha watched him. 'How were Sally and Pierre?'

Ben tipped back his head and finished the bottle. 'Sorry?'

'Sally and Pierre in the bar, they must be very busy if the football's on.'

'They seemed to be managing,' he said after a brief pause.

Martha indicated to the food on the table. 'I think your chicken wrap might be past its best, but Alice has brought some clafoutis for us to try.' Martha held out the plate.

'It's not turned out quite as it's meant to be,' Alice said quickly.

Ben stepped forward and picked up the sticky pudding with his

70

hand before returning to his position against the doorframe. He took a bite.

'It's good,' he said and took another bite. 'Did you use ground almonds?'

Alice nodded. 'I didn't add as much sugar as I normally would because Paula nearly had kittens when she saw me adding what she called "vast quantities" to the batter.'

'Sounds like a case of too many cooks,' Martha said.

'I know how that feels.' Ben had finished what was left and licked his fingers. 'Especially when one cook thinks he's king of the world.'

'Have you ever worked in a restaurant?' asked Alice.

'Oh yes,' Ben said with a wry smile. 'I'm a chef, for my sins.' He wiped his hands on his jeans and didn't expand on his answer. 'Is it OK to have another beer?'

'Of course, help yourself,' Martha called. Ben was already inside. 'I've said Alice can come here tomorrow to make a lemon tart. It might be a bit of a squeeze with us trying to cook the dinner as well but I'm sure we'll manage.'

'I might feel daunted cooking with a professional.' Alice took another sip of wine.

Ben returned with the new bottle and grinned in Alice's direction.

'If your clafoutis is anything to go by you'll be able to teach me a thing or two.'

Josh suddenly appeared around the corner. He looked briefly from Alice to Martha and then to Ben before putting his hand on Alice's shoulder.

'Here you are, gorgeous. I've been looking everywhere. You missed Ranjit's hilarious impersonation of me dancing in Ibiza the summer we graduated.'

'I'm just finishing this.' Alice held up her wine glass. Josh took it from her and put it on the table.

'Paula is threatening to go to bed, and you can't leave me on my own with Ranjit, he's out to get completely wasted on that local plonk from the village. And you know how easily led I am.'

71

'Actually, I didn't know,' Alice said.

Josh grinned. 'I'm afraid I have very little self-control.' He ran his hand up and down her back. Alice stood up.

'I'm very tired. I might go to bed myself.'

Josh's grin widened. 'Now that I think about it, I am rather sleepy.'

'That'll be the effects of the Chateau du Nob,' Ben said with a smirk.

'Mm, it is rather potent,' Josh mused. 'But very good.'

Alice pressed her hand against her mouth as though trying to wipe away a smile.

'Are you sure it's OK about tomorrow, Martha?' she asked.

Martha nodded. 'We'll look forward to sharing it with you.'

'What are you sharing?' Josh looked from Ben to Martha to Alice. No one offered him an explanation.

'Well, our bed awaits,' Josh said after a few moments, and with a wave he steered Alice away from the table and up the path. Ben shook his head and muttered something under his breath. Martha couldn't quite hear what he said but she had a fair idea that she could guess.

Chapter 9

Monday

Martha worked methodically along the rose bush. Snipping with the secateurs as far as she could reach, up and down each long stem, dropping the fading flowers into a basket at her feet. Deep pink and heavily scented, the roses scrambled up the back wall of *Le Couvent des Cerises*. Martha liked to imagine the nuns planting the bush many years before, lifting up their long black habits to dig into the rich soil at the base of the house. Now the branches seemed integral to the yellow render, growing into the walls and across the cracks, as though the plant was trying to hold the house together.

A light breeze blew through Martha's own long black clothes making the heat of the morning more bearable. At last *Le Couvent des Cerises* was blissfully quiet. Josh and Alice had borrowed the Range Rover and taken the two boys into town to buy croissants for breakfast; the screams and splashes, almost non-stop for the previous two hours, had been replaced by cicadas and the occasional banging of Ben's hammer, as he repaired a row of roof tiles dislodged by the storm.

It took a while for the soft murmuring that Martha could hear above her to become distinct.

'I'm not surprised you have a hangover. How many bottles did you and Josh get through?'

'It's not a hangover, I think I just ate too much.'

'Probably that funny pudding. I thought it was a bit sickly.'

'I thought it was delicious.'

'You and your sweet tooth.'

Martha stopped deadheading the roses and listened. Paula and Ranjit were on the balcony of the bedroom. She could hear Tilly chuntering as if trying to join in the conversation and imagined the baby cradled tightly in Paula's arms, longing to be allowed to crawl.

'It was a pudding. Puddings are meant to be sweet. Josh told me she has ambitions to write a cookery book.'

'Confessions of a Fondant Fancy.'

'Paula! You are very naughty!'

The husband and wife both laughed. The baby laughed too.

'It's nice to hear you laughing, Paula. It's not a sound I've heard for a while.'

There was a pause and Martha resumed her snipping.

'Do you think he left Carla *for* her?' Paula said after a few minutes. 'Has Josh said anything about the break-up?'

'No, just that Carla moved out a month or so ago.'

'Probably discovered he was having an affair. Poor Carla. I feel bad that I haven't been in touch. I've been so busy with Tilly, and the extension.'

The rest of Paula's words were drowned out by the sound of hammering coming from the roof.

Martha glanced towards Ben. He had his shirt off. She noticed his tattooed skin looked slightly red and wondered if he had any sun cream on. She didn't have any to offer as she always kept herself so well covered up.

There was another sound. Martha turned and saw a car at the top of the drive. For a moment she thought it was Josh and Alice returning but then she saw that it was a small copper-coloured hatchback. Even from a distance she could see there was a large dent in the bonnet and that the car was very dirty. It turned in through the tall stone gateposts and stopped. Martha waited for it to come down the drive but instead it reversed and then disappeared down the winding road towards the village.

She glanced back at Ben and saw him staring in the direction that the car had gone, hammer poised, mid-strike. As the noise of the engine died away, Ben brought the hammer down with a loud crack.

'Shite!'

The broken tile slid down the roof and fell onto the grass beneath him.

'Thank God the children aren't here to hear that!' Paula's voice drifted back into Martha's consciousness. 'Reuben is already copying the Scottish accent and I found Noah drawing in felt tips all over his chest – he said it was a dragon!'

Ranjit laughed. 'Well, Noah is a handful. I caught him trying to put the rabbit in the swimming pool to see if it could swim.'

Martha made a mental note to keep a closer eye on Pippa.

The baby made a hiccupping sound.

'I must go down and get Tilly's breakfast. Do you really think the peaches are safe to eat without peeling them?'

'I'm sure they are fine. Just rinse them in the sink.'

'The sink is so grimy, have you seen that black stuff round the plughole?'

'It is just old. I don't think there are germs.'

'And I've noticed the fridge is mouldy around the seal.'

'But it is clean inside.'

'I looked under the units – I'm sure I saw some rabbit droppings!' Paula made a shuddering noise.

'Why were you looking under the units?'

'I'm going to start a list. Points to raise with Dordogne Dreams.'

'But, darling . . .'

'You said Tamara has asked for a review and you've agreed we'll give one. I think we have to be honest.'

'Martha is trying her best. And she has made us two excellent meals.'

'She looks so grumpy every time I see her – like she doesn't want us here.'

Martha couldn't bear to hear any more. She picked up the basket of flower heads and walked away as fast as she could.

Fussy-pots British, Martha echoed Pierre's words as she headed for the chapel. *Mouldy! Grimy!* A small stone skipped in front of her as she limped down the path. *Grumpy!*

The crunch of gravel beneath wheels heralded the return of the rest of the party. A car door slammed. A child screamed.

'It's only a wasp, Reuben.'

'I think the ice cream's dripped on Ranjit's lovely leather seats.'

'Noah, leave that rabbit alone.'

'She's running away.'

'Don't chase her. I said don't . . .'

Martha stepped into the semi-darkness of the chapel kitchen; Pippa raced in and squeezed herself under the dresser. Martha slammed the door shut and locked it. Outside she could hear children's voices.

'Where did she go?'

'In here.' The door handle rattled as small hands tried to open it.

'Let's go swimming.'

'Last one in the pool is a loser!'

Martha went into the bedroom. Picking up the postcard on the bedside table she read it for the thousandth time, taking in every slant and curve of Owen's handwriting. It was addressed to 'Mum'. This, she reminded herself, was why she'd let these people invade her home.

Chapter 10

Martha lay on the sunlounger outside the chapel, a nauseous headache pulsing in her temples. She imagined Paula's list of complaints for Dordogne Dreams. The list grew longer in her mind.

33. There is a small spider's web in the downstairs toilet.
34. The cutlery appears to be mismatched.
35. There are too many French people in the village.

Martha was aware of noises coming from the house; the scrape of the lunchtime crockery being cleared away, Ben hammering, Ranjit laughing, someone whistling, the baby crying, another rendition of 'Ode to Joy'.

'The cars are like ovens,' she heard Paula say.

36. Complete lack of shade in the allocated parking area.

Something buzzed in Martha's face; she batted it away.

37. There are too many bees.

With relief she heard the cars leaving for the canoeing trip. Martha knew that Paula had decided to stay behind with Tilly for a nap but hopefully the rest of the guests would be out for hours.

Martha wondered if she ought to bleach the kitchen and hoover under the cupboards. She definitely should be making a start on the dinner. But her eyes felt heavy; they slowly closed, the sound of Ben's hammering becoming fainter.

She dreamed of Abertrulli and the ice-cream shop on the seafront and the woman that used to sell buckets and spades from the back of a van.

'Martha.'

A hand on her shoulder woke her. She was looking into Andrew's face.

'Martha, darling,' his voice sounded soothing in her ear, like the early days when he would wake her with a kiss. 'I've brought him with me.'

Looking up the drive, Martha saw the blue BMW, its blacked-out windows tightly closed. Andrew was pressing the car key into her hand. She tried to put her fingers around it, but he was increasing the pressure. It hurt her palm.

'You'd better let him out. It's very hot,' he whispered.

'OWEN!'

She sat up with a jolt. Bright sunlight blinded her momentarily. She looked for the car. But there was no BMW. She looked down at her hand. There was no key. As the dream faded only the sound of Owen's name on her lips remained.

After a few seconds Martha realised that she was not alone. Elodie was sitting on the edge of the grass stroking Pippa on her knee. Her black T-shirt spoke for her: 'So Bored'.

'I thought you'd gone with the others,' Martha said. Had she actually shouted Owen's name out loud?

'I hate boats,' Elodie said, not looking up from the rabbit's fur.

Martha lay back and tried to calm her racing heart. She clung to Elodie's words, repeating them in her head like some kind of mantra = *I hate boats, I hate boats* and after a few minutes she felt her body start to relax.

The sun was hot on Martha's face. Normally she would have fetched her straw hat but Elodie's presence stopped her from moving.

She peered through half-closed eyes at the teenage girl still attentively stroking the rabbit. Martha tried to remember what it had been like to be fourteen.

That was the year Cat started at her school, the new girl from England; she seemed so exotic. Together they had formed 'The Bay City Rollers Are Crap Club', scorning classmates who scratched *I love Woody* into their desks. Instead of Woody, Martha and Cat sighed over pictures of David Essex in *Jackie* magazine and saved up pocket money for the platform shoes they coveted in Cat's mum's *Kays* catalogue. By the end of that school year, David Essex had been replaced in their hearts by David Bowie and *Jackie* had been eschewed for *Cosmopolitan*; from its glossy pages they learned about orgasms and how to apply lip gloss like Jessica Lange.

On Saturday nights, Cat's older brother would buy them cider at The Sailor's Arms. In return Martha taught him useful Welsh phrases like 'you have lovely hair' and 'do you want to go out with me?' Martha remembered gate-crashing a sixth-form end of term party; she and Cat standing in the kitchen of one of the big houses on the edge of Abertrulli, swigging White Lightning from the bottle. Cat had her first kiss, Martha had her first cigarette and on the way home they were both sick.

She and Cat had spent much of the long summer holiday lying in the sand dunes trying to get a tan under the watery Welsh sun. They would have hated boats.

'Hi, Martha.'

Martha looked up to see Alice carrying a cardboard box.

'Sorry to disturb you, I thought I'd start the tart. I found a wonderful greengrocers in the village.' She delved into the box. 'Look at the size of this!'

Martha squinted at the knobbly lemon in the young woman's hand. Alice was wearing a dress printed with strawberries; with her peachy skin and radiant smile she looked like an advert for fruit yogurt.

'You didn't change your mind about the canoeing then?'

'No, I thought it best for Josh to spend time with Noah . . . and to be honest I don't really like boats.'

'Then you and Elodie have something in common.'

Alice glanced round at Elodie, who was stoically stroking Pippa.

'I get terribly seasick,' Alice said. 'Even in the smallest dingy.'

Elodie sighed disdainfully.

'Please do go into the kitchen.' Martha struggled to stand, her leg was stiff, and her head still hurt. 'It's pretty basic, but as I said, the oven is good. I'll come and explain how it works.'

'Stay there, I'll be fine.'

Martha sat back down. 'I was going to start chopping onions for dinner, but I have a bit of a headache that I'm trying to get rid of.'

'Then I'll get you a cup of tea.' Alice smiled. 'Elodie, a cup of tea? Or coffee perhaps?'

Elodie shook her head but didn't look up.

'Glass of water?'

'I don't want anything from you.'

Alice sighed and walked into the chapel.

Martha watched Elodie hunched over the rabbit, hostility as pungent as any perfume.

'I think Alice is trying her best, you know.'

'I didn't even know he had a *girlfriend*!' Pippa sprang away from Elodie's angry voice and ran beneath the sunlounger.

Martha tried to think of something encouraging to say but her head was now thumping and she couldn't think.

'I'm sure things will seem better soon.'

'No, they won't.' Elodie stood up. 'They're both as bad as each other. Dad with that woman and Mum with . . .' Elodie stopped and bit her lip. 'Mum is just as bad,' she said quietly. Then she turned around and stomped up the path.

Chapter 11

The afternoon grew hotter. Martha resumed her position on the sunlounger. She had asked Alice to bring out her straw hat when the young woman had brought out the cup of tea. Lying down she used the hat to cover her face. Her headache began to subside.

She liked the smell of the straw; it reminded her of her mother's shopping bag. Martha remembered the summer evenings when her mother would fill the bag with sandwiches and cans of Fanta. She'd let Martha carry one handle while she held the other and they'd walk to the end of the row of council houses, down the steep hill, past the multicoloured cottages, swinging the bag between them, singing Motown songs until they reached the beach. Martha's mother would spread out a chequered cloth – which was actually half of a pair of old curtains – and they'd have a picnic on the sand. They'd had picnics on the beach with Owen, when Martha used to visit from London; the same shopping basket, the same chequered curtain. They had sung the baby the same songs.

Martha shifted on the sunlounger and thought about her mother dashing in and out of the waves, even when Owen had been little – so different from the frail, confused old woman she had been in the years before she died. Martha had phoned every other day, despite the staff in the nursing home gently suggesting that Miss Morgan could no longer remember who Martha was. It had been a comfort to know that her mother was on the other end of the line, even though she rarely spoke. Martha liked to let herself believe that she was still talking to the plump young woman in the Abertrulli kitchen, slapping fish paste onto bread for sandwiches as Marvin Gaye played on the Dansette.

The hours drifted by and the smell of baking coming from the chapel intensified; it wafted through the open door, wakening Martha's taste buds. At five o'clock the church bell chimed, and Ben came down from the house. He pointed towards the roof.

'I think the whole thing needs replacing.'

'You don't need to tell me,' Martha muttered.

Alice came outside carrying a plate of golden biscuits.

'I got a bit carried away.' She smiled. 'I've made the tart, these almond shortbreads and two loafs of focaccia to have with dinner, though I wasn't sure what's on the menu?'

'Chorizo risotto,' said Ben. 'Focaccia is great.' He grinned at Alice.

Martha sat up. 'I'd better start chopping the onions.'

'Don't worry,' Ben and Alice said together.

'I'll do it.' They spoke together again and then both laughed.

'I don't think there's enough room for three,' said Alice.

'We'd be tripping over each other in that small space,' added Ben.

Martha smiled. 'If you insist.'

As the sun began to slip behind the house, the canoeing party returned. It didn't take long for *Le Couvent des Cerises* to fill with noise. The children intermittently laughing or wailing and Paula calling out admonishments and cautions as if refereeing a football match.

'Don't put your wet clothes on top of my hat!'

'No, you can't go in the pool.'

'Hang up the towels.'

'Noah!'

'I just don't understand how the boys got so wet?'

'Josh, please stop Noah!'

'My hat is ruined!'

'Ranjee, go and ask about the Wi-Fi.'

Martha sat up and waited. It wasn't long before Ranjit came striding down the path, his white shirt looking rather grubby and his linen shorts a little damp.

'No, it's not,' Martha said.

Ranjit smiled. 'What's not, Mrs. Morgan, I mean Martha?'

'The Wi-Fi. It's not fixed.'

'Oh. Wonderful news. Another day of peace in paradise.' Ranjit spread his arms wide to the view across the valley. 'I can feel the pressures of work melting away.' Ranjit paused. 'But what shall I tell Paula?'

Martha lit a cigarette. 'I don't know, tell her to add it to her list of complaints for Dordogne Dreams?'

Ranjit shifted nervously, then sniffed the air.

'I'm sorry.' Martha waved away the smoke with her hand.

'No, no, it's not the smoke, it's those lovely smells coming from your little shed.'

'It's not a shed, it's the chapel that belonged to the convent. It dates back to the sixteenth century.'

Martha hoped that Ranjit might leave for fear of a history lesson. Instead he sat down on a canvas chair, stretched out his long brown legs and let out a contented sigh.

'It's nice to have a break.' He leant back in the chair indicating his wet shirt. 'I don't know who was worst, Noah, Reuben or Josh – it was like taking a basketful of puppies out on the river – chaos!' He shook his head and smiled.

There was a long pause during which Martha wondered when he would be going back up to the house. Ranjit leant forward and Martha got ready to politely say goodbye, instead Ranjit pointed to the plate on the table.

'Those biscuits look very nice. Are they from the local patisserie?'

'Alice,' Martha gestured towards the chapel. 'She's using my kitchen.'

'I understand – no kids running around, no silly men spilling wine.' Then he added in a hushed tone, 'and no food police.'

Ranjit helped himself to a circle of shortbread and sat back. Martha felt the headache coming back.

'It's gone very quiet up there.' Ranjit nodded towards the house. 'I think Paula must have got the boys into the bath.'

Pippa appeared from under the sunlounger; Martha scooped the rabbit up and stroked her crooked ear.

'These are delicious.' Ranjit took another biscuit. It was halfway into his mouth when he stopped and looked at Martha. 'You won't tell Paula, will you?' He patted the slight mound of his stomach. 'She wants me to give up cake and biscuits. But you have to have something to look forward to when you're sitting at your laptop all day trying to . . .' He stopped again. 'I mean, when you spend all day commuting back and forth to the City, dealing with high-powered clients.'

'I won't breathe a word about the biscuits.'

Ranjit made a thumbs up sign with one hand as the other pushed the rest of the biscuit into his mouth. After a few moments he suddenly sprang to his feet.

'Are you going to help with bath time?' asked Martha.

'I'm going to make us a little treat.' He grinned and rubbed his hands together. 'To thank you for letting me unwind on your delightful terrace, just wait here, I'll be back very soon.'

Martha shook her head.

'I'm afraid I really ought to go and help with dinner.'

Ranjit took a couple of strides towards the chapel and popped his head quickly around the kitchen door, waving at the occupants inside.

'Alice and your son seem to have it all in hand,' he grinned at Martha.

'He's not my son,' Martha said firmly.

'Oh, I'm so sorry. Your partner?'

'He's not my partner!' Martha flushed. 'He works for me! He's half my age and . . .'

'I'm so sorry, it's really none of my business.' Ranjit's own face was colouring too. He quickly changed the subject. 'I noticed the mint by the kitchen door. Could I help myself to a few sprigs?'

Before Martha could answer, Ranjit had bounded away up the

path. Martha pressed her fingers to her temples; she hoped that Paula would find him lots of chores to do and prevent his return, but a few minutes later Ranjit was back, holding a large jug filled with ice and foliage. Josh followed behind with a tray of glasses.

Ranjit waved the jug in the air with a smile.

'Mojito, Martha?'

Alice appeared with a plate of cheese straws.

'Ah, there you are, darling' Josh put down the tray of glasses and kissed her cheek. He glanced at Ben who had followed Alice out of the chapel. 'Ranjit said you were in the kitchen with the handyman.'

'A mojito for our resident Domestic Goddess?' Ranjit was pouring liquid and leaves into the glasses.

'Oh, yes please.' Alice rescued some cheese straws that had rolled off the plate and onto the table.

Ben stood, framed in the doorway taking in the scene in front of him.

'Mojito?' Josh held up a glass.

Ben shook his head. 'I'll stick to beer, thanks.'

'I don't suppose a chap like you would be seen dead drinking one of these.' Josh placed his arm around Alice's waist. 'I expect whisky with a shot of Irn-Bru is more your sort of cocktail?'

Ben nodded slowly. 'I was raised on it.'

Josh laughed. 'I hear Alice has been helping you in the kitchen.'

'She's been deep-frying Mars bars with me all afternoon.'

'Really!'

'He's just teasing.' Alice sat down on the bench. 'Ben's made risotto.'

'Oh, very manly!' Josh said.

Ben returned with a bottle of beer and Martha waved to a chair. 'Bring that over and sit down.'

'I'm fine here.' Ben stayed where he was and took a swig of beer.

'May I propose a toast?' Ranjit held up his glass, then stopped. 'There's a wasp trying to drink my mojito!' Ranjit tried to blow it away. 'My God, it's huge.'

'There's another one on the jug.' Josh drew back in his seat.

Ben stepped forward and deftly flicked the wasps away before resuming his position in the doorway.

Ranjit and Josh seemed to be settling in for the night. They reminded Martha of the boys in the band, easy and relaxed in each other's company. They started competing to see who could recount the most outrageous exploits of their college days. There seemed to have been endless parties and holidays; windsurfing, mountain climbing, hitch-hiking across Europe, scuba diving in Thailand. All the stories had some additional tale involving getting lost, or alcohol, or hangovers, or girls they'd met along the way.

Martha couldn't help laughing. Ranjit topped up her glass and she noticed his eyes darting to the cigarette packet on the table in front of her. She made a move to hide it out of site.

'No, no,' Ranjit protested. 'It's fine.' On a hunch, Martha pushed the pack towards him. Ranjit glanced towards the house and then reached across and took a cigarette.

'I don't really smoke,' he said as Martha held out the lighter. 'Not since I met Paula anyway. She had me tamed from our first date. No more wild nights, no more crazy parties. She made me into the fine, upstanding man you see before you,' he laughed, lit the cigarette and inhaled deeply. 'From the minute I laid eyes on her I changed my ways.'

Ranjit sat back and blew a smoke ring.

Martha noticed another large wasp crawling up the side of his glass towards his mouth. She started to warn him, but he had already put the glass back down and the wasp flew away.

'What on earth are you doing?' Paula had appeared from nowhere, Tilly on her hip. 'The wet clothes are still in a heap and you two are sitting here giggling like schoolboys – I can hear you from the terrace.'

'Sorry, Paula.' Ranjit dropped the cigarette on the ground.

'Sorry, Paula,' Josh mumbled.

'And Noah is running around stark naked and won't put his clothes on.'

'Sorry, Paula,' Josh mumbled again.

Paula swatted at something in front of her face. 'These wasps are everywhere!'

'I'll sort them out,' said Martha.

'Thank you.' She looked at the jug and the glasses and then at her husband and Josh. 'Are you coming?'

'Yes,' the two men said in unison.

Paula turned on her heels and set off back towards the house. Josh and Ranjit got up quickly and followed.

Just as they were disappearing from view, Paula stopped, causing the men to bump into one another on the path. 'Just to let you know,' Paula called back towards Martha. 'The tap on the other bath is leaking.'

Martha sighed. 'That's two leaky taps now.' She looked at Ben. 'Do you know anything about plumbing?'

'A bit,' Ben shrugged. 'I'll have a look at them tomorrow.'

Alice picked up the empty plates. 'Sorry, Martha, I bet you just wanted a bit of peace.'

Martha shrugged. 'It was all quite entertaining really.'

Alice turned to Ben who was clearing away the glasses. 'I'll take the bread and salads up to the house and set the table. Will you be up soon to serve the risotto?'

'In a minute.' Ben gave Alice one of his lop-sided grins. 'But first, I thought I might deep fry that leftover Toblerone as a special treat for your man.'

Alice didn't answer, but Martha noticed the slight smile on her pretty face before she set off after the others.

Chapter 12

Tuesday

Another restless night left Martha with a powerful urge to go and find Jean-Paul. Her dreams had been full of Owen. He was coming to stay, Martha cooked a pot of pasta sauce that overflowed and turned the swimming pool tomato red. Owen arrived on a motorbike. He stopped at the top of the drive and waved from the gates. Martha ran to meet him, repeatedly slipping backwards on the gravel and rocks so that she ended up scrabbling on all fours like an animal. At last she reached the bike, breathless and covered in sweat. Owen removed his helmet and his face was Andrew's, his expression one of contempt. Martha woke up with a jolt.

Yesterday's headache was back, and her leg throbbed with pain. As dawn broke, she gave up trying to sleep and, after tugging off her sweat-soaked nightdress, pulled on a pair of wide linen trousers and a black T-shirt.

Keys, keys, where are the bloody car keys?

Martha searched frantically through her bag and then amongst the clutter of the kitchen dresser, before deciding she must have left them in the car.

She opened the front door and stepped into the morning mist. It was difficult to see more than a few metres ahead. Insects were buzzing everywhere and something large collided with her face. As Martha swiped it away, she heard a voice. She peered through the mist towards the orchard. Between the trees she could just make out a figure running.

At first she thought it was Josh, on his morning exercise routine, but as she turned away, she heard an angry shout. Looking back, she saw two figures; even through the mist Martha was sure neither was Josh. They were too tall, one had a scarlet T-shirt on, the other wore blue. They seemed to be standing very close, almost head to head, and then one pushed the other. They grappled for a few seconds until one fell to the ground. The figure in blue turned and ran towards the high, yellow wall that marked Martha's boundary with the neighbouring farm. The figure on the ground struggled to his feet and shouted, but the crowing of a distant cockerel drowned his words.

Martha rushed to the chapel to fetch the shotgun from the top of the dresser. She had found it in the house when she moved in. She knew it didn't work, the lock was broken, and she would never dream of loading it, but the gun made her feel safe. She'd brought it down to the chapel with her when she moved from the house.

It only took moments to retrieve but when she came back there was no sign of either figure. Martha scanned the orchard, the barrel following her line of sight. She stood, heart hammering for several minutes, looking for the men.

'Everything OK?' Ben came down the path, bare chested. He seemed unfazed by the sight of Martha cradling a twelve bore.

'I saw men fighting in the orchard.' She began to laugh nervously, feeling ridiculous, the shotgun suddenly very heavy in her hands. 'I thought I might scare them off. Did you see them?'

'No.' Ben shook his head. 'I've just been having a quick wash. I didn't see anything.'

'One of them pushed the other over and ran off, he looked like he was going to climb the wall down there.' Martha gestured with the gun.

Ben peered towards the orchard; the mist was lifting, the rising sun bringing the valley into technicolour focus.

'I can't see anything. Shall I?' Ben gently took the shotgun from her hands. 'You look very pale. Maybe you should rest?'

Martha closed her eyes, perhaps he was right. Her sleep had been fragmented, thoughts and dreams mixing together in a cauldron of angst. A snippet from another dream came back to her. A car, a crying child inside, people trying to open the doors.

The arguing men could have just been another dream she'd somehow confused with reality. She'd imagined so many things in the past, seen so many things that were not there; the tablets had fuelled illusions that had become a way of life.

Often Owen was with her; toddling at her side in the garden, pointing at the lizards as they darted over the walls, sniffing at the lavender heads. She'd lift him onto the swing and push him back and forth for hours. He slept curled up with her in her bed at night and sipped hot chocolate beside her as she drank her coffee in the morning. He held her hand as she bought vegetables in the market and they ate their tea together, dipping their toes in the murky water of the swimming pool as they chewed sausage sandwiches and cakes from the patisserie. Reality and fantasy mingled; the little boy who never grew up and the woman who was making a perfect home for her son.

'Perhaps I was mistaken, about the men?' Martha murmured.

'Well, the mist was very thick.' Ben guided her gently into the chapel and laid the gun on the kitchen table.

'I think you're right about getting more rest.'

'An extra few hours of sleep might make you feel better, but I need to talk to you about the wasps.'

'I'll put some sugar traps out later on,' Martha replied. 'That usually sorts them out.'

'They're not wasps, they're hornets.'

'Oh.' Martha felt any energy she had left seeping away. 'No wonder they're so big. I'll have to go into town and phone the pest control department.'

'It's OK,' Ben said with a smile. 'I'll find the nest and sort them out.' He walked towards the front door. 'Don't worry, I haven't

forgotten about fixing the leaky taps either. And I thought beef bourguignon would be good for tonight. I bought the ingredients
yesterday.' He stepped through the door and gave a wave.

The sun seemed to cast a golden halo around his head. Martha
resisted the urge to tell him he was an angel again. She suspected
there were only so many times a Scottish man covered in tattoos
would want to hear it.

In the bedroom, Martha gently eased herself onto the unmade bed.
Pippa lay stretched out where Martha had left her. Martha stroked
her velvet fur and Pippa made a little purring sound in response.

Martha picked up the postcard on the bedside table and studied
the familiar picture. A seaside town in the sunshine; touched up in
the photographer's studio the sea looked like the Caribbean. Martha
thought about the little boy who had kept her company for all those
years, replacing her absent son. They used to talk about the beach.

'Do you remember the sea, Owen?'

He'd kick at the water in the pool and laugh.

Sally had brought the postcard with the annual Christmas card from
Sledge, the one band member who made an attempt to stay in touch
with Martha. For years there had been so little post for *Le Couvent des
Cerises* that the postman left letters in the bar rather than cycling up
the long steep hill to the house, though of late the slim white letters
from the bank were arriving with increasing frequency.

'It seems a funny thing to send at Christmas,' Sally had said as
she'd handed Martha the postcard. She'd done her usual whirl around
the kitchen putting mugs into the dishwasher and sluicing away the
ancient coffee grounds in the sink. Her face broke into a smile. 'I've
brought cake from the patisserie. *Bûche de Noël*, though in Rochdale
we'd just call it chocolate log.'

Martha was staring at the postcard.

'Is it another one of your fans?' Sally asked.

Sally took two thick discs of chocolate sponge and buttercream
from a box and put them onto plates with spoons.

'No.' Martha looked up.

'Are they from Wales? The picture's of some place called Abertoffee.'

'Abertrulli,' corrected Martha.

'Is it from someone in the band?' Sally licked cream from her fingers and pushed a plate towards Martha.

Martha shook her head.

'Who is it from then?' asked Sally, tucking into her slice of cake.

'It's from my son.' Martha's voice sounded flat though inside her body was shaking.

'You have a son?' Sally choked, a spray of chocolate sponge spattering her cleavage.

'Didn't you know?'

'No!'

'I thought everybody knew.' Martha tried not to think about the newspaper headlines all those years ago.

'I had no idea.'

'I thought you and Pierre were being tactful never mentioning him.'

'For God's sake, Martha, I couldn't be *that* tactful! Why didn't you tell me about him?'

Martha put the postcard down and pressed her hands against her face.

Sally put her spoon down.

'What happened?'

Martha sighed. 'I was a terrible mother, I let him down, I wasn't fit to look after a child.'

'You can't have been that bad,' Sally nodded at the postcard on the table between them. 'Or he wouldn't be writing to you.'

Martha let her fingers trace the letters of his name, the same way that her fingers had traced his name every day for over six months. The postcards' dog-eared corners and smudged ink were evidence of all the times she had picked it up. The phone number at the bottom had started to fade. Martha sighed. She still hadn't answered. She hadn't found the courage to reply to the breezy message that seemed more like something written by a brief acquaintance than a son writing to his mother.

Hello Mum,

I know it's been a long time. Would it be OK to come and visit you in France? I'd like to see you. Catch up on what's been happening in our lives. There's someone very special I'd like you to meet. Let me know when would suit you. I hope you are well.

Owen.

'Owen,' she whispered into the stillness of the room.

Martha stared down at the picture on the front of the postcard. Abertrulli. Did Owen really remember? Long journeys on the motorway, miles of winding country lanes? Could he remember Martha and his grandmother singing to him in the pushchair on the sand? Martha could see Owen laughing; his first word had been 'more'. She turned the postcard over, rounded letters, black ink, slightly sloping; Owen's name was underlined, not once but twice.

She thought of the young man on the LinkedIn page and tried to imagine him walking beside her on the sand, what it might be like to look up into his smiling face. But his smile was too set, his suit and tie too formal for the beach at Abertrulli. He didn't laugh or say 'more', he didn't have a voice at all.

She imagined the person Owen had said he'd like her to meet. A girl, probably very like his stepmother, the beautiful Amelia; blonde hair, long legs, a cut-glass accent unable to disguise disdain. Martha's heart began to beat wildly at the thought, not just of Owen but Owen and a girlfriend – maybe even a wife. She'd never be good enough for either of them.

Suddenly a high-pitched scream broke through her thoughts, then another and another. Martha dropped the postcard and ran outside.

Chapter 13

The adults were huddled together at the bottom of the drive surrounding the source of the screams. Reuben was skirting around the adults, peering through their legs trying to get a better look, his body still glistening from the pool.

As Martha hurried towards the group, she heard Ranjit's voice. 'Calm down, we need to see.'

'They're everywhere!' Paula sounded on the verge of hysteria. 'I'm going to get Tilly inside.'

'Take Reuben with you,' Ranjit said. 'And shut the doors and windows.'

Paula rushed past Martha, the baby in her arms, herding Reuben towards the house, urging him on with her free hand.

'What's the matter?' Martha asked.

Paula didn't reply, she took her son's hand and started to run up the path.

Martha approached the edge of the group. The screaming seemed to be getting louder. Martha could see Ranjit, squatting down, holding something pink and writhing in his arms. The first thing Martha thought of was a pig, though of course she knew it was a child.

'He's covered in them,' Ranjit said. 'Twenty stings at least.'

Josh had a tube of ointment and was attempting to smear it onto the child's body. He glanced up at Ranjit.

'Are you sure it's going to work?'

Ranjit nodded. 'Paula swears by it.'

Alice stood slightly apart, watching, eyes wide, cheeks drained of their usual rosy glow.

'Whatever has happened?' Martha asked her.

'It's Noah.' Alice turned to Martha. 'I told the boys to keep well away but . . .' Her voice trailed off as Noah started screaming even louder than before.

'We can't help you if you won't let us put this cream on,' Josh said.

'Away from what?' Martha shouted to Alice above the increasing noise.

'The hornet's nest.' Alice pointed towards the cherry orchard. In the distance, Martha could see black dots zooming angrily between the twisted trees.

'Ben found the nest,' Alice continued, her voice wavering.

'Noah! No! Don't kick,' Josh shouted as the child lashed out and Ranjit struggled to keep hold of the boy's squirming body.

'Ben told me about it on his way to find the ladder.' Alice looked on the verge of tears. 'I was on pool duty while the others were clearing breakfast. I just thought that I ought to tell the boys to stay away from the trees. So stupid – that was obviously asking for trouble!' Alice shook her head. 'And I wasn't watching them properly. I was writing about the different cheeses that I'd seen at the supermarket in my notebook. I didn't see Noah get out of the pool or get the stick and . . .'

Martha sighed.

'I can guess the rest.'

'It's all my fault.'

'No. It is my fault.' Martha ran her fingers through her hair. 'I should have spotted the nest before you arrived or at least got pest control this morning. I thought Ben had it under control.' She looked around. 'Where is he?'

'I don't know,' said Alice.

At that moment, Elodie appeared, dressed in pyjamas printed with faded pink unicorns; the arms and legs were too short and her skinny wrists and ankles poked out like twigs.

'What's going on?' She yawned. 'Is that Noah?'

At the sight of his sister, Noah stopped screaming. Slick with oint-ment he slid out of Ranjit's arms and threw himself against Elodie. His back and arms were covered in red welts.

'It hurts, it hurts,' he repeated over and over, sobbing as Elodie crouched down to hold him.

She looked up at the others. 'His hands, his arms, they're like . . . balloons?'

Martha felt sick; an awful memory surfaced in her mind.

'My mouth feels funny.' Noah's voice sounded thick between the sniffles. 'My tongue is . . .' He stopped, suddenly quiet.

Martha remembered the hot afternoon in Germany, her friend lying on the stage.

'He needs to go to hospital.' Everybody turned to Martha as she spoke.

Josh looked astonished. 'Surely it's not that bad?'

'If I could just get more of the cream on him,' Ranjit said. 'It always works for bites or stings.'

Martha's voice was firm. 'He needs to go to hospital right now – he's going into anaphylactic shock. I've seen it before.'

Noah made a rasping sound.

'Oh my goodness,' Ranjit exclaimed. 'His lips are swelling up.'

'And his eyes are like golf balls' Josh looked pale. 'What are we going to do?'

'I'll get the car keys.' Ranjit took off towards the house.

Alice turned to Martha. 'Where's the nearest hospital?'

'Bergerac . . . but it's too far.'

Josh was trying to take Noah's pulse but the child was twisting his wrist away from him. Josh let him go.

'Has he had a reaction to wasp stings before?' Ranjit asked.

'Umm, I don't know, I don't think so . . .' Josh was running his hands through his hair repeatedly. 'Elodie?'

'No, Dad, never. He was fine when that wasp stung his leg at Legoland, he hardly even cried. And the time he tried to Sello-tape a bee to his remote-control car he was fine too.'

'We have to act quickly.' Martha's heart was hammering. How

stupid to leave it to Ben to deal with a nest of hornets. 'He needs adrenaline. As soon as possible.'

'We'll have to get him to Bergerac,' Alice said. 'It's his only hope.'

'There isn't time.' Martha shook her head. 'There is a doctor in the village. He only has evening surgeries, but you could go to his house and see if he's there, if not, there's only the chemist, they might be able to help.'

'OK, that's the plan.' Ranjit had run back from the house with the car keys; sweat ran down his forehead and his face was puce. 'Get him in the back of my car. Where's the doctor's house, Martha?'

'To the right of the square.' Martha tried to make her brain work faster; she hadn't had much need for a doctor. Jean-Paul had supplied the only medication she was interested in.

'It's the second avenue of big houses; the house is in the middle. I'll come with you; it will be easier if I direct.' Ranjit was already running towards the Range Rover, Josh was close behind carrying Noah who was clinging to his sister's hand, moaning. His face was very swollen, his cheeks and eyelids puffed up so that you could no longer see his eyes.

Martha struggled to keep up.

'Alice,' Ranjit called back as he reached the car. 'Please make sure that Paula is OK, tell her what's happening.'

Martha managed to scramble into the passenger seat just as the car started to move. Ranjit shot off, creating a swirling cloud of yellow dust. Martha glanced at the back seats and saw that Elodie was beside her father. Noah lay half across Josh's lap and half across his sister's. His face had taken on a bluish tinge. Elodie stroked his hair. 'Hush, hush,' she whispered, even though, for once, her little brother wasn't making any sound.

Chapter 14

'*Antiparasitaire* are on their way.' Sally placed the coffee cup in front of Martha. Steam curled towards the ceiling of the quiet bar. 'They'll sort the hornets out in no time.'

It wasn't yet lunchtime, but Martha felt that a whole day must have passed, at least. Martha pressed her palm against her forehead, trying to hold back the headache that threatened to return with a vengeance.

'If only I'd got them in to sort out the nest sooner.'

'Are you sure you don't want something stronger than coffee?' Sally asked. 'You still look very pale.'

'Cognac?' Pierre said, pointing to a shelf of colourful bottles. 'Is good for le shock.'

Martha shook her head and searched her pockets for a lighter.

'No, a coffee and a cigarette are fine.' She gave up her search as Sally offered her a box of matches and sat down next to her.

'Something sweet *peut-etre*?' Pierre began to cut a slice from a tart on a glass stand on the counter. 'I will not hear no. You have had *le jour terrible*.' He made a tutting sound. 'Hornets are bloody evil baggers.'

'Buggers,' corrected Sally.

Martha struck a match, letting the flame blaze for a few seconds before lighting her cigarette.

'I can just imagine this added to the list of complaints – lack of air conditioning, lack of Wi-Fi, leaky taps and killer hornets!'

'But the little boy is going to be alright, isn't he?' Sally put her hand on Martha's arm.

Martha nodded. 'Yes, thank God. The doctor gave him a shot of adrenaline and five minutes later Noah was well enough to find a biro and deface a poster showing the parts of the body affected by yeast infections.'

'Dr. Dubois, he is good,' Pierre said, placing a slice of lemon tart on a side plate with a fork beside Martha. He gave Sally's shoulder an affectionate squeeze. 'For us he never gives up the hope.'

'But hope never gets us anywhere, does it!' Sally shrugged his hand away. 'He and his specialist friends still don't know why I keep losing our babies.'

'Cherie.' Pierre's hand returned to Sally's shoulder.

'Just don't,' she said, shrugging him away again.

Pierre retreated back behind the bar and started to dry a row of glasses; he looked miserable. Sally picked up the fork and took a bite of the tart intended for Martha.

Martha wanted to reach out and take Sally's hand, but Sally stiffened.

'Where's Noah now?' she asked.

'Dr. Dubois sent Noah to the hospital in Bergerac for a check-up. Just in case. I didn't think they needed me any more and Noah was much better by then.'

'It is very good luck you knew what is happening to the boy.' Pierre looked up from the glass he was drying.

'When I was in the band, Posh Paul was stung by a bee at an outdoor gig in Berlin. He nearly died, right there on the stage. After that he always carried an EpiPen with him and we all learned what to do if he got stung again.'

'Imagine if no one had taken Noah to the doctor.' Sally shuddered.

'Today you are a hero,' Pierre smiled.

Martha shook her head. 'It's my fault. I shouldn't have left Ben to sort it out.'

'Ben?' Sally stopped halfway through putting a forkful of tart into her mouth.

Martha stubbed out her cigarette.

99

'I forgot, I haven't seen you for a few days. Ben is a young man who's been helping me. He came up to the house looking for work. He's been wonderful around the house and garden. He works hard and cooks as well.'

'Where did he come from?' Sally asked.

'He saw the handyman advert, you know, the one I put up in here months ago.'

Sally and Pierre turned towards the collection of curling cards and fading flyers pinned to the wooden panelling beside the door.

'You've met him,' Martha continued.

Sally looked at Pierre. Pierre shrugged. 'I do not know a Ben.'

'What does he look like?' Sally asked.

'Shaggy blond hair. Piercings. Tattoos up his arms. Rides a motorbike.'

Sally's eyes widened. The tart, still suspended on the fork, wobbled and she clamped her rosy lips around it before it could slip back onto the plate.

'He came to see you on Sunday?' Martha went on. 'To tell you that the phone line was down.' Martha looked from one to the other. 'He's Scottish.'

'Ah *oui, oui*, I remember this boy,' Pierre said. 'He is staying with you and I think that he is one of your holiday people. Sally, I tell you about him and say he did not look like what I expect of Martha's guests.'

Sally nodded. 'That was the night of the quarter-final, the bar was packed. I don't remember him.'

'*Mais oui*, I remember,' Pierre said. 'I serve him a beer and when I hear he is Scottish I made joke about Scotland is never in the World Cup. He was not laughing.'

'Is he staying in the village?' Sally asked.

'No, he's staying with me.'

Sally choked a little. 'But you've only just met him.'

Martha shrugged. 'I have a house full of people I don't know anything about. And to get money from them I need all the help I can get.'

100

'Well, he hasn't helped with the hornets!'

Martha sighed. 'It was too much. I should have got the professionals straight away.'

Sally licked icing sugar from the plate with her finger.

'I'll give you a lift back up the hill. I want to get a better look at him.'

'You really don't need to worry, he's just a young man looking to earn a bit of money to fund his travelling.'

'Do you know anything about him at all?'

Martha thought for a few moments. 'Not really, he's a man of few words – it's one of the things I like about him.'

'I think he is a doggy one.' Pierre cleared away the tart plate before Sally could start licking it with her tongue.

'Dodgy,' Sally interpreted.

'*Oui*,' Pierre continued. 'This is what I said. In the bar, he is looking like he is waiting for someone, always watching the door. He is not even looking at the football on the television – a man who is not interested in the World Cup – that to me is very doggy indeed.'

Chapter 15

'Your driving doesn't get any better.' Martha grabbed the dashboard as Sally's small Fiat screeched around the tight bends leading out of the village.

'It's these French roads,' Sally laughed. 'They're like Scalextric tracks.'

'Maybe if you went a little slower?' Martha suggested.

The sunflower fields and little farms were speeding by at an alarming rate.

'You don't think this Ben might actually be your son?' Sally asked, veering sharply round another bend.

'What?'

'Well, Owen said on the postcard he wanted to see you; maybe he's come but hasn't had the courage to tell you who he really is?'

'You read too many novels, Sally! Ben is Scottish, for a start, and I don't think Owen would have quite so many tattoos and earrings – my ex-husband would have a fit.'

'OK, but when *are* you going to get in touch with Owen, it's been ages.'

'I just can't seem to . . .' Martha tried to find the words to express the fear that paralysed her every time she thought of contacting her son. 'I may not be what he's expecting,' she said quietly. 'Especially if I lose the house. Who would want a penniless, homeless addict for a mother.'

Sally put out a hand to touch Martha's arm, and the car swerved as the next bend approached.

'Hands on the wheel!' Martha shouted.

'OK, keep your hair on! You're worse than Pierre.'

Martha shut her eyes and thought of the last time she'd seen Owen. It had been his third birthday; she'd been allowed to visit for half an hour.

'Ex-addict,' Sally said.

'Whatever.' Martha opened her eyes a fraction.

'I can't imagine how awful it must have been for you not to be able to see your child. How could your husband have been so cruel?'

'Andrew's lawyer made such a big thing about me taking painkillers, completely disregarding the fact that I'd been prescribed them by Andrew's family's private doctor after the accident. It was Andrew himself who insisted that I had Vicodin. He said that his friend in the States swore by them for pain relief. He denied that in court – of course. I just seemed like a hopeless mother who was completely out of it most of the time. Andrew was only too happy to detail all the times I'd fallen asleep in charge of Owen or forgotten mealtimes and appointments. Once, I left Owen in a clothes shop on the King's Road.'

As they veered around another corner Martha tried not to think about the time she'd crashed her Mini with Owen in the back; she could have killed him. The memory of it still had the power to make her want to curl up with shame and self-loathing.

'Did Andrew not suggest rehab?' Sally asked.

Martha shook her head. 'My little problem suited him very well. He already had his eye on his next wife.' Martha thought about Amelia with her long blonde hair and doe-like eyes. Her Norland nanny uniform seemed to accentuate her curves and long tanned legs.

'Your husband sounds like a right knob,' Sally said. The car juddered as the steepness of the hill increased. 'Why did you ever marry him?'

Martha sighed. 'After the band broke up, I was miserable. I waited and waited for Lucas to get in touch; he never did. So, I suppose when I met Andrew, he seemed like an escape from all that pain. He offered me a completely different life, far removed from the music industry. Something stable. A proper home. A fridge full of healthy food instead of vodka and champagne. Nights at the theatre instead of nightclubs.'

'Sounds a bit dull,' said Sally.

'In the beginning we were happy. We bought a big house in Kensington. I threw myself into decorating it – choosing the brightly coloured paints and curtains and bits and pieces I picked up from Portobello Market. When Owen was born it was wonderful, I had a baby, I had a beautiful home. But after I had the accident, Andrew changed. It was as though he didn't trust me to look after Owen any more, or want me to. He hired the nanny while I was in the hospital. When I finally came home I felt like a visitor rather than Owen's mother and Andrew's wife.'

'But how could Andrew stop you from seeing your little boy for so long?' Sally asked.

Martha looked down at her hands; her knuckles were white from gripping the black upholstery. She forced herself to relax and put them in her lap.

'Andrew promised he'd bring Owen to see me. The divorce was awful but afterwards he was actually quite nice. He even paid the deposit for *Le Couvent des Cerises*. I was so grateful. He said it would be great for Owen to come to France for holidays, said it would be good for him to experience another country, another language.'

Sally slowed down as the *Antiparasitaire* van sped past, going in the opposite direction.

'What happened? Did Owen ever come here?' Sally asked.

'No. There was always an excuse; a cold, a change of holiday dates, a family bereavement. I sent Owen letters, presents on his birthday, get well soon cards when he had, yet another, bout of flu or chickenpox, an extra big present at Christmas – I was always searching for things I thought he'd like. Andrew would write and say that Owen said thank you, but I never heard from Owen himself. I asked Andrew for photographs, but he didn't send a single one.'

'Bastard,' Sally muttered.

'I've tried to keep the house and garden nice for Owen. I'd think of things we could do together; in town I'd pick up leaflets about kayaking on the river, trips to caves, camping by the lake. I bought a wicker hamper for the picnics I hoped we'd have one day. I put up the swing.'

Sally crunched the gears. 'I don't understand why you couldn't have just gone to England to visit Owen yourself.'

Martha swallowed. She opened her mouth to answer but the words refused to form. She had gone, she'd made the trip two years after she'd moved to France. It had been Owen's birthday. She had stood on the Kensington doorstep and rung the bell. Amelia had answered, billowing in silk and immaculately blow-dried hair. She'd looked Martha up and down as if she was some vagrant from the streets.

'What do you want?' she'd asked in a voice more like a sneer.

Inside Martha had been able to see balloons and bunting and children running around in party clothes, a fat man in bright clothing and a red nose. The décor had changed, white and beige instead of the vibrant colours Martha had chosen.

A child had come to stand at Amelia's side, a little boy with golden curls. He'd taken Amelia's hand in his and looked up into the woman's perfectly made-up face.

'Are you coming?' he'd asked her. 'The clown is going to start.'

'Of course, darling.' Amelia had lifted Owen in her arms. 'Nothing is going to spoil your special day.'

Then she'd slammed the door in Martha's face. Martha had stood on the step for a long time, listening to the children's laughter inside, then she'd turned and walked back down the street to the hotel she'd booked. She'd taken a whole strip of tablets, washed down with half the contents of the minibar. She'd gone back to the house.

This time it was Andrew who opened the door. Martha remembered she'd been swaying, her vision blurred, her voice thick and slurred.

'Look at you,' he'd said. 'What makes you think you're fit to see my son? What makes you think you're fit to be a mother?'

He'd told her he'd take her to court if she ever turned up again. When she got back to France there was a solicitor's letter waiting, threatening to take away all her rights to see her son if she didn't keep away. She never went to London again.

She had stayed at home and taken more and more Vicodin. Momentarily Martha thought of how the tablets had made her feel; a warm bath in which she had been able to escape reality. She thought how lovely it would be to escape like that again.

'At least Owen has got in touch now.' Sally's voice broke through Martha's thoughts.

'Just as the home I made for him is falling apart,' Martha sighed.

'For goodness' sake!' Sally narrowly missed one of the gateposts as she swung the little car into the driveway of *Le Couvent des Cerises*. 'It's not falling apart. As soon as you got that postcard you booked yourself into the rehab clinic. Now you're off the painkillers and you're doing something positive to keep your home. Trust me, it'll all work out.'

It was true. The postcard had spurred Martha into action, and she had been off the painkillers for more than six months now.

'Wait till Dordogne Dreams hears about the hornets,' Martha said through gritted teeth. Each jolt and jar of the car was sending a spasm of pain through her leg. 'I'll never get paid. I'll never get any more guests. The bank will repossess the house . . . and then I'll . . .' Martha's voice trailed away into an unimaginable future.

The car skidded to a stop on the dusty stones, narrowly avoiding Josh's Porsche. Sally pulled on the handbrake and turned to Martha with a smile.

'Well, you might just have to go for plan B.'

'Plan B?'

'The brothel!' Sally winked. 'Like Pierre said, *Madame Martha* has a ring to it.'

Martha shook her head as she opened the car door. 'I promised myself after the divorce – no more men!'

'Even if they pay you?' Sally was laughing.

'No way.'

'Even if they pay you a lot?'

'It doesn't matter how much they pay.' Martha slammed the car door. 'No men! Not for business. Not for pleasure! Ever!'

'I think I get the message.' Sally leant out of the car window, still laughing. 'The checkout at the Intermarché it is!'

Chapter 16

All was quiet.

No shrieks and splashes came from the pool; no chatter or noise from the terrace.

'My God, it's hot.' Sally squeezed herself out of the little car. She nodded towards the Porsche. 'Someone having a mid-roof crisis?'

Martha rolled her eyes. 'That's Josh's car. Newly separated from his wife and trying to impress his younger girlfriend.'

'Well, it looks like he's having trouble getting it up,' giggled Sally.

Martha looked about the deserted garden. There was no sign of Alice or Paula and thankfully no sign of the hornets either.

Sally fanned her face with her hand. 'It must be the hottest day of the year so far.'

Martha turned towards the terrace and spotted Alice sat at one end of the long mosaic table, half hidden in the dappled shade of the vine. She hoped that Alice hadn't heard Sally, though the expression on the young woman's face seemed to signify misery rather than indignation or embarrassment.

She looked up as they approached. Martha noticed a scrunched tissue in one hand.

'How's Noah?' she asked.

'Noah is absolutely fine.' Removing a child's sock from the seat of a chair, Martha sat down.

A silver candlestick from the drawing room was standing in the middle of the table in a pool of melted wax. Around it, remnants of the breakfast that must have been partly cleared when Noah let out his first scream; a pile of jammy plates, an open box of sugar-free muesli, and croissant crumbs swept into a heap on the mosaic surface.

'Really?' Alice sounded doubtful.

'Really.' Martha could see a wobbly letter N scratched into the wooden edging of the table.

Alice sighed. She had a mug beside her and a plate of her short-bread biscuits; the biscuits didn't look like they'd been touched.

'I should have realised I'd have to watch him at all times.'

'It's his father that should have been watching him!' Sally said.

Martha prodded her with her elbow.

'Well, he should have been.' Sally reached across the table to pick up a biscuit.

'I suppose Noah must be completely traumatised,' Alice said, pushing the plate of biscuits nearer to Sally.

'When I last saw him, he was trying to climb the monument in the village square shouting "Look at me, I'm Spider-man," while Josh and Ranjit begged him to get into the car.'

Martha recounted Noah's rapid recovery, then she asked where Paula was.

'Indoors with Tilly and Reuben. I did go up and tell her that the pest control men had been. They filled the orchard with smoky stuff and then afterwards they came up here and they seemed to be saying the hornets were no more. Though my French is not very good, they might have been asking for a cup of coffee.'

'And Ben?' asked Martha.

'I haven't seen him since before Noah got stung,' Alice said.

Sally raised her eyebrows and looked pointedly at Martha.

'I can still see his tent. And his rucksack, so he must be going to come back.'

'I love these biscuits,' said Sally.

'I have an idea for something really special for pudding tonight.' Alice scrunched her tissue into a smaller ball and smiled. 'Josh's favourite, to make up for his awful day. Pavlova.'

'Ooh, I love a bit of pav.' Sally licked biscuit crumbs from her lips. 'I bet you make a really good one.'

'Alice?' a small voice said. Reuben was standing beside the table, a miniature replica of Ranjit.

Alice smiled gently at him. 'What is it?'

'Will you come swimming with me?'

'Yes, of course, in a minute. What have you been up to?'

'I've been being very quiet.'

'For your mum to get a rest?' asked Alice.

Reuben shook his head. 'I've been being very quiet for the man.'

'What man?' Martha felt a tingle in her spine.

'The man at the window,' the little boy said. 'In the living room.'

'What kind of a man?' Alice asked.

'A man with no hair. And a white face. He told me to be quiet.'

'He spoke to you?' Martha shifted in her seat.

'He went like this,' Reuben made a shushing action with his finger against his mouth.

Martha recalled the men she thought she had seen fighting in the orchard that morning. 'Could it have been one of the pest control men?'

'They both had long hair in ponytails and big bushy beards,' said Alice.

'Could it have been Ben?' Sally asked.

Reuben shook his head again.

'He would have recognised him,' Martha said to Sally.

'And he doesn't fit the description,' Alice said.

'Ben has lots of hair,' said Martha.

'And he doesn't have a mean face,' Alice added.

'He looked like a ghost,' Reuben said.

'There are no ghosts here,' Martha said firmly.

'Yesterday Noah saw a ghost.' Reuben's voice was very solemn.

Sally glanced at Martha.

'You know what they say in the village about this place,' she whispered under her breath. 'The wandering nun!'

'Where did Noah see the ghost?' Martha asked Reuben.

'In the trees.' He pointed at the cherry orchard. 'He said it was a pretty ghost with long blonde hair and a white dress.'

'Bride of Christ,' Sally murmured with a slight tremble in her voice.

Martha glanced towards the orchard – the little copse shimmered in the afternoon heat.

'I'll be back to check out this Ben tomorrow, and your ghosts.' Sally stood up. 'But I'd better go and help get ready for the quarter-final this evening. Pierre says we'll be getting a crowd.' She waved goodbye and descended the stone steps towards the drive, her flowery skirt flouncing over her curvaceous hips. At the bottom of the steps she turned. 'Save me a slice of pavlova.' Then she was gone.

'Is it alright if I use the kitchen later?' Alice asked.

'Of course.' Martha glanced up the drive, looking for signs of Ben's motorbike. She hoped she wouldn't have to make the main course all alone.

'There you are, Reuben!' A loud voice came from the kitchen door.

Paula was peering around, batting invisible insects away from her face. Her eyes alighted on her son.

'I told you to stay indoors and read your book.'

'I was bored,' Reuben said petulantly.

Martha hoped that Reuben wouldn't tell his mother about the ghostly man at the window. It would not help to endear Paula to her holiday home.

'How is poor Noah?' Paula turned her gaze to Martha. 'Alice told me you saved his life.'

'Well, I think that's a bit strong,' Martha said. 'I just recognised the symptoms of a severe allergic reaction. He was right as rain when I last saw him.'

Paula shook her head. 'I don't think we've ever had a holiday when there hasn't been some trauma with that child. Though you really should have sent the professionals to deal with the nest much sooner. Imagine if little Tilly had been stung.'

'I don't think Tilly would have been up a tree poking the nest with a stick,' said Alice.

Paula shot her a look of disdain and disappeared back inside.

'Ready for our swim?' Alice asked Reuben. 'I know I am. I've done nothing all day but sit here worrying. I feel like a bit of exercise.'

Reuben nodded enthusiastically.

'I'll see you later,' Alice said to Martha and the young woman and the little boy set off towards the pool.

Martha picked the candle wax off the table. She thought about what Reuben had said. A strange man lurking around was the last thing she needed to add to the week's list of calamities.

'Martha!' Paula was back. Martha jumped at the woman's loud enunciation of her name.

'I have another question.'

'Yes?'

'What's on the menu tonight?' Paula smiled. Martha wasn't sure if she'd really seen her smile before even though the expression on the woman's lip was tight.

Martha desperately tried to remember what Ben had said he'd bought the ingredients for.

'Beef bourguignon.' Martha anticipated that she would be told that Paula didn't eat red meat but instead Paula's smile widened.

'Oh, that's one of my favourites – if it's cooked correctly. I shall look forward to seeing what yours is like.'

'Great,' Martha muttered through gritted teeth as Paula disappeared inside again.

Before going down to the chapel she walked tentatively around the perimeter of the house looking for signs of an intruder. The bamboo thicket outside the living room had a broken branch, but the storm, or the two boys, could easily have done the damage.

She passed the broken swing, the seat still hanging desolately from one rope. Ben had offered to mend it, but Martha had said no. The thought of other little boys playing on it hurt. She had put it up for Owen.

'You silly woman,' she said out loud as she walked down to the chapel. Would the young man she'd seen in the LinkedIn photo really want to use a swing? The thought made her smile as she imagined him kicking out his legs in his formal dark suit; his tie flapping behind him as he flew backwards and forwards through the air.

112

Chapter 17

The last few hours had been exhausting, yet surprisingly exhilarating. Martha and Alice had worked on separate sides of the little kitchen. Alice whisked and folded and carefully arranged the cream and fruit, while Martha chopped, stirred and splashed and added more and more red wine to the chunks of meat simmering on the stove. Alice got used to Martha's profanities as the stew bubbled over or the garlic bulbs proved impossible to peel.

As they worked, Alice had told her about the string of terrible boyfriends she'd had in the past; Martha had to agree that compared to Bodo, Gideon and Bean, Josh did seem like an improvement. Alice told her about her family in Sussex and her perfect older sister: a Cambridge medical school graduate that Alice's parents thought could do no wrong. She was also a champion triathlete and played the flute and violin exceptionally well. She and her fiancé had recently climbed Everest to raise money for defibrillators for schools in developing nations. Alice's parents were throwing a party the following weekend to celebrate their achievement.

'They asked if I'd make cupcakes.' Alice sliced a cherry in half and prised out the stone. 'With little icing replicas of Everest on top!'

Martha waited for her to say more but Alice just went on chopping the cherry into smaller and smaller pieces.

For a while the two women worked in silence. Now and then Martha glanced outside the door, watching for Ben.

'Do you think he's OK?' Alice asked after a while.

'I hope so.' Martha didn't know whether to be worried or angry that Ben had left her to do the cooking alone. She hadn't seen him all afternoon.

'Do you think he realised what had happened to Noah and feels so bad he doesn't want to come back?' Alice stopped slicing up cherries and looked at Martha. 'I'd hate to think he might blame himself, when really it was all my fault.'

Martha put down her wooden spoon.

'It wasn't your fault. It was mine.'

'You were great though; so calm and sensible.'

Martha raised her eyebrows; she'd never been called calm or sensible before.

Dried leaves crunched beneath Martha's feet as she walked up the path with the beef stew. She looked down at the meaty chunks in the aromatic dark brown gravy and felt the way she did when she finished a painting that she was pleased with, or how she'd used to feel when she'd written a good song. Her beef bourguignon had been a success. She offered up a prayer of silent thanks for the previously unused cookery book that her mother had given her thirty years before.

Martha stopped at the sound of an engine – could it be Ben's bike? But it was the Range Rover, lumbering slowly down the drive. Alice had also stopped and the two women watched Ranjit slide the car in between Martha's Citroën and Josh's Porsche.

Reuben had been loitering at the bottom of the drive for hours, waiting for Noah's return. The car stopped and Reuben tugged the passenger door open. Noah sprang out like a coil released and the boys ran in circles whooping and screaming like tiny warriors.

The rest of the party took longer to emerge. Josh climbed out looking slightly dazed.

'Noah, please take it easy,' he called out weakly. 'You know the doctor said you might feel tired for a few days.'

Noah let out an extra loud war cry followed by 'Let's go on a rabbit hunt!' as he led a full-speed charge towards the house. Martha was relieved that Pippa was safely shut inside the chapel.

114

'I saw another ghost,' Reuben shouted after him. 'A man ghost with no hair.'

Noah began to sing the theme from *Ghostbusters* at the top of his voice twirling around as though holding an imaginary proton pack.

Ranjit emerged and leant against the open car door. He yawned.

'I think that adrenaline injection has made Noah even more hyper than before.'

'I think you're right.' Josh was yawning too. 'I wish I could have had one.'

He spotted Alice and walked towards her.

'Well, here's a vision as good as an adrenaline shot.' He leant over the pavlova to give her a kiss. Whipped cream and cherry sauce smeared his pale blue shirt.

'I'm so sorry . . .' Alice began. Josh shook his head.

'Don't worry. You've seen Noah. He's absolutely fine.'

'That's a huge relief, but . . .' She nodded towards the pocket of his shirt.

'Oh no! It's new!' He started trying to rub the cream and cherry stain away; it only served to make it worse.

'Where's Elodie?' Alice asked. Josh looked around as if he had forgotten that Elodie had been with them.

'I'm here,' a voice came from the depths of the car and slowly Elodie climbed out, still in her tiny unicorn pyjamas but now wearing enormous wellington boots on her feet. She started to kick one of the boots off.

'Keep them on,' Josh said. 'At least until you get to the house. If you step on a hornet, we'll have to go through the whole palaver again.'

Elodie glared at her father. 'I look stupid.'

'They're Paula's new Le Chameaus!' said Ranjit. 'They cost a fortune. I think they were more expensive than this holiday.' He laughed and then suddenly looked mortified as he noticed Martha. He hastily turned back to the girl. 'Anyway, they were all we had. You couldn't go into the hospital in your bare feet.'

Elodie stomped up the path ignoring Alice, Martha and her father (who was very busy rubbing his shirt).

'You're just in time.' Alice smiled at Josh and Ranjit. 'Martha's made a wonderful stew and I made pavlova especially for you, Josh.'

'I need a shower first,' said Josh, 'and I'll have to try to sort this blasted stain out. Do you think a bit of salt might do it?' He looked to Alice and then to Martha.

Martha shrugged. 'I haven't a clue.' She smiled at Alice. 'Come on, we'd better get that magnificent pudding onto the table before anyone else damages it.'

Josh hurried on ahead while Ranjit locked the car.

'You can't be too careful,' he said. 'Josh said he saw a man lurking near the gates when he went for his run this morning.'

Alice and Martha exchanged a glance.

'What is it?' Ranjit asked. 'Do you have a problem with crime round here?'

'Look at the lovely roses by the pool,' Alice said quickly. 'They've all come out today, you wouldn't think they'd do that in this heat.'

'Ah, yellow roses,' said Ranjit. 'They always remind me of my . . .' his voice trailed off, his big brown eyes looked sad. He stared at the roses for a few more seconds and then walked away towards the house.

'Thank you,' Martha mouthed to Alice and the two women set off after Ranjit's retreating back.

'Well, I didn't think you'd want to give them something new to worry about,' Alice said. 'And after spending the afternoon in the pool with Reuben I have begun to realise he has a very vivid imagination. He told me he has a grandfather with long hair who rides a big motorbike and draws cartoons of talking dogs!'

'I somehow can't imagine that,' Martha laughed. 'Let's hope the mean-faced man was just another one of his stories.'

When they got to the terrace, Ranjit seemed more like his cheerful self. He rubbed his hands together as he looked at the table.

'Looks like a delicious spread.' He was smiling. 'You are eating with us, aren't you, Martha? You should join us, especially after everything you did to help Noah.'

'Well, I ought to wait for Ben to come back.'

'He can have something with us when he gets here. Please say yes.'

Martha felt her heart begin to beat faster, she wasn't sure if it was the slope of the path or anxiety. It had been years since she had been part of a dinner party or any social event. Even during her week at the clinic in Lyon she'd refused to eat with the other patients, preferring the seclusion of her white-walled room.

The summer that she had first arrived at *Le Couvent des Cerises* she'd been asked to attend the mayor's annual summer celebration. She'd taken a double dose of tablets and sat quietly at one of the long trestle tables in the village square, eating thin chips fried in goose fat and slices of spit-roasted pork. Garlands of brightly coloured paper flowers hung between the ancient buildings and children in traditional costumes ran about the cobbled streets.

Martha had initially been entranced but it wasn't long before she became aware of the darting glances and whispers: *la chanteuse du groupe anglais, Moondancing, accident, drogue*. Martha had found an excuse to leave as soon as she could and never went again, despite the gold-edged invitation that arrived each year.

But Martha wasn't entirely a recluse. She had lunch with Sally and Pierre from time to time, and in the past her mother had always come at Christmas. Martha would light the big fire in the living room and the two women would open their parcels in front of it (they used to compete with lavish gift wrapping) and then eat dinner on their laps watching *It's A Wonderful Life* or *Miracle on 34th Street*. Afterwards, they listened to Motown on the Dansette as they washed up, dancing around the kitchen, tea towels waving in the air.

'Just like the old days,' her mother would say.

But Martha's mother became too frail to travel and Jean-Paul became the only visitor to the house on Christmas Day, his small packets of white pills the only present Martha received – and they didn't come gift-wrapped or without a price.

'I'm really tired,' Martha said to Alice. 'I think I'll get an early night.' She put the beef down beside the sliced baguette and salad.

'That's a shame,' said Ranjit. 'I feel so bad that you're doing all this cooking, we are wearing you out.'

'Don't wait for me.' Josh appeared from the house brandishing a bottle of beer. He had taken his shirt off; presumably he was soaking it in the sink in an attempt to remove the stain. Martha noticed the beginnings of a paunch above the waistband of his shorts. 'I had a burger in the *aire de service* when we stopped for petrol,' Josh continued. 'I don't think I can eat another thing.'

Martha took the pavlova from Alice's hands before it slipped to the floor. The young woman stared after Josh as he went back inside the kitchen.

'Actually, I think I will join you,' said Martha taking a deep breath. 'It would be a shame not to taste this wonderful pudding.'

'Fantastic,' Ranjit said. 'You must sit here, at the top of the table.'

Martha let Ranjit guide her to the chair. He put a velvet cushion on the seat, one of Martha's favourites from the living room.

'Just to make it nice and comfy.'

Ranjit flipped the cushion over before Martha could sit down.

'Whoops, I think someone's been wiping their chocolatey little hands on this.'

Martha thought of all her precious clothes in the cupboard and hoped that no chocolatey little hands had been near them. She made a mental note to go upstairs and check as soon as all the guests were out of the house again.

Chapter 18

The meal was a chaotic affair. The group seemed so much larger sitting down. Even though Martha was at the top of the table it was narrow; Ranjit was seated beside her and his elbows kept knocking against hers as she ate. Ranjit ate one-handed holding Tilly on his lap. Paula sat beside him feeding the baby something mushy from a jar of organic baby food in between forkfuls of stew for herself. She kept looking upwards.

'What was that?' she said.

'Just a moth,' Ranjit reassured her.

Ranjit ate the bourguignon with gusto; his arm next to Martha seemed like a piston, mechanically shovelling the rich stew into his mouth.

'This is so good,' he kept repeating and to her surprise Martha found that she agreed with him; the beef was tender and the red wine sauce was full of flavour.

'It is good,' Paula said when she had nearly finished. 'I'm impressed.'

Martha felt ridiculously pleased with herself.

Josh had reappeared after his shower wearing a fresh white shirt and pale linen shorts. The shower and rest had restored a more youthful appearance to his face, and he seemed to have forgotten about the burger he'd had earlier. He sat down next to Alice and helped himself to a ginormous portion of stew. Like Ranjit he ate with one hand, his other permanently under the table, presumably caressing Alice's knee.

'Where's your Scotsman tonight?' he asked Martha.

'He's gone out,' Martha replied.

'Hot date with some pretty mademoiselle in the village?' Josh took a second helping of potatoes. 'I expect in a small place like this the girls can't afford to be too choosy.' A tiny potato skittered from the spoon onto Josh's lap. 'Oh my God, I don't believe it!' He stood up and started rubbing at the buttery stain on his crotch.

'Not in front of the children!' laughed Ranjit. He passed Tilly to Paula and stood up to refill the glasses around the table with wine. Martha noticed they were using the champagne flutes from the cocktail bar. She made a mental note to tell the next guests to only use the glasses in the kitchen.

Next guests! Martha wondered if there would be any more. She realised that Paula had asked her a question.

'Sorry?' she said. 'What did you say?'

'I just wondered how you came to be living at *Le Couvent des Cerises*?'

Martha froze, a forkful of stew halfway to her mouth.

'Did you find it tricky buying abroad?' Paula asked. 'We're looking for a place in Chamonix at the moment, aren't we, Ranjee?'

Ranjit overfilled Josh's glass. Dark red Merlot splashed onto the table.

'Careful, mate,' Josh said. 'I don't want any more stains on my clothes today.'

He turned to Martha. 'Do you have to pay stamp duty over here?'

Martha had put down her forkful of stew and was trying to think of an excuse to leave.

'Did you find it online?' Paula enquired. 'Is it very difficult to get planning?'

With relief Martha realised it was only the history of the purchase they were interested in. She wouldn't need to mention the band, or the accident, or her divorce from Andrew, or even how, as a child, France had been her fantasyland. The safe place where nothing bad would ever happen. The home of the father she had never known.

'I saw it advertised in the back of *The Sunday Times*,' she said, but it was hard to be heard above the noise of the children. The children had the other end of the table exclusively to themselves, Noah presiding at the head, perched on a golden cocktail bar stool, above everybody else. Martha wondered that they hadn't provided him with a small crown and an ermine robe.

In terms of table manners, parenting seemed to range from strict to tolerant to non-existent. Paula regularly admonished Reuben for having his elbows on the table and eating with his mouth full, while Ranjit vaguely issued suggestions to his son along the lines of, 'maybe you don't need to scream every time Noah makes you laugh'. Josh seemed to have forgotten he had any paternal duty at all, though he once joined the boys' conversation and told them a joke about a farting dog, which heralded louder screams from Reuben, and an even ruder joke from Noah.

Elodie sat with the four younger children but slightly away from the table so that she had to balance her plate on her lap. She had changed out of the unicorn pyjamas and was back in black with 'Suck It Up Buttercup' written across her chest.

Martha felt awful as she remembered, too late, that Elodie was a vegan; she wondered if Ben had planned anything special for the teenager. Instead, Elodie's plate consisted of salad leaves and a slice of baguette; she had picked a hole in the centre of the baguette and was slowly rolling the soft dough between her fingers to make a ball.

Noah had been watching his sister and started to make little balls out of his own bread, which he then rolled across the table to Reuben. Reuben copied Noah and then Noah made a larger dough ball and flicked it with his spoon at Reuben. The ensuing dough ball battle was accompanied by whoops and shrieks completely unchecked by the adults, who were now keenly discussing property prices in Wimbledon. They asked Martha how much she thought *Le Couvent des Cerises* might be worth.

She shifted uncomfortably on her cushioned seat. She didn't know. All she knew was how much she owed the bank – and that was a lot.

'Maybe you should think about getting a place round here,' Josh said to Ranjit, his voice rising to be heard above the children. 'You could live here permanently, work from home, fly over to the office every couple of weeks.'

Ranjit poured himself another glass of wine and took a large gulp.

'A lovely dream,' he said, filling his glass once more. 'But I am needed in the office, it's a very busy firm, and I have so many clients now . . .'

'And what about schools?' interrupted Paula. 'We only moved to Wimbledon for the excellent prep school near the common. We couldn't possibly move Reuben.'

'Goal!' Noah shouted. 'Right between your eyes, Roo Poo!'

'Don't call me that, Noah . . .' Reuben screwed up his face in the effort of thinking up a retaliatory name. 'Noah Rower!'

'I like that,' squealed Noah. 'I'm a good rower, aren't I, Dad? I was good in the canoe, wasn't I? Dad? Dad?'

But Josh was busy talking to Ranjit and Paula about the benefits of a second home when it came to tax, though Ranjit looked as though he wanted to leave the table as much as Martha did.

Martha started to think about cigarettes; she had a feeling Ranjit might be thinking about them too.

'Enough talk of houses, darling.' Ranjit filled his wife's glass. 'Have another glass of wine.'

Martha drained her own glass; Ranjit reached across the table and filled it again.

'It's not like you have far to get home,' he laughed.

Martha forced herself to return the laugh and decided to excuse herself as soon as she'd had a few more sips of wine. The sky was dark now, thick with stars. She wondered if Josh was right. Had Ben really gone to see a girl? Why wouldn't he have let her know?

'We have a visitor,' Josh pointed towards the gateway.

Martha twisted in her chair and saw that light was flooding the top of the drive. Ben was back. But, after a few seconds, Martha realised it wasn't the single beam of a motorbike coming slowly down the bumpy track but two headlights.

Conversation at the table stopped. The brightness of the lights in the darkness made it impossible to discern the make or colour of the vehicle though now it was closer it looked bigger than a car. It wasn't until it came to a stop and the security light came on that it became apparent that it was a camper van. A vintage VW model, complete with a split screen and white wall tyres.

'Shit,' Josh whispered, his wine-flushed face suddenly becoming very pale.

After a few seconds, two women emerged from the camper van. Both were tall. One of them had a mane of long, blonde corkscrew curls tied back with a flowing scarlet scarf. A floral skirt and an off-the-shoulder blouse enhanced the gypsy effect. The other woman was older and larger; statuesque, with brown skin and braids of purple hair coiled on top of her head. She wore wide, white linen trousers and layers of green, yellow and turquoise silk. As she began to walk towards the terrace the silken layers floated behind her, like some sort of bird of paradise.

All eyes were on the women. Everyone was silent. Josh stood up, knocking over his drink; the wine washed across the table, spattering his shirt. The glass rolled off onto the flagstones with a smash. No one took their eyes off the women.

'My goodness!' Ranjit was the first to speak, exhaling slowly.

'Well, well,' Paula said under her breath.

'Hi!' The blonde woman waved as the pair reached the top of the terrace steps. 'How's the gang?'

Paula and Ranjit exchanged glances while Alice looked from Josh to the two women and then to Martha. Martha shrugged and glanced at Elodie. Elodie's face was completely obscured by her hair and her salad was sliding leaf by leaf onto the floor.

Noah had taken advantage of the arrival of the camper van to slip unnoticed into the kitchen. He now appeared at the doorway, one hand deep in an enormous bag of crisps.

'Mummy!' He let out a roar, crisps flying in the air as he ran towards the blonde woman. She scooped him up and held him tight against her. So, this was Carla, Josh's ex-wife.

'My darling boy!' She put him down, held his face between both

123

her hands and kissed his cheeks over and over again. 'What a terrible time you've had!'

'I was attacked by giant wasps,' Noah said, pulling himself away from his mother's grip and holding out his hands to show how big the hornets had been – at least two feet long it seemed. 'I nearly died. Like this.' Noah rolled his eyes back into his head and collapsed back into his mother's arms. He made a gurgling sound. 'I'm dead.'

'Oh Noah!' The other woman put her hands onto her wide hips. 'What a shame when we had a present and everything.'

'A present!' Noah sprang back to life. 'Where is it?'

The woman let out a deep throaty laugh. 'Give me a hug and I'll go and fetch it from the van.'

'OK, Mrs. Clementine.' Noah threw himself against the woman's multicoloured clothes. He looked up at her and grinned.

She ruffled his hair. 'Don't call me Mrs. Clementine, sweetie. How many times do I have to tell you that my name is Flora.'

'OK, Mrs. Clementine. Can I have my present?' Noah was hopping from foot to foot.

Reuben had got down from his chair and was staring at Flora, creeping forward and then retreating backwards when she looked like she might notice him.

'Where's your magic handbag?' he suddenly shouted out.

Flora smiled. 'I leave it at home for the holidays.'

'She'd never get it through customs,' Carla said. 'With all those magical things inside!'

'Are you really Mrs. Clementine?' Reuben asked, looking up at her. 'From *Mrs. Clementine's Magic Handbag*?'

Flora's smile broadened. 'I *am* Mrs. Clementine! But only on the television; in real life I'm just Flora.'

'Though sometimes *I* call her Mrs. Clementine.' Carla slipped her arm through Flora's. They both grinned at each other.

Carla looked down at Reuben. 'What's happened to you? You've grown ginormous!' She detached herself from Flora and kissed Reuben's cheek. 'You're all at least a foot taller since I saw you in Kefalonia.'

Josh had remained standing, transfixed, his mouth silently opening and closing like a fish.

'Carla!' he managed at last. 'What are you doing here?'

Carla smiled at him. 'I like the beard.'

Josh touched his chin as if surprised to find he had a beard. He glanced at the others sitting around the dining table and then approached Carla.

'I can't believe this.' He spoke in an ineffective whisper. 'Why, how, why . . .?' He couldn't form a sentence.

'Josh. How lovely to meet you at last.' Flora extended her hand. Josh briefly looked her up and down and turned back to Carla.

'How dare you come here with that, that . . .' He stammered several times before he managed to blurt out, 'woman.'

'When Noah texted me from the hospital I simply had to come.'

'Noah?' Josh looked bewilderedly from Carla to his son. 'Noah texted you?'

'You thought I was playing a game on your phone.' Noah sounded very proud of himself. 'But really I was telling Mummy to come because I might be going to die.'

'We were in Brittany for the week,' Flora explained. 'When we got Noah's text, we packed up immediately and headed for the hospital in Bergerac.'

'Did Noah tell you he was in hospital in Bergerac?'

'No, silly,' Carla shook her head. 'I still have "find your phone" on my iPhone so it's always easy to know where you are.'

Josh's mouth dropped open again.

'When we got to the hospital, they told us he'd already been discharged and when I said I was Noah's mother they gave me this address.' Carla bent down again to give Noah another hug. 'Of course, I had to see my precious boy.'

Josh stopped touching his beard and ran his hand through his hair creating two little tufts on either side of his head.

'But what were you doing in Brittany?'

'Camping.' Carla stood up. 'In the van.' She linked arms with Flora again. 'We've been having a wonderful time staying on the coast. I'm writing an article for the *Telegraph*: *Gallic Glamping – Starry Nights in Beautiful Brest*. It was the perfect place, just close enough to the Dordogne in case of an emergency – like this one!'

'You didn't trust me with the children?'

Carla laughed again. 'Well, it is the first time you've looked after them since I left you.'

Josh's face flushed a darker shade of tangerine; his little hair tufts made him look like a confused highland heifer.

'I took them kite flying on the Common.'

'Like Mr. Banks from *Mary Poppins*!' Carla said to Flora with a laugh. 'After half an hour Noah fell out of a tree and I spent the rest of the day with him in A&E waiting to get his head sewn up while Josh got pissed in the local pub.'

'I bought Elodie a lemonade to cheer her up and just happened to have a pint myself,' Josh protested.

'Elodie said you had three.' Carla acknowledged her daughter for the first time with a wave. 'Hi, darling.'

Elodie didn't respond.

The security light on the driveway clicked on again as one of the camper van's rear doors opened.

'Ah Zac, you've woken up at last,' Carla called down from the terrace as a teenage boy climbed out of the van.

The boy stretched and yawned and looked about. He wore a pair of long denim shorts and very white trainers and nothing else; his skin was as smooth and brown as Flora's and his hair was a complex pattern of shaved tracks at the sides and a mop of mini dreadlocks on the top. He stretched again and revealed the elasticised waistband of his underpants.

Flora bustled down the steps and ran down the path.

'Cover yourself up, Zac, you're not on the beach now.' She disappeared into the van and came out with a T-shirt. 'Get this on and come and say hello.'

'Who to?'

Flora pushed him up the path. 'Everybody.'

He was pulling his T-shirt over his head as he climbed the steps onto the terrace; Flora yanked it down from behind.

'For goodness' sake, try to look half decent.'

'Yeah, yeah, Mr. Respectable, that's my name.' He grinned and surveyed the group of people distributed around the terrace with a confidence that belied his youth. His eyes alighted on Elodie and lingered for a moment. Elodie's face was still obscured by her wall of hair.

Flora beamed an all-encompassing smile.

'Everybody, this is Zac, my nephew. Carla and I have been looking after him for a few weeks for his mother, who is at her wits' end with his . . .' She seemed to search for words in the warm air above her head. 'Entrepreneurial adventures at home! And it's been quite an adventure for us all, hasn't it, Zac?'

'Yeah,' Zac replied with yet another stretch, reaching his arms above his head so that his stomach was revealed again.

Flora yanked at the waistband of his shorts. 'Pull your shorts up, you're not in Peckham now.'

'Hey! Leave the clothes alone.' Zac batted his aunt's hand away, and he glanced at Elodie again, one eye now partially visible through her hair.

Paula stood up. 'So lovely to see you after all this time.' Tilly was balanced on her hip as she air-kissed Carla's cheeks.

'What a poppet!' Carla tickled the baby under the chin and Tilly laughed. 'I'm so pleased for you, Paula, I know how hard it's been since . . .'

'Have some wine,' Ranjit interrupted. He leant in with a glass and another kiss for Carla.

Then he handed Flora a glass and shook her hand enthusiastically.

'Come and sit down,' he gestured at the table. 'We've got lots of food.'

'Ooh, looks scrumptious,' Carla said as Noah pulled her over to the stool he had been sitting on and clambered onto her knee as she sat down.

'I'm absolutely starving.' Flora pulled up a chair next to Carla.

'Cool.' Zac bent down and picked up the bag of crisps from the floor. 'Smoky barbecue, my favourite.'

'Mine!' Noah shouted as he reached forward grabbing for the crisps.

'Whoa, scary child!' Zac cautiously handed the packet to the little boy. 'Did no one teach you manners?'

'Zachery,' Flora cautioned. 'Don't be rude.'

'I'll get some more plates,' Ranjit said.

'They're not staying,' Josh protested. He looked at Carla. 'Are you?'

Noah was trying to push a crisp into his mother's mouth; she laughed.

'I can't leave Noah now.' She opened her mouth and bit down hard on the crisp, sending crumbs flying in all directions. Noah laughed and crammed his own mouth full of crisps.

'But you can see he's fine.' Josh pointed at his son. 'I dealt with the emergency, I took him to a doctor, he had the correct treatment, no damage done – look at him.'

'I'm dead again.' Noah collapsed in Carla's arms for the second time, tongue lolling, eyes rolled back, half-chewed crisps dribbling down his chin.

'I'll have to carry out a medical procedure just to check for any signs of life.' Carla tickled Noah's stomach. He squealed and wriggled upright again, throwing his arms around his mother's neck.

'Don't go, Mummy, please stay.'

'She can't possibly stay,' said Josh firmly.

'There are ghost's here,' Noah's voice quivered. 'I'm frightened.'

Carla looked up at Josh with solemn eyes. 'I don't think I can possibly leave my little boy – suppose he has a relapse?'

Josh pressed his hands against his eyes and sank down on his seat next to Alice.

'I must be having a nightmare.'

'It's so lovely that you can all meet Flora at last.' The whole table watched as Carla reached out a hand to Flora and tenderly began to caress her neck. Martha noticed Ranjit whisper something to Paula, Paula nodded and whispered something back.

Martha pushed her chair away from the table, wondering if this might be a good time to escape the unfolding drama, but her movement only served to draw attention to herself.

'Let me introduce you ladies to our hostess.' Ranjit jumped up and put his hand on Martha's shoulder. 'Mrs., I mean Ms. Martha Morgan.'

Martha wished that she had left before the women had arrived. They were both now staring at her far too quizzically.

'Martha Morgan,' Flora repeated her name. '*The* Martha Morgan?'

Carla untangled Noah's arms from around her neck to lean across the table.

'We were only talking about you in the van today.' She sounded excited. 'We heard that song on the radio.'

Martha felt her whole body begin to stiffen.

'What song?' Ranjit asked, looking confused.

'You know, that On The Waterfront song – sing it, Flora.'

Flora broke into a resonant rendition of the first line of 'Moondancing'.

'*I touch your face and watch your eyes, I see myself reflected in the stars.*'

'I know that song,' Ranjit said.

'My dad used to play it all the time,' said Paula, as though recalling something from long ago.

Carla nodded. 'Yes, it's a really old one.'

Martha wanted to protest but speech seemed to have deserted her.

Carla continued speaking. 'Flora said whatever happened to On The Waterfront, didn't you, Flora?'

This time Flora nodded. 'We were trying to remember the name of the band, it took a while.'

'Man, it was so much fun!' Zac, who was piling stew onto his plate, yawned in an exaggerated manner.

'Zac!' his aunt admonished.

'What did I say?' Zac protested.

'We remembered the drummer was called Sledge,' Carla said.

'Yes, and Lucas Oats, of course.' Flora fanned her face. 'He was gorgeous.'

'I wouldn't have thought he was your type,' Josh mumbled.

'And there were two girls.'

'More up your street,' Josh said under his breath.

'Just get over it, Josh,' Carla hissed.

Flora didn't seem to hear him or care. 'One was called Cat, the blonde one with the spiky hair, I remembered that much.'

'Everyone knows her,' said Carla. 'She's still producing hits. She's amazing!'

'But I couldn't remember the name of the dark one with the flicked fringe,' Flora mused and then she beamed at Martha. 'But of course. It was Martha Morgan! And here you are, alive and well and living in France.' Flora spread out her arms to encompass their surroundings.

'You said she was a junkie,' Zac said.

'We were talking about a different band by then.'

Martha tried to move but she seemed rooted to her chair.

'On The Waterfront,' Ranjit said. He was still standing beside Martha, staring at her, as though seeing her for the first time. Paula was staring too. It seemed as though she was trying to re-evaluate everything she thought she knew about Martha.

'Bloody hell,' Josh said, temporarily seeming to forget his estranged-wife worries. 'A real-life pop star, and you've been cooking us our dinner every night. Wait till I tell the guys at work.'

Martha's longing for nicotine was intense. It was exactly the scenario she had dreaded.

'I think we need another drink to celebrate,' said Ranjit, picking up an unopened bottle of Merlot from the table.

Carla clapped her hands together. 'This is so exciting. I can include it in the article – maybe it could be a whole new spin. What about *Gallic Glamping – New Romantic Nights*.'

Martha felt her body turn to lead. She wondered if she'd ever be able to move again.

'You're not camping here!' Josh sat upright in his chair.

'Well, where else are we going to stay?'

'There are hundreds of campsites nearby.' Josh glared at Carla.

Carla raised her glass. 'This is my third. Thank you, Ranjit.' She blew him a kiss. 'I can't drive anywhere. And Flora doesn't drive.'

'I'll drive,' said Zac.

'Don't be silly, Zachery,' said Flora. 'You're not even seventeen.'

'I'll drive you.' Josh stood up.

Alice touched his arm. 'You've had a few glasses yourself.'

'Oh, hello.' Carla looked at Alice as though she hadn't realised she was there before.

'You must be Josh's new girlfriend. He told me he'd met someone much younger than me.' She smiled and continued slightly breathlessly. 'But he didn't tell me you were so pretty. You have such lovely hair.'

'Stop looking at her.' Josh sat down and put his arm around Alice's shoulder.

Noah looked up at his mother from her lap. 'Can I sleep with you in the van?'

'Yes, darling, of course.'

'No!' Josh blurted. 'He can't sleep with you and, and your . . .' he stammered as he tried to search for an appropriate word for Flora. He made another attempt, 'Your . . .'

'It's OK, man,' said Zac. 'It's not like they're doing their lady love *all* the time.'

Josh's head fell forward onto his hands and he groaned.

'I still haven't had my present,' Noah said.

'You can have it when you go to bed, sweetie,' said Carla. 'If you go and get your pyjamas on, we'll get you tucked up very soon.'

'Maybe we should check with Martha if it's OK?' Flora said. 'She may not want her garden used as a campsite.'

'There's already someone camping over there.' Carla pointed beyond the chapel. A yellow light emanated from the tent. In the commotion of Carla and Flora's arrival no one had noticed Ben return.

'You can stay if you want,' Martha said, finally managing to find the strength to stand up.

'Fantastic!' Carla reached to refill her glass.

131

'Tell me, Martha,' Flora said as Martha took her first steps away from the table. 'Do you still sing?'

Martha stopped. She stared at the woman's genial smile and sparkling eyes and thought about the last time. The stage at The Scala, the solo show Big Bryn had arranged after her divorce. It was supposed to be a new start. Martha's mother hadn't cut out those reviews: *Mumbling Martha Forgets Her Lines*, *Moondancing Musician Medicated to the Max*.

'No,' she said. 'I don't sing.' And then without another word she walked away.

Chapter 19

Wednesday

The old Saab juddered reluctantly into life. Martha pushed her sun-glasses up her nose and squinted against the morning sun. She hadn't been out for days but today was market day and she needed food and cigarettes. She also needed arnica, paracetamol and some antiseptic cream.

The car lurched slowly up the potholed drive. Martha thought about the large bruise on Ben's eye, and the cut that looked like it needed stitches just below his bottom lip. He'd told her that he had fallen off his bike. Peering at him through the lamplight it had been hard to see the full extent of the injuries.

The night before, she'd found him sitting on the grass outside his tent, hunched and motionless, knees drawn up to his chest, his arms clasped tight around them. He reminded her of a wounded animal; his body coiled against the pain, one eye swollen shut and blood congealing on the corner of his mouth.

Martha wanted to reach out and comfort him, but she hesitated, frightened of rejection, or misinterpretation. He refused her offers of a cup of tea or something to eat and in the end, she had left him alone.

She couldn't sleep. She washed the pots and pans she'd used to cook the stew and wiped the surfaces until she couldn't find anything else to clean. Ben remained silhouetted in the light outside his tent. At two o'clock Martha had wrapped a shawl around her shoulders and crossed the meadow to suggest that he should go to sleep. He seemed to ignore her but when Martha looked out again at half past two the lamp was out and the tent in darkness.

Martha rose at dawn. The air in the chapel felt thick, already hot. She went outside and peered towards the tent. It looked like some sort of ancient shelter, camouflaged amongst the ryegrass and poppies that already consumed the thin canvas.

Martha heard the tent being unzipped. Ben slowly emerged, like a moth from a cocoon. She could tell from the awkwardness of his movements that he had more injuries than just those on his face. He wore the same dark stained T-shirt he'd had on the night before. He stood unsteadily, unaware that she was watching. Martha went into the chapel to make coffee.

When she returned, Ben was sitting on the bench. He'd changed his T-shirt, but his face was still smeared with dried blood. The wounds looked worse in daylight, the bruising darker and the cut on his lip deeper. Martha offered him a mug. He reached for it, his movements slow and measured as he gulped the coffee. He asked for a cigarette.

'I thought you didn't smoke.' Martha offered him her Marlboro packet.

'I'll go into town and get my own in a bit,' Ben mumbled, sliding out a cigarette.

'You're not fit to go anywhere.' Martha lit the cigarette that balanced precariously between his swollen lips. 'I'll go to town myself and get you something for those cuts.'

Martha lit a cigarette as well and they sat and smoked in silence.

When she had finished, Martha fetched a bowl of water and a flannel. She put it down for him to clean his face but made no move to start.

After a few moments, Martha picked up the cloth. She dipped a corner of it in the water and tentatively touched Ben's face. His eyes flicked momentarily towards her, but he didn't protest. His gaze returned to the orchard as if expecting someone, or something to appear. Martha dabbed at the gash through his eyebrow. Ben mumbled briefly but didn't flinch. She pushed his hair from his forehead and started on the other eye. It was almost completely closed with swelling.

'This one's nasty,' she said. 'Maybe we should get it checked by a doctor? And the cut on your lip could do with a few stitches . . .'

'No!' Ben stiffened. 'No doctor.'

'OK, no doctor.' Martha touched his shoulder with her free hand; he winced. 'Does it hurt?'

'Just a bruise.'

'Is the bike damaged?'

Ben ignored the question.

Martha dipped the flannel into the bowl again, squeezing out the excess water. The drips sounded loud in the quiet morning air.

'You should have been wearing a helmet.'

She wiped the flannel over the deep wound on his mouth; the blood was too congealed to clean it properly. She dipped the flannel again; the water swirled with shades of pink and red.

'The hornets,' Ben said, as though suddenly remembering.

'They've been dealt with,' Martha said.

'I'm sorry, I was in the middle of sorting them out.'

'Where did you go?'

'I just had to . . .' Ben paused. 'Something came up and I . . .'

'You bin in a fight?' The South London accent interrupted Ben's explanation.

Zac stood in front of them, his hands in the pockets of his long shorts; his narrow torso was bare and his shoulders moved to an inaudible beat.

'Where did he come from?' Ben mumbled, turning his head to Martha.

'Just there.' Zac pointed to the VW camper with his thumb.

Ben looked towards the van.

'It's my aunty's girlfriend's,' Zac explained. 'So, where d'ya have the fight, man?'

'I fell off my motorbike,' Ben replied through swollen flesh.

'Oh. Right.' Zac turned to Martha. 'So, what happens round here? You got a gym?'

135

'I have a pool,' offered Martha. 'You're welcome to use it.'

'I saw a small one. Just water. No slides.' Zac stared hopefully at her as though waiting to be told where the larger more exciting pool might be.

'It is just water,' Martha said. 'No slides.'

'Oh. Right.' Zac kept staring and then added. 'You got anything happening at night? A DJ?'

'It's not a Eurocamp, mate,' Ben muttered thickly and picked up the flannel to hold it against the cut on his mouth himself.

'Oh, I just thought . . .' Zac's words trailed off. 'I'm a bit of a DJ myself,' he added with a sudden smile in Martha's direction. 'You used to be in the music biz, didn't you? What was your scene? Old school? East Coast, West Coast, Gangster, Bounce? I do Grime, but you just tell me what you like and I'll get it on my phone. I've got some speakers, maybe I can do a set and liven it up round here?' His smile broadened as he took an iPhone from his pocket. 'Very reasonable rates.'

'Zac, you stop hassling those good people.' Flora emerged from the camper van swathed in a fuchsia pink robe. Her purple braids were pulled back in a high ponytail. 'I'm so sorry about my nephew,' she called out to Martha. 'I hope he's being polite.'

'Just trying to do a bit of business,' Zac shouted across to his aunt.

Flora bustled towards them, her bright robe billowing behind like a massive cushion. 'I know your kind of business, Zachery! And the kind of trouble that it got you into.'

Zac threw his hands up in the air. 'Aw, man! Why won't anyone believe me? I'm not hanging with that crew no more.'

Flora folded her arms. 'Well, let's just hope so for your mother's sanity.'

'Just to let you know,' Martha said hastily. 'There is no phone signal.'

'Aw, what!' Zac's arms were up in the air again. 'Where have you brought me now, Aunty Flo?' He stared hard at his phone.

'No Wi-Fi either,' Martha added. 'I know how hard that will be to believe.'

Zac's mouth dropped open, he shoved his phone into his pocket and turned to Flora. 'I think it's time to hit the mac.'

'English Zachery!'

'It's yute talk – get with it, Aunty!'

Flora rolled her eyes.

'What can you do?' she said to Martha. 'He used to be such a sweet little thing.'

'I'm still sweet.' Zac's cheeky grin returned and he wrapped his arms around Flora. 'I'll always be your favourite nephew – right?'

Flora laughed as she returned his hug. 'You're my only nephew, Zachery.'

'I'd better get to work,' Ben said suddenly. 'I'll start on the potholes on the drive.'

'I don't think you should be doing anything in the state you're in.' Martha's face was full of concern.

'I'm fine.' Ben stood up and took a few steps forward. 'I'll just get the wheelbarrow.' He stopped mid step and started to sway.

'Timber!' Zac cried out and between them he and Flora caught Ben as he crumpled. They managed to sit him back down onto the seat; Flora pushed his head between his knees.

'I'm just a bit woozy, that's all.' Ben struggled to sit up and rested his head against the wall behind him. He closed his eyes.

'You need to get horizontal, dude,' Zac said.

'Yeah, you're right,' Ben mumbled. 'I'll go and lie down in the tent for ten minutes.'

'You'll roast in there.' Martha felt his forehead. 'You're already burning hot.' She turned to Flora and Zac. 'Let's get him inside.'

Between them they got Ben into the chapel and onto Martha's bed where he fell into a deep sleep.

As Martha drove down the long windy hill, she looked for skid marks or some evidence of Ben's accident. She saw nothing.

It was market day. Tourists thronged the pavements, mainly Brits, faces flushed and clothes crumpled. French women in chic linen shifts and French men with loose white shirts and designer jeans stood out in the sweltering crowds.

Martha, avoiding the main car park, negotiated tiny cobbled

streets and parked the car under the shade of a lime tree in a residential lane. It was quiet away from the crowds. She got out of the car and took her wicker basket from the back seat. Washing hung between the houses and geraniums cascaded from window boxes. One of the houses had a bronze plaque on its wall where six members of the French resistance had been executed in the war. Martha shuddered at the sight of the bullet holes that were still evident.

She thought of Ben's injuries. She'd seen enough fights – when the band had been on the road – to know what it looked like when a fist had been hammered over and over into someone's face. She just didn't understand why Ben would lie about it. What could have possibly happened? Who would have beaten him up in a sleepy French town on a Tuesday night?

Chapter 20

The first thing Martha noticed was the top hat. She nearly ran over it as she returned through the gates of *Le Couvent des Cerises*. It had lost its silver ribbon and the once shiny plush was dull and grey with dust. A child darted out from the bamboo thicket and ran down the drive in front of her, naked, apart from a pair of angel's wings and apricot tinted sunglasses. The mop of golden hair could only belong to Noah. A few seconds later Reuben burst from a bush, velvet cape flying, a pink wig on his head. Both boys were trailing long silk scarves and singing the *Ghostbusters* theme at the tops of their voices. Martha brought the car to a halt and struggled out.

'What are you doing? Where did you get those clothes? Put them back where you found them.'

'Who ya gonna call?' the boys shouted and then they were gone, disappearing back towards the house. Martha followed, marching towards the terrace as quickly as her leg would allow.

At the pool she paused and stared. She took off her sunglasses to see better. The once turquoise water was covered with multi-coloured bobbing objects. It took her a few seconds to realise that the swimming pool was in fact completely covered in a layer of hats.

Straw hats, sailor hats, bowler hats, flat caps, baseball caps, Stetsons and fedoras; and a huge conical swirl of scarlet netting that Martha had worn for the cover of On The Waterfront's *Techno Purple* album. An armada of headgear. Anger bubbled inside Martha. She marched on, passing a long silk glove draped over the broken swing and a string of pearls hanging from a branch. A plastic bangle was snapped in two on the steps and a lipstick had been used to scrawl *Noah* across the terrace flagstones.

A solitary figure sat at the table beneath the vine, wearing large-rimmed reading glasses and the pink robe that Flora had been wearing earlier. But it wasn't Flora, it was Carla. She glanced up from her laptop.

'Oh, hi. I didn't hear you coming – now tell me, Martha, have you ever glamped?'

'My clothes!' Martha ignored Carla's question. 'They're all over the garden. The children are wearing them! My hats are in the swimming pool!'

Carla took off her glasses and peered at Martha. 'Sorry?'

'My clothes, my costumes, my . . .' Martha could hardly get the words out. 'They're everywhere.' She turned around and noticed a gold lamé evening dress in a crumpled heap under the table and a single stiletto, skewered into a pot of rosemary.

At that moment the boys ran out of the house, Reuben now sporting a pair of Ray-Bans and Noah a silver Stetson. Carla laughed as they raced down the steps.

'I love to see Noah having such fun with his friend.'

'But they're wearing my costumes.'

'I'm sure they'll put them back in the dressing-up box when they're finished.'

'They're not from a dressing-up box!' Martha reached under the table and picked up the evening dress. She shook it; dried vine leaves had attached themselves to the sparkling fabric, a grape was squashed onto the sleeve. 'They're my costumes.'

Carla shrugged. 'They've been wearing different outfits all morning.'

'But the clothes were put away in a cupboard. I'd asked Josh and Ranjit and Paula to tell the boys not to touch them. Did they forget?'

Carla shrugged again and put her glasses back on.

'I'll ask them when they get back. They're all at the market.' Her fingers were poised over her keyboard ready to start typing again. 'I

140

said I'd stay here and look after the boys; they might have got into all sorts of mischief while everyone was trying to shop.'

Martha had seen the others in the market earlier. She had crossed the square to avoid Ranjit and Paula at a cheese stall. Then she had spotted Josh sitting morosely outside Sally and Pierre's bar drinking beer, while Alice perused a nearby rail of vintage dresses. Sally had come out to replenish Josh's glass and beckoned Martha over; Martha had pretended not to see her and ducked into the musty darkness of the florist's shop.

As she lingered over the tubs of hydrangea heads and gaudily coloured gladioli she noticed Elodie and Zac outside. Elodie was looking at a hat stall while Zac loitered nearby studying a knife display. He had picked up a large hunting knife and seemed to be examining it, but Martha could see him stealing glances at Elodie, who seemed engrossed in a display of bandanas. After a few minutes Flora bustled up to Zac and pulled him away from the knives just as Paula and Ranjit appeared beside Elodie. Paula tried on a small straw hat that made her look like a donkey and Ranjit tried on several berets.

Later, as Martha queued in the pharmacy, she heard English voices behind her.

'So *she* left *him*?'

'I'm beginning to think so.'

'For a woman.'

'I never knew she was . . .'

'A lesbian?'

'Ranjee, keep your voice down.'

'There's nothing wrong with being a lesbian, Paula.'

Martha furtively looked round and saw that Paula and Ranjit were queuing behind her with Tilly perched, as usual, on Paula's hip. Ranjit now wore a beret and Paula was wearing the donkey hat. Both seemed unaware that Tilly was trying to grab sunglasses from a tall revolving display.

They didn't notice Martha either.

'I know there's nothing wrong with it, I just didn't know that Carla was . . . one!'

'I expect she's gender fluid.'

'What on earth is gender fluid? It sounds like something that might help Josh get his roof up.'

There was a clattering sound followed by a large crash as the carousel of sunglasses fell onto a display of lavender soap and hand cream.

Other tourists stared and tutted and a shop assistant rushed to help. Tilly started to howl and Martha, who had already paid for the arnica and a tube of Savlon, slipped out unnoticed.

'I have to get my article finished ASAP otherwise I would help you tidy up,' Carla smiled.

Martha levered the stiletto from the plant pot. 'Don't trouble yourself,' she muttered and went inside the house leaving the tap, tap, tap sound of Carla's keyboard behind her.

The kitchen was in chaos. Strawberry jam had been smeared on the fridge door and a carton of orange juice lay on its side dripping down onto a white lace shirt scrunched on a chair. The shirt appeared to have been used as a cloth to mop up something red and sticky. Martha remembered wearing it the first time On The Waterfront had appeared on *Top of the Pops*; her mother had kept it for all those years and now it was ruined.

The drawing room was in a similar state. Discarded food and more of Martha's precious costumes were dotted around. Her old make-up box was on the cocktail bar and someone had drawn a smiley face in scarlet lipstick on the cocktail bar's mirrored front. Elvis had been draped in scarves and beads, and a pork-pie hat sat jauntily on his head making his normally ferocious expression seem comical.

Martha took the hat off Elvis and wearily climbed the stairs gathering clothing and jewellery as she went. On the landing of the first floor she stopped. There was a photograph of Lucas on the wooden floorboards. He gazed nonchalantly up at her, arms crossed, wearing fingerless gloves and a leather jacket; collar turned up, sleeves pushed

142

back to the elbow. Martha let the clothes and jewellery fall to the ground. She picked up the photograph; Lucas stared at her through thirty decades. His hair was swept to one side; thick and lustrous with a purple steak running through the long dark fringe. Despite the eyeliner and glossy lipstick, he exuded macho sex appeal, though the dimples on his cheeks gave him an impish youthfulness that made him so irresistible.

In the years before he died, Lucas hadn't looked much like the young man in the picture. Martha had seen him on the Internet. A rare photograph taken as he got out of a car in Harley Street; completely bald, his dimples no longer visible, a little pouch of sagging skin beneath each eye and a complexion that suggested too much wine and whisky. Martha had still felt a jolt of affection.

Martha looked towards the winding wooden stairs leading to the attic. She let out a gasp. A cascade of papers, vinyl records and photographs flowed down the steps like a waterfall. Ribbons of unwound cassette tape had pooled on the bottom step like a big pile of spaghetti. Martha carefully picked her way up through the debris to the top of the attic steps. At the top she could see immediately that the cupboard door was open wide, clothes and papers spilling out onto the floor. Martha's past lay spread around as if a whirlwind had merrily twirled across the landing, randomly blowing through her carefully parcelled memories, opening them up, confronting her with everything she tried not to think about. Martha's fists clenched. Looking down at her hand she realised that she had crushed the picture of Lucas, creasing his beautiful face, adding lines to the smooth skin.

'Oh no!' The voice was a whisper. Martha turned and found Elodie standing behind her, a black bandana tied around her forehead; for once you could actually see her eyes.

'I told you not to touch my things,' Martha said, anger building.

Elodie didn't seem to hear; she crouched down to pick up a photograph, a head and shoulders studio shot of the band, ruffled shirts and diamanté jewellery for them all.

'Is that you on the left?' Elodie asked.

'I said don't touch!'

Elodie let the picture flutter to the floor.

'You knew what was in there,' Martha pointed at the open cupboard. 'You saw me putting it away.'

Elodie was staring as Martha's voice got louder.

'I saw the way you touched my boots the other day. I bet you just couldn't resist having a look?'

'No,' Elodie's voice wavered.

'Did you try them on?'

'No.'

'Did you clomp round up here in my DMs and party dresses? Admiring yourself in the mirror? Or taking pictures? I bet you thought it was all a great big selfie opportunity!'

'What?'

'Then you left it all out for Noah and Reuben to make this lovely mess.' Martha gestured around. 'How am I ever going to get everything back in the right boxes? My clothes, my jewellery, my hats . . .'

'What's happened?' Alice appeared at the top of the stairs. She gaped at the maelstrom.

Martha picked up a cardboard record cover. As she slid the single out it fell into two pieces.

'Everything is ruined!' Martha cried.

'I don't understand, who did this?' Alice said.

'I think I understand only too well' Martha pointed at Elodie.

'No!' Elodie shook her head. 'It's nothing to do with me' Elodie's voice was now as loud as Martha's. 'Why would I want to look at all this old crap anyway?'

'Calm down, Elodie.' Alice tried to touch Elodie's arm. 'Maybe you should go downstairs while I help Martha tidy up.' Elodie jerked her arm away and stared at Alice with ferocious eyes.

'You can't tell me what to do!' The girl was shouting now. 'My dad doesn't really want to be with you. He loves my mum!'

'I understand that the situation is difficult.' Alice kept her voice calm.

'Difficult!' Elodie kicked at a file of press cuttings sending it spinning into the air. It landed open exposing a cover from *Smash Hits*

144

magazine: On The Waterfront were swinging from rigging like a bunch of moody pirates.

'Stop wrecking my things.' Martha was shouting too.

Elodie ignored her; she was glaring at Alice, tears streaming down her face.

'You don't know what it's like for me at school – everybody saying my mum's shagging Mrs. Clementine! And now my dad's shagging someone who wears stupid dresses like a little girl!' With that Elodie turned and clattered down the stairs, skidding on some photographs so that she surfed the last few steps, landing at the bottom with a bang.

'Are you alright?' Alice called down.

'Fuck off!' Elodie shouted and there was the sound of her running down the lower flight of stairs, and then a juddering crash as the French windows out into the garden slammed.

Alice winced. 'Oh dear!'

Martha let out a long sigh and sank down against the wall.

'What a mess!' Alice crouched down beside her and picked up a copy of *Jackie*. Martha and Cat pouted on the cover with glossy purple lips. Cat was winking one heavily made-up eye. 'I'm so sorry this has happened.' Alice continued gesturing around. 'All your happy memories.'

Martha glanced at the magazine Alice was holding; she could see her own face on the cover, just behind Cat, a little in the shadow.

Were they happy memories?

There had been so many complications. Her feelings for Lucas for a start. Her turbulent friendship with Cat. All the beautiful ballads that poured out of her only for Cat and Lucas to turn them into boppy pop songs.

She wasn't sure why she'd kept so much of their stuff. She didn't like looking at it, and she certainly didn't want to see it now, strewn around the floor.

'Shall I go and find Ben?' Alice asked. 'I'm sure he'd give us a hand sorting everything out.'

'Ben!' Martha struggled stiffly to her feet. 'I must check on him.'

'Why?'

'I left him in my bed.'

Alice's eyes opened wide.

'No! It's not like that!' Martha felt a flush of heat across her cheeks. 'He had an accident. I left him sleeping in my bed because it seemed better than letting him sleep in the tent. It's nearly forty degrees today.'

'Is he OK?'

'I think so, just cuts and bruises. But I'd better go and check.'

'There's some food left over from last night in the fridge. Do you want some for his lunch?'

Martha took the magazine from Alice's hands and placed it on an upturned box.

'Come and see him yourself, you might cheer him up.'

Alice smiled.

'Alice,' a voice called from below. 'Where are you?'

'It's Josh.' Alice struggled to her feet with a sigh. 'He's pretty upset about Carla turning up.'

'I bet he is!'

'I feel sorry for him – he seems to find being left for another woman as some sort of insult to his manhood.'

'Would he rather she left him for another man?' Martha asked.

'He thinks the others are laughing at him.' Alice lowered her voice to a whisper. 'He says they'll say he turned Carla gay.'

'Alice!' Josh's voice called again.

'I'd better go.' Alice picked her way through the chaos to the bannister. 'But I'll be back to help as soon as I can.'

As Alice disappeared down the stairs Martha looked down at the picture of Lucas. She wondered what it might have been like if Cat had never moved from England to Abertrulli. Would Lucas ever have asked Martha to be in the band on her own? Would he have chosen her to be his lover? She remembered the precious few days in Amsterdam, when Cat had walked out in the middle of recording the last album. Lucas had consoled himself with Martha, and Martha had been too love-struck and grateful to understand the game he was playing. Martha had written 'Moondancing' that week. But then, of course, Cat had come back and all Martha was left with was the chance to finally sing on her own.

A few months later, when Cat had packed her bags and left for good, Lucas chose the whisky bottle for comfort instead of Martha. He hadn't even answered her phone calls or responded to the letters she sent.

Martha put the photograph down on the box beside the *Jackie* magazine. From the cover Cat winked at Lucas's crumpled face. She started to go downstairs. But then she stopped and turned back to the landing. She picked up the photograph of Lucas and scrunched it up into an even smaller ball, and then she tore the cover of the magazine in half and ripped Cat's beautiful face into a hundred tiny pieces.

Chapter 21

As Martha passed through the empty kitchen, she flung the little bits of Cat's face into the rubbish bin along with Lucas and stepped through the kitchen door onto the sun-dappled terrace.

She stopped at the sight of the group assembled around the table. Ranjit was wearing his new beret and slicing an enormous loaf of bread. Beside him Flora was peeling the wrapper of a huge wheel of Brie. They were both singing along to Édith Piaf. Édith's voice crackled from the little record player that sat precariously on the stone balustrade.

Paula was arranging circles of salami on a plate, with Tilly balanced in her usual place on her hip. Ranjit was feeding the baby some bread. Carla sat at the end of the table pouring Orangina into the cocktail glasses; she passed the little boys a glass each. Reuben didn't notice, he was gazing at Flora, obviously still somewhat star-struck. Noah was back on his golden throne wearing only a pair of pants and the glittery Stetson. He downed his drink in one gulp and let out a loud burp.

Zac sat beside him leaning back on his chair. 'Your bro has no manners,' he said to Elodie who was sitting opposite him.

'Sit up properly, Zachery,' Flora tutted.

'Keep your dreds on, Aunty Flo' Zac winked at Elodie. Elodie's eyes were red and puffy. Martha felt a wave of guilt wash over her for blaming the young girl for opening the cupboard.

'Martha!' Ranjit strode towards her, the breadknife still in his hand, his arms outstretched in welcome. 'Come and join the feast. The market has such a wonderful range of food and we bought this record at the vinyl stall, we were looking for one of On The Waterfront's albums, but we couldn't find one. We bought Édith instead – I hope you don't mind us bringing the record player out here.' He cupped his hand to his ear. 'Don't you just love her voice? Though I'm sure yours is just as good.'

'Look. We're drying out the hats.' Flora pointed at the lawn below. 'I found the bamboo canes in the shed, I hope it was OK to use them.'

Martha looked at the lawn. The hats had been fished out of the swimming pool and placed on top of the bamboo canes, which were planted into the lawn. It looked as if a crowd of skinny figures were advancing on the house.

Martha's attention moved back to the table. Josh and Alice were nowhere to be seen.

'More!' Noah pushed his empty glass back towards his mother.

'Of course, sweetie,' Carla cooed across the table.

Martha watched the blonde-haired woman, now dressed in a low-cut linen dress, pour out more Orangina into the pretty long-stemmed glass. The blue rose that Flora had worn in her hair the night before was pinned to her cleavage.

Martha remembered the newspaper articles that journalists had written during the custody trial; horrible stories – day after day there had been twisted facts and lies. Reporters had camped outside the little flat that Martha was renting; they posed as meter readers, they went through her rubbish bags. Carla didn't look like the middle-aged men that Martha had peeked at through the Roman blinds, but she was a journalist.

'We are so sorry about the mess the boys made,' Ranjit said. 'They didn't know the clothes and hats were yours.'

'We've gathered everything up into a pile in the living room,' Paula added. 'And we've wiped the lipstick off the drinks bar and the jewellery is in a basket on the kitchen table.'

Carla started picking at a bowl of olives. She spat an olive pip into her hand.

149

'If the cupboard hadn't been left open, they wouldn't have got it all out in the first place.'

'It wasn't *left* open. Someone opened it,' Martha glowered at Carla. 'Someone who was poking about where they shouldn't have been.'

Carla's eyes opened wide in surprise. 'You think it was me!'

'I know what you journalists are like. You'll do anything for a story.'

'Hang on a minute,' Carla protested.

'Martha, please,' Ranjit's voice was soothing. 'Don't jump to conclusions.'

'Carla isn't that kind of journalist,' Paula said. 'She's won awards for her investigative stories.'

'Like *Gallic Glamping*!' Zac said.

Elodie let out a snort.

Carla stood up. 'Do you really think I'd go through your cupboard just to get some kind of lead? What could possibly be gleaned from a load of old clothes?'

'It's not just the clothes.' Martha was staring at Carla. 'Someone's been through all my papers and photographs too, as if they were looking for something. Maybe they were looking for information? Maybe they were looking for some secrets to write an article about?'

'Why?' Carla gesticulated with her hands. 'Why? Who would be interested in a story about a washed-up 80s pop star living in the middle of nowhere? Obviously in need of money, no love life, no children, no career. You're not anyone of interest any more.' Carla's long curls swished as her gestures became more exaggerated. 'Yesterday, we couldn't even remember your name!'

Martha felt heat rising in her cheeks; her own angry words seemed to shrivel in her throat.

'Perhaps we should leave,' Flora said. 'We said we'd go after lunch anyway.'

'No! Mummy, don't go!' Noah cried out and slipping down from his seat threw his arms around Carla's waist.

'Look what you've done!' Carla glared at Martha. 'Not only have you accused me of being some sort of gutter hack, but you've upset my little boy as well.'

Martha wanted to walk away but her feet seemed rooted to the spot, glued down by Carla's harsh words.

'Carla! A gutter hack! As if!' Josh came up the terrace steps wiping his hands on a glittery silk scarf.

'I think that might be Martha's,' Flora said, nodding at the scarf.

Josh looked bewildered. 'I found it in a bush! I've been fixing the soft top and I didn't want to get dirt on this shirt, it's Prada.'

'*It's Prada*,' Carla mimicked.

Ranjit proffered Josh a beer. 'Any luck with the car?'

Josh made a triumphant punching movement in the air with his fist. 'The roof is finally down!'

'Good man,' said Ranjit.

'I'm going to take Alice for a spin . . .' Josh looked behind him. 'Where's she gone? She was helping me with the car a minute ago.'

'Josh.' Carla was stroking Noah's head as he clung to her. 'Let's just try to be friends for the sake of Elodie and Noah.'

'Good idea.' Josh took a swig of beer. 'After all, the well-being of the children is our priority.' He nodded as though very pleased with his words of wisdom.

'So, can I trust you to look after them properly for the rest of the week?' Carla was stroking Noah under the chin as if he were a cat.

'Of course I'll look after them.'

'Mummy, please stay!' Noah pleaded.

'Come on, big boy. We're going to have a great time.' Josh tried to pull Noah towards him. 'You could come out in the car too – it's cool with the top down.'

'Cool.' Martha noticed Elodie mouth the word to Zac and make a face.

'I want to go with Mummy!' Noah clung tighter to his mother.

'Oh, darling,' Carla let out a little cry. 'It breaks my heart to leave you.'

Josh tried to pull Noah away again. 'Mummy has made her

151

choice,' he indicated towards Flora. 'She has to realise there are the consequences to her actions.'

'You're such a prat!' Carla hissed. 'Come on, Flora, come on, Zac. Let's just go.'

'Hey, I don't want to move on just yet.' Zac rocked back in his chair again and grinned at Elodie.

A loud coughing noise came from the direction of the baby.

'Oh my God! Tilly!' Paula held the baby out in front of her with both hands. 'She's choking!'

'The bread!' Ranjit tried to put his fingers inside the baby's mouth to get it out.

'You shouldn't have given it to her!' Paula started frantically rubbing the baby's back, bouncing her up and down at the same time.

Tilly made a rasping noise, her face turned purple.

'Turn her upside down?' suggested Flora.

'Do the Braxton Hicks,' Josh volunteered.

'I think you mean Heimlich,' Carla sneered.

'For God's sake, someone, please do something,' Paula screamed, tears welling.

As though in a dream Martha moved swiftly round the table and took the baby from Paula's arms. Ignoring Paula's protestations, she sat down on a chair, lay Tilly face down on her lap and slapped her firmly on the back. A nugget of white dough shot from the baby's mouth.

'Oh, my poor poppet.' Paula scooped Tilly from Martha's lap as the baby retched and then projectile vomited across the terrace.

'My dress!'

'My shirt!'

Josh and Carla were splattered with milky white vomit. Somehow it missed Noah and he stared from one parent to the other.

'Gross!'

'Poor Tilly.' Paula cradled the baby in her arms.

'What about my shirt?'

Elodie began to giggle. Zac joined in, their sniggering getting louder as Josh and Carla's indignation increased.

'Zachery, stop laughing this minute!' Flora started dabbing at Carla's dripping dress with a napkin.

But Zac and Elodie couldn't stop, and first Noah then Reuben and then Ranjit joined in. Even Paula was smiling, looking relieved, and as though she didn't know whether to laugh or cry. Then Flora's mouth turned into a grin as she dabbed the rose at Carla's cleavage, then her shoulders began to shake, her breasts began to heave and she released a peal of laughter. Carla looked at her and burst out laughing too.

'It's not funny,' Josh protested, mopping at his shirt with Martha's scarf.

Ranjit tried to help him using another napkin.

'I'm sorry my friend . . .' but the words turned to louder guffaws as Josh's face turned red with indignation.

'Oh dear.' Carla clutched at Flora, doubling over with laughter, tears streaming down her face. 'I think I'm going to wet my pants!'

'This is just typical of Carla, you never could take anything seriously!' Regurgitated milk dripped from Josh's sleeve onto the floor. 'You don't care when something's ruined.'

'It's just a shirt,' Carla managed to say.

'I'm talking about our marriage!'

The laughter grew louder. Even Tilly was laughing now, gummy mouth open, saliva dangling from her little lips.

Martha wasn't laughing. She snatched the scarf from Josh's hand and stomped down the steps. Carla's words swirled round and round. She was nothing, nobody, not even worth thanking for saving the baby's life.

Chapter 22

Martha could still hear them laughing on the terrace as she made her way down the path. Like the laughing at The Scala club all those years before. She twisted the dirty scarf between her hands, trying not to remember that awful night; there had only been a handful of people in the audience but they hadn't been kind. The heat was unbearable. Martha's clothes were clammy on her back.

Passing the pool, she longed to strip off and float in the cool water. Did it matter what the guests would think? After all, as Carla said, she was a nobody; washed up, forgotten. Would anyone even notice her floating naked in the pool?

But she continued on, pushing through the branches of the fig tree that spread across the path. Something brightly coloured glinted at her feet. Martha bent to pick it up, imagining another piece of jewellery from the cupboard. Instead she found a crinkly golden wrapper. She smoothed it in her hands; a picture of a little elephant and the name of a chocolate manufacturer. Another empty wrapper poked out from a fig leaf just beside it. Milka, the largest bar you could buy in the Intermarché. Martha sighed. The guests didn't even have enough respect to clear up their rubbish. She picked up the wrappers and turned the corner to the chapel.

She heard the kettle rattling to the boil inside the kitchen. As she stepped through the front door it let out a high whistle. Martha threw the chocolate wrappers into the bin along with the scarf and removed the kettle from the heat.

154

A woman's voice came from the bedroom. Martha peeked around the door. Ben was sitting up in the bed and Alice was perched on the edge. Pippa lay stretched between them. Ben had one hand on the rabbit's head, tickling behind her long ears, Alice was tickling her stomach; Pippa rolled ecstatically.

'She loves the fuss,' Alice laughed.

Ben's grin was made more lopsided by the cut.

They both looked up, realising that Martha was standing in the doorway.

'I thought I'd just pop in and see if Ben was alright,' Alice said.

'And how is the patient?' Martha asked.

'I'm sorry I'm still in your bed.' Ben's Scottish accent was made more pronounced by his swollen mouth. 'I didn't wake up until Alice came in.'

'I was shocked when I saw him,' Alice said. 'It must have been quite a crash.'

'I'm much better now' Ben struggled to sit up further.

'I think you need more rest,' Alice said gently.

'I agree with Alice.' Martha walked over to the bed and plumped up the pillows. 'You shouldn't rush it.'

'I'm fine.'

'You've been in an accident,' Alice said. 'You need to give your body time to recover.'

'But . . .'

'Just lie down,' Martha interrupted.

Ben obediently lay back down.

'I'll make coffee,' Martha said.

'I'll do it.' Alice stood up.

Martha opened the window then drew the thin muslin curtains to stop the glare of the midday sun. She turned back to Ben. His face looked a little less dramatic even though the bruising had turned from yellow to dark purple; the swelling round his eye had gone down.

'I feel pathetic lying here, being waited on.'

A clink of crockery and the squeak of the fridge door being opened and closed came from the other room. Martha sat down on the bed; she lowered her voice.

'Did you really come off the bike?'

There was a pause, a heartbeat. Ben looked at her. 'I misjudged the bend before the house.'

'Here we are.' Alice came back now carrying a tray. 'I found some of the shortbread biscuits I made the other day.'

Martha looked away from Ben as Alice passed the coffee cups. A gust of wind blew through the open window making the curtains billow and Owen's postcard fell from the bedside table onto the floor. Martha bent and picked it up wondering if Ben, or Alice, had read it.

'I was telling Ben all about your things being taken from the cupboard' Alice took a biscuit from the plate and dunked it in her coffee. 'I said you thought that Elodie had done it.'

'I don't think it was Elodie' Martha shook her head. 'I have just accused Carla. I thought she might have been looking for a story.'

Alice stared at her, the soggy end of the biscuit drooping slightly in her hand.

'Do you really think so?'

Martha shrugged. 'I don't know. As she said to me, who'd be interested in a washed–up 80s pop star?'

'Goodness!' The end of Alice's biscuit fell back in the coffee with a splash. 'What a bitch!'

Martha found herself relaying Carla's words. They didn't sound quite so bad, especially when Alice began to giggle.

'She's the one who's washed up! Josh told me that she made up a story about Jeremy Corbyn's socks and was sacked from her job as a political correspondent at the *Guardian*.'

'Socks!' Martha said.

Alice laughed. 'I can't remember the details, something to do with elderly CND supporters and exploitation. Anyway, it wasn't true.'

'Hence the freelance articles about glamping,' said Martha.

'Tell her to glamp-off, she's not even meant to be here.' Ben was leaning back on the pillows, eyes closed.

'Are you OK?' Martha asked.

'Just resting my eyelids.'

'Maybe you've been burgled.' Alice took another sip of coffee. 'Didn't Reuben say he saw someone strange at the window yesterday?'

Ben's eyes flicked open. 'Who did he see?'

'Oh, I think he was just being silly,' Martha said. 'He seems to be a bit of a storyteller.'

Ben didn't look convinced. Martha took the half-empty cup of coffee from his hand. 'You need more sleep.'

In the distance the church bell chimed. Outside someone shouted Alice's name.

'There's Josh,' Alice said. 'I said I'd go out for a drive now the roof's working.'

Ben smiled, though his eyes were still closed. 'He's finally fixed it then?'

'Well, actually I suggested it might just be a fuse.' She grinned. 'And I was right!'

'Alice.' The voice was nearer.

'You could ignore him,' Martha suggested.

'I'd feel bad doing that. I'm sure we won't be out for long. I heard someone in the market say there's more bad weather coming this afternoon.'

Martha sighed. 'That's the way it goes here. It gets hotter and hotter until a big thunderstorm arrives, though this year there have been more storms than I ever remember being before.'

There were footsteps outside the window. 'Alice? Are you in there?'

'I'd better go.' Alice stood up and stepped through the door with a brief wave.

'There you are!' Martha heard Josh through the open window.

'I was just having a chat with Martha and . . .'

'You won't believe what happened to my shirt!' Josh interrupted.

'God knows what she's doing with him,' Martha said as Josh and Alice's voices faded.

Ben didn't answer. He seemed to be asleep again. Martha watched him for a few moments. His face looked very young despite the bruises and swollen lip. She looked down at Owen's postcard still in her hand. After a few moments she slipped it into the drawer of the bedside table and quietly left the room.

Chapter 23

Martha emerged from the chapel into the bright sunlight of the early afternoon. A loud splash, then a shriek, came from the direction of the pool. Several more shrieks followed, then laughter, and then an even bigger splash.

Someone was singing, a voice rich and smooth, like treacle running from a spoon. Martha turned the corner and found Flora beside the camper van, surrounded by piles of clothes and bags of food.

'I'm having a sort-out before we go,' the woman smiled cheerfully. 'You can't imagine the mess with three of us in there.' She nodded at the van, purple braids swinging.

'Where's Carla?' Martha asked.

'Oh, she's in the pool with Noah. Look, I am so sorry about what she said to you earlier.'

'I shouldn't have been so quick to accuse her of breaking into the cupboard,' Martha mumbled and turned to walk away.

'It's understandable. They're your precious things.'

Martha paused. They were precious; only old clothes and bits of paper but they were precious to her. From nowhere tears came. Martha blinked them back.

'I have to get my shopping from my car.'

'And I must get on with sorting the van.' Flora picked up a bag and started to sing again, a Motown song she recognised, about a heatwave burning in her heart.

★

Martha hurried away. She could remember her mother singing the same song as she stood at the sink in the little council-house kitchen; hands submerged in soapy water, hips swaying in time to the tune on the radio.

'Come on, cariad, sing along.'

Martha had joined in with Martha and the Vandellas and her mother had laughed. 'You could go far with a voice like that.'

Martha took a deep breath and opened the door to the Saab. There were too many people in her house and too many memories in her head. She reached into the car to retrieve the wicker shopping basket. Through the rear window she could see Zac standing on the edge of the orchard. Elodie was a few feet from him, leaning back against the gnarled trunk of a tree. They appeared to be ignoring each other until Zac pulled a cherry from a branch and threw it at Elodie.

'Catch.' It hit Elodie on the head.

'Hey!' Elodie picked up cherries from the ground and threw one back at Zac.

Zac began to run, Elodie in pursuit, pelting Zac with cherries as they zigzagged through the twisted trees.

'Watch out for the nun,' Zac called behind him.

'I don't believe in ghosts,' shouted Elodie.

Martha straightened and shut the car door. Flora had disappeared from view, but her voice emanated from within the camper van, a different song this time.

Martha began to negotiate the rocky path to get back to the chapel.

Ben's motorbike was parked on the edge of the line of cars. Martha stared at it, squinting against the glare of sunlight on the metallic surface. There wasn't a scratch on the paintwork, let alone a dent.

A noise caused Martha to turn. Sally's little Fiat bounced erratically down the drive and lurched to a halt next to the bike; she leant out of the open window.

'What happened to you earlier? I saw you in the square but you didn't come in for coffee.'

'I was in a hurry.'

Sally squeezed out of the car. 'Are those guests of yours making life busy?'

'It's worse than that! They're turning my life upside down – literally.'

Sally laughed.

'It's not funny,' Martha protested. 'I'm beginning to realise that you and Pierre were right about how difficult it would be. They've made a bloody big mess of all my things; you should see the attic. I feel like telling them to leave.'

'Why don't you then?' Sally was still laughing. 'Tell them to bugger off and go somewhere else.'

She handed Martha a slim white envelope; Martha's name was neatly printed underneath a transparent rectangle, *Confidential and Urgent* was stamped in red on the front and also on the back.

'It came this morning.'

Martha didn't need to open it to know who it was from. It was the fourth letter she'd had from the bank in as many weeks. This one looked more urgent than the previous three.

'This is why I can't tell them to leave.' She folded the unopened envelope and slid it into her pocket.

There was a pause as the two women looked at each other.

'Come on.' Sally took Martha's arm. 'Show me this bloody big mess. It's probably not as bad as it seems.'

Chapter 24

'It's pretty bad.' Sally looked around at the chaos on the attic landing. She picked up a lace glove from the floor. 'It looks like someone's had a great time flinging this lot around.'

'It's hard to tell if anything is missing,' Martha said taking the glove from Sally and searching fruitlessly for its partner.

Sally sighed. 'I wish I had more time and I could stay and help. But France are playing this afternoon so it's all hands on deck in the bar. I think the match has started already.'

'Don't worry, I ought to sort through it all anyway, there's probably loads I could chuck away.'

'Who do you think did it?' Sally looked around again.

'I don't know. I've already accused a teenage girl and a lesbian journalist.'

'A lesbian! Where did she come from?'

Martha shook her head. 'Don't ask.' She picked up a pink fur coat.

'Did that Scottish bloke ever turn up?' Sally asked.

'Ben? Yes, he came back last night.'

'Pierre said he saw him in the village yesterday, talking to a man.'

Martha slid the coat onto a hanger; the nylon fur gave her the tiniest of static shocks.

'Pierre said they seemed to be arguing. He couldn't see who the man was because he had the hood up on his jacket despite the heat.'

'Hi, guys.' Carla appeared at the top of the wooden stairs. She was back in her gypsy outfit. 'It's getting hotter.' She pushed her blonde curls back from her forehead. 'I thought I heard thunder just now.'

'Maybe it was a cheer for a French goal,' Sally laughed. 'I'd better get back. I'll be in trouble if there's a run on the bar.'

After a few more pleasantries about the weather and the football, Sally left, promising to come back the next day.

Martha didn't look at Carla but she knew that the woman was staring at the mess.

'My goodness! I can see why you'd be upset,' Carla said.

Martha touched the envelope in her pocket and took a deep breath. 'I'm sorry I accused you of breaking into the cupboard.'

'Don't worry about it. I understand that a journalist might be a potential suspect, but I really wouldn't stoop so low.'

'I shouldn't have jumped to conclusions.' Martha began folding clothes, waiting for Carla's apology for her own mean words.

Instead Carla said, 'I forgive you.' She twisted one of her curls around her finger. 'Anyway, Flora and I have to go so I just wanted to say goodbye and to thank you for letting us stay.' Carla peered through the little window looking down at the garden. 'How lovely, Noah's playing boules with Reuben.' She sat down on the window-sill. 'It's nice to see him looking happy. Sometimes I just feel . . .' She pressed her hand to her chest, 'like I've ruined the children's lives.'

Martha turned away. She smoothed down a rose-covered skirt that she'd worn in the video of 'I Don't Need You Anymore'.

It had been an awful song; Cat had changed the lyrics of a beautiful love song Martha had composed, to suit an angry mood she was in after an argument with Lucas.

> *You'll never get me in your bed,*
> *You'll never make me toast your bread*

Martha had cringed when she'd had to sing them, but Lucas had added a good electronic beat to Martha's initial piano tune and the song eventually reached number fifteen.

'I've let them down, broken up their home.' Martha realised Carla was still talking. 'Changed their lives for ever because of my own need for happiness.'

163

Martha folded the skirt and put it into a box and thought of Owen. She hadn't meant to break up his home, and it certainly hadn't been for her happiness.

'It wasn't that Josh was a bad husband,' Carla continued. 'We talked, we laughed, well, I laughed – at him mostly!'

Martha started to gather photographs from the floor. She glanced at one: the Royal Variety Performance 1985. The Queen hadn't had a clue who On The Waterfront were, but she said their performance had been very nice. Martha remembered how much coke Cat and the boys had snorted in the dressing room; it had been a miracle they could perform at all. But not Martha. She never touched drugs. Throughout Martha's childhood her mother had listed all the musical careers ruined by cocaine and heroin and acid. Martha had stuck stoically to champagne and vodka, not even tempted by a spliff or a slice of a hash brownie. How ironic that she was the only one to end up in rehab.

'Flora is such an amazing person.' Carla was leaning back with her eyes closed. Martha studied her face. Something about Carla reminded her of Cat; a raw feline quality, a slight air of the feral no matter how many diamonds she wore. Martha suspected that like Cat, Carla would always land on her feet.

A cry came from down in the garden; Carla opened her eyes and peered outside. 'Oh dear, I think Noah just threw a boule at Reuben. Here comes Ranjit to sort it out.'

There was a louder cry. 'Oh dear! Noah has thrown a ball at Ranjit.'

'Caaarla!' Flora's elongated call came from the bottom of the stairs.

Carla stood up. 'Now, Martha,' she sounded businesslike. 'Before I go. I've been thinking about what I said earlier.'

Martha turned to her; the apology was on its way.

Carla lowered her voice. 'I know I said no one would be interested in a washed-up 80s pop star.'

Martha gave a brief nod.

'But actually, on second thoughts I think they might be.' Carla's hands mimed a newspaper headline. '*Martha Morgan – Where is She*

Now? *On The Waterfront's Martha is Alive and Well and Living East of Bordeaux.* I could offer an exclusive interview. The *Daily Mail* would love it, I'm sure.'

Martha's back crawled, hot needles of fear pricking her spine. 'I really don't think . . .'

'Ah, here you are.' Flora appeared at the top of the stairs. Her braids were back in their high purple cone and she was wearing a long silk scarf embroidered with butterflies. 'We'd better get going. I've managed to get Zac into the van. All that complaining about coming here and now he doesn't want to leave.'

Carla slid her arm through Flora's.

'I'm just suggesting that I do an interview with Martha.' Carla beamed up at Flora then turned back to Martha. 'That's how Flora and I met. I was writing about children's TV personalities.'

'Martha might not want to be thrust into the spotlight,' Flora said, looking at Martha with concern.

'Don't be silly, sweetie, everyone loves a bit of press coverage.' Carla gave Flora a kiss on the cheek and turned back to Martha. 'You don't need to decide now. I can email you the questions, but before that I'll do some research into your background; where you came from, your time with the band, why the band broke up, what happened to you afterwards, how you came to be living in France – that sort of basic information.'

The photographs in Martha's hand slipped back onto the floor.

At that moment there was a loud banging noise as Elodie stomped up the wooden stairs. She ignored the three women standing on the landing and disappeared into her room, slamming the door shut behind her. The aged floorboards shuddered.

'Darling,' Carla called after her. 'Aren't you going to say goodbye?'

She detached herself from Flora and knocked on the bedroom door. 'Sweetie, can I come in?'

'No!'

Carla's shoulders drooped in despair. 'My daughter hates me.'

'Of course she doesn't hate you. She's a teenager. They care about no one but themselves.'

Flora wiped Carla's eyes with her multicoloured scarf.

'Elodie will be home next week, by then she'll be delighted to see you.'

Carla nodded.

'Come on; let's hit the mac, as my nephew likes to say. We need to find a campsite before dark.'

'Don't forget about the interview, Martha.' Carla suddenly sounded more cheerful. 'I'll be in touch.' The two women descended the stairs and disappeared.

Martha stood very still. Through the open window she heard the van start up and slowly crunch its way up the drive. In the distance thunder rumbled like the introduction to a song.

Chapter 25

Elodie's door remained firmly shut all afternoon. Every now and then Martha heard a slight shuffling, or a sniff. Apart from that the house was quiet – no sound from the children or the adults, only a rustling from the vine beneath the open window. Martha supposed the guests were lounging on the veranda, or perhaps collapsed in the cool of the thick-walled living room. It was too hot and humid even for Noah to run around.

Martha wondered if she should ask Elodie if she was alright. Her hand hovered a few inches from the door. The dull thump of music started up and Martha's hand fell to her side.

She had almost finished clearing up the mess, only a few items remained scattered on the wooden floor. She picked up a single diamanté earring; at least half the bits of glass had fallen out. She dropped it and it skittered under the cupboard. Martha was just contemplating kicking everything else under the cupboard when a gust of wind blew through the window and ruffled the pages of a notebook Martha hadn't noticed on the floor before.

She bent to pick up the book. It had a red cardboard cover and the paper inside felt thin and cheap. She flicked through it. At first glance it appeared that the pages were blank but turning to the back Martha saw a series of squiggles and dashes. She reached into her pocket for her glasses and put them on. The squiggles and dashes became musical chords.

There were words written under the chords; scribbled in a

scrawling hand. Martha peered more closely and read 'The Child in My Eyes'. It appeared to be a title.

Then there were more lines of nearly indecipherable handwriting. Martha squinted and held the notebook at arm's length.

> *As you drew breath, I made my wish*
> *As you held my hand, I gave my kiss*

Martha whispered the words out loud; slowly at first then faster as she became more familiar with the scribbly style. She could see now that it was a very messy version of her own handwriting.

> *The seeds we planted in the garden never got to grow*
> *But they blossom in my heart*
> *Roots deeper than you know*

> *At night I wander and silently cry*
> *The air holds a whisper*
> *The wind holds my sigh*

Martha began to hum as she worked out the melody.

> *I wonder if you walk under darkening skies*
> *I look for your star*
> *Child in my eyes*

She had no memory of writing the song, but it was definitely her handwriting. Turning the pages Martha found more chords and melodies, more words and different songs. They were beautiful tunes. Heart-wrenching lyrics.

Martha took off her glasses and rubbed her eyes. She didn't remember writing any of them.

The little landing had become dark. Martha hadn't heard the last Angelus ring so it couldn't be past six o'clock. She slid the notebook onto the top shelf of the cupboard, pushing it back as far as it would go, shutting the door. She wished that she could lock the door.

At the sound of thunder, she closed the window and peered through the small criss-cross panes. Grey clouds were steadily advancing from the other side of the valley, an inky cloak of gloom that swallowed the sky and blocked out the sun.

A movement in the garden made Martha look down. A figure was standing on the grass, someone wearing a motorbike helmet and a full set of leathers, despite the humidity. She thought it was Ben but then realised the figure was too tall. The stranger took off the biker jacket to reveal broad shoulders and lean yet muscular arms. It was a man. He looked up at the house – the helmet's visor was still down, a huge single eye swivelling to and fro. She thought of the intruders she'd seen in the orchard and was glad that the guests were just downstairs. She opened the window.

'Hello?'

The man raised the visor and looked up at her. She saw two eyes now, crinkled at the corners in a smile.

'Can I help you?'

Lightning shot across the sky, followed by a roll of thunder. The man placed both of his hands on the sides of the helmet and eased it off. She could see the man's face despite the fading light. The ruddy brown skin of someone who spends a lot of time outside, a short stubbly beard, long, thick dishevelled hair, dark but greying around the temples. He had a nose that looked like it had once been broken and a strong, well-defined jaw. Martha thought of the gypsies who had camped on the edge of Abertrulli one wonderful summer, 'proper Romani', her mother had said. Large drops of rain began to fall.

'I'm looking for my daughter,' the man called up, wiping raindrops from his eyes. He sounded Irish.

'What's she called?'

'Orla. Orla Rose.'

Martha shook her head.

Suddenly a white flash lit the garden and the French windows of the living room were flung open. Paula ran out into the gathering storm, wind blowing her perfect bob into an auburn nest.

'For God's sake, dad, what are you doing here?'

'Well, that's a fine welcome for your old da, Orla!'

'Paula, it's Paula, Dad. It has been for many years.'

'Well, as you well know that's not what your mother would have wanted, but . . .'

'Why are you here?' Paula interrupted. 'You're supposed to be in London. With the builders.'

'I know, I know, but I had a query and Ranjit wasn't answering his phone, so I just thought I'd hop on the bike and pop over.'

'Pop over! To the Dordogne! From Wimbledon!'

'Sure, it was a grand ride down.'

Paula's hands were on her hips. 'But you're meant to be looking after the house! What about the extension?'

'Ah, well, that's the thing.'

'Is there a problem with the Aga?'

'I just need a word with Ranjit.'

'There's nothing you can't say to me about the building project,' said Paula, raising her voice against the sound of the increasing rain. 'We're not in 1970s Dublin now!'

'Well, I know that, Orla, but I think Ranjit might be best in this case, it's just a little query about the measurements. You know how good he is at maths.'

'So, you came all this way to ask Ranjit a question about measurements?'

'And I miss the little fella too, and Tilly, of course. Thought I'd have a ride down to see them while the job's a bit quiet.'

'Quiet! It shouldn't be quiet! The limestone flags are going down on the floor this week. And the Aga splash-back tiles are being—'

'Grandpa, Grandpa.' A small figure shot out through the French windows and hurled himself into the man's arms. The man squatted down and hugged Reuben tightly.

'The little fella himself. Are you having a lovely time?'

'I dressed up in funny hats and I saw a ghost.'

'Sounds like a blast,' Paula's father laughed.

Thunder crashed again. Reuben screamed.

'Come on,' Paula shouted above the sound of the now torrential rain. 'Get inside, Dad, you're making us get wet!'

Martha shut the window as another flash illuminated the small group dashing across the grass into the house. The landing was plunged into semi-darkness and Martha put on the light. A bang like a gun-shot shook the room. The lights flicked off and then back on again. Wind whistled through the closed window with a whine that matched the wail of Tilly crying far away in the kitchen. Above the high-pitched noise Martha could hear the sound of voices on the landing below. She leant over the bannister.

'You'll have to tell her, Ranjit,' the Irish man was talking softly.

'I will, I promise, but not now,' Ranjit spoke hurriedly. 'Max, please, I beg you, just let us have this holiday. Paula needs a rest. She's been getting worse since Tilly was born, if she could just relax a bit – get back to normal.'

'She's going to realise what's going on soon enough.'

'I can't tell her at the moment.'

'She wants to know why I've come all this way. She doesn't buy the story about the measurements or that I missed Reuben and Tilly – though of course I did.'

'Say that Buster is dead.'

'Reuben's gerbil?'

'Say you forgot to feed him and now he's died!'

'That's culpable homicide! I don't want to be mixed up in that!'

'It's just pretend, Max. Of course you hadn't really killed him.'

'No, I've been giving him his nuggets religiously, water and my old apple cores too.'

'Of course, but just for now, please say that you had to come to tell Reuben that poor Buster has passed away. Maybe a sudden heart attack would be the kindest option.'

'For God's sake, Ranjit . . .'

'Ranjit! Dad!' Paula's voice came from the ground floor. 'What are you doing up there? There's coffee on the kitchen table, come and get it before it gets cold.'

'Coming, Paula,' said Ranjit.

'Coming, Orla,' said Max.

Martha stepped back from the bannister. There was another clap of thunder and an explosion of bright light. The door to Elodie's room flew open. Elodie stood, white faced, on the threshold.

Martha held up her hands. 'It's alright. It's just a thunderstorm.'

'I don't like it.' Elodie was trembling. The rain hammered on the roof above them. The next crash was even louder than before. Elodie jumped. The light flickered off and on and then off again. Elodie stumbled forwards towards Martha, leaning against her as though expecting an embrace. The thunder crashed again.

Martha patted Elodie's back, it had been so many years since she'd given comfort to anyone, she felt awkward, clumsy. 'It will be over soon.'

'Martha!' The shout came from the bottom of the stairs, and a few seconds later Ben appeared, his battered face flushed, his hair dripping.

'The chapel.' He paused to take a deep breath. 'The chapel is flooding.'

Chapter 26

Pippa hopped around Martha's feet as she lit the candles in the tall candelabra that she'd fetched from the living room. The flames cast a sickly glow on the faces gathered around the kitchen table. Everyone's expressions were grim, the candlelight highlighting the weariness in their faces. Even the children seemed exhausted. Reuben sat on his grandfather's lap, sobbing into Max's denim shirt. Max took a handkerchief from his pocket and wiped Reuben's face.

'There there, we'll get you another gerbil. Just the same as poor Buster. Identical. In fact, you'll never know the difference.'

'But Buster was special,' Reuben wailed.

Max grimaced at Ranjit who was opening a bottle of red wine.

'Buster had a peaceful end,' Ranjit said soothingly. 'Your grandpa says he just didn't wake up.'

'Like Alisha?' Reuben said.

Ranjit froze, his hand hovering over the glass he was about to pick up.

From the other side of the table Paula made a small noise and buried her face into Tilly's hair. The baby whimpered in her sleep.

Max let out a long sigh and hugged Reuben close to him. 'Have I ever told you about the raven we found on a building site in Spitalfields? I think he'd escaped from the Tower of London. We taught him how to say *Line the bloody Guinness up.* We'd take him round the pubs at lunchtime – we always got served for free.'

'Dad, that's not a suitable story for Reuben.' Paula lifted her head.

'It's a distraction, Orla love, that's all it is.'

'Line the bloody Guinness up,' Reuben mumbled with a sniff.

'Line the bloody Guinness up!' Noah suddenly sat up from his position slouched against his sister's shoulder. He let out a laugh. 'Bloody Guinness, like *your bloody father*. Mummy says that, doesn't she, Elodie?'

Elodie shrugged and beside her Josh groaned.

'What a nightmare,' he muttered.

'Here, Josh, have this.' Ranjit pushed a glass of wine across the table. When he didn't move to take it, Alice picked it up and put it in front of him.

'Come on, Josh, you might feel better with a drink. You've had a shock.'

Josh groaned again.

'You must sleep here in the house,' Ranjit addressed Martha as she sat down beside Alice. 'And Max, you must stay too.' He nodded at Paula's father.

'Well, it doesn't look like I'll be getting back on the road tonight.' Max helped himself to more wine with a satisfied sigh. 'There's no point digging out the bike until this rain stops.'

Martha felt her heart sink at the word *digging*. She thought of the devastation at the bottom of the drive and felt sick.

Josh buried his head in his hands and let out a noise more like a sob than a groan.

'I can't believe it! It's ruined.'

'Well. You should have put the roof up,' Paula snapped.

'I was having a lie-down. I didn't hear the storm.'

'That thunder was loud enough to raise the dead,' Paula said. 'You must have been *very* tired – or maybe you weren't sleeping.'

Alice put her own glass down a little too hard; wine splashed onto the table, glistening in a tiny candlelit pool.

'It was Carla. She sucked away all my energy,' Josh muttered. 'After she left, I collapsed into a deep sleep, a coma really, stress induced.'

'Only to be woken by me thumping on your door to tell you your car had turned into a dumper truck.' Ranjit tried to hide a small smile. 'It gives convertible a whole new meaning.'

'It's not funny!' Josh sounded indignant.

'It's not just you,' Paula retorted. 'We've got a tree on our roof! And a shattered windscreen.'

'It's a branch,' Ranjit corrected. 'And the windscreen is cracked.'

Paula rocked the sleeping Tilly back and forth on her lap.

'Imagine if the children had been playing on the drive.'

'Everyone is safe.' Ranjit touched his wife's arm. 'It was much too wet to be outside.'

'But supposing they had been.' Paula's voice sounded pained.

Martha lifted Pippa from the floor onto her lap. She took a large gulp of wine. She had been thinking just the same. The surge of water coming down the drive must have been a force. It had washed away the surface, taking with it the piles of stones and gravel that had been waiting to fill in the potholes. The neat line of cars at the bottom had been swamped. Only a vague outline of Ben's bike was visible under the thick deluge of mud. Max's motorbike had got off lightly; it was covered with a fine layer of mud but only its wing mirror seemed to have been damaged. Martha's car had miraculously escaped, a point that Paula had raised several times.

'You must have known there was a risk to cars parked anywhere else.'

'It was purely chance,' Martha had sighed. 'There's never been a landslide on the drive before.'

Martha wondered if the public liability insurance Dordogne Dreams had arranged would cover the claims. It wasn't just the cars. Martha had hoped that Ben's description of the flood in the chapel had been an exaggeration. It wasn't. Water had been swirling through the two small rooms, ankle deep. Martha and Elodie got to work immediately. Elodie helped Alice pull up the rugs and baskets. They put chairs on top of tables and rescued shoes floating forlornly around the furniture. Martha and Ben bailed water with bowls and buckets, throwing it out of the doors and windows as quickly as they could. It had been no good. The water was coming in as fast as they could get it out.

★

They seemed to have been sitting at the table for hours. The rain fell relentlessly; the noise was like the beat of a never-ending song.

'Shouldn't we have something to eat?' Paula stared pointedly at Ranjit as he opened a fourth bottle of wine.

'Is it too wet for a barbecue?' he asked.

'Don't be facetious,' Paula sniffed.

'A bit more wine then.' Ranjit topped up the glasses. 'And what about some biscuits?'

'Yeah,' Reuben and Noah cheered in unison.

Paula got up and peered into the darkened fridge. 'We don't need biscuits. I think I can see some radicchio and three carrots.'

'Ugh,' the little boys chorused.

'What about those sausages we bought in the market?' asked Ranjit looking into the fridge himself.

Paula wrinkled up her nose. 'They will have gone bad by now. The fridge has been off for hours.'

'I'm sure they'll be fine.' Ranjit gently touched his wife's arm.

'I thought you are meant to be feeding us, Martha?' Paula sat back down at the table.

Martha stared at her. Surely the guests didn't expect a two-course dinner in the middle of a power cut.

'There's plenty of bread and cheese,' Alice said. 'Enough for everyone.' She had got up too and fetched a packet of salted almonds from the cupboard. She poured them into a little porcelain bowl.

'Bread and cheese sounds grand to me.' Max took an almond from the bowl, placed it on his palm and, with the finger from his other hand, flicked it into his open mouth. Martha remembered how Lucas used to do the same with peanuts on the tour bus. She wondered how old Max was, not much older than herself, she thought. She tried to imagine what it would be like to have grandchildren. Maybe she did have them. For all she knew Owen might have a child of his own, he was old enough to have several. She felt a tingle of excitement as she imagined a baby on her lap instead of a rabbit.

Max performed the almond trick again. Noah watched him with

wide eyes then he tried to throw a nut in the air himself; it missed his mouth and hit Elodie on the nose.

'For God's sake, Dad,' Paula cried. 'You're already setting a bad example.'

Max caught Martha's eye and grinned.

'I'll fetch the plates.' Martha stood up.

'No,' Ranjit protested. 'You stay where you are, Martha. In fact, all you ladies just enjoy your wine. We men will get you everything you need.'

Max gently eased Reuben off his lap and stood up. He rubbed his hands.

'I can do wonders with a few carrots, some radicchio and a mountain of cheese. That's what comes of being an artist.'

'You're not an artist, Dad.' Paula sighed. 'You're a stonemason.'

'He is an artist,' said Reuben vehemently. 'He does really good drawings for . . .'

'Look at my new knife,' Max interrupted. He produced a Swiss Army knife from his pocket.

'Cool,' said Reuben and Noah together.

'I bought it on the ferry. It'll be grand for a bit of sculpting. Bring me the cheese and I'll get to work.'

'There you go.' Max placed his cheese board triumphantly in the centre of the table. He'd cut the carrots into little spirals like orange roses with radicchio cut up for the flower's purple leaves. The cheese had been sliced into undulating waves graduating in colour across the wooden board from creamy Camembert to bright yellow Emmental, and blue speckled Roquefort had been crumbled round the edges like a frame. The vegetable roses were scattered across the sea of cheese as if floating in the waves. The whole effect was unlike anything Martha had ever seen before.

Noah and Reuben stretched across the table, jostling to see the cheese display.

'I want the big rose,' they said together.

'No, I want the big rose,' said Reuben.

'That rose is mine.' Noah put his finger up his nose and then into the middle of a carved carrot.

Reuben started to cry again.

'Now look what you've done, Dad.' Paula shook her head.

Suddenly a shriek came from outside. Everyone's eyes turned to the door.

'The ghost!' Noah and Reuben looked at each other with wide eyes.

Across the darkened patio a torch beam wavered in the distance. A voice called out, 'I'm slipping!'

Another shouted, 'Wait for me.'

The voices got closer.

'My skirt is ruined.'

'Watch the potholes, you two, this mud is terrible.'

'Chill out, Aunty, it's worse at Glastonbury.'

'When have you ever been to Glastonbury?'

'In my dreams, Aunty, in my dreams.'

In the kitchen Noah sat up and Elodie pushed her hair back from her eyes. Josh stared towards the door, a look of horror spreading across his face.

'Mummy!' Noah sprang from his seat as Carla, Flora and Zac arrived at the door. The small boy threw himself into Carla's arms then sprung back. 'You're wet!'

'We're all wet,' Flora laughed. Her hair had unravelled from its coil; purple braids jumbled around her shoulders. A bulging holdall was slung over one shoulder, dripping water onto her colourful sandals. In her other hand she clutched a wicker shopping basket. Zac held more bags and dragged a suitcase behind him; the wheels had come off and the bottom was ripped and muddy. Carla wasn't carrying anything, her hands occupied by holding up the hem of her long, red skirt. All three looked as if they had been swimming, fully dressed. Carla stepped through the door first shaking her curls like a dog; droplets of water sprayed the cheese board on the table.

'We've had a terrible time,' her voice wavered.

Flora dropped her bags on the floor with relief. 'Well! We've certainly had an adventure.'

Zac looked down at his feet. 'My trainers are fucked.'

'Zac! What have I said about your language?'

'Chill, Aunty Flo, we've been through stress.'

'Zac's right.' Carla's shoulders drooped. 'We've been through more stress than any of you could imagine.'

'Come in and have a glass of wine and something to eat.' Ranjit stood up and found chairs for the dishevelled trio. 'It looks like you might need a bed for the night as well.'

Josh put his head in his hands and groaned again.

Chapter 27

Thursday

'Happy bloody birthday, Martha Morgan.'

Martha said the words aloud as she stepped out onto the battered terrace. She put Pippa on the ground, picked up the golden stool from the cocktail bar and set it upright. The stool had blown over in the high wind that had followed the rain; its little padded back had snapped off and one of the legs was twisted, making it rock from side to side. Martha balanced precariously and lit her first cigarette of the day. Blowing out a stream of smoke she surveyed the scene around her. The trellis had stayed upright, and the shutters were still secure, but roof slates littered the paving slabs and a pot of geraniums lay smashed on the steps in a heap.

Martha looked across the garden. The water in the pool was crusted with leaves and debris; a sunlounger bobbed, upside down, in the middle of it like a barge on a dirty canal. At the bottom of the driveway deep mud was studded with sticks and stones. The devastation seemed incongruous against the perfection of the still, blue morning.

Martha hated to think what the chapel would be like.

In her pocket the letter from the bank crackled; a reminder, a prod. Martha took one last drag on her cigarette and dropped it to the floor. There was no way the guests would be giving her a good review now and there was no point imagining Dordogne Dreams would be taking any more bookings, let alone paying her for the disastrous visit. The bank would never get their money, the house would have to be sold, and Owen would never . . . Martha pressed her hand to her eyes as she thought of her son. Owen would never want to see her now.

'Happy birthday,' the voice came from behind her.

Martha jumped. She had thought that she was alone on the terrace. She turned to find Max filling the kitchen doorway with his tall physique and broad shoulders. His weathered hands nursed a steaming cup of coffee. Martha inched forward on the high stool, preparing to make an excuse and leave; the last thing she wanted was a conversation.

'Do you want one of these?' Max nodded at his cup.

Martha shook her head, even though coffee was what she longed for more than anything.

'I doubt it's feeling like much of a happy birthday right now.' Max sat down on the low wall that ran along the edge of the terrace, and stretched out his long legs. Pippa, who had been snuffling around the fallen vine leaves hopped over to him. Max stroked her head.

'How do you know it's my birthday?' Martha asked, suspiciously.

Max's Irish accent was deep and smooth. 'I heard you from the kitchen. You wished yourself a happy bloody birthday.'

'I thought everyone was asleep.'

'The others are and there's someone snoring like they'd wake the blessed dead.'

Martha couldn't help smiling; he could only be referring to Carla. She lit another cigarette. 'It's been a long night.'

Drinking had seemed easier than deciding where everyone would sleep. Martha wasn't sure if she should be the one to accommodate the extra guests or if the others should decide where she and Max would sleep. And surely they would take responsibility for Carla, Flora and Zac? In the end, just after midnight, as the last of the storm died down, Martha had taken a candle up to the big walk-in cupboard on the first floor where she kept the bed linen.

She came back down with a heavy pile of bedding just as people were stumbling to their feet, mutterings of goodnight coming from those who already had beds while those that didn't were looking hopefully at the sofa in the kitchen.

Ben had appeared, wet and exhausted.

He nodded at the pile of blankets and pillows in Martha's arms.

'Do you need a hand?'

'Now then, where to put you all.' Ranjit swayed. He was in no fit state for dormitory logistics.

'Women in the sitting room, men in the kitchen,' Martha announced. She started handing out the blankets and pillows that Ben was now holding.

The night had been uncomfortable. There were two sofas in the living room and somehow Carla had ended up on the largest one. Flora insisted that Martha have the other while she slept on the zebra rug on the floor.

'I can sleep anywhere,' she proclaimed as she lay down and drew a thin cotton blanket over her curves. 'And through anything.'

Throughout the night Martha marvelled at Flora's abilities to sleep as she herself shifted around on the narrow sofa. Her leg ached, and Carla's incessant snoring and snuffling kept her awake. Pippa was in a box beside Martha. Paula had insisted that the rabbit be contained. 'She can't just run around, she'll poo all over our things.'

Constrained in the box, Pippa made nearly as much noise as Carla, beating her back legs as though demanding to be let out.

Through the kitchen door, Martha heard the heavy breathing of Max, Ben and Zac. In the middle of the night Ben had shouted out, though Martha couldn't make out the words.

At some point, just before dawn, the electricity had come back on and *Finding Nemo* blared dramatically into life. Martha had sat up with a start to be confronted with an orange and black fish talking to her through the TV screen. She'd fumbled for the remote control, stubbing her toe on the coffee table and knocking over a glass of water before finally turning off the film. As she lay back down on the sofa Carla grumbled something about 'not being able to sleep a bloody wink all night', then promptly rolled onto her back and started to snore more loudly than before.

Earlier, Carla had wasted no time in telling everyone the sacrifices she had made to get back to *Le Couvent des Cerises*.

'I just had to be sure that my babies were safe in this terrible storm. I couldn't drive another mile without knowing how they were.'

'And the van had a puncture,' added Flora. 'And we couldn't change the tyre as we didn't have a jack.'

'It was a sign that we simply had to come back.' Carla stroked Noah's curls as he sat on her lap sucking his thumb. 'I couldn't leave my little ones to face the weather alone.'

'Then why did we sit there for three hours waiting for help?' asked Zac sitting down next to Elodie. 'You said there was no bloody way I'm going back to that house to face that twat of a . . .'

'Zachery!' Flora glared at her nephew.

'When the storm started, I knew I had to get here no matter what,' Carla continued. She took a large gulp of wine. 'We walked for miles.'

'About a mile,' smirked Zac. 'We were only halfway down the hill.'

'We trekked through torrential rain, and thunder and lightning, we could have been struck down at any time.'

'You insisted we waited in the van until the thunder stopped,' said Zac.

Carla wasn't listening to Zac. She addressed Noah. 'Great big bangs. Huge flashes. Like bonfire night on Clapham Common, only much, much louder.'

Noah looked up at his mother.

'It was like that here.'

Carla ignored him and carried on.

'As we climbed higher, darkness fell. It was pitch black; all we had was the torch on Zac's phone. The charge was dangerously low, at any second it could have died and we would have been plunged into darkness. After nearly an hour . . .'

'About fifteen minutes,' Zac whispered loudly to Elodie. She giggled.

'We turned one particularly steep corner and found the whole hillside had collapsed; huge boulders were blocking the road. We had to scramble over them. It was very hard.'

'That bit's true,' Zac said.

'The threat of a further landslide was ever present.' Carla shivered dramatically. 'Then I got my foot trapped between two slabs of rock. I told Flora and Zac to go on without me, "Save yourselves," I said.'

Zac opened his mouth to speak.

'Zachery!' Flora said with a brief shake of her head.

'Then, miraculously, I managed to free my foot and struggle on, through the pain.' Carla pushed Noah from her lap, kicked off her sandal and began to examine her foot. 'I think it's swollen, just here.' She swung her muddy foot up and onto the table with remarkable agility. 'Look!' She pointed at her big toe. 'It might be broken.'

Zac let out a long sigh. Flora gave him a glare.

'I could write an article about it,' Carla said, wiggling the toe with apparent ease. '*When your Dordogne Dream becomes a Nightmare.*'

'We can all contribute to that one,' muttered Paula.

Carla looked up.

'Why? Have you had a hard time too?'

Martha and Max sat in silence on the terrace. Martha tried to think through a plan of action, but her thoughts veered wildly from sweeping the terrace to jumping off the village clock tower. In the orchard she saw a figure crouched down on the ground, apparently smoothing out a large piece of blue fabric.

She turned around to Max.

'Was Ben still in the kitchen when you got up?'

'The young Scottish fella?'

Martha nodded.

'I didn't notice.' Max stood up. 'I'll have a look.'

'There's no need.'

But Max was already on his feet. Martha watched him stoop as he passed through the kitchen doorway. She could see where Paula got her height though little else of the genial Irishman seemed to have been passed on to his daughter.

Looking back towards the orchard she saw the figure stand up, raise a hand and wave. She could see now it was Ben and was about to wave back, when she realised that he wasn't waving at her but at someone in the garden below the terrace. Martha watched as Alice ran down the path towards him, her thick hair swinging out behind her as she skipped between the muddy puddles and broken twigs and foliage.

'He's not in the kitchen.' Max was back.

'I can see him now.' Martha nodded towards the orchard where Alice had now joined Ben; together they were picking up the thin, blue tent fabric, tipping water from it and then hanging it on the lower branches of a cherry tree to dry.

'I thought you might be ready for this.' Max handed Martha a cup of coffee.

She took it and the warmth spread through her like a soothing balm.

'I'm sorry about your bike,' she said.

'Ah, with a bit of a hose down and some gaffer tape she'll be fine.'

'She?'

'I call her Fionnuala.'

'Fionnuala,' Martha repeated. 'An unusual name.'

'My wife's name,' Max said.

'Does she mind you calling your bike after her?'

Max smiled sadly. 'She's been dead for thirty years.'

Martha took a sip of coffee and tried to formulate a suitable response.

'She loved you,' Max said.

Martha looked up at him in surprise.

'And your band.' When Martha didn't say anything, Max added, 'You were in On The Waterfront, weren't you?'

Martha took another sip of coffee and didn't reply.

'Sure, I remember you on *Top of the Pops* – we saw you for the first time on the little TV we had in our bedsit in Dublin. Fionnuala was heavily pregnant with Orla but she was always one for fashion and style. She said, *I want my hair like that girl*. She asked the hairdresser in Ballymun but she couldn't do the fringe at all. Fionnuala used to joke she only agreed to move to England for the hairdressers, but they couldn't get it right in Kilburn either.' Max smiled. 'After the chemo she found a wig that had the perfect flick – she was delighted.'

Martha looked down at the mug in her hand.

'She would have liked your hair now.' Max nodded towards Martha.

'You must have been young,' Martha said, changing the subject. 'When you had Paula. I mean Orla.'

'Ah, don't worry about her name. She always wanted to be English. Ever since she was a little girl, she's wanted to fit in with the posh girls,' he sighed. 'Wasn't it bad enough to be the child with the dead mother and a father who worked on the building sites, without being the one with the funny Irish name?'

'At school I was the one with no dad, the mum with no money and the name that no one else had in those days.'

'Then you'll have some sympathy for my poor Orla.' He fell silent for a moment. 'I was a hopeless father,' Max continued. 'Worse at being a mother – I couldn't plait hair or cook a fish finger. And we had no money after the rent had been paid, well, not enough for all the swanky clothes Orla wanted, or the pony or the skiing holidays.' He paused, the smile falling from his eyes. 'I never saw anyone so determined to make a better life for themselves. She couldn't wait to get away to make it happen on her own.' Max sighed again. 'I wasn't able to give her a fancy house or the holidays, but I've always tried to be there for her when she's needed me.' He looked at Martha. 'And isn't being there the most important thing?'

There was a shriek and a roar and Noah and Reuben came running out of the house wearing their trunks.

'Grandpa, come and watch us swim.' Reuben threw himself into Max's arms. Max returned the hug then pointed towards the pool.

'I don't think there'll be much swimming going on in there. It looks like a bowl of my old granny's stew.'

The children groaned. 'But we want to swim,' they wailed in unison.

Max stood up.

'If you both help I'm sure we could get the leaves out with that great big net on the side. It would be a grand game, like fishing on a lake.'

'Fishing is boring,' said Noah.

Max pressed his finger to his lips and looked thoughtful. He started patting the pockets of his jeans, looking for something. After a few moments he pulled out a packet of fruit Polos.

'A prize for the person who collects the most leaves.'

The boys let out a cheer and together they dragged and pushed Max down the steps towards the pool.

Martha was left alone.

Isn't being there the most important thing? She repeated Max's words.

She hadn't been there for her child. Even when she had been with him, she hadn't been fully present, letting him down again and again. She wanted to be there for him now. To make things right. It was why she was so desperate that this should work. But it was Owen she wanted here with her, not these strangers.

Isn't being there the most important thing? An hour later Martha still couldn't get Max's words out of her mind.

Chapter 28

'I've been down to check the car.'

Ranjit's voice came from the kitchen. Martha had been putting off returning to the chapel by finishing tidying the cupboard in the attic. Now she was in the living room, folding bedding from the night before. Martha took a few steps towards the partially open kitchen door so that she could hear just how big the insurance claim might be.

'Do you want the good news or the bad news?' Ranjit put his arms around his wife but she shrugged him away.

'Tell me the bad news,' said Paula.

'There is no bad news really, only minor damage. A crack on the windscreen, and a dent on the roof, and just a few minor scratches. We were lucky. Poor Josh's car is written off.'

'There's still all the faff of the insurance forms and getting the dent repaired,' Paula said. 'And what about Dad's bike? When will he be able to leave?'

'Your dad's bike's not too bad. But no one can go anywhere till that landslide is cleared.'

Tilly began to whimper as Paula reached across the sink and turned the tap on, and off, then on again.

'The water is brown.'

'Martha told me that the well gets silted up sometimes. I expect it's just a bit murky from the storm.'

'You didn't tell me that the water came from a well!' Paula shuddered.

'Don't worry, darling.' Ranjit leant across her and turned the tap on again. 'It will run clear soon, I'm sure.' The pipes juddered as Ranjit turned the tap on full. 'It's looking better already?'

Paula didn't answer. She was filling the kettle with Evian, jigging up and down sporadically as Tilly's whimpers turned into a high-pitched wail.

'I'm so sorry, Paula.' Ranjit put his arms around his wife; this time she let him hold her. 'I know it's not been the holiday you wanted.'

'It's been awful. I can't wait to go home.'

'Only two more nights.' Ranjit kissed the top of Paula's head. 'Then it will all be over.'

In the living room, Martha's leg began to ache; she shifted position leaning on the door for support. As she did so she lost her balance and the door swung open so that she staggered into the kitchen, almost on her knees.

Paula and Ranjit stared at her; even Tilly stopped crying.

'Oh Martha.' Ranjit began to wring his hands. 'I hope you didn't hear what we said. We don't want you to think that we're at all ungrateful.' He looked at Paula. Paula didn't speak.

'We're having a wonderful time,' Ranjit continued. 'It's been . . .' His voice trailed away as Paula glared at him.

'It's quite alright.' Martha crossed the kitchen. 'As you said, only two more nights and then you can leave this awful place.'

She stepped out onto the terrace. As she shut the door behind her, she heard Ranjit say, 'Now I feel really bad.'

Outside, Martha could hear singing. Voices getting more enthusiastic by the second. She started to walk down the path and the singing got louder. She recognised the tune and lyrics: 'Love Roller Coaster'. It had been at number three for five weeks in a row in 1982.

The singing was coming from the swimming pool. Max and Flora were standing on the edge, scooping out debris with the pool net and a bucket while Noah and Reuben helped using bamboo sticks to guide leaves and flowers. They were all singing the old On The Waterfront song as loudly as they could.

The song trailed off as Max and Flora seemed to forget the words to the last two verses. Flora laughed.

'It reminds me of school discos.'

Max started to sing again from the start. '*Come on! Hop on board the shiver ride.*'

From behind the fig tree Martha winced. She'd always hated the lyrics that Lucas and Cat had changed from the ones Martha had originally written.

'*You're going to feel me slip and slide.*' Flora energetically sung the second line with a wiggle of her hips.

Noah and Reuben repeated the line and shook their hips from side to side with exaggerated enthusiasm.

'*Buckle up, you're in for a treat,*' Max and Flora sang together. '*You've not known love till you feel this heat.*'

They started to sway in time. Martha watched as Max and Flora attempted another verse, making up some of the lyrics, imitating the bump and grind dancing that she and Cat used to do as they crooned the chorus into a microphone. Flora wore a long embroidered tunic over wide silk trousers, and huge hoop earrings. Silver sandals sparkled on her feet. She looked as though she was ready to go on stage – she had obviously got her priorities right about what to rescue from the camper van.

They didn't notice Martha watching through the leaves.

'Do you remember this one?' Flora began to hum.

From behind the fig tree, Martha shifted awkwardly. She recognised the tune.

The hum turned into a song.

And then I'm Moondancing again

'Ah, "Moondancing".' Max smiled. 'That's a very special song.'

'I remember Martha in that beautiful video, she looked stunning. Though you'd hardly recognise her now.'

'She reminds me of a nun in all those long black clothes.'

Martha didn't want to hear any more, she moved to walk away. The leaves of the fig tree rustled.

'There's someone in the bushes,' Noah pointed.

Reuben screamed. 'The ghost!'

Flora and Max peered towards the fig tree.

Martha stepped out from behind the leaves.

'Oh Martha.' Flora sounded horrified. 'I'm sorry . . .'

Max shook his head. 'I didn't mean . . .'

But Martha was already moving on down the path as quickly as she could. She concentrated on the noise of the cicadas so that she didn't have to hear any more of Flora and Max's excruciating apologies.

At the bottom of the drive she could see Josh picking rubble out of the Porsche. Carla was beside him, leaning against the boot. Martha paused, but she couldn't go back past the pool or go into the house again.

She braced herself.

As Martha approached, she heard Carla's voice.

'I'm just saying. You should have invested the money in a course of counselling instead of this ridiculous car. Worked on your inner self before growing a beard and running around London picking up young women. Such a cliché.'

Martha relaxed. At least their conversation wasn't about her.

Carla picked a small pebble from the bonnet and flicked it towards the pile of rocks beside the car.

'You're the one with the problems,' Josh muttered.

'Are you sure about that?'

'Well, at least I'm not lusting after women!'

'Really?' Carla laughed, and threw another pebble at the pile.

The midday Angelis rang out across the valley.

'Do you think it's for the tourists,' Carla pondered. 'Or do people really go to church round here?'

Josh heaved a rock from the driver's side and threw it on the ground. It missed the pile and squelched into the surrounding mud.

'Anyway.' Carla turned back to Josh. 'Why am I the one helping you? Where's your girlfriend?'

Josh hesitated. 'I'm not sure.'

'I saw her earlier.' Carla raised her eyebrows. 'Helping that young Scottish man with his bike.' She nodded towards where the bike stood, pristinely clean, beside the cars. 'Polishing his great big muffler with her pretty little hands.'

Josh threw a large rock so hard that it shattered as it hit the pile.

Martha carried on around the corner that led to the chapel.

She was confronted with a mountain of furniture. Everything, apart from the bed, had been piled outside the back door in a sprawling heap. Rugs and bedding and items of clothing had been laid out on top of the heap to dry in the sun. Distracted by the sight, she almost bumped straight into Elodie, who was leaning against the rough stone wall. The young girl held a bougainvillea flower in her hand, slowly tearing off the petals, one by one. Pippa sat beside her feet, nibbling the petals as they fell. Martha wondered how much of her parents' exchange Elodie had heard.

'Come on,' Martha said, nodding towards the door of the chapel. 'Let's go and see the damage.'

Elodie threw a handful of petals up in the air so that they showered her head like confetti and followed Martha through the door, Pippa hopping at her heels.

Inside, Zac was sweeping mud from the floor. 'Nearly there, Mrs. M,' said Zac cheerily.

'You don't have to do this.' Martha couldn't believe the teenage boy could have done so much.

'There's not much else to do round here.' Zac made a couple of exaggerated sweeps followed by a twirl as though the broom were his dance partner. 'When Alice asked for help, I thought I might as well show off my va-va-vroom with a br-br-broom.' He flipped the broom and tried to balance its end on the tip of his finger. It fell, with a clatter, to the floor. 'Whoops!'

'Alice?' Martha said.

Zac nodded towards the bedroom. 'She's in there, where the mud is really gross.' He made a face and glanced at Elodie. A few of the bougainvillea petals had caught in her hair; they looked very pretty

192

against the turquoise stripes. The petals drifted from her hair onto the floor.

'Hey, mind what your doing.' Zac recovered the broom. 'You're ruining my work.'

'There you are, Zachery, I knew you'd be up to mischief somewhere.'

Flora stood in the doorway.

'Don't sweat, Aunty! I'm helping the lady.' Zac nodded towards Martha and began pushing the broom across the floor again.

Flora pursed her lips. 'Oh Martha, I just wanted to say that whatever you heard earlier . . .'

'Zac has been wonderful,' Martha interjected, lifting Pippa from the floor to stop her from being swept up in Zac's enthusiasm. 'He's swept out all the mud from this room.'

Elodie was looking down at the floor. Zac started brushing around her feet until she looked up at him.

'Leave the poor girl alone,' scolded Flora.

'She likes it.'

'No, she doesn't, do you, darling?'

Elodie scowled at Flora. Zac made some smaller sweeping movements towards the girl's toes.

'That's enough of you acting like a giddy goat.' Flora grabbed the brush and leant it against the wall.

Zac winked at Elodie. Elodie smiled.

'I think I've got the worst of the mud up.' Alice came out from the bedroom holding a mop and bucket. 'It wasn't nearly as bad as it looked.'

'I don't know what to say,' said Martha. 'You've been so kind.'

Alice smiled. 'It's the least I can do, you've been so kind to me.'

Martha blinked. 'But I haven't done anything.'

'Oh yes, you have.' Alice stepped forward and gave her a hug. 'You've made it all bearable.'

Martha's body stiffened as the young woman's sun-freckled arms encircled her, but after a few moments she felt herself relax. It was good to be held, it had been such a long time.

'Thank you,' she said quietly. Then she peered over Alice's shoulder into the bedroom.

'Is Ben in there?'

Alice released Martha from the embrace. 'No, he's gone into the village.'

'How? His bike is here, and the landslide's blocking the road.'

'He said he was going to walk across the fields. He had to do something important.'

'I love these paintings.' Flora was admiring the canvases that lined a shelf in the kitchen; the flood hadn't reached that high. 'Who is the artist?'

'Martha,' Elodie answered quickly. 'She's really good.'

Zac tilted his head to one side and studied the pictures with the air of a professional critic.

'They're well sick, Mrs. M.'

'I think he means they're beautiful,' Flora translated. 'The oranges in this one look almost real, they make me feel hungry.'

'Good,' said Alice, untying her apron. 'Because my next plan is to bake a big batch of cookies to cheer everyone up.'

'Cool,' said Zac.

'I liked those cookies you brought with you,' said Elodie. Alice's eyes widened.

'But I thought you . . .' she began, then stopped. 'Good, I'm glad you enjoyed them.'

'I think it might be difficult to cook in here?' Martha looked around the empty kitchen.

'Don't worry,' Alice said. 'I'll cook up in the house and leave you in peace. Perhaps you'd like to help me, Elodie?'

Elodie shrugged, then after a second, gave a nod.

'I'll help too,' Zac offered.

'When have you ever cooked anything?' Flora folded her arms.

'I'm a ninja in the kitchen, Aunty.' Zac made a series of chopping movements with his hand. 'I make Gordon Ramsay look like a burger flipper at McDonald's.'

Flora rolled her eyes.

194

'You'll be in charge then,' said Alice. 'But I'll make you a hot chocolate first . . . as a reward for all your hard work. I got some lovely cocoa powder from the market.'

'You got marshmallows?' Zac asked as they stepped outside. 'That swirly cream? A Cadbury Flake?'

'Unfortunately not.'

Flora hovered in the doorway.

'Please,' Martha sighed. 'No more apologies.'

'OK,' Flora smiled. She paused. 'I hope you managed to get some sleep last night, I know Carla snores like a little pig sometimes.'

Martha resisted the temptation to say more like a ginormous warthog.

'It was fine,' she lied. 'Though I'll be glad to be back in here tonight.'

'I'll come round later and help put the furniture back when it's dry.' Flora flashed a brilliant smile as Martha started to protest. 'It's no trouble. I'm sure the landslide won't be clear for hours so I might as well give you a hand while we're still here. It's the least I can do. Besides, as Alice said, you've been so kind.'

With a wave of her ring-adorned fingers, Flora billowed away leaving Martha standing alone in the empty chapel.

Martha went out into the sunshine and sat down on a bench; Pippa hopped onto her knee. She lifted her face and felt the warmth of the sun on her skin. She closed her eyes, her fingers rhythmically stroking the rabbit's soft fur.

You've been so kind. Flora's words echoed in her head, then Alice's. *You've made it all bearable.*

The women's words made her heart glow. Andrew used to call her unbearable. Selfish. A typical addict, he said. A loser. A waster. She'd let herself believe him, let herself believe she was incapable of caring for anyone. Not even herself.

'You poor thing!'

Martha's eyes sprang open. Carla stood in front of her, blocking out the sun.

'Sorry?' Martha peered at the outline.

'You poor thing,' Carla repeated. 'I feel really sorry for you. The hornets, your stuff being ransacked and now all this devastation.' She swept her arm around, taking in the drive and Martha's possessions heaped outside the chapel. 'You must wish you'd never let your house out for the summer.'

Carla sat down on the bench. Pippa jumped from Martha's lap.

'You don't mind, do you? If I sit down.' Carla didn't pause for a response.

'It's just I have a question to ask you; don't worry it's not about your personal life this time. Just a little favour – something for me, because I'm a bit wound up by that bloody fool of an ex-husband of mine – the divorce seems as though it's going to take for ever – unfortunately. He makes me feel so cross, on and on about his own problems, all he thinks about is himself, selfish is an understatement and he's so rude and so crass – actually, crass is a good word for him, I'm going to call him crass next time I see him, *You crass bastard*, that's what I'm going to say.'

'What do you want?' Martha interrupted.

Carla looked at her, as though she had forgotten that she was going to ask for anything.

'Oh, yes.' She opened her big blue eyes wide. 'I just wondered if you could possibly spare one of your cigarettes?'

Martha sighed. 'I only have two left.'

Carla widened her eyes. 'But I'd only want one. It's not that I smoke, never have, not really, but when I'm upset or stressed or really, really annoyed, like now . . . when I have to listen to Josh going on and on and see him doing such a terrible job of looking after our children, I mean, he is supposed to be an adult! He's more upset about that car of his than he is about poor Noah. He doesn't seem to realise how quiet and withdrawn our little boy has become.'

Martha took the packet of cigarettes from her pocket and handed one to Carla hoping it would shut her up and make her go away. She lit it and then lit her own.

'Children are such a worry, aren't they?' Carla blew a cloud of smoke. Martha didn't answer.

Carla arranged her features into a thoughtful expression.

'Flora says she seems to remember something about you having a son. Didn't you crash into a Nando's or something with him in the back of your car?'

It was Pizza Express, Martha wanted to say, *not Nando's!* But did it really matter where it was. It was meant to have been a trip to Battersea Park on a sunny Saturday afternoon. But somehow Martha had missed the entrance to the park, driven too fast down a busy shopping street, failed to stop at two red lights, mounted the pavement and crashed into the plate-glass window of the restaurant. She had no recollection of the accident, but the pictures had been in all the papers – fuzzy images of Martha climbing out of the crumpled Mini, passersby helping to get Owen out. The horrified customers behind the shattered glass. Owen crying.

'Drug-addled Martha In Crash Drama With Son'

'Ex-Singer Wasted At The Wheel'

'Pizza Panic As Martha Nearly Kills Her Baby'

Martha's mother hadn't kept those press cuttings.

'Do you see much of your son?' Carla asked. When Martha didn't answer she gave a little sigh. 'That must be hard.'

Martha swallowed, nausea rising from her stomach. It would only take an Internet search for the whole awful story to appear. Supposing Carla decided to write an article about incompetent mothers, using her as an example. Supposing Owen read it.

Carla stood up, dropping her cigarette to the ground.

'Thanks for that, I feel much better now.'

'Please don't write anything about me.' Martha hated the pleading tone in her voice. 'Or my son.'

'Oh Martha – you seem to think I'm some sort of awful tabloid predator.' She smiled. 'I have a very kind heart, you know, all I really want to do is help.'

With a wave of her hand, Carla walked away. Martha watched as she stopped to pick the last rose from the bush that grew beside the drive; the only rose that had survived the battering of the storm.

Martha desperately wanted another cigarette. She peered across the fields, hoping to spot Ben returning from the village so that she could ask for one of his, but there was no sign of him.

She could see his tent and sleeping bag still hanging in the cherry trees to dry. His rucksack was propped against one of the trunks. Martha wondered if he might have left the packet of cigarettes she'd bought him the day before in his bag.

Martha stood up and made her way through the long grass towards the rucksack. It felt damp. Martha patted the outside pockets feeling for the familiar rectangular shape. It was hard to feel anything through the thick fabric and the multitude of buckles and straps. She pushed her hand inside a pocket and felt the soft pages of a paperback book. Curious, she eased it out just enough to read the title, *French Country Cooking* by Elizabeth David; it looked like it had been published a long time ago. The cover was faded and torn and the pages well thumbed. Martha pushed it back into the rucksack. The pocket on the other side contained a passport and a creased and battered photograph.

Martha studied the photograph: a young woman with a round, pretty face was laughing, eyes squinting against the sun. She had her arms around a toddler with a mop of pale hair. He held a swirling ice cream, pink sauce dribbling down its cone onto his chubby fingers. They were standing against a hazy sky, a strip of sand and sea just visible in the distance. Martha imagined a man behind the camera, encouraging big smiles; proud of his young son, in love with his wife.

Martha slid the picture back into the pocket and clipped the buckle back together with a snap.

Her longing for a cigarette intensified. She had no intention of reaching into the rucksack itself but there was one more pocket running along the front that she hadn't touched. It bulged. Martha pushed her hand against the outside and thought she could just feel the corner of a box.

A shout came from behind her, she jumped and turned, but there was no one there. The splashing that followed assured her that it was just the children playing in the pool.

She quickly unzipped the pocket. As soon as it was open a string of plastic pearls slid out, followed by a huge fake sapphire brooch and a diamanté necklace. Martha recognised them immediately; old costume jewellery that she had once worn on stage, cheap and worthless but pieces that she had kept and stored together with the clothes and boots and hats and photographs up in the little attic room. Ben had helped her store the jewellery away in the cupboard only a few days before.

Martha's shoulder's stiffened. It had been Ben who had opened the cupboard, not Elodie or Carla.

She pushed her hand into the pocket, feeling more beads and bracelets. A thin metallic belt shaped like a serpent slithered onto the grass, its clasp a head with ruby eyes that glinted up at Martha and seemed to tell her what a fool she'd been. She sat back heavily on the grass. The little heap of jewellery glittered beside her in the sunlight, glass and plastic and imitation gold.

Martha wondered if Ben could really have thought that any of it would be worth stealing. She tried to imagine him riffling through the contents of the cupboard, throwing it around, betraying her trust. She had tended to his wounded face that day; let him rest in her bed, gone to town to buy him ointment. While she had been gone, he had ransacked her possessions, stolen from her and then gone back to bed.

Martha twisted the belt between her hands, coiling it tightly into a circle.

How could you have been such a fool, Martha Morgan? she thought.

She needed to find Ben. She would intercept him in the village and tell him what she'd found. It would be better to confront him somewhere public in case he turned nasty. Martha stood up and went into the chapel to retrieve her purse from the shopping basket.

After she found Ben, she'd have a cup of coffee with Sally. Sally would want her to go to the police; Martha knew she wouldn't do that. But one thing that she did know for sure was that once the land-slide was cleared Ben would have to take his bike, and his belongings, and go.

Chapter 29

Martha pushed her way through a gap in the hedge to the field next door. Anger was building inside her, small at first, a ripple, but then swelling into a wave; she had let Ben into her life, let him stay on her property, fed him, paid him, trusted him.

Bastard!

Her shirt caught on a bramble; as she yanked it free, she realised she hadn't changed her clothes since the day before. There was mud on the hem of her skirt, her hair was sticking up in all directions and she could smell the slight trace of stale sweat. For a moment she thought of turning back to change and have a shower but the determination to find Ben pushed her on.

She hobbled through the rows of sunflowers that lined the hillside, their big round faces seemed to mock her as she passed. Martha stumbled over the ruts the tractor had made when the seeds were planted, she heard the crunch of breaking stems and cursed but she didn't stop, she didn't look back.

She entered a small oak copse. Martha tripped on the root of an old tree; a bolt of pain shot through her leg. Steadying herself on the trunk she somehow managed not to fall. She leant against the trunk and looked back up the way she'd come. The house seemed very far away already.

Martha looked down the valley; she'd have to get to the bottom then start the steep climb up to the village. It was so much further than it looked from the house. Sweat trickled down Martha's back. The church bell struck three.

Martha took a deep breath and stood up straight. She noticed that the ground around the trunk had been dug up; it looked dark and rich. She could smell damp soil. In January this was where the truffles could be found. Martha looked around. She wondered if the ground had been dug up by a wild pig, or a boar snuffling for them much too early. She knew wild boars roamed this part of France. She'd never seen one but once Sally had told her that Pierre had been chased as a boy. She looked around again.

In the distance she could see more sunflowers, heads up, turned toward the sun. She could also see the bright red roof of the little shack where Jean-Paul lived, so much nearer than the village. If she cut across the next field, she could be there in a matter of minutes. He might give her a lift – if she paid him? Maybe he would sell her a cigarette? Maybe he would sell her . . . *No!* Martha wouldn't even let the thought into her mind. But . . . it was her birthday. Didn't she deserve something, especially after all the months of coping with the letters from the bank, the worry and the hard work on the house and then the demands of the guests, and now Ben . . . and her leg was very painful. Just one? Or two? Maybe they would help her sleep?

What would Sally say?

'Bugger Sally,' Martha muttered. There really wasn't any need to see her anyway. She set off towards the shack, then stopped.

'NO!'

She shouted the word out loud and thought of the mantra that they'd taught her at the clinic.

I am in control. I will not give in.

Martha took a deep breath.

I am in control. I will not give in.

Martha started to walk.

I am in control.

Her pace quickened.

I am in control. I will not give in.

Jean-Paul's shack got nearer.

Bloody mantra! Bloody clinic!

I will give in if I want to!

★

It didn't take long to get across the field. Opening a wooden gate, she found herself on the rough dirt track that led directly towards the back of Jean-Paul's ugly, breeze-block home. The neglected walls were rough and grey. One end of the building was covered in an ancient tarpaulin; a rusting cement mixer stood beside it, almost completely covered in weeds. An Alsatian dog was chained to the cement mixer; it didn't bark as Martha had expected it to. It whimpered, straining against the studded collar round its neck. Martha felt sorry for it.

Martha passed a little copper-coloured hatchback parked on the patch of earth in front of the house. It was just like the car Martha had seen at the top of the drive earlier on in the week. She vaguely wondered whose car it was but within seconds she had forgotten all about it, and as she reached the front door, she forgot everything else as well: Ben, the bank, the house, the guests, even Owen. All she could think of were the small white pills and the drifting, fuzzy, lovely escape they would bring.

Jean-Paul answered the door in nothing but a pair of striped boxer shorts. Draped against the peeling paint of the doorframe he reminded Martha of a lizard. A slow smile spread across his pale angular face, his hooded eyes slithered over Martha's body making her aware of her bedraggled appearance and dirty clothes. She noticed that his head was closely shaved revealing a large white scar that in the past had been hidden by long greasy hair. She could see little indentations on each side where stitches had been put in long ago.

'Madame Morgan, what a nice surprise,' Jean-Paul said, drawing out the words in his heavy French accent.

Martha noticed a bruise around his left eye; in the past she might have asked about it, now she wanted to complete the transaction as quickly as possible.

'I only want one tablet,' she said. 'Actually two.'

Jean-Paul looked Martha up and down again, his eyes lingering on the muddy skirt and ripped shirt.

'Tell me, how are you? How is it with all your . . .?' He paused as though trying to decide on the word. 'Visitors.'

Martha stiffened. 'I don't think my visitors are any of your business.'

'But I am only asking. Your big house full of people, it must seem strange?'

'As I said, it really is none of your business.'

Jean-Paul raised one eyebrow. '*Mais non*, I am your old friend.' His mouth turned down in a parody of melancholy. 'I miss you calling me. *Please, Jean-Paul, please come over, I need you.*'

Martha winced at his demeaning impersonation. She had forgotten just how much she disliked him. She could smell the scent of stale coffee, dogs and marijuana coming from inside the house.

'Jean-Paul.' A woman's voice, from the darkness beyond the open door. 'Are you coming back?' She spoke in English. Jean-Paul answered her in French, too fast for Martha to understand.

Martha unzipped her purse.

'How much are you going to charge for two tablets? A fortune, I presume.'

Jean-Paul looked affronted. 'A fortune – to you? Always in the past I am doing special offers, but now because you are back, I will do a very extra special offer for one hundred tablets.'

Martha shook her head. 'I only want two. Just tell me how much. I need to get home to my guests.'

She peered into her purse to hide her desperation. Jean-Paul shouted into the house then turned back to Martha.

'Ben tells me that you have to cook.'

Martha's head shot up at the mention of Ben's name. 'How do you know Ben?'

Jean-Paul didn't answer.

The woman appeared at Jean-Paul's side, more of a girl than a woman; heavy kohl around her eyes, pale skin, long blonde hair straggling down her back. She wore a white, muslin dress that was far too big for her; it slipped off her shoulders and the sleeves fell over her hands.

The girl held a cigarette in one hand and a silver strip of tablets in the other.

Jean-Paul took the strip of tablets from her and pressed two out onto his palm.

'Sixty Euros.'

Martha pursed her lips and searched for the cash, trying to imagine how Ben could possibly know Jean-Paul and then trying to ignore the answer that sprung too easily into her mind.

'There is no rush,' Jean-Paul said. 'I am not the impatient man like Ben.' Jean-Paul touched his bruised eye.

Martha looked away quickly. She could hear her heart beating as she fumbled through the compartments in her purse.

'What is on the menu for your guests tonight, I wonder?' Jean-Paul mused.

Martha had taken one hundred Euros from the cash point the day before but now she could find only ten. 'I have tomatoes if you are interested.' Jean-Paul nodded towards a dilapidated greenhouse; for a drug dealer he had an incongruous proclivity for vegetable-growing. In the past, Martha had bought beans and courgettes and beautifully coloured squashes from him as well as painkillers. 'Or would your guests like a little weed instead. Thirty Euros, it is good. Very gentle, very nice.'

Martha ignored him and searched back and forth through her purse, sickness rising in her stomach. The money was gone, only the single note remained. She looked up at Jean-Paul.

'I have ten.'

He laughed and handed the tablets back to the girl.

'There is no deal for ten.'

Martha stared at the girl.

'Would you sell me one of your cigarettes?'

The girl sold her a whole packet. She'd taken it from a large airport multipack. Jean-Paul had become surly, arguing with the girl in French before casting one last disparaging look at Martha and disappearing into the gloom of the house.

The girl had given Martha a small smile, pity in her smudged blue eyes, and then she had followed Jean-Paul inside, leaving Martha standing on the doorstep.

Martha limped back up the dirt track. She felt soiled; the smell of Jean-Paul's shack lingered in her nostrils, his look of disdain seared into her mind. Her humiliation was mixed with horror at the realisation that Ben must have stolen money from her purse. And Ben knew Jean-Paul. Ben had hit Jean-Paul. Ben must be a user, Ben must be an addict, desperate to fund his habit, he was a thief, a petty criminal. Martha felt like a fool, she'd been deceived, taken in. She had liked Ben, even let herself imagine her own son might be like him. She shuddered, now Ben was the last person she wanted her son to be like.

Martha pushed through the gate, blinking back the tears that were swimming in her eyes. She retraced her steps across the fields; uphill was harder. She didn't stop. The tears began to run down her cheeks; she brushed them away and opened the packet of cigarettes, lighting one without slowing. Up and up, one foot after another, inhaling deeply, trying to make the nicotine relieve her pain. The tears kept coming, running into her mouth, salt mixing with the taste of the cigarette. Everything seemed hopeless, the house, the money, the addiction that refused to let her go to start afresh. It was too late to change anything. She knew now there would never be a time when she'd be ready to get in touch with Owen. She'd never be the kind of mother that anyone could possibly want.

Martha longed to be lying on the big sleigh bed in her peacock coloured bedroom, a sheet pulled over her head, the world and other people far away. She climbed towards this dream of solitude even though she knew that it would be impossible; her home was full of people, her bed taken, the silence and seclusion she craved no longer there. She finished one cigarette and lit another. Looking up she could see *Le Couvent des Cerises* far above her; she looked back the way she'd come. The dirt track was a thread, Jean-Paul's red roof a smear. Pin-pricks darted in front of her, tiny flies, or stars, she brushed them away but more were coming; they were stars, the night was closing in and the steep hillside seemed to be rushing towards her, tilting, tipping, long grass smothering her face, darkness washing over her in a wave . . .

Martha opened her eyes. She was face down on the ground. She tried to lift her head, but it felt like it was spinning. Slowly she rolled over and lay, eyes closed, on her back.

As the dizziness passed, Martha opened one eye and looked up. A buzzard soared above her, its wings spread against the clear blue sky. Martha closed her eye and tried to imagine gliding over the countryside. Weightless, painless, she circled upwards, higher and higher. She was a speck, a dot. Invisible.

'Are you OK?'

Martha's eyes sprang open. It was a man. His face was very close. He was crouching over her, his hand on her shoulder.

Martha jerked upright, struggling into a seated position, pushing the man's hand away.

'Get off me.'

'It's OK, Martha, it's OK.' The man stood up and stepped back. 'I was just worried about you, that's all. Are you alright?'

Martha squinted; the man's large frame was silhouetted against the bright sun but his Irish accent was familiar.

'Max?'

'Yes.' He stepped forward and she could see his face, he looked concerned. 'Are you alright?' he repeated. 'Has something happened? Have you had a fall?'

'No! I have not had a fall.' Martha scowled. 'I am perfectly alright.'

'I didn't mean to startle you. I came out for a walk, I wanted to see the sunflower field.' He held up three sunflowers. 'Then I saw you lying on the grass and ran over. I should have given you more warning. God knows what you think of me?'

'It's OK' Martha shifted her position so that she felt more comfortable. 'I just got a bit of a fright.'

Max laughed.

'I got a bit of a fright too. Seeing you laid out like that. I thought . . .' He paused.

'You thought I was dead?'

'No!' Max paused again. 'Well, that would have been the worst of all the terrible stuff going through my mind.'

'Heart attack? Stroke? Concussion? Snakebite?'

Max nodded 'Yes, they were all there, though not the snakebite. Or you could have been worse for wear on a bottle of Tia Maria.' Max looked at her with a smile. 'Or just having a bit of a doze in the sun.'

'The doze is more like it.'

'Are there any snakes around here?' Max asked.

Martha looked towards Jean-Paul's shack.

'A few.'

'I was going to ask if you'd mind if I sat down, but in that case, I'll stay standing up.'

Martha peered up at him, her hand shielding her eyes against the sun.

'I didn't think a big man like you would be such a wuss.'

'Oh, I'm a terrible coward when it comes to snakes. We don't have them in Ireland. It was my biggest worry about moving to England – the adders.' He gave a shudder. 'Terrifying! Luckily there were very few in Kilburn.'

Somewhere in the distance a dog barked.

'That'll be the wolves,' said Martha. 'They're worse than the snakes.'

'Really?'

Martha smiled as more dogs joined in as a repeated banging sound rang out across the valley.

'They come marauding in a big pack. The villagers are erecting a fence to keep them out.'

Max peered into the distance. 'I can see a man on top of a ladder by the church tower, he'll be the lookout, I suppose?'

'You've got it.'

'I'd never have come if I'd known the Dordogne is such a danger-ous place.'

'Actually, there may be some wild boar about,' Martha added.

Max laughed. 'You're very funny.' After a few moments of silence he nodded towards the church. 'What's really going on over there?'

'Fireworks,' Martha said. 'There's a big display tomorrow night. They do it every year to mark the beginning of the flower festival. The man on the ladder will be nailing Catherine wheels to the church tower – it looks amazing when they all go off, sparks cascade down the walls like a waterfall.'

'The boys will love that.'

Martha had forgotten to tell the guests about the annual fireworks. From *Le Couvent des Cerises* it always looked incredible, the night sky alight with fizzing rockets, the whole village exploding into bursts of glittering colour. Martha liked to watch it from the terrace. This year she would have to settle for watching it from outside the chapel. The guests would get the terrace view; it would be their last night.

'I think I'll risk the snakes.' Max sat down on the grass, drawing up his long legs and resting his arms on his knees as he stared at the view. He glanced at Martha. 'Look, I'm sorry about earlier. I don't know how much you overheard but I didn't mean . . .'

A deep rumbling noise drowned out Max's words. Martha looked towards the road from the village. Two diggers trundled slowly down it, men in high-vis jackets hanging from the sides, shouting and yelling as if they were off to fight a battle rather than clear a landslide.

As the men's shouts died away, Martha caught the last of Max's words.

'. . . a nun. I'm mortified.'

Martha glanced down; the sunflowers looked incongruous in his large weathered hands.

'Don't worry about it,' she said, looking back up to meet his gaze.

His eyes still looked concerned. 'It's just you look as though you've been upset.'

Martha touched her face, her eyes stung from the tears, her nose felt blocked.

'Hay fever,' she said quickly.

Max nodded. 'My wife had that. She went around with tissues

stuffed down her bra all summer, constantly wiping her nose.' He smiled.

Martha smiled too.

Max let the sunflowers droop to the ground. He stopped smiling.

'It's funny, I can remember those bits of scrunched-up tissue so clearly, but I can't see her face. Sometimes I imagine her laugh or feel the touch of her hand on mine and I can see her for a second, then like a wisp she's gone.'

Martha thought of Owen's laugh, the weight of him in her arms, his fingers curling round her own. She could still feel his warm skin.

Max turned to her. 'Do you have anyone in your life? Some suave Frenchman or a fellow musician perhaps, to keep you company?'

Martha shook her head. 'Us nuns aren't allowed relationships with men, you know.'

'I knew I had offended you.' Max ran his fingers through his hair. 'I didn't mean to say that you're really like a nun, not that there's anything wrong with nuns, apart from their hideous black clothes.'

Martha brushed the grass seed off her own black skirt.

Max looked apologetic. '*Your* black clothes are very nice. Not nun-like at all. Despite what I said. I only meant that your clothes are long . . . and black.'

'Like a nun's,' Martha said.

'Oh God, you must think I'm an idiot.'

Martha stood up. 'We're all idiots sometimes,' she said. 'Though some of us are more idiotic than the others.'

'You mean me?'

'No, I mean myself.'

'Why would you say that?'

'It doesn't matter' Martha turned and peered up the hill towards the house. It looked so far away.

'Can I walk with you?' Max asked, standing up.

'Suit yourself; it's nearly time for vespers and Mother Superior gets very cross if I'm late.'

Martha set off, Max's voice behind her.

'I really am so very sorry. And you of all people. Fionnuala would be furious with me, she was such a fan. We both were. It was such a shame that the band broke up.'

Martha wished that he'd stop talking. She tried to walk faster but Max was very good at keeping up.

'I suppose that business at the BRIT Awards was a sign that things weren't going well.'

Martha stopped. 'Please don't mention the BRIT Awards.'

'Ah, it wasn't your fault, anyone could see those heels were far too high for her and she was the one who started it, trying to snatch the statue and she gave the first shove.'

Martha looked at Max's face, his eyes were kind, his smile sympathetic. She bit her lip.

'I didn't mean to push her.'

'I expect she was jealous,' Max said. 'You sang "Moondancing" so beautifully.'

Martha set off up the hill again. Slower this time, suddenly wanting to talk about the painful memories that all the clothes and pictures had stirred up.

'She couldn't bear that Lucas let me sing instead of her.'

'But you wrote it.'

'That was another thing she couldn't bear. But it was the one and only time Lucas acknowledged my input on a song.'

'How many did you write?'

'Most of them started with me coming up with a tune on the piano, writing a few lyrics, but then Cat and Lucas would take over and change them so much that they'd insist they were their songs.'

'I hope you got the royalties?'

'No. It didn't seem important at the time. I wasn't interested in money.'

'You were interested in Lucas.'

Martha stopped again. 'Why do you say that?'

'It was what Fionnuala used to say. *The redhead fancies the pants off the lead singer but he's getting off with the blonde one and doesn't realise he'd be much better off with the other.*'

'Fionnuala was very perceptive.'

Max nodded. 'She was.'

'It was complicated, Cat was my best friend – or I thought she was.'

'But just imagine if you had the royalty money from all those songs.'

'Well, I wouldn't be bloody well letting out my house to strangers, that's for sure.'

Martha walked on, faster this time. What was the point of getting angry now? It didn't take long for Max to catch her up again, his stride carefully paced to match her limping step.

'Do you never think of having another go at the singing career?'

'No,' Martha wheezed, she was getting out of breath.

'I bet you'd be just as good as that Cat. I saw her on the telly the other day – she doesn't have a line on her face, it's like she's made of plastic.'

'I think I've lost the battle with the wrinkles' Martha patted her face.

'But you look much better than her. You're beautiful.'

Martha didn't answer and if Max said anything else it was drowned out by the clanking and the rumbling across the valley as the landslide clearance started.

The noise died down as they neared the top of the hill.

'There was all sorts of commotion going on at the house when I left,' Max said. 'Paula's lost her diamond ring.' Martha's chest suddenly felt very tight, she took a deep breath. 'They've been taking the place apart looking for it.' Martha felt like she might pass out again. 'Took it off when she was washing the dishes in the kitchen sink. She's sure she left it on the draining board, but it's vanished, there's no sign of it at all. Ranjit was talking about taking the U-bend off the sink when I left . . .'

Martha couldn't take in any more, all she could think about now was Ben. She hadn't seen him up at the house since early in the morning, though that didn't mean he hadn't sneaked back up before he went to the village. She thought of the bags and phones and iPads strewn around. Ranjit had an expensive-looking camera; Paula's sunglasses didn't look cheap. He'd probably take anything to fund his drug habit; after all, he'd even stolen her cheap costume jewellery.

'I just wondered if you had anything special planned for it?'

Martha struggled to re-join the conversation.

'For the U-bend?'

'No, for your birthday. Are you having a bit of a do? Anyone coming over?'

Martha shook her head. 'It's been a long time since I celebrated a birthday.'

'Well, maybe you should give it a try.'

Martha looked at Max's broad back; he was slightly ahead now. She wanted to tell him that celebrating was the very last thing she wanted to do, but the climb was steep and it was hard enough for Martha to breath let alone speak.

Chapter 30

Max pushed his way through the hedge. Martha followed. The garden was very quiet. Ben's tent and rucksack were still where Martha had left them; there were no sounds of shrieks and splashes coming from the pool. Martha felt an ominous sense of dread; she wondered what was going on up at the house.

Max seemed unaffected by the steep climb.

'That was a grand stretch of the legs.'

Martha's shirt stuck to her back and sweat prickled on her hairline.

'Water!' she panted.

'I'll get it.' Max pulled a wooden chair from the pile of furniture outside the door. 'You sit down.'

She shook her head and pointed inside. 'Shower.'

Max raised his eyebrows.

'Ah well, I can't help you with that.'

He began to walk away then stopped. He turned around and held out the sunflowers.

'Here.' He stepped forward and handed them to Martha. 'A birthday present.'

Martha stumbled through the chapel door. In the coolness of the kitchen she put the sunflowers in the sink, filled a glass of water from the tap and gulped it down. The chapel smelled musty from the flood, earthy and damp; it made Martha feel sick. She had two more glasses of water, her breathing gradually returning to normal. Pippa sat in the middle of the empty room watching her.

Martha scooped her up. She thought she could see reproach in the beady black eyes.

'I know.' She kissed the rabbit's head. 'You don't need to tell me. I've been a fool.'

Martha fetched a carrot from the fridge and gave it to Pippa. She put her back down on the floor and went into the tiny bathroom. Holding the enamel sink for support she stripped off her clothes, kicking them into a pile in the corner before stepping into the shower cubicle. She leant against the tiled wall while the cool water flowed over her body, washing away the dust and mud and the sweat.

In the bedroom she opened a built-in cupboard and found a pair of black linen trousers amongst a pile of many black linen trousers. Her hand hovered over a well-worn black T-shirt, but then she stopped. Closing the cupboard door with a bang she opened a little door underneath and pulled out a black silk shirt.

'After all, it is my birthday.'

Martha did up the row of covered buttons and looked in the mottled mirror on the bedroom wall.

Max had told her she was beautiful. She studied her face searching for the girl from the front of *Jackie* magazine. But it didn't matter how long she looked into the glass, that girl was nowhere to be seen.

'Fool,' Martha said to her reflection and went outside.

She sat on the bench; Ben seemed to be everywhere. His bike parked at the bottom of the drive, his tent and sleeping bag still hanging from the trees. The rucksack taunted Martha with its bulging pockets.

Martha lit a cigarette. She thought about dinner and blew out a stream of smoke with a sigh. No doubt she'd be expected to make up for her lack of enthusiasm the previous night by producing something decent in her soggy kitchen, and now with no more help from Ben. Martha decided she would drive into the village and buy a pile of pizzas from the pizzeria on the square. There seemed little point in trying to impress anyone any more.

A shroud of revulsion wrapped itself around her shoulders as she remembered hoping that Owen had turned into a young man as kind and amiable as Ben. Now she hoped that however selfish and unpleasant her son might have become in the hands of the Frazer family, he wouldn't be conning his way into women's homes, exploiting them and stealing to feed a sleazy drug habit.

Why had she trusted Ben? What a hopeless judge of character she was. Andrew had always criticised her choice of friends. He said she was instinctively drawn to the wrong type of person. At the North Kensington baby group, she had made friends with a woman who turned out to be the mistress of a thuggish Russian gangster, and then she'd employed a cleaner who Andrew's mother discovered had been in prison for fraud.

Martha shook herself, hoping that the shroud of revulsion would fall; but it seemed to wrap itself tighter, squeezing out any hope that she might be capable of having a future with her son.

Chapter 31

Martha stood at the kitchen sink and splashed water on her face then turned and looked around the room; it was as grey and empty as she felt. The only colour came from the paintings lining the shelf on the wall and the sunflowers sitting in the sink.

Martha picked up the sunflowers and took them outside. She put them on the garden table and hunted amongst the furniture pile for her easel. She took out her paints and brushes and a canvas. Pippa appeared from underneath a rosemary bush and stretched herself out in the shade of the table. Martha squeezed paint onto a palette and arranged the sunflowers, so their big brown faces looked straight at her. After fetching a pot of water, Martha placed the canvas on the easel, sat down on the chair that Max had pulled out for her earlier and began to paint.

Martha wasn't sure how much time had passed. The diggers hammered and clanked in the background while Martha's paintbrush worked furiously across the canvas, recreating the flowers in the thick acrylic paint. But Martha wasn't even thinking about the painting. She was completely absorbed in thoughts of Ben and what she would say when he came back. Would she tell him that she'd found the jewellery in his bag? Would he deny it if she accused him of taking the money from her purse? Would he deny having taken Paula's ring?

The diggers had stopped. A faint smell of sewage wafted on the gentle breeze. Martha looked towards the septic tank in the meadow.

It had probably flooded again with all the rain. This time Ben wouldn't be around to sort it out.

Martha heard raised voices. Peering up the drive she could see Carla and Josh stomping up the drive towards the gates.

'Of course I know how to change a tyre.' Josh sounded indignant. 'Now we've got Ranjit's jack it'll be easy.'

'The last time it took you an hour to work out how to get the spare out of the boot.'

'Who else is going to do it – your *girlfriend*? She can't even drive a car!'

'Shut up. I'll show you how it's done myself!'

'Why do you have to be so pig-headed?'

'Me!'

The voices faded.

Martha added a few extra streaks of red to the edge of the petals and put down her brush.

'That's gorgeous,' a cheerful voice rang out beside Martha. She looked up into Flora's beaming face.

'I've come to help get this lot back inside.' She walked over to the furniture and ran her hand across a Persian rug. 'Lovely and dry.'

'You really don't need to do that,' Martha objected. But Flora already had a leather pouf in her arms.

'It won't take long.' Flora flashed her brilliant smile; she was in and out with surprising speed given her long nails and glittery footwear.

Flora disappeared into the chapel again, this time with the little bedside table. Martha started clearing her paints and brushes away.

Flora came back out and sniffed. 'Can you smell something a little odd out here?'

'Probably just the cherries.' Martha thought she ought to change the subject. 'Will you and Carla be staying another night?'

'Carla wants to hang around here a bit longer to find out what Josh intends to ask for in the divorce. She's worried he might go for custody.'

Martha swirled a paintbrush in the water pot.

'But Carla's a fighter,' Flora continued, picking up a chair. 'She'd never let him have her kids.'

Martha's fingers slipped and she knocked the paint pot so that the cloudy water gushed across the table.

'Hey,' Flora said. 'Are you OK?'

Martha didn't answer. She rubbed her eyes; they stung from all the earlier tears. Flora sat down on the chair she had been carrying.

'Tell me something, Martha. Why don't you sing any more?'

Martha thought about that last humiliating concert, standing on the dusty stage, desperately trying to remember the words, trying not to slur.

'I promised myself I'd never do that again.'

Flora considered her. 'I promised myself I'd never work in children's TV and I ended up as a crazy lady with a magic handbag for nearly a decade. Definitely not part of my career plan. When I left drama college, I played Desdemona at the Bristol Old Vic, then I was in a Mike Leigh film – I thought I was headed for stardom.'

'Judging by Reuben's reaction, Mrs. Clementine is a star.'

Flora folded her arms. 'The programme has just been axed by the BBC. Too dull – apparently! So, as of last month, I'm officially unemployed.'

'I'm sorry.'

'Don't be sorry. It's a chance – an opportunity.'

'For what?'

'For the next chapter. Life doesn't stand still. I haven't a clue what's next but I'm going to grab whatever opportunity comes along.' Flora stood up and shimmied her hips to an imaginary tune. 'You've gotta move your butt or get stuck in a rut.' She laughed at Martha's bemused expression.

'Do you need some help?' Max strode towards them down the path. He was wearing an Iron Maiden T-shirt. The black fabric seemed to be covered in white powder.

'What have you got all over you?' Flora asked.

Max looked down. 'Ah, that'll be the cocaine.' He brushed at the fabric. 'The house is awash with drugs.'

219

Martha stiffened.

'Silly joke,' Max said.

'I thought you'd been allocated an important job up there,' Flora said, gesturing towards the house.

'They seem to have everything in hand, though I think the kids are more in charge than anyone.'

'What's going on?' asked Martha.

'Bath time.'

'Teatime.'

Max and Flora spoke at once.

'Teatime.'

'Bath time.'

They spoke in unison again and laughed.

Max looked at the painting on the easel. 'You're good.'

There was a shriek as Noah and Reuben raced down the path towards the chapel.

'Grandpa, Grandpa, you have to come and help,' Reuben shouted.

Noah skidded to a halt in front of the easel, stones and dust rising in a cloud around his feet; Reuben failed to stop and catapulted into Noah and they both fell against the easel. It wobbled forward then back then forward again – Martha rushed towards it and grabbed her painting just as it was about to slide onto the dirty ground, hugging the canvas to her chest as she caught it.

'Sorry,' the boys chorused, disentangling their limbs from each other and getting to their feet.

'Oh no!' Martha held the smudged picture at arm's length.

'Oh dear!' Flora had her hand on her mouth.

Martha looked down. The silk shirt was covered in yellow and brown paint.

'Bollocks, shit and twiddling twats!'

'I think that's Welsh for what a shame,' Max whispered to the children.

Martha held the hem of the shirt out to see the extent of the damage.

'Go and change and we'll finish putting your things back.' Flora gently steered Martha towards the door of the chapel.

'And these young troublemakers can help us.' Max looked at the children, who were staring wide-eyed at Martha.

'No!' Martha's voice came out much louder than she'd meant it to. 'Leave everything alone. I can manage on my own.'

Inside the kitchen Martha threw the picture of the sunflowers onto the floor. She wanted to scream. The painting was ruined, her favourite shirt was ruined and she'd sworn in front of the children – again; no doubt one of them would tell their parents.

She stood at the sink and turned on the tap. The ancient pipes groaned and grumbled. Nothing happened. Martha turned the tap off then on again and off and on once more. Suddenly water gushed out in a belching burst, drenching the shirt and also her trousers.

'Bloody hell!'

Martha pulled off the wet trousers and tugged the soggy shirt over her head; little buttons flew across the room.

'Bollocks!'

She plunged the shirt into the water. The silk ballooned like a dejected jellyfish. She gave it a poke with her finger.

The shirt let out an indignant burp.

Martha went into the bedroom to fetch a T-shirt and a new pair of trousers, but at the sight of the bed she collapsed onto it. After all, she thought, what else was there to do?

Martha dozed, then finally slept. Fragmented dreams turned into vivid nightmares; she was in a field of sunflowers, Owen was running ahead of her, a small boy weaving in and out of the long green stems. Martha called out, desperate to warn him there were snakes in the field. At last he turned and looked at her. 'You're not my mother, you're just Martha . . .'

Martha, Martha.

She opened her eyes and saw Flora standing in the doorway.

'Martha, are you awake?'

Martha fumbled for the sheet to cover herself, aware that she was only wearing her bra and pants.

'What's the matter?' she said.

'I wondered if you wanted a cup of tea?'

'No.'

'Coffee?'

'No.'

'A glass of wine?'

Martha drew the sheet over her head. 'Please, I just want to be left alone.'

She heard the slight rustle of fabric as Flora turned to leave and the soft click of the latch as Flora shut the kitchen door.

The next time Martha opened her eyes the light was fading, it seemed like days ago that she'd walked all the way to the bottom of the valley.

She sat up with a start. The dinner! She had forgotten that she had to go and get the pizzas. The guests were probably sitting around the table, knives and forks in hand – waiting.

'Hello,' a voice was calling from the kitchen.

'Dinner will be ready in half an hour.' Martha swung her legs out of the bed, sitting on the edge, trying to coordinate her brain.

'That's nice but I ate with Pierre before we opened up the bar.'

Martha looked up to find Sally standing in the doorway now, eyes wide as she stared at Martha sitting on the edge of the bed.

'Bloody hell! When did you last buy any new underwear?'

Martha looked down at her bra.

'About 1997,' she said. She noticed a large pink envelope in Sally's hand.

'What's that?'

Sally handed it to Martha and sat down beside her on the bed.

'If you hadn't told me that you don't have a birthday, I'd think it was a birthday card!'

Martha opened the envelope; she knew it would be from Sledge. Christmas and birthdays, he always sent a card; no news, no message, no reminiscences. Just his name and the name of his latest wife and ever-expanding tribe of children.

The card had a picture of Elvis on the front with *A Hunka, Hunka, Birthday Love* written in large pink letters across the top.

'I knew it!' Sally threw her arms around Martha, crushing her to her ample bosom in a huge hug. 'Happy birthday!'

'Hello, Martha. Are you there?'

Before Martha had a chance to disentangle herself, Ranjit walked into the room.

'Martha, you must come quickly . . .' He stopped and covered his eyes. 'Oh, Ms. Morgan, I am so sorry. I didn't know. I didn't realise. Oh my goodness, I should have knocked.'

Martha looked at Sally, who still had her arms around her, and then down at her underwear.

'I know what you're thinking,' Sally said to Ranjit.

'I'm not thinking anything.' Ranjit had covered his eyes and was trying to walk backwards through the door but instead he was backing into the wall. 'But there's a lot of it about at the moment.'

'It's not like that, Ranjit.' Martha pulled herself away from Sally.

'She's not my type.' Sally gave Martha a nudge. 'Not in that old bra anyway.'

Martha pulled the sheet around herself; Sally helped her arrange it so that she was covered up.

'It's alright. I'm decent now.'

Ranjit tentatively uncovered his eyes.

'What was it you were trying to tell me?' Martha asked.

'I just wanted to tell you that we need you up at the house.'

Martha sighed. 'I was about to go and get the dinner. Only pizzas I'm afraid but I'll be as quick as I can.'

'It's not about the dinner.' Ranjit wrung his hands. 'I think it would be best if you come to the house first.'

'Is it an emergency?'

He hesitated, and then began nodding vigorously.

'Yes, it is a very big emergency indeed.'

Chapter 32

Friday

Martha opened one eye. Light pierced her skull like a laser and she became aware of a thumping beat of pain inside her head. She swallowed. Her mouth felt as though it had been rubbed with sandpaper and her tongue seemed to have swollen to twice its usual size. Martha realised that she was fully dressed; her trousers twisted uncomfortably and her T-shirt stuck to her back. She closed her eye and shifted; her leg sent a jolt of pain up to meet the pain in her head.

A loud snuffling noise seemed to intensify the pain. It was followed by a grunt and a prolonged moan. Martha's first thought was that there was some sort of animal in her room. It happened again and she opened both eyes just a fraction. She shut them quickly, trying to process what she had seen. Carla's face was inches from her own. Martha re-opened her eyes, slowly this time. Carla was in profile, mouth wide open, a thin line of saliva dribbling from the corner. She appeared to be wearing a pair of children's plastic swimming goggles. Another snore reverberated through the slice of air between Martha and the sleeping woman.

'Hi,' a voice said from the end of the bed.

Martha peered downwards. Elodie lay at the bottom of the bed, half covered by a floral quilt. She was propped up on one elbow looking at her phone.

'Wi-Fi's working.' She smiled at Martha. 'I'm just putting some pictures onto Instagram.'

'Too loud,' another voice. Martha tried to move her eyes towards it, but her head hurt too much.

'Alice has a hangover,' Elodie whispered towards Martha.

With difficulty Martha turned to see Alice lying on the pillow on her other side. The girl's normally pink cheeks were very pale and one arm was thrown across her eyes.

'I don't feel very well.'

Slowly Martha began to pick out objects in her limited line of sight. A painting of a row of poplar trees, an elaborately carved dressing table, thick embroidered curtains hanging at a mullioned window. She realised that this was not her little bedroom in the chapel or even her peacock-coloured bedroom in the house. From somewhere in her fuzzy brain she recalled that this was the room she'd furnished for her mother's visits; yellow walls, an enormous wooden bed from an auction in Brontome, a mahogany chest of drawers and matching wardrobe from an antique shop in Périgueux. This was the room that Alice and Josh were sharing. But why was she in it and why was she in bed with two women and a teenage girl? The more she thought, the more her head hurt. Martha pulled the quilt over her face to block the sunlight coming through the open curtains; she wondered what had ever possessed her to paint the walls that dazzling colour.

A crashing noise came from somewhere in the distance, followed by a *Merde!*

Martha peered out from under the quilt.

'Oh, that's just Pierre.' Elodie didn't look up from her phone. 'He's cleaning cake off the ceiling.'

'Cake?' Martha had difficulty speaking; her tongue seemed to fill her mouth. 'Pierre?'

'He and Sally had to sleep in my room.' Elodie sounded nonchalant. 'They were much too drunk to drive back to the village.'

'Cake? Pierre?' Martha repeated, pulling back the quilt from her face. 'Drunk?'

'Don't you remember last night?' Elodie looked up and grinned. 'It was epic!'

*

Martha remembered being in the chapel with Sally. She remembered Ranjit saying there was an emergency. She remembered throwing on a T-shirt and trousers and rushing up the path.

'I think I know what this is about,' she'd muttered to Sally, who followed behind. In her mind she prepared herself for an interrogation about the missing diamond ring and possibly missing laptops, wallets, credit cards and goodness knows what else.

Ranjit had ushered them towards the house. It was very dark.

A flickering lantern lit the way across the gloomy patio.

'Is there another power cut?' Martha called to Ranjit.

He didn't answer, instead he guided Martha through the kitchen door into the pitch-black room. The smell hit Martha first, a delicious warm aroma that reminded her that she hadn't eaten a thing all day. Then there was a scuffling noise and the room was flooded with light and cheers and *Happy Birthday!* shouted at the tops of voices, Noah and Reuben screaming it out until Martha's ears buzzed.

Alice embraced her followed by Flora, and Zac held up her hand and gave Martha a high five.

'Congratulations, Mrs. M.'

Elodie showed Martha a long banner on the wall that she'd made with the boys. *Happy Birthday Martha* was written in large letters and coloured in with scratchy felt-tip pens. At each end they'd drawn rabbits; the left-hand rabbit seemed a bit more like a vampire.

'I did that one.' Noah was jumping up and down with excitement, pointing at the fang-toothed bunny.

Martha stared around her at the smiling faces and wondered if she was still dreaming.

'How did you know?'

'Ah, that was me, I'm afraid.' Max stepped forward. 'I couldn't resist telling the others it was your birthday, and then Alice wanted to make you a cake and we were all up for a party to thank you for all your help and hospitality.'

'Help?' Martha repeated doubtfully. 'Hospitality?' She wasn't sure she had been that hospitable – she certainly hadn't felt it for most of the week.

'We drew you a card.' Reuben handed her a folded piece of paper with a child's interpretation of *Le Couvent des Cerises*, the roof tiles picked out in accurate crookedness. There were even some on the ground.

'Look at the cake!' Noah pointed at the table. Martha turned and saw a tall and slightly wonky chocolate cake, oozing cream from its many layers. It was covered in a pyramid of sugar-frosted cherries; each one sparkled, jewel-like, in the electric light.

'It was a joint creation,' Alice said.

'Even I helped,' Max added. 'And I've never baked a cake in my life.'

'He spilt the flour,' Reuben said.

'Everywhere,' said Noah.

Martha looked at his shirt – that explained the white powder.

Max laughed.

'The layers didn't rise properly,' Alice said. 'That's why it looks squiffy.'

'Noah kept opening the oven door,' said Elodie. 'He was very excited about eating it!'

Suddenly there was the thump of rap music as Zac turned on his speakers.

'Let's get this party started!' he shouted.

'Stop!' Ranjit signalled that he should turn the music off. 'Give Martha a chance to speak.'

Martha gripped the edge of the table. Surely she wouldn't be expected to give a speech? She glanced at the door.

Sally had been standing at the entrance to the kitchen, watching the scene with a huge smile on her face. She stepped forward and linked her arm through Martha's, as though she knew Martha would otherwise flee the room.

'Just say thank you,' she whispered. 'They've gone to a lot of trouble.'

Ranjit handed Martha a glass of red wine. Everyone was looking at her; she could feel her cheeks beginning to burn.

She took a deep breath.

'Well, I wasn't expecting this! What a kind gesture.' From the corner of her eye she saw Paula and Carla sitting on the sofa, they didn't look like it had been their idea at all. Martha couldn't see Paula's left hand but from her miserable expression she assumed that they still hadn't found the ring. Josh stood moodily against the kitchen table. It didn't look like it had been his idea either.

'I, I don't know what else to say.' Martha stumbled over her words, clutching the stem of her glass so tightly with her hand she felt it might break. The room was silent. Sally squeezed her arm.

'Thank you,' Martha said and took such a big swig of her wine that she nearly finished it.

'A toast to Martha.' Ranjit raised his glass. Everyone followed with a murmur of *Martha, Martha, Martha.*

Ranjit clinked his glass to call for silence again and began a speech of his own.

'Martha Morgan. You have made us welcome in your beautiful home.' He glanced down at his glass, suddenly looking a bit embarrassed. 'I know you may have overheard us sounding a little ungrateful earlier . . .' he paused. 'But we want you to know . . .' he nodded towards the women on the sofa and then put his hand on Josh's shoulder. 'That we are really very appreciative of everything you have done.'

'It's quite alright.' Martha felt her face flush with heat. 'You don't need to do all this for me.'

'Please,' Ranjit interrupted. 'We do. You have put up with all our requests and all the noise and chaos. You have saved two of the children's lives with your quick thinking and you have helped us when we needed extra beds for unexpected additions to our group,' he indicated Josh and then Carla, Flora, Zac and Max. 'You have cooked us delicious meals and most of all you have kindly given up your home for us to enjoy.'

Paula muttered something Martha couldn't quite hear. She saw Max frown at his daughter.

Ranjit raised his glass again. 'Martha Morgan, you were once a 1980s pop sensation – from what I'm told by my father-in-law, as it was a little before my time. But to us you are still a superstar!'

More cheering followed with a couple of whoops from Zac and a scream from Noah.

Sally put her arm around Martha. 'Hear that – you're a superstar!'

Ranjit topped up Martha's glass.

'It should be something sparkling,' he said. 'But with the road being blocked we didn't make it into town before the shops shut so we'll have to make do with the local red.'

'Hang on,' Sally said. 'I'll go back to the bar and get champagne. We've got crates of the stuff and, unfortunately, we never get the kind of customers who drink it.'

Martha held on to Sally's arm.

'Don't leave me,' she hissed.

Sally patted her hand. 'You'll be fine, just drink the wine and keep smiling. You never know, you might even enjoy it!'

Martha drank the wine as Sally had instructed. Her second glass not quite as quickly as the first, but it was swiftly followed by another one and then one more. She tried to smile as much as possible, but she was relieved when Sally returned. Pierre followed her into the kitchen carrying a box of champagne.

'I can't believe you got Pierre to come,' Martha said to Sally as they took out the bottles and put them on the table.

'I know! It's the first time I've known him shut the bar before midnight – the match wasn't even finished.'

Pierre put down the box of champagne and kissed Martha heartily on both cheeks.

'It is very important for your birthday. You are a good friend to us, especially to Sally. You have helped her so much when she is sad about . . .' He lowered his voice, 'our problems.'

Martha stared at him. She'd always felt completely useless when Sally had yet another miscarriage, painfully aware of her own ability to have a child then overwhelmed with guilt at her inability to care for it.

There followed a popping of corks and champagne was passed around, fizzing over the edge of glasses amidst increasing laughter.

Ranjit proposed another toast to Martha and 'Happy Birthday' was sung. A tealight had been placed on top of the cake and Martha could vaguely remember blowing it out and making a wish. Cake had been eaten then Zac had turned his music up and everyone, apart from Elodie, protested about it.

'Call that music.' Max went to fetch the old record player in its red leather case.

'This is more like it!' He opened the lid and held up *Motown Magic*.

Max plugged the record player into a nearby socket and let the needle drop onto the record. After an initial scratching the opening bars of 'Dancing in the Street' rang out.

'Martha and the Vandellas!' cried Flora as she began to tap her feet. 'Your namesake, Martha, come and dance.' She tried to take Martha's hand, but Martha pulled away. Flora shrugged and moved into the centre of the room, swivelling her ample hips and throwing her arms up in the air as Alice and Elodie pushed the large farmhouse table to one side, leaving Josh toppling backwards. Noah and Reuben followed Flora, copying her moves, rotating their hips exaggeratedly and clapping their hands in time to the music. Max joined Flora and the boys for 'Going to a Go-Go' and 'Papa Was A Rolling Stone'. With a smile Martha watched his dancing; long limbs moving in all directions like a crane performing a mating dance. Paula was watching Max too, shaking her head and peeping through her fingers, which were covering her eyes.

'Jimmy Mack' came on, the dancing grew more exuberant, the little boys leaping up and down, vying with each other to jump higher.

Martha stood on the edge of the room beside Ranjit and sipped her champagne wondering if it would seem rude to go outside and have a cigarette.

After a few minutes, Max appeared beside her. He leant against the table, legs sprawled in front of him, his hand clutched to his chest.

'They've worn me out,' he panted.

'You are a good dancer,' said Ranjit.

'I'm an embarrassing dancer.' Max nodded towards Paula sitting on the edge of the sofa with her arms folded and lips pursed.

Ranjit laughed. 'Ah, dad-dancing, the curse of the younger generation.'

'Embarrassing your offspring?' Max said between deep breaths. 'It's a parent's prerogative.'

Martha put down her glass on the edge of the table; the desire for nicotine was overwhelming.

'Excuse me,' she said to Max so that she could get past his long legs and escape.

'Of course.' He sprung to his feet and bowed a little. 'I'd be delighted.' He placed his hand on her arm and gently guided her towards the centre of the room.

'I wasn't asking you to dance.' Martha tried to pull away, but Zac had turned the music up and Max didn't seem to hear her above The Supremes.

'I just want to go outside,' she protested.

But Max was counting the beat, mouthing *one, two, three, one, two, three*, before he proceeded to lead Martha in a sort of slow waltz. Martha started to laugh. It seemed impossible to get away.

'I hope it's not too fast for you,' he said.

'I'm not that ancient,' Martha replied.

Max looked abashed. 'I wasn't suggesting that you are. I'm the one that can't keep up with those mad youngsters,' he nodded towards the pogoing children. 'I was only thinking of your . . .' Max nodded down towards Martha's leg.

'The champagne is working wonders,' she said.

'Let's go then!' Max grinned and started to speed up, until they were doing something more like a jive.

'Hang on,' Martha gasped. 'This is a bit *too* fast.' But Max kept twirling her round and round until her head spun and the faces in the room became a blur. She could just make out Ranjit who was jumping up and down with the children. And Carla and Paula still scowling on the sofa. When the song ended everyone stopped and

Noah unexpectedly catapulted himself off Ranjit's stomach. Ranjit fell over and the boys fell on top of him in a heap of arms and legs.

Carla rushed to scoop up Noah from the floor. He immediately began to cry.

'Reuben fell on my arm,' he sobbed. 'It hurts.'

'My poor boy.' Carla carried him back to the sofa and rocked him back and forth on her lap, while at the same time kissing his outstretched arm. Max went to help Reuben who was protesting that it wasn't his fault and Martha escaped to the edge of the room, flopping down on a chair, breathless.

She gulped down a glass of champagne which she was no longer sure was hers. The first bars of 'You Are The Sunshine Of My Life' wafted from the record player. Ranjit and Flora appeared to be doing some sort of ballet while Sally and Pierre were glued together in a fluid tango.

Stevie Wonder finished and Pierre and Sally threw themselves enthusiastically into 'Needle In A Haystack'. Flora and Ranjit followed, Flora's neat cone of hair collapsed as she jigged up and down to the beat; her purple braids flew out behind her like the tail feathers on a magnificent bird and she began to spin around.

'Come on, Carla,' she called out. 'Come and dance.' Carla shook her head.

'I have to look after Noah,' she said pointing at her son who was sprawled proprietorially across her lap. Carla stroked his hair, pushing back the tangle of curls from his angelic face. Despite his supine demeanor, Martha could see the way he watched his father.

Alice and Josh had been standing together by the table in its new position, Alice sipping her champagne while Josh repeatedly topped up his glass from the bottle beside him. Martha saw his eyes slide towards Carla but it was hard to tell if his expression was one of disdain or warmth. He put his arm around Alice, only to have her yanked away from him by Reuben.

'Come and dance, Alice.'

Liberated, Alice seemed to burst into life, raising up her arms and pirouetting round and round as the little boy followed her. Flora and Max joined them, and they all took it in turns to dance as outrageously as possible. Noah broke away from his mother's embrace to join in the fun. If a prize had been given for the most frenzied dancing, Noah would definitely have won, though Ranjit would have come a close second. She'd never quite seen anything like his dance moves before.

'It's called "The Running Man",' Ranjit shouted across to her. 'We used to do it at Uni. 'If you think that's cool, look at this one.'

Ranjit grabbed his neck with his left hand, and his left leg with his right hand and began hopping on the spot.

'Come on, Josh' Ranjit beckoned to Josh who was still loitering by the table. 'Don't you remember "The Sprinkler"?'

Josh shook his head, pouring more champagne.

'He hasn't got it in him any more,' Carla shouted.

Josh scowled at her then downed the champagne and strode across the room to join his friend. Within seconds the two men were performing a sequence of complex moves throwing their arms up and down and jigging around with only a modicum of coordination.

Meanwhile Zac and Elodie stood in the corner swigging champagne from a bottle they had purloined for themselves. Elodie seemed to be taking lots of photographs and the pair giggled as they looked through the results, no doubt disdainful of the older generation's idea of a party. But when the opening chords of 'The Shoop Shoop Song' began, the two teenagers started their own exaggerated 1960s-style routine. Max encouraged them to get out of the corner and soon the pair were dancing with everyone gathered around trying to follow their moves. Martha took the opportunity to step out onto the terrace for a cigarette.

The warm night air was still. She sniffed, relieved that the smell from the septic tank hadn't reached the terrace, and lit her cigarette. Someone had turned the swimming pool lights on. The illuminated water looked like a patch of turquoise silk. Martha thought she could almost reach out and pick it up, 'Like a handkerchief,' she said out loud and realised she was quite drunk.

Martha took a drag on her cigarette, her feet tapping in time to the distant music. How many years since she had danced? She blew a long stream of smoke towards the pool. There had been dancing on the night of her accident. She had held Owen in her arms, spinning him round and round as he laughed, mouth open wide, the white ridge of his first tooth breaking through his gum.

Martha leant against the stone balustrade and turned her face up to the moon. It looked like a perfect sphere in the dark blue sky. There had been a moon that night too. It had glinted on the frost, glimmered on the icy pavement. She remembered staring at it as the paramedics strapped her onto the stretcher and wheeled her towards the ambulance.

Suddenly above the music and the cicadas Martha heard the rustle of leaves behind her. She turned towards the dark bushes that lined the drive. Then there was another sound, the shuffle of gravel, the skip of a small stone. Martha thought she heard an intake of breath.

'Ben?' Martha peered into the gloom.

There was no answer.

'Ben?' she called again. Martha looked up and down. The pool light gave an eerie glow to the cars parked at the bottom of the drive. Martha could see that Ben's bike was still there. She peered back up towards the gates. Leaves rustled again, a crack like a twig snapping underfoot.

'Is that you?'

'Maybe it's the ghost.' A whispered voice made Martha spin around. Ranjit handed her a glass brimming with champagne. 'I thought you might need this.' Martha took the glass, but her eyes returned to the bushes; she'd been so sure that someone had been there.

'Also, I have a favour to ask.' Ranjit was still whispering.

'What is it?'

'I just wondered if you had any spare?' Ranjit nodded at the cigarette in Martha's hand.

234

Martha took the packet from her pocket and held it out. Ranjit took a cigarette and glanced anxiously at the kitchen door.

'Paula would be very cross.' He lit the cigarette and inhaled deeply. 'She worries about things.'

Martha resisted the urge to point out that this was an understatement. Instead she said, 'She must be very worried about her ring.'

Ranjit waved his hand dismissively. 'I keep telling her we will claim on the insurance, but she's still upset.' He paused. 'She never used to be like this, or not so bad. She was ambitious and motivated, maybe a little controlling – but she was happy. When Alisha died, she became the opposite.'

'Alisha?'

'We named her after my grandmother. Ten pounds when she was born. The midwife said she could join a rugby team.' Ranjit inhaled and blew out a long stream of smoke. 'She was four months old. Always laughing. She loved it when I blew raspberries on her tummy.' Ranjit stubbed his cigarette on the balustrade, specks of orange sparked into the darkness. 'It was only a slight cough, a bit of a temperature. Hardly anything. She seemed fine when Paula put her in her cot for the night.' Ranjit pinched his eyes. 'We'd never even heard of sepsis.'

Martha offered Ranjit another cigarette. He took it.

'You never imagine you can lose a child so easily.'

Martha had to look away.

'And now I feel that I have lost my Paula too. We never talk about Alisha but we never can forget. Paula is not the happy woman she was. There is someone sad in her place. I thought having another baby would make her better but : . . Maybe it was too soon. She is getting worse. I try to help but I can't get anything right.' He paused and looked across the dark garden. 'I miss her. I miss my wife.'

'Give her time,' Martha said quietly.

Ranjit turned to Martha with a sigh.

'Sorry, I am spoiling the party spirit.' He slipped the unlit cigarette into the pocket of his shirt. 'I'll save this for later if you don't mind?' He made a hushing gesture with his finger.

'It's alright, Ranjit.' Paula was silhouetted in the kitchen door-way, Tilly perched on her hip.

'Oh Paula, sorry, I was just . . .' Ranjit sounded flustered.

Paula walked across the patio and kissed her husband on the lips.

'I don't mind,' she said as she stepped back, her hand on Ranjit's cheek. 'Whatever helps.'

'Really?' Ranjit took the cigarette from his shirt pocket. 'I'm probably not going to smoke it for days.' Tilly reached out and grabbed it. Ranjit managed to snatch the cigarette back again before the baby had a chance to stuff it into her mouth.

Tilly let out a wail of protest at having her prize removed. She pulled at Ranjit's hair.

'Ow!'

Paula laughed. Her eyes seemed brighter, her smile wider. Martha could see a glimmer of the more carefree younger woman that Ranjit must have met at university.

'I'm not surprised you need cigarettes,' Paula said. 'I know I must be very hard to live with.'

'No,' Ranjit started to protest but Paula stopped him, taking his hand in her free one.

'I'm going to try . . .' She seemed to be searching for the right words. Her face became serious and she looked into Ranjit's eyes. 'I've been horrible to you the whole holiday.'

'No, darling, I wouldn't say that,' Ranjit protested.

'Yes, I have. As you know, this place isn't my dream holiday destin-ation.' Paula glanced at Martha. 'Sorry – but I can see that it is beautiful. I've realised that sometimes things might not be how you want them to be, but they can still be something good. It's a shame not to appreciate what you have in your life, or where you are.'

'Or who you are with,' added Ranjit.

'I have been a bitch,' Paula said quietly. 'It's just that I miss Alisha so much, I blame myself for what happened every day . . .'

'It wasn't your fault,' Ranjit interjected.

'It's OK.' Paula looked up into Ranjit's face. 'I'm not going to think that way any more. It's part of what I've realised since I've been here. I have so much to be thankful for – Tilly, Reuben, you – even my dad; it was so kind of him to come all this way to tell Reuben about Buster. I can't sacrifice his happiness or your happiness just because I am angry and sad. I need to move on. I will move on, or at least I'm going to try.'

Ranjit kissed her hand. 'We'll try together.' He stroked Tilly's pink cheek; she was still determinedly reaching for Ranjit's pocket. 'But there is something I must tell you, Paula.'

Against the soft rhythmic beat of the cicadas, Martha heard Paula whisper, 'Not tonight, don't tell me anything tonight.' She kissed him again. 'Tonight I think I'd very much like to dance.'

'Come on, you party poopers!' Josh stood in the kitchen doorway, swaying slightly, a glass of champagne in each hand. 'What are you doing out there? "Nutbush City Limits"!' With a whoop, Josh disappeared.

Ranjit held out one arm to Paula and the other to Martha.

'Come on, ladies, the party awaits.'

Back inside, Carla was the only one not dancing. Josh was bopping energetically in front of Alice, stealing glances at Carla to make sure she was watching. Alice was swaying half-heartedly, her eyes watching the door.

Zac and Elodie were still giving their masterclass, Flora, Max and the boys were their enthusiastic students, putting their own interpretations on the teenager's inventive moves.

Pierre and Sally didn't need lessons; they seemed to have their own intimate routine. Martha wondered if they practised in the bar and imagined Pierre sweeping Sally into his arms after the last customer had left, twirling her around the tables, collecting empty glasses as they went.

Ranjit took Tilly from Paula and swayed his daughter from side to side in time to the music. Tilly giggled every time he swooped her up and down and started to cry every time he stopped. Beside them Paula was dancing too, holding on to Tilly's chubby hand, stepping from side to side, an ever-broadening smile on her face.

Josh swayed over to Carla and tried to pull her from the sofa. She shook her head vigorously, clutching her glass to her chest.

'I'm not in the mood, darling.' Carla reached for the champagne bottle beside her.

Josh turned his attention to Martha instead. This time she didn't protest. She downed the rest of her glass and staggering slightly, stood up. Josh steadied her with an 'Oops-a-daisy, Birthday Girl' then led her onto the dance floor.

Halfway through the song Josh disappeared and returned with a bag brimming with the children's swimming things; swimsuits, armbands, snorkels and goggles. He placed it in the middle of the floor.

'It's a handbag,' he shouted. 'For us to dance around.'

'Very 1980s,' Ranjit called. 'Wouldn't you say, Martha?'

Martha didn't answer; she was watching Paula's face. The anxious expression seemed to be melting away and she looked ten years younger. Ranjit still held the giggling Tilly but he had one arm around his wife's shoulder as the three of them swayed from side to side. Ranjit performed a sudden spin, twirling his wife and baby round until they were all laughing. Reuben joined them, taking hold of his mother's hand.

'Spin with me,' he pleaded. 'Spin with me.' And they did. As Paula smiled down at her laughing son, Martha thought it was the first time she'd seen her take her eyes off Tilly for more than a few seconds all week.

Josh and Zac were now engaged in some sort of crazy dancing competition, arms and legs thrashing wildly in impossible directions – Josh seemed to have forgotten about impressing Alice or Carla. He bent down and fished a pair of goggles from the wicker bag. Putting them on he began to perform a sort of front-crawl dance move.

'Prat,' Martha saw Elodie mouth the words to Zac as she pointed to her father, but Zac was already reaching for the snorkel. Elodie shook her head but she was laughing. Zac handed her a pair of armbands, which she duly put on and joined in Josh's dance moves with Zac as if they were all in some underwater disco.

The song changed, Chuck Berry picked up the pace.

'Come on, Mummy,' Noah shouted.

'What the hell.' Gulping the last of her champagne, Carla stood up and walked, unsteadily, across to the dance floor. She started to sway, arms above her head, head thrown back so that her curls swung to and fro in time to the music.

'You go, girl!' Flora clapped her hands.

'She's not your girl, she's my wife.' Josh's words were slurred as he stepped in-between the two women. The goggles made him look like a startled frog.

'Now, now, you two, no fighting over me.' Carla turned around to face Josh tossing her hair over her shoulder before turning back to Flora, only to find that Flora had joined a conga line and was disappearing through the kitchen door onto the patio.

The song stopped.

'It's the end of the album.' Zac peered at the record player through the snorkel mask.

'Turn it over,' Josh called.

'What?' Zac shouted back.

'There's more on the other side.' Josh was swigging champagne from the bottle. 'It's vinyl not a CD! You youngsters have no idea.'

'Keep your beard on.' Zac grinned as he flipped the disc in his hands and placed the needle on the edge of the vinyl. 'I love vinyl, CDs are for grandads.'

'Grandads?' Josh looked incredulous. Ranjit laughed, he shouted something, but Zac turned the sound up making what Ranjit said inaudible. 'Signed, Sealed, Delivered, I'm Yours' blared out of the record player.

The conga line came back inside, and Martha found herself caught at the front, Flora's hands pressed to her waist. Max handed Martha something murky in a mug.

'We've run out of glasses,' he shouted above the music. 'I think you'll like it. I thought we could do with a cocktail and I found a load of spirits in the cabinet in the living room.'

'It's meant to be locked,' Martha said, but she took a swig of the sickly liquid; it burned her throat. She wanted to sit down but Flora and the rest of the conga line pushed her into the living room where Carla was dancing in front of Elvis, thrusting her hips towards his furry legs. Max peered inside the cocktail cabinet and pulled out an ancient bottle of Baileys. He took off the lid to give it a sniff. *Help*, Martha mouthed as she passed and Max took her by the arm and prised her away from the line.

'I need a rest,' she panted, but Gloria Gaynor was singing.

At first I was afraid . . .

Max began theatrically acting out the words, the bottle of Baileys still in one hand as though it was a microphone. Martha couldn't stop herself from laughing.

'Told you you'd enjoy it,' Sally shouted in Martha's ear as she twirled past with Pierre.

Then Max put the bottle down, took Martha's hands in his and suddenly she found she had all the energy in the world to dance again.

Chapter 33

Martha tried to remember more but the rest was a blur. She had vague memories of someone playing the piano and she thought at one point she had been wearing a hat, but every time Martha remembered something solid, the memory disappeared like a puff of smoke in a breeze.

'Coffee, ladies?' Flora appeared, tray of mugs rattling.

'Too loud,' whispered Alice.

Martha glanced at Flora's turquoise robe and closed her eyes.

Too bright, she wanted to say.

Elodie covered herself with the flowery quilt as though she didn't want to be seen.

Carla went on snoring, mouth wide open. The swimming goggles were misted up and her hair a tangled mess above the elastic strap.

Flora set the tray down on the bedside table.

'This will see you right, girls.' She began pouring coffee from a big enamel pot, adding spoonfuls of sugar to the mugs and copious amounts of milk.

'Black,' Martha mumbled as she struggled to sit up, her throat hurt, speaking was an immense effort. 'No sugar.'

'You need it sweet and white today, girl!' Flora handed her a steaming coffee.

Martha whispered 'Thank you', grateful for the hot sugary liquid.

'You can go and find Zac now.' Flora addressed the bulge at the bottom of the bed that was Elodie. The glow of the girl's screen radiated through the quilt giving her whereabouts away. 'He's still cross that I marched him off to the camper van so early.'

Elodie pulled back the quilt, her cheeks flushed bright pink. Clutching her phone, she slipped off the bed and disappeared from the room.

'Don't worry, Martha, when I found them in the chapel it was more innocent than I feared.' She passed a mug to Alice. 'All Zac was doing was persuading the girl to eat a massive slice of chocolate cake – and Lord knows that child needs some fat on her bones.'

'Why don't you have a hangover?' Alice asked.

'Me? I can drink champagne for ever and feel just fine the next day. If I'd touched those cocktails Max was making, I'd be like you.'

'Oh no,' Alice groaned. 'The Dordogne Detonators.'

'Uh-huh,' Flora nodded. 'And The Villa Killers. And The Cherry Bomber Slings, and The Ghostly G&Ts and then after Martha's performance we had the Singing Sensation Slides – vodka and crème du menthe with a dash of Baileys.'

Alice flopped back onto her pillow, then sat back up as a loud snorting sound reverberated around the room.

'Oh my God.' Alice peered over to the other side of the bed. 'Is that Carla? Why is she here? Why is she wearing goggles?'

'What performance?' Martha asked.

Her words were drowned as Carla snorted and snuffled before sitting bolt upright and manically starting to scratch at her eyes.

'Get off! Get off! Help me!'

'Hey, it's alright.' Flora removed the goggles as gently as she could while Carla batted at her hands.

Carla lay back, panting on the pillows; beads of sweat dotted her forehead; her hair wilder than before.

'I thought my eyes were being sucked out by an alien. It was horrific.' She groped for Flora's hand and clung to it. Martha slurped her coffee and tried to stifle a laugh, which turned into a splutter, and then a cough. Carla turned her head and looked askance at Martha.

'What are you doing here?' Then she noticed Alice. 'And you? What are you doing in my bed?'

242

'This is *my* bed,' Alice answered. 'I've been sleeping here with Josh all week.'

'With Josh?' Carla sounded as though the idea was highly unlikely. Then she peered closer at Alice. 'Oh yes, of course. You're his *girlfriend*. I didn't recognise you. You don't look very well.'

'You're not looking so good yourself,' Alice said weakly.

Carla took another deep breath. 'Well, I am feeling a bit fluey.'

Flora let out one of her long, rich chuckles.

'I think hung-over is the word, sweetie.'

Carla closed her eyes. 'I only had two glasses of champagne.'

Flora shook her head and poured more coffee.

Noah burst into the room. 'Daddy's lying down outside!' He jumped onto a little art deco armchair Martha had bought from a Ribérac antique shop and from there bounced onto the bed. Martha's head pounded from the motion and coffee sloshed onto the sheet.

'Oh, my lovely boy, come here.' Carla opened her arms and Noah threw himself on top of her. 'Is Daddy alright?'

'Yes, Max is with him.' Noah squirmed his way down the bed between his mother and Martha. 'They are both lying down. Max says everyone was "fecking poleaxed" last night.'

'Max said that to you?' Carla's eyes widened. 'I'll have to have a word with him about his language.'

'No. I heard him say it to that Frenchman. When he was up the ladder scraping the cake off the ceiling.'

'How did the cake get on the ceiling . . .?' Martha managed to mumble.

'It wasn't me,' said Noah quickly.

'Well, that's not strictly true, is it?' said Flora.

'I think it was Josh who started cake juggling,' Alice said weakly.

'And Zachery and Ranjit wanted to see how high they could throw the slices,' said Flora. 'But then Noah and Reuben stood on the work-surface and threw cake at the ceiling.'

'We were making a world map!' said Noah.

Martha's brain felt addled.

'On my kitchen ceiling?'

'Oh, my little cherub, you are so creative.' Carla cuddled Noah tight against her. 'Just like me.'

Noah wriggled out of his mother's embrace. 'Why were you swimming with no clothes on, Mummy?'

Carla frowned and then she laughed.

'I remember! We were skinny-dipping.'

Alice put her hand over her face.

'I saw your boobies,' Noah pointed at Alice, then at Flora. 'And yours.'

'I thought you'd gone to bed,' Flora said.

'And I saw you.' He stopped and regarded Martha with serious eyes. 'I saw your funny leg.'

Martha felt like she might be sick.

Carla laughed, 'Oh yes, it's coming back to me now. Paula jumped in too.'

Martha closed her eyes. Carla chirped on. 'It was so funny when that Suzie woman from the village flung herself onto the lilo and it rolled over and she thought she was trapped underneath.'

'Sally,' corrected Martha.

'Sally, Suzie, whatever. My God, I've never seen such huge tits, has she had them done? I've got a great byline for an article about boob jobs that have gone too far – *My Cups Overfloweth*.'

'Mummy,' Noah interrupted. He looked up at Carla with his huge blue eyes.

'Yes, darling.' Carla smiled benignly and coiled his hair around her finger.

'I saw you kissing Daddy behind a bush.'

Carla let go of Noah's curl; it pinged back like a golden spring.

'You were probably dreaming.'

'Reuben was with me. We both saw.'

There was a pause. Alice stared down at the quilt, pushing her nail along the stitching between the printed roses. Flora's smile melted away. She sat down heavily on the bed and sighed.

'Oh Carla.'

Carla rubbed her eyes; they were rimmed in red from wearing the tight goggles all night.

'Maybe I had a bit more champagne than I thought.'

'There you are, Martha.' Sally appeared in the doorway holding Tilly. 'Look who I managed to prise out of her mum's arms.' She gave Tilly a little squeeze and Tilly let out a squeal of delight. 'Isn't she gorgeous?'

'Hi Suzie,' said Carla.

Sally looked at the four women on the big double bed.

'Bloody hell, what's going on here then?'

'Not what it looks like,' Martha said faintly.

'I can see that. You all look too ill to be up to anything naughty. It must have been those cocktails.'

'Please don't talk about the cocktails.' Alice's face went paler. Sally shook her head.

'Max was a right Tom Cruise with that shaker, we should get him to do a special night in the bar.'

'You don't seem very hung-over, Suzie,' said Carla.

'Sally,' Martha muttered again.

'I only had one Cherry Bomber Sling,' Sally said. 'Pierre stopped me having any more after I had that panic attack in the pool.'

'I'm hungry,' Noah announced.

'So am I,' the voice came from under the bed. Reuben crawled out holding an iPad.

'How long have you been under there?' Flora asked.

'Since Elodie showed me how to use the Internet,' Reuben replied. 'I've been looking at grumpy cats on YouTube. And dogs that wee in toilets.'

'Your mum will probably have some croissants in the oven by now,' Carla said. 'You and Noah should go and find her in the kitchen.'

'I'm afraid there are no croissants in the oven today.' Sally jiggled Tilly up and down on her hip. 'Because I persuaded this little beauty's mummy that I could look after her for an hour while she took Tilly's daddy a nice cup of tea in bed.' She gave Tilly a kiss on the cheek.

Carla rolled her eyes. 'Then I suppose I'll have to get up and get the children something to eat.'

Martha felt relief flood through her as Carla got off the bed.

'Carla, I think we need to talk.' Flora's voice was serious as she followed Carla and the children out of the room.

'I'd better go and give this one back to her mum,' Sally said. 'Pierre and I will be off soon to open up the bar for lunch.'

Martha raised her hand weakly as Sally disappeared. She looked at Alice.

'Are you OK?'

'My head,' Alice groaned and turned over so her face was buried in the pillow.

Martha stared at the ceiling trying to stop the pounding in her own head. She focused on a mottled patch in the corner and made a mental note to ask Ben to look at it later.

Ben.

'Did Ben come back last night?' she asked Alice.

The young woman rolled onto her back, eyes open, staring at the ceiling too.

'I made such a fool of myself,' she said.

Martha turned her head. Alice looked like she might cry.

'I flung myself at him like some sort of drunken bimbo.'

'What happened?' Martha asked.

'The children weren't the only ones who saw Carla and Josh kissing. I was outside, getting some air. Ben was walking up the path. He asked where you were, I told you were dancing and tried to persuade him to come up to the house, I told him about Max's cocktails, I told him they were amazing.' Alice shuddered. 'Ben was just about to follow me onto the terrace when there was a noise in the bushes and Josh and Carla stumbled onto the path with their arms around each other. They didn't even notice us as they staggered past. Ben asked me if I was alright and I just sort of lunged at his face and tried to kiss him.'

'What did he do?'

'He kissed me back for a few seconds, at least I think he did, but

246

then he stopped and said that things were very complicated and then he just left me standing there. I was so embarrassed. He must have thought I was reacting to seeing Josh with Carla, but it wasn't like that at all. It was a relief, to be honest. I knew it was over with Josh days ago. I wanted to tell Ben how much I liked him, but I just did it all too fast and too drunkenly. The last thing I remember is him zooming off up the drive.' Alice covered her eyes with both her hands. 'I feel so stupid!'

Martha took a deep breath.

'There are things about Ben that I think you need to know.'

Chapter 34

'Why do I always pick the losers?' Alice had groaned repeatedly. Martha found herself trying to placate her with the same phrase she used to say to Cat after village discos and drunken Saturday nights in Abertrulli.

'Perhaps you have to kiss a few frogs . . .'

Alice hid her face amongst the pillows. 'But all my frogs turn into toads.'

'I was taken in too.' Martha rubbed her eyes. 'He seemed like such a nice man. I should have realised that he was too kind and helpful, he was bound to have an ulterior motive.'

'I should never have come on this holiday,' moaned Alice. 'I really just wanted to escape my sister's stupid party. I couldn't bear the thought of all my parents' friends telling me how charming my little cupcakes were and then turning round to my sister to congratulate her on scaling the highest mountain in the world.' Alice paused and took a deep breath. 'For charity.' She took another deep breath. 'With her fiancé!'

'Oh Alice.' Martha patted her hand. 'You mustn't compare yourself to your sister. We all have different talents.'

'Mmm,' Alice mused. 'Dumpy baking blogger versus athletic doctor with a gift for music and finding just the right man!'

'Come on,' said Martha. 'I need to survey the party damage and you need to get up and get some fresh air.'

'I can't.' Alice covered her face with her hands. 'I think someone has actually nailed my head to the pillow.'

*

As Martha limped back down the drive towards the chapel the Angelus bell rang out for midday mass.

No more drinking, Martha thought as she reached the bottom of the path. *No more dancing.*

Her head ached more than her leg and her leg ached a lot.

Martha stared up and down the drive. Max's motorbike, with its slightly skew-whiff mirror and dented fender was there but Ben's motorbike was nowhere to be seen. Martha peered down towards the cherry orchard. The tent was gone and the rucksack too. Alice had been right; it looked as if Ben really had left for good.

The small pile of jewellery glinted in the shafts of sunlight streaming through the open door of the chapel. It was the first thing that Martha noticed as she entered the kitchen. She picked up the diamanté necklace and then let it fall back onto the kitchen table. It was the jewellery from the rucksack and a few more things she hadn't found in the pocket. There was the cheap gold ring that her mother used to wear when she needed to appear to be married and a little jade dragon that Cat had given her for her eighteenth birthday. There was no sign of Paula's diamond ring. Ben had obviously kept that and decided to give Martha back what he considered worthless. He probably thought he was being generous. But Martha didn't want them back. They felt sullied, spoilt.

She swept the glittering heap into her shopping basket; she would give it to one of the junk shops that lined the twisting backstreets of the village.

Martha pressed her hand to her aching head. There was something sticky in her hair. Looking at her fingers, Martha found bits of chocolate cake and cherry jam.

She went into the bathroom and ran the shower. Her clothes from the day before were still strewn across the floor. As she waited for the water to warm she undressed, then gathered all the clothes and shoved them into the linen basket. Something crinkled amongst the fabric. Searching amongst the T-shirts and trousers, Martha pulled out the letter from the bank; creased and damp it drooped in her hand and seemed to signify defeat. Even if the guests did write a good review and Dordogne Dreams put her permanently on their books, in reality she could never get enough money to pay what she owed the bank. She crushed the letter into a ball.

'Bugger off and leave me alone.' She threw the ball of paper through the door as hard as she could.

'Ow!' a man's indignant voice called from the kitchen. 'I only came to say goodbye.'

Martha turned off the shower and stood naked in the middle of the tiny tiled room. The voice had sounded like Max. She tried to remember if Max had said he'd be leaving in the morning. All she could remember was the dancing and the laughing, Max jitterbugging her around the living room. Had he really picked her up in his arms? She suddenly remembered it was Max who had helped her to the bed when she'd felt too dizzy to stand up; he'd made her a cup of tea and told her a story about a donkey his father had once won in a raffle. Wrapping herself in a towel, Martha peered around the door.

There was no one there. Martha went to the front door and stepped out onto the patch of bare earth. She could see Max disappearing around the corner.

'Hey,' she shouted, hobbling on the stones towards the path in her bare feet.

Max stopped and turned.

He raised his hand in a wave. 'Don't worry, I'm buggering off.'

'I didn't mean you. I meant . . . It doesn't matter who I meant. But I didn't mean you.'

He smiled. 'You're a good shot.' He held up the crushed envelope. 'You got me right on the nose.' He threw the paper ball back to her and Martha caught it but nearly dropped her towel.

As Martha regained her grip on the towel, Max took a few steps backwards, averting his eyes.

'Don't let me stop your bath.'

'Shower,' Martha corrected. She paused. 'Are you really leaving?'

Max nodded towards his bike. Martha noticed the panniers neatly positioned on the back, his helmet waiting on the seat.

'I think it's best I leave Paula and Ranjit to have the last day of their holiday in peace. They don't need me.'

'I thought you were all having such a good time together last night. Paula seemed to have finally relaxed.'

'Ah well, she needs to make the best of it.' Max looked down at his boots, his toe pushed at the dry earth on the path dislodging a small pebble. 'Ranjit's got some news to break when they get home.'

'What is it?'

Max sighed. 'I don't want to say, but things are going to get tough for them.'

'Ranjit told me about their baby.'

'Poor Alisha, it was a tragedy. I think that's why Ranjit . . .' Max stopped, as though he didn't want to give away too much. 'I think that's why Paula's so anxious around Tilly, I think she thinks it's going to happen again.'

Martha clutched the towel tightly to her chest.

'At least she has you. As you said, it's the being there that's important.'

'Well, apparently it's best that I'm not *here*.' Max gestured around him. 'I've promised Ranjit I won't tell Paula myself, and I think Ranjit will find it awkward having me hanging around looking reproachful.'

'About what?'

Max ran his hand through his long hair.

'I wish I could tell you. I feel like I'm such a useless parent. I'd love to ask you for your advice.'

Martha squeezed the crushed-up envelope in her hand.

'You're a much better parent than me: running away, hiding in a convent.'

Max looked apologetically at Martha. 'Ah now, you know I didn't mean to imply that you were living . . .'

'Well, I think you might be right,' Martha interrupted. 'Maybe I have been living like a nun. Worse than living like a nun. I don't even have a higher calling – apart from nicotine. At least you were always there for Paula in the past . . .' Her voice trailed away as she swallowed; a hard lump had formed in her throat and the infuriating tears threatened to start. She took a deep breath and more words came tumbling out. 'I didn't even have the strength to stick around and fight for my child. I could have challenged the custody decision, showed Andrew that I could be a good mother. But instead I hid. I wallowed in self-pity. I stuffed myself with drugs. Pretended I was waiting for the right time. I thought that buying rugs and paintings and Rococo chairs would make a good home for my son, when I eventually saw him – as if it would make up for not being there on his first day at school, his birthdays, all those Christmas mornings. I don't even have the courage to be there for him now.' She stopped and whispered the last words. 'And that makes me wonder what the point of my life has been.'

'Martha . . .' Max started to speak, his expression full of sympathy.

'I need to have my shower,' Martha interrupted.

'Ah, Martha, you shouldn't be feeling like that about yourself.' Max's eyes looked concerned.

Martha shifted and felt the small stones on the path dig into the soles of her bare feet. She wiped her eyes with the corner of the towel.

'Sorry, I shouldn't have said anything, you're the one with all the worries about your daughter.'

'Ah, no, we all have our worries.'

'But you don't need me wallowing in self-pity.'

Max stepped forward; he was just a couple of feet away. 'What you said just now . . .'

'Please, just forget it.'

'I'd like to tell you something.'

'Please, don't.'

'If I tell you, you might feel better.'

Martha shook her head. 'I think you should just go.'

Max sighed. 'Do you mean just bugger off and leave you alone?'

Martha's voice cracked. 'Yes.'

'OK, I'll leave you to it.' Max held out his hand. 'It was very nice to meet you.'

Martha remained very still, clutching her towel.

Max let his hand fall and turned and walked towards the bike. When he reached it, he picked up his helmet and straddled the seat.

'The new song is great,' he called, just before pulling the helmet over his head.

'What?'

The sound of the motorbike engine starting up drowned Martha's voice.

The bike began to move away.

'What new song?' Martha shouted, but it was too late. The bike was going up the drive. As it reached the top, Max raised his hand in a salute, then disappeared through the gates.

The stones dug deeper into Martha's feet as the sound of the engine faded. After a few minutes she saw the bike again, a tiny toy on the twisting road. It turned a bend and then it was gone. Martha watched the road, willing Max to come back, wanting to apologise for being so rude, wanting to thank him for looking after her the night before, for being so much fun. But the road remained empty. After a few minutes, Martha turned and began to slowly pick her way through all the painful pebbles back to the door.

Chapter 35

Martha showered quickly, dressed and made her way up the path towards the house, all the while trying to ignore the empty feeling in her heart she had had since Max had left.

She passed the pool. Ranjit was in the water while Tilly bobbed about in a blow-up yellow rubber ring. She was being pulled around by Reuben, squealing with delight as her brother twirled her in a circle and her father splashed her. Paula lay on a sunlounger laughing at the chaotic scene. They looked like the perfect family.

'Hi Martha,' Paula called out. 'You were spectacular last night.'

Martha stopped.

Ranjit said something too but Martha couldn't hear above the noise of Tilly's squealing. She carried on towards the house.

Noah was on the terrace trying to coax Pippa from under the table with a piece of chocolate cake.

'Leave her alone,' Martha scolded as she scooped the rabbit up and went inside the house.

In the kitchen, Flora and Carla were making an attempt at washing up. Neither of them seemed to notice Martha looking around the cluttered surfaces for her cigarettes with Pippa under one arm.

'I wouldn't mind so much if it wasn't for all the awful things you've said about him.' Flora banged a pile of dirty plates onto the draining board with a clatter.

Carla stood at the sink, her arms submerged in bubbles.

'People change,' she said, dreamily.

'They certainly do!' Flora threw a squeezed lemon into the rubbish bin and walked out.

In the living room, Elvis was wearing a sailor hat at a jaunty angle. Empty glasses covered every surface. The cocktail cabinet doors were open, the contents of it largely gone. On top of the bar empty bottles were tipped over and flies buzzed around a congealed puddle of crème de menthe.

Sally and Pierre came down the staircase. Pierre took the sailor hat from Elvis's head.

'We did not spot this one.'

'We've put the hats and records back in the cupboard as tidily as we could,' said Sally.

'Hats? Records?'

Pierre grinned.

'It is the big honour to be wearing the cowboy hat from 'Roller Coaster Love' video last night.'

'Really?' Martha tried to imagine Pierre in the large pink cowboy hat covered in glitter.

'And it is also the honour to be hearing you sing.'

Martha swallowed. 'Sing?'

'You were amazing.' Sally touched Martha's arm.

'What did I sing?'

'Come on, Sally.' Pierre was looking at his watch. 'It is the festival tonight. We must be back to get ready for the business.' He took Martha by the shoulders and kissed her on both cheeks. *'Merci pour tout le plaisir.'* He handed her the sailor hat and turned to open the French windows.

'I'll see you later,' Sally said as she followed Pierre outside. 'Are you coming into town for the fireworks?'

'I doubt it.' Martha put the hat back on Elvis's head and started to climb the stairs. On the landing she put Pippa down on the floor and let her hop along the corridor till they reached the yellow bedroom.

Alice still lay in the enormous wooden bed, her head covered by the quilt. But she wasn't alone. Beside her Josh was stretched out on top of the covers. He wore sunglasses and there were grass stains on his Prada shirt.

'The last thing I ever wanted to do was to hurt you, Alice.'

'You haven't.' The flowery quilt muffled Alice's response.

'I hope you don't think I'm some sort of *player*,' Josh continued, making quotation marks with his fingers around the word player.

'I don't.'

'If I'd known Carla still had feelings for me, I would never have asked you to come here in the first place.'

'Sorry to interrupt,' said Martha. Josh looked towards her and took off the sunglasses revealing bloodshot eyes.

'Can I help?' he asked.

Alice lowered the quilt. 'Hi Martha.' She squinted against the light. 'Sorry I got so upset earlier.'

'It was perfectly understandable, Ben seemed like such a lovely young man.'

'Ben?' Josh looked from Alice to Martha and back again. 'What about Ben?'

'I kissed him,' Alice said. 'Last night. I snogged him. It was lovely.'

Josh sat up and glared at Alice. 'You did what?'

Alice looked at him through her half-closed eyes. 'I don't think you're in any position to be annoyed.'

Josh swung his legs off the bed and stood up.

'I can't believe this! I bring you on a holiday,' he folded his arms, 'I introduce you to my children, and my best friends. I pay for everything . . .'

'I paid for my own ferry ticket, and our room at the hotel the first night, and lunch the other day, and all the beers and cups of coffee you've had.'

'I drove you down here in my brand-new sports car.'

'It's hardly brand new, is it?' said Martha. Josh ignored her.

'I hope you haven't done anything more than snog the odd-job man, you don't know where he's been.'

'Just shut up, Josh,' Martha said, suddenly spotting the cigarette packet on the dressing table.

Josh pulled himself up so that he was just a little taller.

'How dare you?' He stared at Martha. 'You can't come barging into my room that I've paid good money for and start telling me to shut up.'

'You haven't.' Martha picked up the cigarette packet and peered inside it.

'Haven't what?'

'Haven't paid for the room.' Martha gave the cigarette packet a little shake. It was definitely empty. 'None of you have paid for anything.'

Josh made a series of huffing, squeaking, stuttering sounds.

'Martha is right,' Alice said. 'Ranjit got that special deal so you didn't have to pay up front and you've gone on and on about all the things wrong with the house that meant you wouldn't have to pay at all. I even saw you twisting the taps to make the leaking worse. Basically, you'd much rather have a lovely free holiday than pay Martha any money for her hard work. And that's the worst thing about you, Josh. Not your vanity, or your pomposity, or the bald patch at the back of your head. You are mean.'

Josh made more squeaking sounds, patting the back of his head.

'You needn't think there's any future for us when we get back to London, Alice.' He twisted trying to see the back of his head in the dressing-table mirror. 'As far as I'm concerned, we are officially finished.' With a final pat of the back of his head he left the room. Martha and Alice listened to him thumping his way along the corridor and down the stairs, making a surprising amount of noise for a man in espadrilles.

'Are you OK?' asked Martha, turning to Alice.

Alice struggled to sit up, then flopped back down against the pillow.

'I'm fine. It was worth snogging Ben, even if he is a loser – the look on Josh's face was more satisfying than anything else he's done for me in the last few weeks.'

'OMG, you're nearly viral!' Elodie burst through the door holding out her phone, closely followed by Zac.

'You've got to look at this!' Elodie held the screen inches from Martha's face.

'I put it on Snapchat and someone uploaded it onto YouTube and you've had ten thousand views already, and people have shared it on Facebook and Twitter and Instagram.' Elodie sounded breathless.

Martha peered at the shaky screen. She couldn't make the image out.

Alice got out of bed.

'Wow!' She steadied Elodie's phone with her hand. 'Can you put the sound up?'

Martha could hear a piano being played, someone singing. A woman. The voice was slightly husky, but it was clear and strong.

> *As you drew your breath I made my wish*
> *As you held my hand I gave my kiss*

Martha recognised the words.

> *I wasn't there to hear your cries*
> *But every step I take you're with me*
> *The child in my eyes*

Martha looked more closely at the screen. The woman was wearing a red trilby hat and sitting at a grand piano.

'Where did this come from?' Martha snatched the phone from Elodie's hand and held it further from her eyes so she could focus better.

'You were amazing.' Elodie was quivering with excitement. 'I thought you were good at the time, but you've had so many likes and shares and people are saying really cool things about you, shall I read some out?'

'No!' Martha's head swam. 'How did this happen? When . . .? Last night . . .?'

As Elodie started to explain, the memory of it all came flooding back. She had brought the On The Waterfront records from the cupboard and they'd danced and sung along until they'd exhausted every song the band had recorded. They'd got the hats out too; everyone had been wearing one.

'Then you sat down at the piano and began to sing,' said Zac. 'It was wicked, everyone went quiet.'

'I remember now,' said Alice. 'It was beautiful.'

'You made Paula and Ranjit cry,' Elodie said. 'And Paula's dad was wiping his eyes, and Zac was too.'

'Hey, man! No, I wasn't!'

Elodie giggled. 'I saw you!'

'OK.' Zac shrugged his narrow shoulders. 'It made me miss my mum.'

Martha stared at the screen, she found couldn't look away.

'Did you really write that?' asked Elodie when the song finished.

Martha nodded.

'Cool!' she and Zac said together.

'Now I really need a cigarette,' Martha said, crushing the empty packet in her hand. 'Who wants to come with me to the village.'

Chapter 36

The narrow streets were festooned with garlands of paper flowers, criss-crossing between the houses like a wonderful fishing net of colour, brilliant against the bright blue sky. Tubs of geraniums and lobelia had been placed on every corner and hanging baskets overflowed with petunias and trailing foliage. The market square had been laid out with trestle tables, and around the edge food stalls were being erected with the ringing clatter of metal poles and vendors exchanging cheerful chat. The surrounding shops had closed for the siesta, the residents resting behind their pale-blue shutters in preparation for the excitement of the festival and fireworks that evening. A few tourists wandered forlornly around, fruitlessly looking for something to do despite the heat.

In the corner of the square, Alice, Elodie and Zac sat outside the bar. Sally served a second round of coffees and put a bowl of nuts onto the table.

Flora emerged from the dark bar where she had been using the toilet.

'It's like an oven out here,' she said, sitting down on one of the ornate wrought-iron chairs. 'It can't be helping your headache, Alice.'

Alice mumbled something incomprehensible from behind a large pair of dark glasses.

Flora patted the young woman's hand.

Zac had persuaded his aunt to join the expedition into town. Flora had been sitting on the steps of the VW van, elbows on her knees, face in her hands, her beautiful smile more of a droop.

'Come on, Aunty Flo,' Zac had said. 'Grab your magic handbag and come with us for coffee.'

Martha fanned her face with a laminated menu and wondered if it might be the hottest day of the year so far. She'd left Pippa in the chapel with all the windows open but the door firmly locked.

'Hey, Martha Morgan, I see you on YouTube singing,' a man called out. He was setting up a large griddle for crepes. 'You are very good.'

Martha moved her chair into the shade.

Sally laughed as she disappeared inside. 'There's no hiding place now.'

'You are out there!' Zac trickled peanuts through his fingers into his mouth.

Martha sank down in her chair. 'I don't like it,' she muttered and lit a cigarette.

Since arriving in the village four people had complimented Martha on the song. The girl in the *tabac* even started singing it herself. She seemed to know the words. An old woman with a wizened apple face had leant out of a window and called, '*Belle chanson.*' A man up a ladder securing a chain of paper flowers had shouted out, 'When can I buy on iTunes?'

'You won't believe what people are saying about you on social media.' Elodie was scrolling down her phone.

'I don't want to know' Martha stubbed out her cigarette. She could imagine the comments. Then and now pictures all over Facebook. *Hasn't she let herself go!*

Elodie's eyes were widening.

'Listen to these comments. *A bewitching performance. Beautiful. Martha Morgan has touched my heart. I love Martha and her song.*' Elodie looked up. 'This is all on Twitter.' She looked back at the screen. 'Here's one that just says *Fanfuckingtastic.*'

'Can I see?' Martha sat up straighter and Elodie passed her the phone.

Breathtaking. Gorgeous. Martha skimmed through the comments. *Waited such a long time to hear from her again – worth every minute.*

'You see,' Alice grinned. 'Everybody loves you.'

'Isn't that the young man who works for you, Martha?' Flora pointed across the cobbled square. This time it was Alice who sank down in her chair, covering her face with a menu.

Martha turned and looked in the direction Flora was pointing.

Ben was on his bike, his helmet off, talking to a girl.

'Do you think that's his girlfriend?' Alice peered over the menu.

Martha had seen the girl before; she recognised the straggly pale hair and the floaty white dress. It was the girl that she had seen at Jean-Paul's house.

Ben took something out of his pocket and handed it to the girl. She slipped it into a battered-looking shoulder bag and gave a small package to Ben in return. They exchanged a few more words and Ben put his helmet back on, started up the bike and sped away down one of the small side roads.

The girl walked quickly across the square. She appeared not to notice the small group gathered round the table, peering into her bag as if checking its contents.

'Doing Jean-Paul's dirty work?' Martha said as the girl passed.

'Pardon?'

Martha nodded towards the street that Ben had disappeared down.

'I'm surprised you dare in broad daylight.'

The girl stopped. She stared at Martha.

'Sorry? I don't understand.'

'I saw you doing a drug deal with Ben.'

The girl tucked a strand of lank hair behind her ear.

'I am not doing a *drug* deal.' She emphasised the word drug. 'Didn't he tell you why he came here?'

A jangling ringtone emanated from the girl's bag. She reached into it, brought out her phone and began to speak quickly in French, twisting her hair between her fingers and looking anxiously around. She stopped talking and put the phone back in her bag.

'Why did he come here?' Martha asked.

The girl was already walking away.

'The black gold,' she called over her shoulder as her phone began to ring again. 'He wanted the black gold.' She began to run, the battered bag slapping against her thigh as she disappeared down a narrow alley.

'Black gold?' Flora looked around the table. 'What does that mean?'

'Is it a term for some sort of drug?' Alice looked at Zac.

'Hey! Don't ask me, man.'

'She said it wasn't drugs,' Martha said. 'Maybe he's not the thieving addict I assumed he was. But what else could it be?'

Alice put her chin in her hands.

'You can't deny he had a rucksack full of your jewellery. Wasn't some of that gold?'

'He's definitely a dodgy dude.' Zac used his finger to pick up the last few peanut crumbs from the bowl. 'Didn't you notice his tattoo?'

'He has lots of tattoos,' Martha said.

Zac sucked his finger and then wiped it on his T-shirt. Flora handed him a napkin.

'On his hand.' Zac indicated the space between his thumb and his forefinger. 'Five little dots. That's the sign.'

'The sign of what?'

'He's done time.'

Martha and Alice exchanged brief glances.

'He's been in prison,' Zac reiterated, as though they might not understand.

'You can tell from five dots?' Martha asked.

'Four walls.' Zac marked out the dots with his finger in the air again. 'And the one in the middle is the prisoner locked up inside.'

'How do you know these things, Zachery?' Flora tutted.

Elodie's phone vibrated on the table. She looked at the message.

'It's my dad. He says he and Mum are trying to talk but Noah's having a meltdown, can I come back?'

Chapter 37

They could hear the wailing even as the car bumped down the rocky drive, but it wasn't Noah having a tantrum, it was Paula.

She was standing by the open boot of the Range Rover throwing bags inside. Josh and Carla were standing a slight distance away while Ranjit hovered anxiously beside his wife.

'I'm so sorry, Paula. I never meant you to find out this way.'

'I just want to go home,' Paula was shouting.

Ranjit tried to put his arm around Paula.

'Come on, we only have one more night. What can we do at home anyway?'

Paula pushed him.

'I can start to sort this whole mess out myself!'

Ranjit looked at Carla and Josh beside him, his eyes pleading for help.

'Please stay, Paula, Noah will miss Reuben if you go.' Carla was holding Tilly, though she held her in the sort of way that suggested she hadn't held a baby for a while.

Cautiously Martha and the others got out of the Saab. They approached the little group around Paula.

'What's going on?' Flora whispered to Carla.

'Ranjit has been sacked,' Carla said. 'He messed up a big account at work.'

'You lied to me, Ranjit!' Paula's shouting grew louder.

'I was trying to protect you!'

'What! Did you really think I'd never find out?!' Paula threw an

264

open holdall into the boot, a pair of Ranjit's boxer shorts fell out onto the dusty drive. 'What about Reuben's school fees? What about the little apartment in Chamonix we've been dreaming of?' Paula scrunched up the boxer shorts and threw them into the car on top of the luggage. 'And what about my beautiful new kitchen.' She made the wailing noise she'd been making as they'd driven down the drive.

'Where's Noah?' Elodie asked her mother. 'Dad said he was having a meltdown.' But Carla wasn't listening to her daughter.

'I could interview you, Paula, and write an article about what it's like when you find out your husband lost his job six months ago and kept it secret. Editors love a riches-to-rags story.'

'Please, Carla,' Ranjit said. 'That's not constructive.'

Carla's eyes opened wide. 'I'm only trying to help. The fact you put your suit on and pretended to go to work is the sort of thing readers can't get enough of. Riding the tube, sitting on park benches, deceiving your family, they love that stuff. *Sacked from The City: My Secret Shame.*'

'You disappeared every day!' Paula shrieked. 'You could at least have been at home changing nappies or hoovering the floor!'

'I keep trying to tell you.' Ranjit's voice was nearly as loud as his wife's. 'I wasn't lazing around doing nothing.'

'I suppose you were feeding the birds, or jogging round the Serpentine.' Paula shoved the wicker swimming bag into the car. 'Or maybe you were helping old ladies cross the road!' She let out another wail. 'How are we going to survive? The mortgage, the cars, the gym membership! You've spent all of our savings. We have no money! I suppose that's why you booked this shitty holiday.'

'You said how lovely it was this morning,' Ranjit objected.

'That was before Reuben told me all about the conversation he'd overheard between you and my father. Imagine how I feel having to find out something like this from my six-year-old son!'

'I would have told you when we got home.'

'When I found out that the builders have walked off site and that the Aga hasn't been installed, let alone those lovely hand-painted tiles?'

'At least the roof is on and the windows are in.' Ranjit gave a weak smile.

Paula glared at him. 'I can't believe my father. All these months he's been lying to me too.'

'I begged him not to tell you. I promised him I'd sort it out. I have been trying to get another job. He let me use his flat as a sort of office.'

'Ahh!' Paula let out a scream. 'How could he not have told me! And now he's just buggered off! Typical! He's never there for me when I need him!'

'He came all this way to try to persuade me to tell you. But I asked him to go back and give us some time together before we went home.'

Paula stopped shoving things in the car and turned to Ranjit, her face inches from his.

'What about Buster? Is he really dead?'

Ranjit took a step back.

'No, not really.'

'For Christ's sake!' Paula threw her hands up in the air. 'Hasn't there been enough grief in this family without you and my dad inventing a dead gerbil!'

'Maybe you could get a job, Paula?' Josh offered.

'Overnight? To pay off all the bills that Ranjit's let mount up, let alone next month's mortgage.'

'But you have a degree.'

'In Medieval Celtic History with an MA in early Irish oral poetry and its relevance to Thomas Becket's demise. That's not going to pay for a trolley-full at Waitrose in the near future! Obviously I'll need to get a job but that will take time! CVs and endless interviews and I'll probably just end up working on the Waitrose checkout anyway.'

'If you'd let me speak, you wouldn't have to be so worried,' Ranjit said taking the swimming bag back out of the car.

'Put it back!' Paula screeched, her face now the colour of her hair.

Tilly began to cry.

'Where's Noah?' Elodie asked again. 'Where's Reuben?'

'The thing is, Paula.' Ranjit tentatively touched his wife's arm but she elbowed him away.

'I'll talk to the mortgage company.' Paula sounded as if she was talking to herself now. 'I'll try and organise a reprieve. I'll sell the cars, I'll sell my jewellery, if only my bloody diamond ring hadn't disappeared!'

'The thing is . . .' Ranjit repeated.

Paula ignored him and started hurling more bags into the boot.

'I'll take whatever job is going. Ranjit can stay at home and look after the children.'

'Paula . . .'

'Maybe the local primary wouldn't be too bad for Reuben.'

'LISTEN TO ME!' Ranjit bellowed at the top of his voice. Paula stopped and stared at him. They all stared at him. 'The thing is – I've checked my emails now that we have the Internet.' He lowered his voice. 'And I've had an email from my agent.'

'Your what?' Paula looked incredulous.

'My agent. My literary agent. Well, she's not just mine, she's your dad's agent too.'

Paula opened her mouth to speak but Ranjit got in first.

'I know you're going to say we don't have a literary agent, but we do, and she's got us a three-book deal in the UK, Australia and Germany and there's a bidding war going on in the US.'

Paula started to make choking noises.

'You're joking,' Carla said. '*You* have written a book!'

'I'm not joking. That's what I've been doing all day for the last six months; Max and I have been writing a children's book. *Billy Bacon, Secret Agent*.' He looked at the startled faces around him. 'I've been going round to Max's flat while he's been at work and written the words and then Max has done the illustrations in the evenings.'

'What's it about?' asked Josh.

'A chubby boy in Year six who is tormented by the school bully and hates his teacher. But in his spare time, he's a spy helping to save the world from a megalomaniac chocolate manufacturer who's putting mind-altering cocoa powder into the chocolate wafer bars his factory produces, so that he can control the population and take over the planet.'

Everybody stared at Ranjit.

'And Billy has a dog called Fat Larry who can talk. And he can also drive a car – but only in an absolute emergency.'

'Cool,' breathed Zac.

'Cool,' whispered Elodie.

'Cool,' echoed Josh.

'We started writing it before I lost my job, when Tilly was born.' Ranjit turned to face Paula. 'We did it for Reuben. He'd been so withdrawn since Alisha died and you were so wrapped up in the new baby. Your dad and I started the story to try to cheer him up. I'd read him each new chapter and your dad would come over and show him the illustrations and then Reuben would suggest changes or come up with ideas.'

'Seems like you've all had secrets,' Paula said with a sniff. She took a deep breath. 'So, you're going to get paid for this story?'

Ranjit nodded.

'How much?'

'Six figures, and there's talk of the film rights being sold.'

'Cool,' Zac, Elodie and Josh repeated together.

Paula's mouth fell open, then it shut and then it opened again.

Ranjit put his arms around her.

'As long as I've got time to write the next two books, we don't have to worry so much about money, though we may need to think about downsizing a bit.'

'Maybe downsizing would be OK,' Paula said slowly.

'It might be fun,' said Ranjit. 'We don't really need a fancy kitchen or big cars, or such a big house, and if I'm not working in the city maybe we don't even have to live in London? The house is worth far more than when we bought it.'

Paula looked up at her husband. 'I suppose it could be an adventure?'

'Yes,' Ranjit nodded enthusiastically. 'We could have a whole new start. We can go anywhere you want.'

'I've always fancied the Cotswolds.' A slow smile spread over Paula's face. 'An old rambling farmhouse, with a few acres of land; herbaceous borders in the garden, maybe we could get a horse?'

Ranjit looked nervous. 'Let's not be too ambitious with the downsizing!'

'Does Dad know about the book deal?' Paula asked.

'No. I saw the email after he left. I've been phoning and texting him, but I've heard nothing.'

The air reverberated with a child's shriek.

'Noah!' Carla and Elodie cried together.

Carla hastily handed Tilly to Paula and ran up the path towards the pool, Elodie was just behind her. The others followed. Martha brought up the rear, her heart sinking at the thought of another hornet attack or some other unforeseen accident that could only happen to Noah.

As she reached the pool, she could hear laughing and Reuben saying *That's so funny*. The laughter was joined cries of *Oh no* coming from the adults.

Martha gasped.

The yellow baby float that Tilly had been in earlier was in the water, with something small and brown and furry perched on the edge.

'Pippa!' Martha cried out the rabbit's name.

'Did you do this?' Josh was shouting at Noah. 'Did you put the rabbit in the float?'

'She likes it.' Noah was laughing.

'He hasn't hurt her.' Carla had her arms around her son. 'It's just a harmless bit of fun.'

'But it's really naughty.' Elodie had her hands on her hips.

'Yes, it is really naughty.' Josh repeated what his daughter had said and glanced at his wife.

Carla took her arms from around Noah and looked stern.

'The poor rabbit.' She looked at her husband and smiled.

'It was the ghost's idea,' Noah said.

Suddenly there was a splash. Pippa was in the water swimming determinedly towards the edge. The children squealed with delight.

'I knew she could swim.' Noah jumped up and down.

Ranjit kneeled down and scooped the rabbit up in his hand. He handed her to Martha. Martha picked up a towel and wrapped it around the dripping rabbit.

'What ghost?' She turned to Noah, cradling the little rabbit in her arms.

'The man ghost,' said Noah. 'Not the lady one. She's gone.'

'Do you mean Ben?' Martha asked.

Noah shook his head. He looked at Reuben. But Reuben had turned away to examine some ants that lined the crack in one of the paving slabs.

Martha felt water seeping from Pippa's soggy fur through the towel into her T-shirt.

'What did the man ghost look like?'

Noah firmly pressed his lips together and shook his head.

Carla put her hand on Noah's shoulder and smiled at Martha.

'He's always had an exceptional imagination.'

In the distance a jazz band began to play.

'Sounds like the festival is starting,' Flora said. 'We really ought to take the children to see the flowers before the fireworks start.'

'We'll all go.' Ranjit smiled. 'We have so many things to celebrate tonight. I have a book deal, Paula is smiling again.' He put his arm around his wife. 'Josh and Carla are back together, and . . .' Ranjit looked awkwardly at Alice and Flora.

'We're getting together ourselves.' Flora took Alice's hand.

'It was love at first sight,' Alice said.

Josh's eyes widened.

'I've realised how much more satisfying a woman can be,' Alice continued.

'Really?' Josh said.

Alice and Flora exchanged a smile.

'They're winding you up,' Carla said to Josh.

'How do you know?' laughed Flora. 'Didn't you say those exact same words to me a few months ago, Carla?'

'Anyway,' Ranjit coughed loudly. 'We can fit an extra person into the Range Rover so you can come with us, Martha.'

'I think I'll stay,' said Martha as Pippa nuzzled into her shoulder. 'I'll make sure Pippa is OK and watch the fireworks from the garden.'

The rumble of thunder joined the sound of the band from across the valley.

'Not another storm,' sighed Paula.

'It's miles away,' said Ranjit, taking his phone out of his pocket. 'It's going to be a clear night here according to BBC Weather.'

Josh took his phone out. 'Google says light showers.'

'It says storms on mine,' said Elodie.

Carla was studying her own screen. 'My weather app says sunshine all night long?'

Soon everyone was consulting their phone, swiping through different pages to find the best forecast.

'It's hot in Peckham.'

'Sandstorms in Northern Africa.'

'Stop!' It was Paula's voice. Everybody stopped and looked at her. 'Wasn't it so much nicer when we didn't have Wi-Fi? We just talked with each other rather than just regurgitating information from the World Wide Web.'

Martha smiled to herself and walked away.

Chapter 38

The night sky exploded with colour; bright sparks corkscrewed into the air and burst into giant balls of stars again and again. A rocket shot across the valley in a high arc, it's tail a myriad of twinkling purple sparks. Martha looked up as each spark multiplied into a hundred more.

Martha took a sip from her glass of wine and stroked Pippa's back. The fur had dried now but it still smelled of chlorine.

The sound of applause drifted across the valley. Martha wondered if the guests were enjoying the firework display. She hoped they were impressed with the flower garlands laced across the streets, and the street vendors selling crepes, and paper plates of sausages and potatoes cooked in cream and garlic.

An allium of purple stars exploded above the village, lighting up the sunflower fields in the valley with a neon glow. A thin veil of smoke and sulphur drifted towards *Le Couvent des Cerises*.

Martha sniffed the air. It reminded her of bonfire night in Abertrulli, sparklers and baked potatoes round a bonfire on the beach, one firework at a time let off painfully slowly in the hotel garden on the headland.

The first time she could remember she had been with her mother, her small hand safe and warm in her mother's gentle grasp. The last time she had been with Owen. He had laughed at the showers of sparks and the whizz of the rockets. He had lost his new mitten; she never had been able to throw away the matching glove.

Martha began to sing, her voice barely more than a whisper.

As you drew your breath I made my wish
As you held my hand I gave my kiss

A bang ricocheted across the valley as a rocket reached its peak; golden stars unfolded from it like a huge umbrella unfurling itself over the village before slowly melting into the velvet darkness of the sky. Drops of rain began to fall, spotting on the dry earth beside Martha's feet.

Another bang and then a rumble that didn't sound like a firework. Martha stood up. With Pippa still in her arms she began to make her way up the path towards the house. The rain was falling properly now, Elodie had been right about the storm.

I wonder if you walk under darkening skies
I look up to the stars
Child in my eyes

The house was in darkness apart from one dim light coming from the second floor. It looked like Reuben and Noah had left a lamp on; Martha sighed at the thought of her electricity bill after her week with all the extra guests.

She hadn't asked them about being paid but it didn't seem likely; even if they had enjoyed their stay, Ranjit's advance might take months to appear. But maybe they would write a good review, maybe more guests would come. The rain was quickening, the drops heavier. Martha reached the terrace.

She turned to look back just as the opposite hillside erupted into a succession of bangs and flashes. A cacophony of multicoloured blasts burst from the rooftops in a prolonged finale to the display. The whole town looked like it was exploding. As the last few fireworks fizzed into the air, the sound of distant cheering drifted over the valley on a smoke-filled breeze.

Martha reached the kitchen doorway and flicked on the lights.

There were already some suitcases waiting by the door for

departure in the morning. A pile of washing sat on the table along-side numerous bottles of sun cream, books and felt-tip pens.

In one corner of the table Martha noticed a plate of unwrapped cheese and a baguette with one end roughly torn away. A few small tomatoes lay beside the bread. Martha put Pippa on the floor and gave her one of the tomatoes.

A noise came from the living room, a rustle, a slight scrape.

'Hello,' Martha called out; she felt sure that no one had stayed behind.

'Hello?' she called again. She heard nothing but the faint hum of the fridge and the rain, which was now beginning to beat against the windowpanes.

Martha made her way through the kitchen to the room beyond. At the doorway she flicked the lights again. Apart from Elvis the room was empty. Martha walked across the oriental carpets to the grand piano and lifted the lid. Her finger lightly touched one key; the ivory felt cool and smooth. She pressed. The sound of the note seemed very loud in the stillness of the empty house. She sat down and placing both hands on the keyboard she played a scale and then Beethoven's 'Fur Elise', the piece she'd practised many times as a child. When she had finished, she put both hands in her lap and closed her eyes. She still had no recollection of playing the night before.

As you drew your breath I made my wish

She murmured the words and opening her eyes put her hands back on the keys, picking out the notes to reproduce the tune. It didn't sound right. She did it again, slightly altering the notes.

As you held my hand I gave my kiss

It still didn't sound quite like the tune. Martha stood up and looked on the top of the piano to see if the notebook with her original scrawled music was there. The candelabra had left a hardened pool of candle wax on the varnished wood and there was a copy of *Marie Claire* with a cover girl sporting a biro-scribbled beard, but nothing else. Martha supposed that Sally and Pierre had tidied the notebook away in the cupboard on the landing. She sat back down and thought she heard the rustling noise again, followed by another noise. It sounded like a cough.

'Pippa?' she called towards the kitchen. She hoped the rabbit hadn't got water in her lungs in the pool. She got up to check but Pippa was sitting under the table, happily nibbling on the tomato. Martha headed for the stairs; she needed to find the notebook.

The wooden treads creaked as she took each step. She could hear the rain on the roof now, the steady drip of water coming from the broken guttering. The guests would be back soon, driven away from the rest of the festival by the storm.

A breeze blew down the stairs; as Martha reached the top, she saw that the little attic window was banging back and forth and realised that this was what she must have heard earlier. She closed it, securing the iron catch before turning to the cupboard.

Suddenly a huge bang shook the house.

A flash of white light illuminated the landing.

Martha thought she saw a figure on the stairs beneath her, an outline of a man, and then darkness. Her first thought was of fireworks, an enormous stray one hitting the roof, though at the same time she knew that was ridiculous. Somewhere very close there was another bang and another flash before everything was plunged back into darkness. This time there was no figure on the stairs. Martha felt along the wall until her fingers found the light switch. Nothing happened.

'Bollocks,' she muttered.

She took her lighter from her pocket and lit it as she felt for the bannister. The little metal wheel against her finger quickly became too hot. She let go and smelled the smoke, the slight whiff of burning; she thought it might be the fireworks, or the lighter. She sniffed again. The smell was stronger now. Martha's eyes began to sting. She looked back and saw a glow coming from Elodie's closed door. Without thinking, Martha opened it.

The room was full of fire. Flames were running up the curtains and across the wooden beams on the ceiling. In a split second they seemed to jump onto the bed and advance like a wave across the duvet, consuming the unicorn pyjamas that lay scrunched up on the pillow. Martha slammed the door shut.

'Bloody hell!'

She stood, motionless on the landing. She couldn't think.

'Bloody hell!' she said again and turning to the cupboard, opened the door. In the darkness her hands felt fabric and paper and the leather of the Dr. Martens boots. A deafening crash from Elodie's room made Martha jump.

'For feck's sake, what are you doing?' A hand grabbed Martha's arm. 'You need to get out. Now.'

Martha turned and in the dim light cast by the fire behind the door she saw Max.

'My things,' she said.

'There's no time.' Max pulled her towards him as another crash came from the room beside them. 'Come on, let's go.'

Martha looked down and saw a tongue of flame shoot out from under the door, searching for something new to burn, the cupboard only inches away.

'My notebook, the songs.'

Max's grip was firm. He pushed Martha in front of him towards the stairs.

'Quickly!'

Martha turned back.

'Owen's mitten.'

'For God's sake, woman, will you get down the stairs!'

This time Martha did as he said, and coughing from the thick smoke she descended into the darkness beneath her.

In the living room, Martha and Max stumbled in the darkness, banging into chairs, tripping on rugs.

Martha felt the cold stem of the candlestick on the piano and lit the wick with her lighter. Max's face looked exhausted.

A crack like a pistol shot came from above them followed by a crash.

'My God, I think the whole staircase is going to go up.'

Max pushed Martha into the kitchen.

'Pippa!' Martha searched under the big pine table, sweeping the candelabra around looking for the little rabbit. 'I can't see her.'

Max was already at the door.

'She's clever, she'll have got out ages ago.'

Together they staggered onto the terrace. Looking up, Martha saw the roof ablaze, flames shooting up into the sky, pieces of debris slipping off and falling onto the flower beds around the house.

'Come on,' Max urged. 'We need to stand well back.'

At the bottom of the driveway they stopped. Martha let out a gasp at the sight of the line of fire that danced its way along the ridge tiles. Max put his arm around her and pulled her towards him.

Something soft brushed against Martha's foot. Looking down she saw Pippa. In the distance she heard a siren. Relief flooded through her.

'It will still be a good ten minutes before they arrive,' Max said.

Martha forced herself to look back to the house. The roof was almost totally alight. The tiles were falling away leaving only the bare outline of the glowing joists, sparks shooting off into the dark sky, horrific, yet as mesmerising as the fireworks display. Martha couldn't take in what she was seeing, it seemed impossible that this could really be happening to her home. Surely it was all a terrible dream, like all the others; soon she would wake up, she always did.

Something made Martha's eyes shift from the roof. Something on the second floor. A movement at a bedroom window; in her mind a lick of flame, a curtain going up. She looked again.

'Oh my God, there's someone in there.' Max had seen it too.

A figure, standing, framed in the window; arms raised as though to wave or maybe try to break the glass.

'Whose room is that?' Max was already moving towards the house.

'The boys. Noah and Reuben. But they're in the village.'

'It looked bigger than a child,' Max called over his shoulder; he was running now. 'It looked like a man.'

Martha followed him; she looked back up at the window. The figure had disappeared.

'You can't go back inside.' Martha stopped as Max mounted the steps to the terrace two at a time. 'Max, don't . . .!' Pippa squirmed, scratching at Martha's bare arm. Martha let her go and saw the rabbit run down towards the cherry orchard. When Martha looked back at the terrace Max had vanished.

Time stood still. Martha wasn't sure if seconds passed or minutes. The sound of the fire engine seemed to get no nearer; at times it sounded fainter amidst the cracks and crashes and the roar of flames as the fire spread. Martha covered her mouth with her hand to try to stop breathing in the choking smoke.

'Max!' she shouted again and again, her voice becoming hoarse. Fear began to build inside her as she realised this wasn't a dream. This was real, her house was on fire and Max was inside amongst the flames.

She looked back to the second-floor window; there was nothing but an eerie glow. She looked towards the kitchen door. There was no sign of Max. Martha turned desperately around. She saw a towel lying in a heap on one of the garden chairs. She picked it up and ran to the pool. She plunged it into the water and wrapped it, sodden and dripping, around her head and shoulders so that only her eyes were left uncovered. The weight of the wet fabric pressed down on her, water poured out of it, dripping down her hands and fingers.

She ran back up the path. Her leg felt no pain, she was as nimble as a child, quick and light on her feet. She took the terrace steps two at a time, then raced through the kitchen door and into the house.

The smoke was thick and dark but instinctively she avoided the chairs and suitcases and steered herself into the living room. She clutched the damp towel as she blindly crossed the floor. Reaching out she touched the bannister. It was scorching hot, the varnish bubbling. She pulled her hand away and peered upwards through the smoke. The second floor glowed ominously. The fire seemed to have a pulse, a heartbeat; rhythmic waves of heat. Stepping forward, Martha's foot touched something soft. She bent down and felt rough fur and claws.

Elvis.

The bear was lying across the bottom of the stairs. There was something underneath him. Martha groped around. Hair and fabric underneath the fur, she felt fingers, then a hand. She heard a groan. Martha pulled. The towel slipped from her head. She pulled again, stepping back and falling over something else. She struggled onto all fours and reaching forwards made out another body, a face, the rough stubble of hair cut close to the head. Martha gasped as a flare of flame made enough light for her to recognise the features. She began to cough, she couldn't get her breath; she thought that she might faint.

Pull your bloody self together, her voice was in her head. *Do something.*

She struggled to stand up and covering her head with the towel again moved forward, hands stretched out in front of her to where she knew the French windows were out to the garden. Her finger-tips felt glass and moving down found the smooth handle of the door. She twisted it but the door didn't seem to move. With her body she pressed against the glass and wood and pushed but nothing happened; she pushed again. It didn't budge.

Think, Martha Morgan, think!

The cocktail chairs. She stumbled over the second body as she crossed the room but managed to stay upright. She knew the cocktail stools were heavy but as her hand reached out to pick one up it felt as though it had no weight at all. Martha made it back to the French window and swung the stool against the glass of one of the doors. It shattered on her third attempt, sending glass showering all around her, the fresh outside air briefly filtering through the smoke. Martha kicked at the remaining glass from the door, she felt it slicing through her toe and cursed herself for wearing sandals, but she kept kicking till the doorframe had no more jagged shards attached.

The sound of the siren was very close now; Martha realised there was more than one. She turned and managed to roll Elvis over so that he was no longer pinioning the body she suspected to be Max to the ground. Fumbling she found both Max's hands and pulled. The towel fell completely away and she felt a surge of heat on her back. Max's body moved a few centimetres. Martha pulled again; the big Irishman seemed impossibly heavy.

Come on, you big oaf, Martha groaned as she pulled again.

She felt her foot slip against the edge of a rug and realised that Max half lay across the zebra-skin. Picking up the edge of the rug it was easier to pull it than pulling at Max's unconscious body. The rug slid across the wooden floorboards like a sledge. Martha managed to heave Max through the empty doorframe hoping that the zebra pelt would protect him from the broken glass.

She got him out onto the lawn and looked around, expecting firefighters to help. But despite the almost deafening siren the blue lights were only just lumbering through the gateway. At her feet Max let out a noise. Martha dropped down to a crouch.

'You silly fool,' she whispered. 'Who did you think you were? Superman?'

'The fella,' Max rasped. 'Is he OK?'

Martha looked back into the living room. She didn't want to save him; she despised everything he was, everything he'd done, not just to her but probably to many others. She saw a burning beam fall, bouncing down the stairs. It landed on top of Elvis. In an instant the one-hundred-year-old fur and sawdust was on fire. She knew he lay inches from the burning bear.

Martha peered towards the flashing lights. The fire engines were still making their way down the drive. Martha looked back towards the body in the living room; his chest was covered in a blanket of flames. There were only seconds left. She stood up. After all, he was somebody's son.

In the light cast by the fire she could just make out the towel lying in a heap on the floor where it had fallen from her shoulders. In a second she was back in the room. She picked up the towel; it was still damp. She threw it onto his chest, hitting the towel with her hands until all the flames were out.

The sofa was on fire now, acrid smoke pouring out of it. Martha's throat felt raw, her eyes were streaming with tears. She couldn't stop coughing; all around her fire seemed to be circling, dancing in a ring-a-roses skip of brilliant orange.

Martha's instincts screamed at her to leave, but instead she spread the towel onto the floor and rolled the body onto it. Using the same technique she'd used for Max she pulled the towel. He moved a foot or two, but something caught the fabric, a nail or a split in the floor. Martha kept pulling and pulling but the towel wouldn't budge. Smoke was filling up her lungs, burning inside, she could no longer breathe; her strength seemed to be seeping away, in her mind she saw Owen as a baby, she was going to die without ever seeing him as a man. She felt the towel rip, one half came away in her hand, then she was being dragged upward, floating, flying through the air. She heard voices speaking hurried French, radios crackling, children crying, a woman shouted *Dad*. Rain was falling, blissful, cool, wet rain. A child's voice cried out *That's the ghost*. Someone was pushing something at Martha's face and then she slipped into a blissfully deep sleep.

Chapter 39

Saturday

'Looks like you've got the Presidential suite.' Martha leant back in the leather chair beside Max's bed. She looked around the large room, taking in the picture window and huge television attached to the wall. 'My room isn't half as grand as this.'

'Ah well, you only have the smoke inhalation and the cut on your foot. I have the smoke inhalation, a broken ankle and concussion.'

'They're sending me home this afternoon,' Martha sighed. 'Not that I have much of a home to go back to. What a bloody disaster. I feel like my whole life is well and truly ruined now.' She put her hands to her face, pressing her fingers on her eyes, trying to get rid of the awful images of the flames consuming *Le Couvent des Cerises* and everything she owned.

Max lifted his head from the starched white pillows.

'Ah, don't be talking like that, Martha. Look! I'm still here and that poor fella in intensive care is here, or over there – just down the corridor.' He pointed towards the frosted glass of the door; stylised birds were etched all over it. 'Two lives saved thanks to you. You were spectacular.'

Martha took her hands from her face.

'Spectacular?' she repeated hesitantly. That was the word Paula had used the day before.

'Yes, that's what you were. I was trying to be the big hero

charging back into the house, thinking I could carry him out, only to go tumbling down the stairs, nearly killing us both.'

'And Elvis,' added Martha.

'I think that poor bear saved us from breaking our necks.'

'He's just ashes now.'

'Well, surely a good cremation is better than being stuffed for eternity?'

Martha laughed. 'Well, yes, poor Elvis always did have rather a pained expression.'

'That's more like it,' Max grinned. 'Look on the bright side. Surely you have insurance?'

Martha nodded. 'Yes, but probably not enough and I can't let the house out now, unless Dordogne Dreams can find a niche market for people who like to stay in burnt-out shells. Oh God, I wonder if Tamara has heard what's happened, I can just imagine her condescending words of condolence.'

'Now, don't start getting all maudlin again.'

'I can't help it, it's very hard to be as positive about life as you seem to be.'

Max took a deep breath. 'Martha, can I tell you why I came back?'

'I thought you must have heard from Ranjit about your deal.'

'My what?'

At that moment, the door swung open and people poured into the room: Noah and Reuben followed by Ranjit and Paula. Ranjit was holding Tilly, and Carla and Josh also pushed in with Elodie and Zac.

'Nice pad,' said Zac, letting out a long whistle.

Behind the group a large nurse in a baggy blue uniform was gesticulating and remonstrating in French.

'I think she's saying there's too many people for visiting,' Martha said.

'There could never be too many visitors for me.' Max opened his arms as Reuben jumped up onto the bed. 'Watch the ankle, mind the head.'

'I explained to her we weren't staying long.' Paula placed a huge box of cream-filled patisserie on the bedside table. 'But I don't think she understands English.'

'Paula.' Max stared at the box of cakes. 'Are you OK?'

'You deserve a treat,' Paula patted her father's hand, 'After everything you've been through.'

Max shook his head in disbelief.

'Let's have some tea and we can share them? I'm sure I can sweet-talk the nurse.' The nurse drew herself up to her full height. 'On second thoughts, maybe we'll forget the tea.'

'Unfortunately, we have to go soon,' said Ranjit, sadly eyeing the box of cakes. 'We're going to try to get the six o'clock ferry.'

'We've had a lovely night at *Château du Pont*,' Paula said. 'But it wasn't as nice as *Le Couvent des Cerises*,' she added hastily.

'Awful soft beds and I could smell the gents from the restaurant,' added Carla.

'And the coq au vin I had last night wasn't a patch on your stew, Martha.' Josh patted his stomach.

'And they don't have much of a view from their terrace.' Ranjit thrust his phone in front of Martha. She could make out some topiary balls and a stone turret. 'Not like your magnificent vista.'

Paula reached across Ranjit and tickled Tilly under her chin.

'Tilly took her first steps in their little playground.'

'That's grand,' beamed Max. 'It's about time that little one tasted a bit of freedom.'

'Where's the other present?' Ranjit asked looking around.

Elodie gently pushed Noah towards Martha.

He was solemnly holding a box of macarons. The box had a see-through lid, revealing rows of multicoloured biscuits, tied with pretty curling ribbons.

'This is a token of our gratitude for the holiday,' said Ranjit. 'We know it's nothing compared to what you have lost but . . .' his voice trailed away.

'Thank you, they're beautiful.' Martha took the box. 'I'm so sorry about all your clothes.' She looked around at the group.

'Actually, I'd already packed ours in the car,' said Paula. 'When I wanted to leave earlier.'

'My suitcase was in the kitchen, the fire didn't reach that room so they're just a bit smoky,' Josh said. 'Nothing that the dry-cleaners can't deal with.'

'Everything of mine got burned.' Elodie sounded surprisingly cheerful.

Carla clapped her hands. 'We'll have such fun shopping for a new wardrobe together. No more of those miserable T-shirts.'

Zac gave Elodie a nudge. 'I'll help. What about some off-the-shoulder tops and them short skirts with the slits up the back?'

Elodie rolled her eyes.

Josh cleared his throat. 'I'll be thinking twice about my offer to give you a lift home in the VW, Zac!'

'Where are Flora and Alice?' Martha asked, looking around the room.

'They stayed with Sally and Pierre,' said Josh. 'We did offer to take them to the hotel.' He shrugged his shoulders. 'But I think they're still trying to pretend that they're a couple. They are pretending, aren't they, Carla?'

'Of course they are, darling.'

Carla gave Josh's cheek a little stroke, then she perched on the end of Max's bed facing Martha.

'What about you?' She leant forward and took Martha's hand. 'You've lost your home, your furniture, all that memorabilia.'

'There's no need to rub it in.' Max shook his head.

'If there is anything I can do,' Carla continued, as behind her Noah was squirting hand sanitiser out of the dispenser and flicking it at Reuben. 'The story would be even better now. *My French Life Up In Flames, My Dordogne Dream Destroyed*, you know the sort of thing?'

Martha withdrew her hand from Carla's grasp.

'I don't want to be interviewed or written about or anything else you're offering.'

'Well, I'm going to think of something I can do to help.'

'*Deux minutes.*' The nurse was still standing in the doorway, hefty forearms folded across her chest.

'Are you sure you'll be alright if we go back to London, Dad?' Paula smoothed the woven blanket on the bed. 'I hope they're looking after you.' She spoke loudly. 'It's hard to know what these foreign hospitals are like.'

'I'm concussed, not deaf,' Max said. 'And the hospital seems very good.' He smiled towards the nurse.

Ranjit patted Max on the shoulder.

'I'll be coming back in a few days with a van to pick you and the bike up.'

'There's no need for that.' Max shook his head. 'I can find my own way back . . . I might stay for a bit and help Martha.'

'Don't be silly,' said Paula. 'We need you home safe and sound. You've got the illustrations to do for the next Billy Bacon book.'

Max stared at Paula.

'Billy Bacon?' Then he stared at Ranjit. 'Did you tell her?'

'He doesn't know.' Josh grinned.

'Know what?' Max said.

'Didn't you get my text?' Ranjit pulled his phone from his pocket. 'I thought that was why you came back?'

'No, I came back because . . .' Max stopped. 'Never mind why I came back, but my phone's been out of charge since I left.'

'So, you don't know?'

'As I just said – know what?'

Everyone, including the children, spoke at once.

Max looked bewildered as each one explained different details of the book deal.

'Am I dreaming this? Is it the concussion?' He touched the large white dressing on his forehead.

He looked at Ranjit. 'Did you tell Orla about the other thing?'

Paula folded her arms. 'I know all about Ranjit losing his job and your dual conspiracy to keep it a secret from me.'

'Ah, Orla love, I was forever going on at him to tell you, but he didn't want you to worry.'

Paula leant forward and kissed her father's cheek.

'It's OK, Dad. I forgive you.' She paused. 'Not just because of the book. You're a great dad, you always have been.'

'Ahh, get away with you!' Max pretended to push her away. 'You don't have to be nice because I nearly died.'

Paula smiled and turned to Martha. 'Thank you for saving him.'

Martha smiled. 'It was nothing.'

Max gave her a wink.

BANG, BANG, BANG.

Noah had discovered a large yellow bin and was busy with his foot on the pedal making the lid thump up and down. The nurse coughed loudly, glaring at Noah.

'*Il est l'heure de partir*,' She steered Noah away from the automatic towel dispenser, which he was eyeing as his next source of entertainment.

'Are we going to see the ghost?' Noah asked.

'How did you know the ghost?' Martha asked.

'He gave us chocolate.'

'Noah!' Reuben exclaimed. 'We promised not to tell!'

'It doesn't matter,' Noah said. 'He doesn't need the stuff now.'

'What stuff?' all the adults said in unison.

'I've told you about accepting sweets from strangers, Reuben,' Max said from the bed. 'It's never a good idea.'

But now the nurse was actually pushing everybody from the room. They stopped listening to the children and waved and shouted goodbyes as they were herded out by two hefty arms.

Paula rushed back to the bed to give Max another kiss.

'I love you, Dad.'

'Go! Now!' the nurse boomed from the doorway.

Paula obediently scuttled out of the room, stopping to give one last wave through the door before Ranjit pulled her away.

And then the door swung shut and they were all gone. As quickly as the guests had arrived in Martha's life, they disappeared.

'Can you believe that?' Max sank back on his pillows with a smile.

'Paula?' Martha asked.

'No, well, yes, Paula too – but me a published author. Isn't that the maddest thing?'

'Shall I get some coffee to celebrate?' Martha stood up, wincing at the pain in her cut foot, putting her hand on the bed to steady herself.

Max's eyes met Martha's.

'What I'd really like is some time to tell you why I came back last night.' His hand moved across the sheet. She felt his fingers graze against her own.

The door to the room swung open again with a swish. The nurse was back.

'Martha Morgan?'

Martha nodded.

'There is someone asking at the desk to see you.'

Chapter 40

Ben sat on a chair in the long corridor. His legs splayed out in front of him on the linoleum floor. His head was back resting against a poster illustrating how to wash your hands and he was staring at the ceiling. Martha noticed the shadow of a beard, and dark circles beneath his eyes. He looked as exhausted as she felt.

Ben turned his head and watched her progressing slowly towards him, the injury to her foot adding to her existing limp. He stood up and made to help her. Martha waved him away and sat down on the chair beside his.

'What are you doing here?' she asked.

Ben sat down again. 'I came back this morning. I saw the house.'

'You know about the fire then?'

Ben nodded. 'I heard in the village that you and Max were in hospital. I want to help, if I can.'

'Did you hear about Jean-Paul?' Martha pointed towards the doors of the intensive care unit.

Ben nodded again. 'Touch and go, the nurse said.'

Martha looked down at the box of macarons still in her hand. The pretty ribbons looked incongruous in the utilitarian surroundings of the corridor.

'I want to explain,' Ben said. 'But I don't know where to start.'

Martha felt sorry for him then. The tattered clothes, his drawn face. He'd lost weight since she'd first met him. It had only been a week, and so much had changed.

'Why don't you start by telling me about yourself, Ben. I know nothing about you.' She continued, a little more sternly, 'Then we can talk about what's been going on.'

Ben was silent. He couldn't meet Martha's eyes.

'How old were you when your mum died?'

Ben looked at her. 'How do you know about my mum?'

'You told me she'd died when you were a kid. Plus, the tattoo on your arm: the dove, the cross, the heart, the word MUM. I was thinking about it after Zac mentioned that he could tell you'd been in prison. I realised that your tattoos could be read like a book about your life.'

Ben gave a brief smile. 'I suppose you're right.'

'I'd like to know about your mum. I would like to know about you.'

Ben took a deep breath.

'She died when I was eight. It had been my birthday the day before. All my cards were on the mantelpiece. I remember the ambulance lady saying I was a lucky boy to get so many.'

'Do you want to talk about what happened?'

Ben was silent for a while, studying his hands as if his story was written on the lines of his palms as well as his body.

'She was an amazing cook. Cordon Bleu trained. She'd worked at The Savoy before marrying my dad. She loved French cooking.'

'Is that her cookbook in your rucksack?'

Ben nodded. 'One of her many cookbooks, but the only one that I managed to take with me.'

'How did she die?' she asked gently.

'She was cooking the tea. My tea. Baked beans.' He laughed. 'When you think what she could have cooked! But I used to beg her for them, they were my favourite. The news was on the television in the kitchen – they were showing all the flowers left for Princess Diana when she died. Mum stood at the cooker, stirring the beans for ages, then there was a crash and she was on the floor.'

Martha couldn't imagine how horrifying that must have been for a child. 'What did you do?'

'I waited for my dad to come home. I thought Mum was asleep.

I kept trying to wake her with kisses. I tried to clean the beans up with a tea towel. She had splashes of sauce on her cheeks.'

Martha realised that she had coiled the curling ribbon from the macaron box so tightly round her finger that the sharp edge had sliced her skin. She imagined Owen trying to wake her up from a drug-addled stupor.

'Afterwards, I waited for people to bring flowers like they had for Princess Diana,' Ben continued. 'But they never did. I picked all the roses in the garden and laid them in a line along the front of the house. When my dad saw what I'd done he went mad. That was the first time he ever hit me, but not the last. I think he started drinking then.'

Ben stopped as two nurses hurried past pushing a trolley with a machine on it. When they'd disappeared through the double doors he sighed.

'In the end social services took me away. To give our dad a *wee rest* they said, like a holiday. They put me in a big house outside Glasgow, a huge rambling place with lots of nooks and crannies where all sorts of horrors could take place out of sight. I saw my dad at weekends but one weekend he didn't come and then, well . . . I never saw him again.'

Martha looked down. A tiny bead of blood had appeared on the curling ribbon cut. Her heart ached for the little boy Ben had been.

'By the time I was fifteen I'd had enough,' Ben continued. 'I smashed up the manager's car with a garden spade and got sent to juvenile prison for twelve months. I know I shouldn't have done it,' Ben grimaced. 'But in the end being sent to prison was the best thing that could have happened to me. I got put on kitchen duty, learned the basics. I was happy there, much more interested in learning how to cook than I ever was at learning anything in school. I remembered a lot of things my mother had taught me about cooking. I suppose it was like a connection with her.

'But when I came out of prison there was nowhere for me to go – I was too old for the children's home, too young to live on my own. My probation officer put me in touch with a place that needed a kitchen porter – a big hotel in Edinburgh. I loved it – you know, the buzz. The head chef, Angus Rosso, was amazing.'

'The name sounds familiar,' Martha said.

'Yeah, he's always on the television and he has a column in *The Sunday Times* – when I started working there, he seemed like a rock star to me, coming up with all these incredible creations – every night was a performance. I got some more training, became a commi, then a junior, after a few years I was made chief legumier, in charge of all the vegetables – I suppose that's when I really came to Angus's attention. He wanted the very best: the freshest, the biggest that were available. I'd go to the market at four in the morning to make sure I got the pick of the day's deliveries. I'd travel for miles on my bike to get suppliers just for the hotel. Angus was really pleased with me. I found him a good mushroom grower for his signature risotto dish and a bloke who grew purple carrots, just for Angus's kitchen. This was a few years ago, around the same time his addiction was really kicking in.'

'Drugs?' Martha asked.

Ben shook his head.

'No, not drugs. Truffles.'

'He was addicted to truffles?!'

Ben laughed. 'Not like that. He started using them in the risotto, then he was adding them to everything, he just couldn't get enough. They made his food taste fantastic, added depths to the flavour, really complimented everything else on the plate. People were raving about the menu; the restaurant was packed every night. It still is.'

'Are you in charge of sourcing the truffles?'

'Yes, I travel the world looking for suppliers that can harvest a truffle that lives up to Angus's high expectations. He's become obsessed. He wants only the best. I think the truffles are driving him mad. I'm constantly at his beck and call to travel all over, looking for the perfect tuber. But he's so demanding. Rude. I used to admire him; we all did in the kitchen. Now we live in fear of his next rage; he shouts and throws things like a child, having a tantrum if a truffle doesn't have absolutely the right flavour.'

'Well, this is the area to get the best ones,' said Martha. 'Perigord truffles are a speciality of the Dordogne. They grow in the orchards; local hunters find them with dogs and dig them up from the roots of oak trees.'

'You don't need to tell me that,' Ben smiled at her. 'From November to March we were getting them shipped over by the crateful. The trouble is the summer months when truffles can't be found in France. I've found wonderful summer truffles in Sardinia and China, but Angus says the taste is nowhere near as good as the Perigord black truffle.'

'So why are you here? There are no truffles now.'

Ben looked at Martha.

'Yes, there are.'

Martha raised her eyebrows.

'In June?'

'It must be because all of the rain this spring. A few, extremely rare black summer truffles have been found, in the oak wood at the bottom of the valley beneath *Le Couvent des Cerises*.'

'That's why you've hung around all week? For truffles?'

'When Angus heard about them, he sent me over. He told me not to come back until I'd got him as many as possible. It turns out he's not the only truffle-crazed chef – there are loads of people after the summer truffles. They're called Black Gold.'

Martha nodded slowly 'Now I understand.'

A nurse hurried past them down the corridor.

'They're worth a fortune,' Ben continued. 'I came expecting to do legitimate business like I usually do, but instead found myself caught up in a black-market racket run by your local drug dealer. It's why I had to be so secretive about it.'

'You mean Jean-Paul?' Martha nodded towards the doors of the Intensive Care Unit.

'Yeah. Mr. Slippery. He was playing me off against several other punters. I gave him a huge wedge of cash for the ones he'd found, and he sold them to someone else before I got them.'

'But kept your cash.'

'Yes. And I had Angus phoning me every five minutes wanting to know if I'd got the truffles yet. That's why I was happy to stay with you. No phone signal was a godsend.'

'And you thought if you stayed nearby you could still persuade Jean-Paul to find truffles for you?'

Ben nodded.

'The trouble was Jean-Paul turned nasty. I went out with him one night to hunt for them; his dog turned up a pile of beauties, but Jean-Paul wanted more money and when I wouldn't give it to him we got into a fight.'

'It wasn't a bike accident, then.'

Ben touched his lip. The cut was still visible.

'I was always lousy in a scrap.'

'But I don't understand why Jean-Paul was hanging round my house? He must have been the man the children saw and decided was a ghost, and I presume his girlfriend was the ghost Noah initially saw in the orchard.'

Ben rubbed his eyes.

'Stupidly I told him that I'd helped you shift all your memorabilia from the band. I realised my mistake when I found all that jewellery in the dashboard of his car when we went out truffle hunting. I recognised it and took it back. I should have told you. I think he kept coming back to look for more.'

'Is that what he was doing at the house last night? Looking for more stuff?'

'Probably. His girlfriend told me that Jean-Paul thought that as Lucas had died anything to do with the band would be worth much more. He was bribing the boys to act as lookout, I think he even had them bringing him things.' Martha thought of Paula's diamond ring.

'He really is a nasty piece of work,' Ben continued with a scowl. 'I saw you with his girlfriend in the village square yesterday morning.'

'She and Jean-Paul had had a row. She sold his latest truffle to me so that she could use the cash to get away from him; he was treating her like shit.'

294

'So now you have your Black Gold.'

Ben nodded and pushed his hand through his thick hair.

'It's a single truffle, huge. The biggest I've ever seen.'

'Then shouldn't you be on your bike heading for Edinburgh? Truffles have a short shelf life, every day they lose a bit more flavour.'

Ben nodded again.

'I know that. By day five you might as well be eating a mushroom from the supermarket.'

'Well? Don't feel you have to hang around here.'

'It's not that. I've done a lot of thinking this week and I'm not sure I really want to go back. There's only so much I can take of being ordered around by an increasingly crazy celebrity chef. And then there's the way I feel about . . .'

'Martha!'

Martha looked up at the sound of her name being called. Three figures were coming down the corridor; shafts of sunlight through the windows gave them a celestial glow. Martha recognised Sally's curves and the high cone of Flora's hair and beside them a slightly smaller figure, long curls bouncing, short skirt swishing. Ben looked up too. His face brightened.

Martha heard the sweep of a door opening; she turned to see a doctor coming out of the intensive-care unit. He walked briskly down the corridor, leather soles click-clacking on the linoleum.

Ben stood up and waved at the women approaching from the other direction. Sally, Flora and Alice's smiles were wide.

'Excuse me,' Martha said as the doctor passed. 'Is there any news about the man with the burns?'

The doctor stopped and wiped a line of perspiration from his forehead.

'In the end there was nothing we could do.'

Chapter 41

All was quiet. No splashing, no shouts or sudden bursts of laughter; no cutlery scraped on plates, no glasses clinking, no corks popping. Even the cicadas had stopped in the midday heat.

Martha sat by the edge of the empty pool; the firemen had used the water to fight the fire. She wanted a cigarette, but her lungs still hurt and her throat felt raw.

She looked up and saw a plane, its white trail drawing a clear line west across the sky. She wondered if Flora was on it, heading back to London.

Sally had said that she would come and visit her after she had taken Flora to the airport. No doubt she would have another go at getting Martha to come and stay with her and Pierre. *It will break your heart looking at your poor home.*

Martha looked at her home. Her heart didn't break.

The house resembled the carcass of a great monster after battle. Charred roof joists silhouetted against the sky like ribs violently exposed.

'She will rise again,' the fire officer had said when he had visited earlier. 'Like *le phénix*.' He had gesticulated enthusiastically with his hands, but Martha had felt nothing but fatigue.

She had no energy left for the house or the things she'd collected within it. It had been her whole life, her sanctuary, her haven. But now, in its present state, it felt like a burden she could no longer carry.

She looked away and then down at the crumpled letter in her

hands, filling in words where Pippa had chewed little holes, smoothing out the creases. She hardly dared to believe it; she was still frightened that it might just be some awful scam.

The sun had already set when Sally had dropped her off at *Le Couvent des Cerises*. All the way up the hill they could smell the smoke; it lingered in the valley and drifted down the winding road.

'I'll come in,' Sally had said as they drew up at the bottom of the drive. 'Make sure staying here is really what you want.'

Martha had been firm and eventually Sally had driven away. Flora, Alice and Ben were at the bar with Pierre, and Martha persuaded Sally that they would be waiting for her to eat supper.

Martha waved as the lights of the little car disappeared. She didn't even have a bag with her. The clothes she had been wearing the day before were ruined and Sally had brought some of her own clothes for Martha at the hospital.

'I'm sorry.' Sally had apologised for the flouncy floral shirt and the elasticated skirt. 'They were the only things I could find that might fit, they've been too small for me for years.'

A breeze blew through the blouson sleeves as Martha walked across the rough track. She saw that Josh's car was still on the drive, full of rocks and rubble. Max's motorbike was parked beside her car; Martha touched the smooth leather seat of the Harley Davidson as she turned towards the chapel.

Hello, Fionnuala.

Behind her the house creaked and groaned like an injured beast. Martha pushed open the door of the chapel and flicked on the light. Nothing happened.

'Bollocks!' Martha swore. Of course the power would be off. Maybe Sally had been right, she should have stayed with the others in the rooms above the bar.

In the half-light she made out Pippa sitting in the middle of the floor nibbling on something. Martha squatted down to stroke her.

'Are you OK, cariad bach?'

Pippa was nibbling on a scrunched-up piece of paper. Martha

took it from her. Smoothing it out she recognised the letter from the bank that she'd inadvertently thrown at Max the day before.

Pippa had already eaten through one corner of the envelope. Martha could see the letter exposed inside. She swallowed and her damaged throat protested with pain. She stood up to get a drink. As she leant against the sink with her glass of water she stared down at the envelope.

What could the bank possibly say that would matter now?

If they really wanted to take back the house, they were welcome to it. She opened the envelope and drew out the piece of paper inside. It was too dark to see. She lit the candle on the dresser and tried to make out the text. Instead of the usual green bank heading she could see orange letters in a rounded font. She didn't have her glasses but holding the letter at arm's length enabled her to make out Proctor and Jones Solicitors at the top.

She coughed and tasted tar and smoke. When the coughing subsided, she went into the bedroom, retrieved her glasses and sitting on the bed, started to read.

Dear Ms. Morgan,

We are writing to you to inform you that the estate of Mr. Lucas Oats has bequeathed to you 50% of all subsequent royalties from the songs that were written and recorded with the band On The Waterfront between the years of 1982 and 1989.

Before his death Mr. Oats stated that he had, in the past, claimed full musical credits with Ms. Catherine Smith. He wishes it to be acknowledged that you also should have had music and writing credits on the songs written and recorded between the above dates.

Five hundred thousand pounds from the estate of Mr. Oats will be issued to you to make amends for loss of previous royalty payments.

Please contact our office for further details.

Yours sincerely,
Nathan Jones

Martha took off her glasses and sat motionless on the bed. At some point in the night the candle had burned out and Martha had crawled underneath the covers. It had been after midday when she'd woken, the letter still in her hand.

Beside the pool she read the letter for the hundredth time. *Thank you, Lucas*, she whispered into the brilliant sky.

Martha looked towards the drive at the sound of a car. A spark of excitement ran through her at the thought of telling Sally about the letter. She skimmed through the words again and felt a dizzying sense of release.

Wheels scrunched the gravel as the car came to a halt, followed by silence after the engine was turned off. After a few moments Martha heard the slam of a car door followed by another slam.

She waited to hear Sally shout her name but instead she heard low voices; two men, their voices deep in hurried conversation. She wondered if it was the fire investigation team the fire officer had told her to expect, or the police.

Martha sat up straighter, folding the letter and slipping it into the pocket of her oversized skirt. She wished she had changed into her own clothes before coming outside.

'It looks bad.' She heard the words distinctly. The accent was English. 'Worse than she said.'

Martha picked up Pippa who had been sitting at her feet.

'My God, poor woman!' The other voice had a Welsh lilt. 'She must be devastated.'

'Come on then.'

'I know you're nervous but it's probably best you go on your own.'

There was a long pause, then, 'OK. Wish me luck.'

Martha heard slow footsteps on the path. Someone heading towards the house. Martha craned her neck to see beyond the fence that encircled the pool. She saw a young man; medium height, loose linen shirt over long khaki shorts, curly fair hair flopping over his face. He was walking up the path with a long lolloping stride. He stopped and turned back.

'Go on,' the Welshman said. 'I'll just be here, admiring the view.'

'OK, I'm going, I'm going.'

'You'll be fine Owe,' the Welshman called.

Martha gasped. It was only a slight inhale, a tiny rasp, but it seemed to draw the man's attention. He turned and looked straight at her.

There was a beat, a heartbeat, a thousand heartbeats; time warped, moments distorted into years and back again. The young man pushed away a lock of hair. His eyes were dark brown pools.

'Owen?' Martha said, breathless.

'Martha?' the man said, and then he very softly whispered, 'Mum?'

Chapter 42

Two Days Later

They sat outside the bar, a lemon-scented candle flickering in the middle of the table, the reflection of the flame glinting on the collection of wine bottles and glasses. A warm breeze blew through the garlands still strung across the square and the paper flowers rustled against the backdrop of a velvet starry sky.

Their plates were scraped clean. It had been the most delicious omelette Martha had ever had. The shavings of truffle had made the simple dish into something divine.

She wiped one last piece of bread around her plate and passed it to the dog under the table. She'd been determined to rescue Jean-Paul's dog as soon as the doctor said Jean-Paul had died. She'd sent Alice and Ben to unchain it from the cement mixer at the squalid shack and it had followed them back to the village as meekly as a lamb.

Max raised his glass.

'I think a toast is in order.' A murmuring went round the table. 'To new beginnings.'

Alice raised her own glass and clinked it against Ben's. He interlaced his fingers with hers, and they smiled at each other.

Martha looked across the table at her son and the dark-haired man. Owen and Rhys had just been telling them all about their marriage plans.

'We're hoping that the wedding will take place in Wales, on Gower, where my parents live,' Rhys said.

301

Owen smiled. 'And after all I'm half Welsh too.'

'I've been trying to teach him the language,' Rhys said to Martha. 'We want to say our vows in Welsh.'

'I'm not very good,' Owen laughed. 'The only word I can remember is *cariad*.'

Rhys looked at Martha.

'Well, cariad is the most important word, isn't it?'

Martha nodded.

'It means love,' she explained to the others and took a sip of wine. Owen hadn't forgotten, even if he said he couldn't really remember all those trips to Abertrulli. It was in him, like all the love that she and her mother had lavished on him. She watched the gentle way he treated his partner. Where had he learned to be like that? Not from Andrew, that was sure. Martha felt a surge of rage at the way her son had been treated by his father. One day she would confront her ex-husband, tell him what she thought of his behaviour towards their child. But not yet. She didn't want to burst the exquisite bubble of happiness that had surrounded her for two whole days.

Martha had been unable to believe that Owen was really standing in front of her, separated only by the little wooden fence between the pool and the path. She felt the softness of Pippa's fur on her hands as the rabbit nuzzled into her neck and she was aware of the unfamiliar flowery fabric billowing in the breeze around her arms. She wondered if she was asleep. It seemed like a dream. She didn't think she could breathe, let alone speak. Could it really be Owen? She wondered how he'd known that this was when she'd need him most.

'I heard about the fire.' He seemed to have read her mind. 'I wanted to come. In case you needed me.'

'Yes,' Martha whispered. She stood up and walked towards the fence. 'I do need you, I always have.'

'I know,' said Owen gently.

'But I feel I have no right' Martha stopped in front of Owen. She shook her head. 'After all the years when I haven't been there for you.'

Owen put his hand onto the fence, long Frazer fingers resting on the pointed picket between them.

'You were there for me. More than you know.'

'I don't understand.'

'When I was twelve, I found your letters and your birthday cards and presents, unopened, stuffed in the cupboard where father kept his hunting rifles. I read every line you wrote to me, over and over again.' He paused. 'I wanted to see you but when I was younger, I didn't know how and when I got older I . . .' His voice trailed away.

Martha reached out to her son but she daren't quite touch him.

'I wanted to see you too. I tried to make a home for you.' She gestured towards the carcass of the house. 'This was meant to be your home. I bought it for you, for us, to share together. I pleaded with your father to bring you here, to let you spend time with me. I waited and waited, stupidly accepted all his excuses. I should have fought harder, I should have forced him to let me see you, I should . . .' Martha stopped to take a breath, she felt her head begin to spin. 'I should have been a better mother.'

Owen reached across the fence and took her hand in his.

'It's OK. I know how difficult my father must have made it. He's not an easy man.'

Martha looked into his face. She saw the Frazers in his handsome features but instead of the ruthless blue steel she saw the deep well of kindness in his large brown eyes.

'I've never stopped loving you.' She tried to squeeze his hand but the ground was beginning to shift beneath her feet, Owen's face began to blur in front of her and the garden behind him fragmented into a kaleidoscopic haze. Pippa jumped from Martha's arms. Owen started shouting, '*Rhys, come and help.*'

Martha became aware of the soft cushion of the sunlounger beneath her body, a young man's concerned face hovering over hers.

'I think she's alright,' the young man was saying. 'She must have got a shock at suddenly seeing you after all these years.'

'We ought to get her water,' Owen said.

'There's a bottle in the car.'

Martha struggled to sit up as she saw Owen going through the gate. She wanted to cry out and tell him not to leave; she cursed her body for its frailty and wondered what Owen must think. She hoped he didn't think that she was drunk or medicated.

She managed to murmur Owen's name.

'Don't worry, he'll be back in a minute,' the young man said. Martha let the man gently push her back down onto the cushion. 'Just rest there and you'll be right as rain soon, you'll see. I'm Rhys, by the way.'

'I've imagined this for twenty-five years, but fainting wasn't part of the plan.'

Rhys smiled, he was very good-looking, with tortoiseshell glasses and slicked-back dark hair.

'Owen has wanted to see you for a long time too; he's talked about you ever since I met him. I suggested he send the postcard but when he didn't hear anything, he thought you didn't want to see him.'

'How could he have thought that?'

'You didn't answer.'

'I was frightened.'

'Owen was frightened too,' Rhys said. 'He said he'd wait. He wanted to make you proud, come and see you when his career had really taken off.'

'In the family business?'

Rhys laughed.

'Yes, I suppose you could call it that. I've told him how proud you'd be of what he does, but his father has undermined his confidence.' Rhys shuddered. 'That man has a lot to answer for.'

Martha's heart contracted at the thought of the hurt that Andrew might have inflicted. But would she have been any better? Martha hoped Owen didn't remember what she had put him through when he had been so young. Her own shambolic parenting, culminating in her disappearance from his life, what must have seemed to a little boy like her abandonment. Martha felt the familiar wave of shame sweep over her. She took a breath.

304

'There has never been a day, an hour, a minute when I haven't wanted to see Owen. I know I should have been stronger, fought battles for him, challenged Andrew. I failed to be there for my son, but I never abandoned him in my heart.'

'I think he knows that,' Rhys said gently. 'He talks about you all the time. When that woman told him about your house, though, nothing was going to stop him coming.'

'What woman?'

'Karen? Carol? I can't remember.' He turned to Owen who was coming back through the gate with a bottle of Evian. 'What was the name of that woman who messaged you?'

Owen crouched down by Martha and handed her the bottle of water.

'She said she'd been on holiday here.' He glanced towards the burnt-out house. 'Carla?'

'Carla?' Martha struggled to sit up again.

'Yes,' Owen nodded.

'How did she find you?'

'Googled me?'

'I've googled Owen Frazer lots of times and never found more than a fuzzy office photograph and sketchy CV.'

'She looked for Owen Morgan,' Rhys explained.

'Morgan?' Martha ran her fingers through her hair, trying to take it all in.

'I changed my name when Dad threatened to disown me after I told him I was gay.'

'Bigoted old dinosaur,' Rhys sniffed, pushing his glasses up his nose.

Owen looked at Martha from under his mop of blond curls.

'I took your name.' He smiled. 'I hope you don't mind.'

'Mind?' Martha shook her head, her heart bursting with joy. 'I'm delighted.'

'Owen is a musician.' Rhys smiled proudly. 'He's in a band. Velvet Couch. You must have heard of them? They get played on Radio 6 Music all the time.'

'We've been played twice,' Owen corrected.

'Owen does lead vocals,' Rhys continued enthusiastically. 'And he plays guitar.'

'You sing?' Martha said, looking up at her son.

He nodded.

'He writes the songs too,' Rhys went on. 'They're fantastic, wait till you hear them, Martha, they'll blow your mind.'

Owen shook his head. 'I think Rhys is exaggerating.'

'No! Speaking as a mega-fan,' Rhys put his arm around Owen's shoulder and grinned at Martha, 'let me tell you that your son really is super-talented.'

Owen pushed Rhys away with a laugh.

'You're just biased!'

'I'm only saying that you're very good.'

Owen looked at Martha through his fringe again.

'You've been my inspiration,' he said quietly.

'He watches your old On The Waterfront videos all the time,' said Rhys.

'I used to go to sleep listening to "Moondancing" on my phone when I was at boarding school,' Owen continued. 'I had a still from that black and white video of you as my screensaver. I used to talk to you under the covers, tell you about the horrible teachers and the bullies and all the things they used to say and do to me.'

'Oh, Owen.' Tears welled up in the corner of Martha's eyes, she couldn't bear to think of him being bullied. All alone.

'When I was older I'd sing you songs I'd written, play you compositions on my guitar. I'd ask you what you thought.'

'What did I say?' Martha whispered.

'You always said I was brilliant.' Owen smiled.

'I'm sure you were. I'm sure you are.'

'I'll never be as good as you.'

'I'm afraid I'm not much to aspire to now.'

'But you're amazing,' Rhys said. 'Carla sent a link to YouTube, didn't she, Owen?'

Owen nodded.

'We watched you singing "Child in My Eyes".'

'It was beautiful,' said Rhys. 'Made me cry.'

'I know it's probably stupid to say this.' Owen pushed his golden hair back from his face, his eyes fixed on Martha's. 'But when I heard the song, I let myself believe that you were singing it to me.'

'I *was* singing it to you.' Martha reached up and took Owen's hand, tears falling freely down her cheeks. 'It's your song, I wrote it for you. All the words I couldn't tell you to your face, all the love I had but couldn't show you. I missed you so much.'

Owen crouched down beside the sunlounger and gently put his arms around Martha.

Martha put her own arms around Owen, breathing in the delicious scent of him, feeling his broad back, marvelling that her baby could have grown into someone so wonderful.

She realised Owen was crying too, and he was saying something over and over again.

'I'm here now, Mum. I'm here. I'm here.'

'How does it feel?' Max asked. 'To have him back?'

Martha grinned. 'I keep having to pinch myself.'

Max poured out the last of the wine. In the corner of the square a small orchestra was playing folk tunes, the last night of the flower festival was nearly over. A huge moon hung above the criss-crossed garlands, lighting up the almost empty square.

The others had gone up to bed. Sally and Pierre were clearing up the bar.

'I cannot believe that we are now the ones with all the paying visitors,' Pierre huffed as he wiped down the table. 'How did this happen when I say I will never do the B&B again?'

'But we are not the fusspots like you had before,' Martha was laughing. 'Alice has been helping in the bar, Ben has been cooking amazing truffle-enhanced meals for your customers, and Owen and Rhys are delighted with the room you've given them overlooking the square. Even Pippa seems happy in that big run you borrowed from the butcher's son and the dog is delighted to be able to sleep inside.' Martha patted the Alsatian's smooth head.

Pierre huffed again. 'He should not be in bedroom, he should be outside in a kennel!'

'Give over with your grumbling.' Sally flicked her husband with a cloth. 'The dog is such a sweetie now he's not with that awful man.' She passed the dog the last slice of baguette from a basket on the table.

'And I'll be no trouble at all.' Max picked up his glass so that Pierre could wipe underneath it.

'I've put you in a room on the first floor, Max.' Sally took away the empty wine bottle. 'It's not many stairs for you with your ankle.' She indicated the crutches leaning against Max's chair. 'Martha's room is next door.' She winked and disappeared into the bar.

'She's a one!' Max laughed.

Martha could feel heat rising in her cheeks. Ever since Sally had brought Max back from the hospital earlier in the afternoon, she had been making insinuating comments.

'It's a good job you have your chaperone.' Max nodded towards the dog who was gazing up adoringly at Martha. 'What are you going to call him?'

'I thought I'd call him Janus, after the Greek god of new beginnings.'

'That's a good name.'

'I hope he'll have a better life with me.'

'Any more thoughts about your own new beginnings?' Max asked after a pause.

Martha twisted the stem of her glass between her fingers.

'Well, finances are less of a problem, thanks to Lucas's legacy.'

'Will you get the house repaired?'

Martha looked around the flower-decorated square; an elderly couple were waltzing to the music by the fountain.

'I think someone else should live in *Le Couvent des Cerises* now – give the place a new lease of life. Actually, I've been thinking about leaving France.' She drained the last few drops from her glass. 'I might move back to Britain. Maybe take Posh Paul up on his offer.'

'Posh Paul?'

'Paul Thomas. We called him posh because he'd spent a year at a private school before coming to our comp.'

'Wasn't he in the band with you?'

Martha nodded.

'Turns out he organises summer festivals now, a bit like mini Glastonburys by the sea. He saw that clip of me singing and he's asked if I'll perform at some of his festivals next year.'

Max grinned. 'That would be grand, a talent like yours should not be wasted.'

Martha patted her pocket for cigarettes and then remembered she had been three days without smoking and was determined to keep going. She put her hand back on her empty wine glass.

'I'm not sure I have the courage to get back on the stage. Maybe I should just leave it to the younger generation.'

'Like your Owen?'

'Velvet Couch are very good. Owen has been playing me some of their music. I'm amazed. All the years that I assumed he was working in the city and really he was playing gigs and writing songs! He's definitely got talent.'

'It must be in the genes.'

Martha flushed with pride. Owen had inherited her gift for music, her voice. She had given that to him, when she had nothing else to offer. And she felt such admiration for him, he was following his passions rather than following obediently in his father's footsteps. He wasn't letting Andrew dictate his life as Martha had.

'Where would you live?' asked Max as the couple disappeared down a tree-lined avenue.

'I rather fancy a little cottage back in Wales?'

'With a sea view?' asked Max.

'Yes, a gorgeous view of Cardigan Bay,' said Martha with a wistful smile. 'And roses round the door.'

'And a vegetable patch?'

Martha nodded. 'Pippa would love that – she could nibble lettuce all day and I'll learn to cook what I grow. Alice and Ben can come to stay and give me lessons.' There were a few moments of silence.

'You can take Janus for long walks along the beach every day,' said Max.

'Yes, me limping along the sand with my gammy leg.'

'And me limping along beside you with my gammy ankle.'

Martha raised her eyebrows. 'I didn't know that you were going to be there.'

'Ah well, I might just be visiting the area on my bike, or maybe I'll buy the little place next door.'

'It will be very secluded. Next door will be at least a mile away.'

Now it was Max who raised his eyebrows.

'Surely there's no need for that any more?'

'For what?'

'For hiding yourself away from the world, burying yourself in a convent and all that.'

'You're not going to start telling me I'm being like a nun again?'

Max smiled and shook his head. 'No. I want to tell you something else.'

'What?'

'I want to tell you the reason I came back.'

'It wasn't just to save my life?'

Max's smile broadened. 'It was you who ended up saving *my* life. Again.'

'Again?'

Max let out a long sigh.

'I'm going to tell you a story.' He laid both hands on the table. 'I've never told anyone this story before, and to be honest, the last person I ever imagined I'd be telling it to was you.'

'Go on then,' prompted Martha. 'Tell me your story before I give up on you and go to bed.'

Max took a deep breath.

'OK, here goes.' He stretched his arms across the table as if

310

limbering up for an exercise session. 'I was on my bike, heading for the ferry and I thought about what you said. I couldn't stop thinking about it.'

'What did I say?'

Max's fingers tapped the table in time to the orchestra's next tune. 'When I was leaving – do you remember? You were upset.'

Martha nodded.

'You said something.' Max's voice was soft. 'You said you wondered what the point of your life had been.'

Martha frowned. 'I was just being silly, feeling sorry for myself.'

'Yes, you were.' Max looked at Martha, holding her eyes with his own. 'Like I was when my wife, Fionnuala, died. I was lost. I was a mess. I was struggling to look after Orla; trying not to cry all over the burnt fish fingers when Orla'd tell me that all she wanted was her mother's shepherd's pie.' Max closed his eyes for a moment. 'Sometimes I thought that I wasn't going to make it.' He lowered his voice. 'I thought that Orla would be better off in a children's home, with me in the grave with Fionnuala.' Max paused and shook his head. 'I can't believe it when I think of it now but there you are, that's what I thought. One morning, after Orla had gone to school, I was feeling particularly bad; I think it started with the plaits and the ribbons and my incompetence with a hairbrush – I'd pulled Orla's hair too hard and she told me she hated me. After I dropped Orla at school, instead of going to work I came home. I remember sitting at the kitchen table seriously thinking the world would be a better place without me, that Orla could find a better home if I wasn't there. Then your song "Moondancing" came on the radio and something in the lyrics and your voice gave me strength. I felt you were talking to me, singing to me, telling me to keep going. You lifted me out of my pit.'

Martha was still frowning.

'You think *I'm* being silly now.' Max smiled. 'But, you know, I got up from the table and went to work, with the lyrics going round and round in my head. And then, on my way home, I bought the single from Woolworths and played the thing over and over again.

311

Every time I felt depressed, I'd put it on our little record player and you'd give me hope. Sometimes Orla and I would dance around the flat to it; I'd waltz her around, singing the words. It made her smile. It made us both smile. Your song kept me going, got me through. It saved my life.'

Max stopped. Martha looked down at his hands on the table; large and brown, calloused from years of working with stone. Scarred where tools had slipped and cut his skin. The tips of his fingers on one hand very nearly touching her own.

'So, you see,' Max said gently. 'When you told me that you didn't know what the point of your life had been, I just wanted you to know that story, because I think that counts as a point, don't you?'

Martha didn't answer. She looked up at the moon so that the tears that swam in her eyes wouldn't fall. She closed the distance between their hands, taking his fingers in hers.

On the little stage across the square a solitary violin began to play. Martha looked at Max as the other instruments began to join in with the familiar tune.

'I can't believe you got them to play this.'

Max was shaking his head.

'I swear I didn't. How could I when I'm sitting all the way over here?'

Martha folded her arms. 'Some sort of Irish magic.'

'Ah, my powers are not that strong. I think the orchestra is playing it especially for you.'

'We are the only people left.'

Max stood up. 'Will you dance with me, Martha Morgan?'

Martha nodded towards his crutches.

'How is that going to work?'

He laughed.

'I can manage with one crutch, if you'd hold on to me.'

Martha came around the table and took Max's arm.

'Come on then, show me your moves.'

They slowly made their way towards the orchestra, laughing as Max wobbled several times; Janus followed them a few steps behind.

They stopped beside the fountain.

'Here?' Max asked.

Martha nodded. Max took Martha in his arms and together they began to slowly sway in time to the music.

Over Max's shoulder, Martha looked back towards the bar; a warm glow came from the rooms on the top floor. A curtain moved and Martha wondered if someone was watching. She smiled; she didn't care.

She let herself relax in Max's embrace. His arms felt strong around her; his cheek was against her own as they danced. Quietly, Max began to murmur the words, his breath soft against Martha's skin. After a few moments, Martha closed her eyes and just as the music of the orchestra swelled to the song's chorus, she took a breath and began to sing.

One Year Later

Abertrulli

The sun slowly set over the sea, turning the horizon a brilliant pink. The week-long heatwave had passed but the air was still warm, and a gentle breeze billowed the banners surrounding the stage. Martha looked out from behind the curtain.

The beach was full of people; they had staked their little areas of sand with towels and deckchairs and opened up picnic hampers. Corks popped at regular intervals and beer bottles clinked as they were taken out of cool boxes. Children ran in and out of the surf while others blew streams of bubbles into the sky. The hotel on the headland was dotted with spectators and the multicoloured houses that lined the seafront had people leaning out of upstairs windows or gathered on the Victorian wrought-iron balconies. The roof terrace of The Sailor's Arms was heaving with customers and in the car park people were standing on the tops of cars and camper vans, waiting patiently for the performance to start.

'I'm nervous!' Martha said as she surveyed the scene.

Behind her Max put his hands on her shoulders.

'You've done four festivals in three months, played live on national television, been interviewed by countless radio stations, "Child In My Eyes" was in the charts. How can you be nervous?'

Martha turned to face him.

'It's just doing it where I grew up. I think I can see the minister's son who used to pull my pigtails and tell me that his dad said my mum was a prostitute because she'd had a baby out of wedlock.'

'What does he look like now?'

Martha looked back through the curtains. 'He's wearing a long purple coat with what looks like satin shorts underneath.'

Max laughed. 'I wonder what his father would have to say about that?'

'I still feel nervous.'

'You'll be fine, Martha,' Flora called out from the makeshift dressing table at the back. She was putting the finishing touches to a sparkling arrangement in her hair. 'You've been wonderful every time you've performed.'

'Thanks to you.' Martha smiled at her. 'You're a great support out there.'

'Well, being a backing singer certainly makes a change from being Mrs. Clementine, I get to have a lot more fun.' She smiled at a short-haired woman with a clipboard on the edge of the stage.

'Ten minutes, everyone,' the woman called out and gave Flora a fleeting wink.

'This is going to be great!' Posh Paul appeared grinning and rubbing his hands together. With his receding hairline and prominent paunch Martha still found it hard to think of him as the baby-faced lead guitarist with the bleached flat-top and super-skinny body. 'I knew it was a good idea to do a one-off gig in Abertrulli. It was fantastic that Idris and Sledge offered to play tonight – and how could I refuse when you all persuaded me to get my guitar out! It's like the old days again.'

'Except Idris and Sledge seem to have about twenty small children with them,' Martha laughed.

'Oh God, I know! I think they're neck and neck on the wife front; both of them are on their fourth families. They're still in the hotel reading bedtime stories and changing nappies. I just hope they're back here in time.' Posh Paul looked at his watch and turned to Max. 'Great that you and Martha had hardly any distance to travel.'

Max nodded. 'The cottage is only half an hour up the road.'

'Martha, can you see anyone we know yet?' Flora called from the dressing table.

Martha scanned the crowd.

'No, I can't. There are so many people.'

Suddenly she spotted Noah, sitting on Josh's shoulders waving a Welsh flag. Ranjit stood beside Josh, Tilly on his shoulders; she looked so grown up with a neatly cut bob and a flower in her hair. Paula was sitting on a blanket with Reuben helping Carla steady plastic cups while she poured out fizzy wine. It had only been a few weeks since Martha and Max had last seen Paula and Ranjit. They were regular visitors to the little rose-covered cottage on the coastal path, especially since they had moved to their own cottage on the Welsh borders – not quite the Cotswolds but there was a Waitrose not too far away and the cottage had come with a vintage Aga that seemed to placate Paula.

Every few weeks, Ranjit came over to Martha and Max's house with new Billy Bacon chapters, and Max would show him the latest illustrations that he drew in the glass-roofed studio extension that he and Martha had built on the side of the cottage.

Paula had a job now too: part time administrator in Reuben's primary school. Tilly was in the nursery next door. Paula and Ranjit had also set up a charity to provide parents and siblings with support after the death of a baby: Alisha's Gift.

Martha scanned the crowd again. A little way away from the others, Elodie and Zac sat on the slipway eating chips out of a cone. Elodie wore a white T-shirt printed with a large golden heart and her hair was in a high ponytail, her body fuller, her cheeks pink. She looked down at something on her phone. Zac gave her a nudge and when she nearly fell off the slipway wall, she grabbed a strand of seaweed and started slapping Zac's head with it. He laughed and covered his hair, even though Martha couldn't hear him she knew he would be saying, *Mind the locks*.

'My nephew, playing the giddy goat as usual.' Flora peered over Martha's shoulder. Martha looked her up and down.

'You look magnificent in that turquoise dress.'

'And you're looking pretty sensational yourself. That red sequined jacket suits your new pink hair.'

'Not so vestal now.' Max put his arm around Martha and kissed her lightly on her lip-glossed lips.

Martha couldn't help her smile. Max kissed her again.

'Hey, enough of all the lovey-dovey stuff,' Posh Paul interrupted. 'You have backstage visitors.'

'Hiya!' a northern voice behind them cried.

Martha turned around to find Sally with her arms outstretched; within seconds Martha was enveloped in a bosomy embrace.

'I haven't seen you for so long.' Sally released her grip. 'Heard you all over the radio, of course.' She stood back. 'You look gorgeous out of all that black!'

'Yes, as I was saying to Flora she's a lot less . . .'

'Enough!' Martha gave Max a stern look.

'Bonjour.' Pierre stepped forward. He had a large floral bag slung over one shoulder and in his arms he held a soft pink bundle.

'Is that who I think it is?' asked Martha with a smile.

Pierre nodded and pulled back the fleecy blanket to reveal a tiny face, eyes closed in a deep sleep. 'May I introduce Celeste.' Pierre beamed proudly. 'Celeste Martha.' He placed the bundle gently into Martha's arms.

'We named her after you,' said Sally.

Martha peered down at the baby; the rosy lips were open in a perfect O. *A blessing*, Sally had told Martha by text the day that she discovered she was four months pregnant.

'She's gorgeous,' Martha whispered.

'She's not always as quiet as that.' Sally hoisted up her blouse. 'She's usually guzzling away, draining me of my most valuable assets!' Sally laughed. 'Oh! I almost forgot. Pierre, have a rummage and find that present we brought with us.'

Pierre crouched down and began to search through the floral bag, throwing out cloths and nappies and baby tights and a plastic Sophie the Giraffe.

'Ah-ha! *C'est ici*.' He pulled out a jam jar with a red polka-dot lid and pretty handwritten label. He handed it to Martha. 'From Alice and Ben.'

Martha read the label. 'Champagne and Cherry Jam.'

'It is selling like the hot cakes at the market,' Pierre said. 'Or should I be saying, like the hot cherries.' He laughed.

Sally rolled her eyes.

'It looks wonderful.' Martha examined the jar; the label had a little printed drawing of cherry blossom and a butterfly underneath the writing.

'The market stall is a big success,' said Sally. 'As well as jam, Alice and Ben are selling cherry chutney, cherry sauce, cherry chocolate brownies, cherry chocolate blondies, cherry tarts and even cherry gin! The new owners of *Le Couvent des Cerises* are only too pleased to have the cherries used by their tenants. And in the autumn Ben is planning to make truffle oils and vinegars. He has a dream to buy a bit of oakwood to start harvesting truffles himself.'

'And Alice and Ben are happy in the chapel?' asked Martha. 'They don't mind all the building noise going on while the renovations go on at the house?'

'It's just right for them,' Sally replied. 'And the house is nearly finished – it looks fab, you'd hardly know there had been a fire.'

'And no more cracks on the wall,' said Pierre. 'No more winky roof.'

'Wonky,' corrected Sally with a tut. She grinned at Martha. 'Have you heard that *Le Couvent des Cerises* is going to be a cookery school? Week-long residential courses.'

'I'll book in,' Martha laughed. 'I still have a lot to learn in that department.'

'Ah, your cooking is grand now.' Max patted her shoulder.

'Here's the best bit,' Sally grinned. 'Alice and Ben have been asked to teach some classes next summer.'

'And stay living at the chapel?'

'Yes, it's all worked out perfectly for them. They would have liked to have been here tonight but when they were offered a stall at the Perigord food festival they couldn't miss the opportunity.' Sally rocked Celeste in her arms and the baby opened her huge blue eyes.

Martha looked at the jam jar again, then at the baby. New life, new beginnings.

'Three minutes,' the short-haired woman shouted.

'We'll be out there watching on the sand.' Sally hugged Martha and then gave Max, Flora and Posh Paul a hug, and then a bemused roadie who happened to be walking past.

On the beach the crowd started chanting *Martha, Martha*, someone screamed out *We love you*. Martha felt the now familiar quickening of her heart, the sudden panic that she'd never remember the words. Her stomach was a knot. Flora squeezed her hand.

'You'll be fine.'

At that moment Idris and Sledge appeared, both out of breath and apologising.

'I had to nip out for Calpol,' said Idris. 'The wife is fretting that Buddy-Blue may have croup.'

'Helsinki lost her favourite teddy so we had to take the hotel room apart,' Sledge said. 'Turned out Odessa had hidden it in the mini-bar.'

'Still living the rock and roll life, guys?' Posh Paul laughed.

'It's alright for you, Mr. Monogamous.' Sledge pretended to do a drum roll on Posh Paul's head with his drumsticks. 'Your children are practically claiming their pensions.'

'Two minutes.'

A roady appeared with a huge bunch of flowers. He handed them to Martha.

'These were just delivered for you,' he said.

Martha took the enormous display and pulled out a little card nestled amongst the roses and white lilies.

I'll be thinking of you tonight, Martha.
You deserve all the success in the world.
All my love,
Cat xxx

Martha smiled as she handed the flowers back to the man.

'Look after them for me,' she said. 'They are from a very special friend.'

'One minute,' the girl with the clipboard called out.

On the stage their intro music played, the sound engineers made thumbs up signs.

Martha had another look through the curtains. Owen had promised that he'd be there.

'I wouldn't miss it for the world, Mum,' he'd said when Martha had told him about the concert. Even though Velvet Couch were on their own festival tour, Owen had come to see Martha perform three times already. But Abertrulli would be special.

'Rhys and I will be there,' he'd assured Martha on the phone.

'One minute.'

Sledge was already air-banging with his drumsticks, Idris clicked his finger joints in preparation for playing and Posh-Paul sucked in his paunch.

'Good luck,' Max whispered into Martha's ear. 'I'll just go and shove my way to the front now.'

Martha nodded, the knot in her stomach tightened.

'Ready?' asked Posh Paul.

'No,' they all replied in unison.

'Then let's go!'

As they stepped out, the crowd let out a roar. Idris and Posh Paul swaggered across the stage and picked up their guitars and Sledge straddled the seat behind his drum kit. Flora took her place at the microphone as the boys began to play their opening chords. The crowd became ecstatic.

Martha put her hand up to her eyes. She peered out at the spectators, still searching for the most important member of the audience. A sprinkling of stars peppered the darkening sky and, as though it were part of the set, a huge orange moon began to rise over the headland.

Martha took her microphone off the stand. Beside her Flora was swaying her hips in time to the music.

'Go, girl,' she mouthed at Martha.

Martha stepped forward, ready to sing. She glanced at the front row, Max was just a few feet away, leaning against the metal barrier, Sally and Pierre were not far from him and Elodie and Zac had also squeezed their way right to the front. They were holding up their phones as high as they could to get good shots. Martha looked out across the sea of people; a searchlight swung across them highlighting expectant faces, raised hands waving in the air. Martha clutched the microphone; she could feel the sweat slippery on her palms.

She looked back down at Max. He nodded at her encouragingly. A banging resonated in her ears. She took a deep breath; Sledge's three drumbeats were her cue. At that moment she saw Rhys, standing on his own. He grinned and pointed. Martha turned her head a little and standing next to Posh Paul she saw another guitarist on the stage; blond curls almost obscuring his face as he picked out the bass chords to match the drumbeats. Owen looked up and smiled at her and Martha realised that she'd missed the first line of the song. It didn't matter; the crowd sang it for her. They got louder as Martha joined in for the second line and they kept going until by the end of the first verse the whole beach seemed to sing as one.

Martha put her head back, raised her hands up to the stars and sang more loudly than she'd ever done before.

And I am dancing on the moon

Read on for an extract from Kate Glanville's
The Peacock House . . .

EVELYN

Dismal. It was the only word that Evelyn could think of.

Dismal, dismal, dismal – it ricocheted around her head as she stared out of the bay window. The rain ran in unrelenting tears down the diamonds of glass and the wind moaned through the gaps around the ancient frame.

Outside there was a world of nothing. The garden had completely disappeared into the thick, grey mist. It was hard to imagine the view; the sea in the distance, the mountains that swept down to the shore, the rooftops of the houses that clustered around the crescent bay.

Evelyn turned and looked around the enormous bedroom; it was much too big for the mean little fire that crackled in the grate.

Flopping down onto the eiderdown she stared at the ornately plastered ceiling. Its Jacobean swirls reminded her of a wedding cake. There had been no cake at her wedding to Howard, rationing had made sure of that. The war had also made sure there had been no white satin dress, or trailing bouquet, though she wasn't sure the war could be blamed for the lack of other things a bride expected.

It had been two years since her wedding day, nearly two years since she had been banished to the land of rain and rocks and shrouding cloud. *Two years*, Evelyn whispered and saw a chilly puff of air escape between her lips.

1

This would be her second Christmas in Wales, in the huge house, with only her mother-in-law for company at the dinner table. So different from the boisterous Christmas dinners at Wilton Terrace where there had been jokes and riddles, and indoor fireworks, and endless bottles of champagne from the cellar. There had always been a huge fir tree in the hall, soaring up through the stairwell; Evelyn and her brother and sister had to stand on ladders to decorate it. At Vaughan Court they didn't have a tree.

'They are unpatriotic!' Lady Vaughan had declared when Evelyn had dared to suggest they put one up in the drawing room. 'We will take no part in Germanic traditions at Vaughan Court.'

She wondered if Howard would come to visit this year. She doubted it. His work in Whitehall was much more important than a wife, especially when he had everything he wanted in London. She tried not to think of the letter; the swirling writing, the sickening scent of violets, the words that had suggested an intimacy Evelyn had no experience of. Instead she glanced over at the jumper she'd been knitting; her mother-in-law had suggested it as a gift for Howard.

'It will give you something to do,' Lady Vaughan had said.

The colour of the wool was hideous, it was all that they had in the town.

Evelyn closed her eyes and wished for something to happen, anything, anything at all, as long as it was something more exciting than the life she had.

She opened her eyes at the sound of the rain beating harder against the windows. The moaning of the wind grew louder, more like a howl, and then a roar. She sat up. The windowpanes started to rattle in their leaden frames and for a moment everything seemed to darken, as though the shadow of some colossal beast had passed by outside. Then there was a bang, an explosion. The whole room seemed to shake; Evelyn thought the windowpanes might shatter. Jumping up from the bed she tried to crane her neck to see from the window, but everything was fog. She heard shouting below her. The boys.

A crash, there's been a crash on the mountain.

2

Without even stopping to think she wrenched open the bedroom door and ran. Racing down the long corridor, she had no time to scowl at the beastly portraits, the Persian rugs slipping beneath her feet. She almost tripped as she took the steps of the marble stair case two at a time. With an ungraceful skid she crossed the black-and-white-tiled hall and pulled at the heavy oak door until it opened and she was outside.

The rain had turned to sleet, slivers of ice pricking at her cheeks; her hands were already turning numb. Ignoring the cold, Evelyn ran around the side of the house. The boys were smudges ahead of her, already scrambling up the steep path.

Peter, Billy.

She called their names and set off as fast as she could, following them upwards, clambering over rocks and boulders. The smell of smoke was thick on the wind and high above her on the mountain-side something was giving off a ghostly glow.

Kate Glanville

THE PEACOCK HOUSE

Available to order now

ACCENT

HEARTSTONES

It's hard to run away from your deepest secrets . . .

When Phoebe's lover dies in a car accident, their hushed affair goes with him to the grave.

Heartbroken, she abandons her life in England and searches out the old boathouse on the west coast of Ireland left to her by her grandmother. Soon she is embraced by the villagers of nearby Carraigmore and slowly begins to heal.

But when Phoebe discovers a collection of old diaries hidden under the floor of the boathouse, she finds herself immersed in a story of family scandal and a passionate affair between her grandmother and a young Irish artist.

With so many unanswered questions, Phoebe turns to the locals who knew her late grandmother best. But when she is met by silence, she realises she's not the only one (in her family) with something to hide . . .

Available to order from

ACCENT

A PERFECT HOME

Is home *really* where the heart is?

Claire appears to have it all – the kind of life you read about in magazines: a beautiful cottage, three gorgeous children, a handsome husband in William and her own flourishing vintage textile business.

But when an interiors magazine sends a good-looking photographer to take pictures of Claire's perfect home, he makes her wonder if the house means more to William than she does . . .

Available to order from

ACCENT

STARGAZING

You can spend a lifetime gazing up at the stars, but reality will bring you down to earth with a bump.

Three women connected by one man.

Daniel is father to Seren, husband to Nesta and lover to Frankie. When he leaves Nesta and their beautiful home in the middle of a party celebrating their fortieth wedding anniversary, Seren's world begins to crumble. Only the continuation of the family ideal can make things right. But Nesta isn't so sure.

And for Frankie, Daniel offers hope for a safe and secure future. But all three women are carrying secrets that they've kept hidden, even from those closest to them. Secrets that might threaten a life . . .

Available to order from

ACCENT